The Dragon Ring

The yellow gem eyes of the dragon suddenly flashed with a pale golden glow. The glow became a shimmering halo, spreading from the eyes, dancing in a miniature borealis around the horned head.

The filament popped out of the open mouth again. A minute dark speck, almost too tiny for the unaided eye to detect, was attached to the end of it.

With a surge of horror, Kane realized that Baptiste's speculation that the dragon ring was a surgical instrument was probably more accurate than she ever dreamed.

The filament had sampled his genetic structure, and whatever stunningly complex and miniaturized mechanism was inside the ring, it had manufactured an implant with his own blood and cells as a nonrejectable sheath.

It wasn't sorcery, but it was no less terrifying.

D0633046

JAMES AXLER

OUTLANDERS™

DESTINY RUN

A GOLD EAGLE BOOK FROM

WORLDWIDE®

TORONTO • NEW YORK • LONDON
AMSTERDAM • PARIS • SYDNEY • HAMBURG
STOCKHOLM • ATHENS • TOKYO • MILAN
MADRID • WARSAW • BUDAPEST • AUCKLAND

Again, for Melissa—
Who understands the
connection (and the difference) between
inspiration and perspiration.

First edition September 1997
ISBN 0-373-63815-9

DESTINY RUN

Printed in U.S.A.

The pangs,
The internal pangs, are ready—
the dread strife
Of poor humanity's afflicted will
Struggling in vain with ruthless destiny.
—Wordsworth

Chapter 1

She came awake slowly. First the black void turned to gray, then to a pale, shimmering yellow.

A cloying pain enwrapped her, pounding at her head rhythmically, in cadence with her heartbeat. She tried to open her eyes, but she couldn't see anything and she wondered rather aloofly if she was blind. For a reason she could not understand, something sticky and thick sealed her eyes shut. Experimentally she touched the tip of her tongue to her lips and she tasted a coppery, salty tang. Her stumbling thoughts groped for what it might be. Finally she realized it was blood, and considering the sharp pain in her head, she knew it had to be her blood.

Brigid Baptiste ground her teeth and tried to move. Cramping needles of agony shot up her shoulders and arms. A persistent pressure compressed her wrists, squeezed them so tightly her hands were no more than numb, half-remembered appendages at the ends of her arms. By a tentative exploration with her fingertips, she felt strands of rawhide wrapped tightly around her wrists. She was helpless, blind and sick. Nausea was a clawed animal trying to tear its way out of her stomach. It was all she could do to swallow the column of burning bile working its way up her throat.

Brigid tested her legs, shifting them slightly. They were not bound, though they were stiff, and she realized they had been crooked in an unnatural position beneath her.

She didn't brace herself with them. Even though her thoughts moved like half-frozen mud, she knew it was best to keep as silent and as motionless as possible. Through her eyelids she saw a wavering yellow-red glow, and over the reek of wood smoke, she smelled mutton boiling. She heard the murmur of voices, speaking incomprehensible words.

She squeezed her left eyelid as though she were squinting fiercely, and a tear formed. By arching her eyebrow as high as she could, she tried to prise her eye open. The effort sparked more pain in her head, along her right temple. She kept up the squinting and eyebrow arching, and fluid oozed from the duct in her left eye. The tears slowly dissolved the dried blood, and on her tenth attempt, her upper eyelid peeled stickily away from the lower.

Flames danced from the bonfire several yards away. Men and women sat around it in a great circle. The wild horde from the mountain valleys of Khaldzan sat with the barely leashed eagerness of great cats, waiting for their prey to move so they could start their cruel game all over again.

Brigid realized she was in the same place, the same position before she had fallen into the pit of unconsciousness. Long spears had been driven deep and lashed together to make a crude framework, and from this frame she hung, wrists tied to the wooden shafts by leather thongs.

Two other makeshift scaffolds stood close by. Adrian and Davis hung limply between them, ragged red scarecrows. On the regular staff of Cerberus redoubt, they had taken the mat-trans jump with her on their information gathering mission. They had been scourged without mercy, and the ground around them glistened damp and bloody.

Bautu had wielded the lash, and Brigid remembered watching him cut both of his victims with great care, the tapered steel tip of the long oiled whip singing and flaying the skin like a flexible flensing knife.

When the scourging of the men had begun, she had cried out in anger, flinging an insult in the Khalkha tongue. She had been surprised that Bautu understood her. She recalled only a fragment of what came next—a leather-shod fist, decorated with wafers of polished steel, driving toward her head.

She had never been knocked unconscious before, so she methodically reviewed what she knew about head trauma induced by a blow. A severe impact on the skull, she told herself, could cause not only a concussion, but also coma, subdural leakages of blood, amnesia, a reduction of intelligence, and death.

Aside from coma, she wasn't sure if she was suffering from any of those conditions, except for the amnesia. She still retained a fairly good, if somewhat hazy idea of who she was, and of the vicious bastard who had rendered her senseless.

Bautu paid no attention to her now. He had stripped off his armor, and his broad chest lifted and fell as he drank in great lungfuls of the chill air. The firelight gleamed dully from his thick, greased braids, and despite the cold, a sheen of sweat glistened on the shaved patch at the top of his head. Etched onto the right side of his broad, low forehead was a small marking she couldn't identify. It didn't look like a scar or a tattoo or even a caste mark, yet it somehow resembled all three.

Bautu's gloved right fist held the coiled whip, and with his left he sipped from a bowl of koumiss, fermented mare's milk. Even at a distance of six yards, she could smell his unwashed-animal odor.

Brigid kept her head bowed, the fall of her thick red-gold hair concealing most of her face. Through her slitted eye, she gazed through the screen of her hair and beyond Bautu and the bonfire.

The camp of the warrior horde spread out across the shallow valley for at least an eighth of a mile. The humped yurts, domelike tents of stretched yak hide, were scattered in no particular order from one end of the valley to the next. The area between the clumps of yurts was cluttered with two-wheeled carts, ox yokes, hobbled ponies and mutton racks. Here and there glowed cook fires.

Farther out oxen, horses and sheep grazed on the scrubby grass growing through the crust of old snow. Beyond the animals lay the Black City of Kharo-Khoto.

Most of the people clustered around the bonfire were men. They were, by and large, warriors, and so dressed accordingly. They were husky, their short legs bowed from years of clutching the barrels of their ponies. They wore yak-skin hauberks and conical, fur-lined caps of discolored leather. Though a few shouldered single-shot muzzle loaders, the standard weapon seemed to be a horn-and-wood bow. Every swarthy face had a sparse mustache or beard.

Although they'd come following up on rumors of a warlord, Brigid, Adrian and Davis hadn't expected to find anyone, much less a horde of warriors, at that location. On foot and underarmed, they had been easily captured by Bautu and a mounted scouting party. Brigid understood a smattering of Khalkha, but almost nothing of their particular dialect, which sounded like a corrupted blend of Chinese, Turkic and colloquial Russian. Therefore, she had been unable to provide satisfactory answers to Bautu's shouted questions.

Once in the shallow valley, Davis and Adrian had been strung up and scourged. Brigid assumed that after Bautu caught his second wind and had his fill of koumiss, she would be next to taste the lash.

As soon as the thought registered, Bautu glanced toward her. She didn't move, body slack and sagging, head lolling. He wiped the sweat from his face and took a step forward. Then he froze, head and eyes lifting, gazing past her. Brigid remained motionless.

A moment later she heard an engine laboring, wheezing and occasionally missing. As the sound grew louder, so did the squeak and creak of an overstressed suspension. Headlights washed over Bautu. He narrowed his eyes and shifted his position as a flatbed truck rattled and jounced over the uneven ground and braked to a stop near the bonfire. Wooden crates, at least a dozen of them, were stacked on the wag's bed, kept in place by hemp netting. Painted on several of the crates in Russian Cyrillic script was a simple legend: 12.

Only one man climbed out of the cab. He was tall, at least a head and a half taller than Bautu. The high fleece cap perched at a jaunty angle made him seem taller. A silver disk, pinned to the front of the cap, glinted with red highlights.

Pulling his calf-length, tan trench coat tighter around him, the man gave the hanging figures a disinterested glance and approached Bautu. In a faint, unintelligible murmur, he spoke to the warrior. Brigid couldn't hear, couldn't understand a word. His manner and tone, however, were very calm.

Bautu's response was the exact opposite. With a savage sweep of his left arm, he gestured to the bodies of the hanging men, and an indecipherable flow of noise burst from his snarling mouth.

He continued the tirade, roaring out each incomprehensible word. The tall man listened to the blizzard of harsh consonants and outraged gutturals politely, hands tucked into the pockets of his coat. He nodded frequently, as if in sympathy.

When Bautu paused to catch his breath, the man turned away, eyeing first Adrian and then Davis. Hands still in his pockets, he stepped to a hide-wrapped bundle on the ground, very near the fire. He toed a flap aside and gazed expressionlessly at the items piled within it—a compass, three H&K VP-70 handblasters, wrist chrons, a small rad counter, plastic containers of water and concentrated food and the trans-comm unit. The little black rectangle of molded plastic and pressed metal held his attention for a very long time.

Lifting his head, the tall man gazed toward Brigid. Four long strides brought him right in front of her. She closed her eye and breathed shallowly. She heard the man chuckle. A gloved hand cupped her chin, raising her head with a surprisingly gentle touch, and he parted her tangle of hair. She did not move, did not react.

"Meno morosch mene golovu." His voice was a rustling, conspiratorial whisper. In Russian he had said, "Don't fuck with me."

Brigid took a breath, got her feet under her and stood up. Once she was relieved of the strain of supporting her weight, the fierce pain in her wrists and shoulders began to seep away.

The man made a *tsk* noise when he saw she could open only one eye and he took a handkerchief from a coat pocket. Wetting it with his tongue, he carefully dabbed at the caked blood on her face, then prised up her right eyelid with a thumb and forefinger.

"Spaseebah," she said.

The man grinned and replied in English, "Quite welcome you are."

Brigid did not reply.

"Your accent gives you away," he said, still speaking in a low tone. "You're not Russian. Where are you from?"

"From far away."

"England." The man snapped his fingers. "No, not England, your teeth are too good. America. I have never met an American before."

"Then we're even. I've never met a Russian. I certainly didn't expect to meet one in Mongolia."

The man smiled. Brigid realized he was older than he looked at first glance. His dark eyes were surrounded by crinkled laugh lines, and the weather-beaten skin on either side of his sharp nose was creased by deep lines.

Crossing the index and middle fingers of his right hand, he declared, "The histories of Mongolia and Mother Russia have been intertwined for over a thousand years, since the days of Temujin, Timur and Babur the Tiger. Sometimes we are enemies, sometimes we are so fond of each other, it would give the shade of Stalin the colic."

"Which is it now?" Brigid asked. She glanced toward the fire. Bautu fingered his lash, glowering at her from beneath a furrowed brow.

"Fairly obvious, is it not? You're the one hung up for flaying, not me."

"Who are you?"

The man put a hand to his chest and bowed. "Sverdlovosk is my name. And you are...?"

She considered giving him a false name, but decided not to bother. Her own name, or a nom de guerre wouldn't make any difference out here. Besides, the pain in her head limited her powers of invention.

"Baptiste."

"An American in Mongolia. Your comrades were American, too, I presume. Sent by one of the baronies to spy on the Tushe Gun."

"You're making a lot of assumptions."

An edge slipped into Sverdlovosk's smooth voice. "Hardly. I doubt there's been an American this close to the Black Gobi in two centuries. I've heard that the intelligence-gathering networks of the American baronies were extending into other countries. You and your comrades are proof of that."

Bautu emitted a bellow, shaking the coiled whip at them.

Sverdlovosk shouted back, ending his retort with two sharp clicking sounds.

Returning his attention to Brigid, he said, "A poor excuse for a language, I must admit. Probably it was a form of a local trading dialect, centuries ago."

"Probably," she agreed. "After the nukecaust, when communications were cut off with other countries, these people slipped back into barbarism and an earlier language, forgetting its roots."

Sverdlovosk eyed her admiringly, flicking his glance up and down her form. She realized her bodysuit was rent and ragged, so much of her bare skin was exposed.

"Impressive, Baptiste. You're obviously educated and obviously very pretty under all that grit and gore on your face. What's not so obvious is how you got here from the Americas."

"Does it matter?"

"Very much. It is the question which consumes Bautu, and he is desperate for an answer before the Tushe Gun arrives."

"I know what those words mean, at least," she said. "It's a title...'the Avenging Lama.'"

A sudden commotion of shouts and yelps erupted from the far end of the valley. Sverdlovosk looked that way, sighed and said, "He is ahead of schedule. If he arrived when he was supposed to have, I might have been able to browbeat Bautu into placing you in my custody. It is too late for that now, I fear."

Trumpets made of rams' horns bleated a discordant fanfare. An ululating wail burst from over a hundred tongues. Firelight glinted from polished sword blades as they were waved in the air. Muskets fired into the night sky, and the valley echoed with a staccato pop-popping. Plumes of powder smoke floated overhead like streamers of gray chiffon.

The chant began slowly at first: "Tushe Gun! Tushe Gun!"

The words were shouted in an ever increasing rhythm until they sounded like a voice tape sped up and on continuous loop: "Tusheguntushegun—"

A harsh blast on a horn silenced the howling throng. The abrupt silence was broken by the clopping of unshod hooves and the squeak of saddle leather. Two mounted men approached the bonfire through a path flanked on either side by warriors and their women standing at respectful attention.

Flames played off the burnished iron scales of armor, winked from the polished helmets. Though the two men rode abreast, Brigid didn't need Sverdlovosk to point out which figure was the Tushe Gun.

He was a head taller than his saddle mate, though the

fanged bear skull mounted on top of his fur-trimmed helmet probably added a few inches to his height. A molded breastplate of leather encased his torso and was reinforced by an interlocking pattern of metal scales. The long sword at his side, its scabbard set with gems, swung in rhythm to his dappled horse's prancing gait.

His face was strangely shaped, strangely shadowed, and it wasn't until he reined his mount to halt that Brigid realized he wore a mask. It was crafted of a thin layer of exquisitely carved jade—at least it looked like jade because of its creamy green hue.

The mask covered his face from his hairline to just above his mouth, leaving only the lower lip and chin exposed. The mask held no particular expression, but from behind the curving eyelets glinted an imperious, hawklike gaze.

Sverdlovosk dropped to one knee and stuck out his tongue in the traditional Mongolian greeting and act of submission. The intent, expressionless scrutiny of the masked face was focused not on the Russian but on Brigid. She tried to return the gaze with the same unblinking intensity.

The Tushe Gun spoke one word, a whisper she didn't understand. Sverdlovosk instantly sprang to his feet and whirled on her. "Grovel before the Avenging Lama," he snapped, and pounded a fist into the pit of her stomach.

Brigid bent double, hanging between the spear hafts, tears of pain clouding her vision but helping to dissolve more of the dried blood. She dragged in raspy lungfuls of air.

When she raised her head again, Bautu stood beside the Tushe Gun's horse, holding up the bundle of ordnance like an offering. The Tushe Gun poked and picked at the blasters with only a mild interest. He held up the trans-comm unit and spoke. His voice was resonant but not particularly deep. It held a peculiar timbre, as if metal were grinding at the back of his throat. The language he used was Russian. "Does this function?"

When Brigid didn't respond, Sverdlovosk side-mouthed to her, "Answer the Avenging Lama."

"I don't know," she said in Russian. She despised the catch in her voice. "It may have been damaged when we were set upon."

The Tushe Gun dropped the trans-comm to the ground as if it were contaminated. He pricked his horse's flanks with his spurs, and the animal lurched forward, hooves stamping on it. The casing broke with a crunch and a crack.

He took the blasters from the bundle, handed one to his companion and kept the other two, looping the gun belts over his saddle horn. Leaning forward, he said, "Tell me at once, woman. Why do you come here?"

"To explore, to trade. We meant no harm."

"How did you get here?"

"By ship."

"From America?"

"No, from China."

The Tushe Gun grunted softly. The blank mask stared. "You did not come from the Great Yurt. I would have heard about three travelers. I see falsehoods in your eyes, woman."

"I see nothing in yours," Brigid replied. "Take off your mask so I may look into your eyes, and perhaps we will talk."

Sverdlovosk's startled intake of breath made a high hissing sound between his teeth. The masked figure slowly stiffened in the saddle. When he spoke, his voice was hollow, toneless. "A thing is not hidden without reason, woman. Nor is it found without reason."

The Tushe Gun turned his horse's head away. "You are here to sap the sacred flame within the Black City. Who sent you?"

"No one."

"I wish only to know that. A fox knows a great many things, a badger knows only one great thing. Who sent you?"

"Are you the badger," she asked, "or the fox?"

The masked man didn't reply to her question. To Sverdlovosk he said, "Bautu will torture her until she speaks the truth. If she does not, she will feel the kiss of the dragon. You will watch and listen and report to me anything she says."

"Wait!" Brigid called. "You haven't heard everything. We sought only to make trading treaties—"

"I have heard enough," the Tushe Gun spoke over his shoulder. "Your people will come, and your treaties will sap our strength and that of the Black City. I swore an oath to Shamos to fulfill our destiny."

Sverdlovosk said loudly, "Great Tushe, I have brought what you requested. Would you not care to inspect it?"

The jade face shifted toward the crates resting on the bed of the wag. "Unload them. Bring them to my yurt." His right hand jabbed toward the far end of the valley, and light glinted briefly from a ring on his gloved index finger. It was a massive ornament, made of thick, hammered silver, designed like a dragon coiled in four loops. The horned head was baleful and demonic of expression. The firelight made tiny iridescent sparks dance within the eyes of yellow gemstones.

With a slight start of surprise, Brigid realized the configuration of the snarling dragon head corresponded to the mark on Bautu's forehead. It was almost as if the ring had been exposed to a flame and the superheated metal pressed into Bautu's flesh.

The Tushe Gun and his companion rode away toward the scattering of yurts. Bautu grinned at Brigid, uncoiling his lash. As the Tushe Gun rode past, he directed a few words toward Bautu, and the grin vanished from his face. The warrior hooked the whip onto his belt. He shouted and gestured to a pair of men at the bonfire, and they joined him at the rear of the truck.

Sverdlovosk tucked his hands back into his pockets, watching the men untying the rope binders around the crates. Without looking at her, he said, "A respite, Baptiste. Not a reprieve."

She didn't answer.

Quietly he said, "Speak to me, Baptiste. Anything. In Russian. Sound angry."

Brigid's mind raced. She groped for a phrase and she blurted, in a loud, sharp tone, "Russian vodka tastes like stump water."

Sverdlovosk wheeled on her, face contorted in anger. He took his right hand out of his pocket and closed it over her bound left wrist, shaking the spear haft. In a threatening whisper he asked, "Can you make it back to the gateway?"

For a moment she was too startled to reply. Then, defiantly she answered, "If I had transportation."

"The keys are in the wag," he said, his tone contemptuous. "God help you if you're recaptured. I'll be howling for your blood just like the rest of these Tartar bastards."

Sverdlovosk removed his hand from her wrist, cuffed her across the face and spun on his heel, marching toward the men laboring to unload the crates. Brigid watched

him go, shouting and gesticulating imperiously with his
arms. She carefully folded her fingers over the small,
open penknife he had slipped into her palm.

Chapter 2

Brigid kept her left arm in position, pressed against the spear haft, though she could tell by the burning pins-and-needles sensation in her hand that circulation was returning to it. Sverdlovosk had sliced through the rawhide thongs.

She watched the unloading of the wag and waited through one of the longest minutes of her life. It felt far longer than the minute preceding her march to the execution wall in the bowels of the Administrative Monolith back in Cobaltville. Three months separated that minute from this one, and she was separated by her old life in Cobaltville by a distance more immense than mere time.

It was still hard to believe the magnitude of change that had taken her from being an archivist living a very confined, sheltered existence to an outcast of the ville society. And it was through Kane bringing her encoded information that she landed in that predicament. It had to do with resistance to the rule in the villes and secret information about the nuclear war of 2001 and the later developments. After the last-minute rescue by Kane, fleeing their way of life was the only choice. Together with Grant, Kane's fellow magistrate, and the outlander girl Domi, they fled beyond the ville's walls.

Just about the only reminder of her former existence was Lakesh at the Project Cerberus redoubt. He'd been her supervisor, the head archivist, but he'd headed up the resistance movement. But to get to that point, they'd first been pursued in the Outlands, then followed up with the discovery of the matter-transfer chamber—the same type of mat-trans jump that landed her in this trouble on the other side of the globe. She'd got out with her skin intact before, she now told herself, and somehow she'd get out now, too, though her heart felt heavy knowing that it was too late for her companions on this ill-fated outing.

She continued to stand motionless until she was sure no eye was cast in her direction. Deftly she brought her left hand away from the spear haft and slashed at the leather thongs around her right wrist. The knife blade was very sharp, and she ignored the fact that she sliced through some skin at the same time. She only prayed she hadn't opened up a major vein or punctured an artery.

After the strands of rawhide parted, she placed her left hand back against the pole. The thongs, half-buried in the flesh of her wrists, stayed in place and would fool a casual glance.

Bautu and the warriors Sverdlovosk had pressed into service walked away from the truck, arms laden with crates. Only a couple were heavy enough to require two men to carry them.

When their backs were to her, Brigid made her move. She lowered her arms and carefully stepped back as far as she could from the perimeter of the firelight. She kept her eyes trained on the warriors. Nothing could be done for Adrian and Davis. They hadn't stirred at all since she regained consciousness.

Moving in a half crouch, half scuttle, she angled her way toward the truck, approaching the driver's door, which faced away from the bonfire. The ground beneath her feet was rocky, patched with snow, and she winced at the slight crunch it made when she walked.

She didn't pause when she reached a point directly in front of the battered grille of the old wag. Three long, swift steps brought her around it, glad the door window was rolled down.

A harsh exclamation hit her like a physical assault. Pivoting on the balls of her feet, Brigid saw a stump-legged man stepping out from between a pair of rock outcroppings. His hands were at his crotch, and she realized he had just relieved himself and couldn't see her clearly in the murk.

She did the first thing that occurred to her, the only thing possible, springing forward and lashing out with her right hand. The knife blade slashed across his broad forehead.

The warrior croaked in dismay and confusion. Blood flowed down his face, into his eyes. With one hand he tried to clear his vision, and with the other he groped for the long dagger sheathed at his hip.

As an outraged scream started up his throat, Brigid kicked him as hard as she could between the legs, hoping to smash his testicle sac against his pelvic bone. The warrior's hands went from his face to his crotch, and he doubled over, the scream turning into an aspirated cough.

She whirled, grabbed the door handle of the cab, threw it down and flung herself behind the wheel. As Sverdlovosk had said, the key was in the ignition. The wag had a standard transmission, much like the Sandcat back at Cerberus, which Domi had taught her to drive. The letters and numbers on the instrument panel were all in Cyrillic, and though she spoke Russian passably, reading it required a concentration and time she didn't have.

Brigid turned the key. Despite the cold, the engine caught on the first try. She worked the clutch, yanked back on the stick shift and floored the accelerator.

With a clanking roar the wag shuddered, nearly died, then lurched forward. She wrestled with the wheel, the foot pedals, trying to upshift without stalling. The gearbox protested, but the wag picked up speed. She couldn't tell by the gauge how much fuel was in the tank, but Sverdlovosk had seemed certain the vehicle would carry her to the gateway.

Over the roar of the engine and the squeak of the suspension, she heard a howled cry behind her. It was echoed by massed voices, and the air around the cab whistled with yard-long arrows. Most were hastily aimed, though she heard at least two thud into the bed.

The terrain was rocky, and rather than risk breaking an axle, she shifted to a lower gear, fighting the wheel, relying on the waning moon to light her way.

Though she no longer had a compass, she didn't need one. Brigid Baptiste possessed an eidetic, or photographic, memory. The overland route she and her companions had taken from the mat-trans installation was indelibly impressed in her mind.

Automatically she glanced at her left wrist and saw only a few leather strands embedded in the skin. She peeled them away, cursing at the pain. Her chron had been taken, so she had only a vague idea of the time. She knew she was several hours overdue for a transcomm check-in. Though Lakesh had instructed Kane and Grant to wait at the installation for twenty-four hours before commencing a search, she prayed she would meet one or both of them halfway.

With each mile the going became smoother. The ground was still rock littered, still fissured and cracked, but once out of the valley the country gave way more and more to sand. Turning on the headlights, she avoided the deeper drifts as best she could, fearing the tires would bog down in the dunes.

The cab wasn't outfitted with rear view mirrors, so the only way to check her backtrail was to roll down the window, twist around and poke her head out of the window. Though the wag couldn't have been traveling at more than thirty miles per hour, the shock of the cold wind made her shiver violently. Her insulated clothing was torn and ragged, so hypothermia was a real possibility.

The plains stretched bleak and empty behind her, but she knew pursuit lay out there. Fuel was the only thing that kept the pursuit from being close. She, Adrian and Davis hadn't been concerned with making time during their journey from the installation, but they had still been out in this stretch of the Gobi for eight hours before their capture.

She tried to calculate how long it would take the wag to cover the same distance, and her best estimate was an hour, probably a little more than that—assuming she maintained the present rate of speed.

The wag churned onward. Brigid relied on her memory, since her eyes couldn't make much geographical sense out of the long, low-lying hills and all the flat, open country. The adrenaline in her system ebbed, and she felt exhaustion overtake her. Her body, muscles pulled and beaten, throbbed with pain. She found herself yawning, her mind straining for clarity, pushing away the wispy folds of inertia, of weariness. She gripped the steering wheel tightly, deliberately averting her gaze from the angry red abrasions encircling her slim wrists.

The landscape once again became rugged, scattered with rock formations sprouting from the sand. Every bump struck by a tire triggered vibrations through her head, feeding the pain. She was concerned about the constant ache, about the frequent blurring of her vision. Knowing she had to keep alert, she rolled down the window, welcoming the chilly chafe of the wind, but fearing its effects on her body temperature.

Then she saw it, the dark bulk of a rocky hill only a mile ahead.

Brigid exhaled a noisy sigh of relief. And the same moment, the drone of the wag's engine faltered, broke its steady rhythm, shuddered and ceased altogether. The vehicle rolled onward, its momentum carrying it across the sandy soil even as the speed dropped. Gently it slid to a complete stop, the sand hissing softly beneath the tires. She knew there was no point in trying to restart it. The fuel was gone. She climbed out of the cab, hugging herself, trying to rub warmth back into her limbs. She looked back the way she had come.

Strung out across the horizon were four—no, *six*—black shapes, bounding over the barren sand-scape. The shapes were warriors astride their sturdy little horses. The riders had to have been pushing the animals to their very limits to be within her range of vision. She estimated they would be upon her in less than half an hour.

Quickly Brigid eyed the distant hill and then the sky. The sun would soon be flooding the Gobi with its lambent light, and if she couldn't reach the installation before then, she would never see another dawn.

Refusing to dwell upon that possibility, Brigid started running. Her booted feet churned up the sand, and she knew she was leaving a trail a blind Dreg could follow, but it couldn't be helped. She ran toward the ridge with a steady lightness and sureness of stride that came of long practice.

Brigid kept looking toward the sky for any sign of the rising sun. Within moments the light of Sol peeped over the rim of the world, staining the blue black backdrop of the sky with a halo of crimson. She continued running. Pain stitched along her left side, the muscles of her legs felt as if they were caught in a vise and her vision was shot through with gray specks.

Over the rasp and gasp of her own labored breathing, Brigid heard the thudding hooves of the horses behind her, then a strident cry of malicious triumph. The skin between her shoulder blades crawled in anticipation of one of the warrior's long arrows planting its barbed head there. She altered direction, heading for the tumble of basalt at the foot of the hill. She knew she wouldn't get to it before the tribesmen reached her.

She hazarded one quick glance behind her. Unsurprisingly the mounted men were gaining. Despite the dim light, she recognized Bautu in the lead, leaning over his horse's neck, teeth bared in a ferocious grin.

Brigid ran across the stone-strewed ground, her feet slipping on the rocks. She dodged among the larger chunks of basalt and granite, banging her knees. She tried to keep her jaws clamped shut on the bleat of terror that tried to force its way out of her mouth.

She heard a piercing, warbling cry behind her and looked over her shoulder. Bautu charged forward, his whip inscribing a humming, hazy circle in the air over his head. His mount galloped at a frightful, reckless speed, hooves kicking up bucketfuls of sand and pebbles.

The snapping of the lash was lost in the thundering hoofbeats. The whip snaked around Brigid's throat, a streak of fire across her chin and neck. She screamed and clawed at it, staggering as Bautu galloped past, intending to pull her off her feet and drag her behind his mount.

As the length of oiled, braided leather stretched taut, Brigid didn't resist the pull. She went with it, kicking herself forward, the penknife gripped in her right fist.

Bautu glimpsed what she was doing and fumblingly tried to transfer the whip from his right to his left hand, seeking to draw his sword. He dropped the reins in the process, twisting on his wooden saddle as Brigid sprang at him.

Though it caused her a brief twinge of guilt, she sank the blade of the knife into the horse's rump, up to the hilt. The animal screamed and exploded forward, rearing and bucking at the same time. Bautu released the whip, grabbing the horse's mane. The flank of the animal slammed into her, bowling her off her feet.

Already off balance because of the horse's wild, bounding gyrations, Bautu tipped from the saddle and fell heavily and gracelessly to the ground. The other riders rushed by in a bustle of shouts, drumming hooves and the clank of unsheathed swords. They pounded on past, almost to the edge of the rock tumble, then wheeled their mounts expertly around. Brigid bounded to her feet quickly and, realizing they had cut off her escape route, began to run in the opposite direction.

Bautu snarled, saliva spraying from his lips as he staggered erect, dragging his sword from its scabbard. His eyes were wide and crazed with the kill-light.

Suddenly a sharp voice cut through the chill air. "Baptiste! *Down!*"

Without an instant's hesitation, Brigid flung herself to the stone-littered ground. Simultaneously the hammering thunder of Sin Eaters on full auto rolled through boulders and scattered rock formations. She heard the 9 mm lead thumping the air over her head.

Scarlet bloomed on the right side of Bautu's head. Pain and anger twisted his face, then it became a befuddled expression of disbelief. Limply he toppled backward to the sand.

The crashing impact of the 248-grain bullets slapped two warriors from their saddles, their arms and legs flopping bonelessly. The remaining three shrieked in fear, and their horses echoed those panicked screams. The horses reared, plunged, and unable to rein their mounts down, two of the riders were thrown. One warrior fell beneath sharp, stamping hooves, his death cry drowned by the staccato reports of the Sin Eaters. Gouts of sand exploded from the desert floor.

The blasterfire abruptly ceased. In the sudden pall of silence that followed, Brigid saw the surviving warriors gazing into the predawn dimness beyond her. Their eyes were wide and their mouths gaped open. Faintly came the steady tramp of boots on sand and stone.

From a wedge of shadow between a pair of upthrusts of rock marched two black figures. They were like statues sculpted from obsidian, somehow given life and movement. The fading starlight struck dim highlights on the molded chest pieces and shoulder pads. Their faces were completely concealed by black helmets except for their mouths and chins. Red-tinted visors masked their eyes. Both armored figures carried autoblasters in their right hands. Their tread was measured, deliberate and menacing.

One of the warriors unlimbered his bow, nocked an arrow, drew back and released a feathered shaft, all within the space of a heartbeat and a half. The arrow struck the larger of the black figures squarely on a molded pectoral. With a crack of wood, the arrow bounced away.

Grant's deep voice rumbled, "Why, you dirty little prick—"

The Sin Eater in his hand spit flame and a roar, and the bowman catapulted backward from a devastating center punch through the breastbone, which not only pulverized his lungs but smashed his spinal column to fragments.

The surviving warrior screamed, shouted and rushed headlong into the desert, following the stampeding horses. Brigid understood one shrieked word: *"Almas!"* It was in the Khalkha tongue and it meant "demon."

She tried to stand, but she swayed and decided to stay on her knees. She was uncoiling the lash from around her neck when Kane crouched down beside her and touched her face with gloved fingers.

"You're a mess, Baptiste."

She managed a whispery chuckle. "This hairbreadth stuff has got to stop."

Kane helped her to her feet, one polycarbonate-encased arm around her waist. She leaned into him gratefully, sagging in exhaustion. Tension drained out of her, leaving her weak and watery kneed.

Grant stepped over to the fallen Bautu, nudging his ribs with the steel-reinforced toe of a boot. He eyed the blood-soaked face and grunted. "Just grazed the bastard. Thought I'd shot straighter than that."

"Straight enough for me," Brigid replied. She felt the cold again, and it required great effort to speak without her teeth chattering.

"Where are Davis and Adrian?" Kane asked.

"Dead." She pointed to Bautu. "That animal chilled them. By half inches."

Grant pointed the blunt barrel of his Sin Eater at the wounded man's head. "Time to rectify my lousy marksmanship, then."

"Don't," Brigid declared. "We didn't learn anything except the warlord's name—not even that actually, just his title. The Tushe Gun."

"The Tooshy Goon?" echoed Kane. "What kind of dumb-ass title is that?"

"Means 'the Avenging Lama.'"

"What about his tech and firepower?" Grant demanded. "Predark?"

Brigid shook her head. "Not from what I saw. But he's getting some kind of material from the Russians— or one Russian, anyway. A man named Sverdlovosk. He wore a silver disk badge and he knew about the gateway."

"An officer of their Internal Security Network," Kane said grimly. "Back in our magistrate days, Grant and I were briefed about them. They supposedly had a base on Kamchatka Peninsula, up around Alaska a few years ago."

"If it's the same briefing I remember," Grant said brusquely, "that intel was pretty damn old. Like eighty or ninety years. That won't meet my definition of a 'few.'"

"Eighty years or a few," snapped Kane, "the rat bastards are still fucking around in other people's countries."

Brigid laughed. Even in her own ears, it sounded forced, with a note of hysteria in it. "We weren't exactly on a bird-watching junket, remember."

Bautu groaned. Blood had trickled into the corner of his mouth, and red bubbles formed on his lips. His eyelids fluttered.

Brigid nodded toward him. "He's our only solid source of Intel. Maybe Lakesh can understand his dialect. Do either of you have anything to keep him under until we get back to Cerberus?"

Grant made a wordless utterance of disgust, then pushed his Sin Eater back into its forearm holster. A cable-spring catch clicked as it locked the handblaster into position. From a pouch on his belt, he withdrew a small squeeze ampoule of liquid. A short hypodermic needle was attached to one end. Pushing Bautu's bloody head roughly to one side, he inserted the needle into the jugular vein and squeezed the ampoule.

"A mixture of morphine and scopolamine," he said. "So if he comes around, he won't feel up to doing anything more violent than picking lice out of his hair."

Grasping the man by his wrists, Grant heaved him up and rolled him over the wide brace of his shoulders. Bautu's head hung down, blood crawling along the length of his braids, dripping sluggishly to the gravel-spotted sand.

"Let's go," he said, marching into the rock tumble. "Getting cold out here."

Kane and Brigid followed him. Though she felt a bit stronger, she didn't object to Kane's armored arm around her waist. To her unasked question, Kane said, "We were just on our way to track you. Good thing you arrived when you did. I hate hikes."

"Saved us both a lot of inconvenience," she replied.

"Avoiding inconvenience is the only part of the Magistrate's oath I still practice, Baptiste." Despite the smile on his lips, she heard the undertone of bitterness in his voice.

They wended their way through the boulders and upthrusts of basalt until they reached the base of what appeared to be a heap of sand, decorated with scraggly vegetation. Kane released Brigid and moved lithely forward, ahead of Grant and his unconscious burden. From a belt pouch he removed a small plastic oval, pulled a thread-thin antenna from it and pointed it at the sand hill.

Instantly a section of the hill collapsed in upon itself, and the entrance door to the gateway installation irised open with a hissing squeak of hydraulics. Dim light spilled out. Kane led the way past the portal and down a short flight of metal stairs. Neither Grant nor Brigid objected. Kane always took the point, regardless of the situation or circumstances.

Brigid brought up the rear, waiting until Grant and Bautu were at the bottom of the stairs before pulling down on the wall lever to close the sec door and reseal the gateway installation. The gateways were major aspects of the predark scientific project known as the Totality Concept. "Gateway" was the colloquial term for a quantum interphase transducer, otherwise referred to as a mat-trans unit.

Most of the units were buried in subterranean military complexes, known as redoubts, in the United States. Only a handful of people knew they even existed, and only half a handful knew all their locations. The knowledge had been lost after the nukecaust, rediscovered a century later, then jealously, ruthlessly guarded. There were, however, units in other countries—among them Japan, England, Canada and this one in Mongolia. The installation wasn't a redoubt. In predark days this region of

the Black Gobi had served as China's principal nuclear-
and weapons-testing site, so its presence was not unusual.
However, the exact purpose of the units and of the Totality Concept itself had vanished when the ultimate nuclear holocaust had destroyed civilization all over the
world.

When Brigid reached the foot of the stairs, Kane and
Grant were already in the mat-trans chamber. Unlike the
layout of most other redoubts, this little installation had
no adjacent control or recovery room. It held only the
six-walled jump chamber, its translucent armaglass walls
colored a rich amber. The floor consisted of a hexagonal,
interlocking pattern of raised metal disks. The same pattern was duplicated on the ceiling.

With a relieved sigh Grant dumped Bautu unceremoniously on the floor. "Son of a bitch is heavier than he
looks. He stinks, too."

Kane undid the chin lock on his helmet and pulled it
up and off his head. His tousled, dark brown hair was
damp with perspiration. Grant removed his own helmet
and wiped at the pebbles of sweat shining on his coffee-
colored skin. He was a few years older than Kane, a few
inches taller and more than a few pounds heavier. His
heavy-jawed face was set in a perpetual scowl.

Brigid had learned that the more Grant frowned, the
more satisfied with circumstances he felt. The sprinkling
of gray in his black hair gave him a patrician air, like
somebody's curmudgeonly but essentially good-hearted
uncle.

In contrast, Kane's high-planed face always mirrored
his emotions. His piercing eyes were gray with enough
blue in them so the color resembled the high sky at sunset. The alert, wary look in them never changed. But

Brigid had seen his face transformed into something ugly and terrible by rage, and then change to the epitome of warm humor when he laughed.

It was difficult to keep in mind that Grant and Kane had spent their entire adult lives as killers—superbly trained and conditioned Magistrates, not only bearing the legal license to deal death, but the spiritual sanction as well. Although she owed both men her life, she still feared them.

When she stepped into the chamber, Kane cast her a sympathetic glance. "Lakesh's judgment was fused out on this one."

She waved away his criticism. "I'm the only archivist and historian at Cerberus. I thought I could speak the language, so his judgment was sound. If he'd sent you and Grant, all we'd have to show for the mission would be a wag-load of dead Mongols."

"Adrian and Davis would still be alive," Grant argued.

Tears suddenly stung her eyes, and she turned away. "Let's make the jump."

By the metal handle affixed to the center of the arma-glass, Kane sealed the chamber. The sec lock clicked, and the automatic transit process began. All of them understood, in theory, that the mat-trans units required a dizzying number of maddeningly intricate electronic procedures, all occurring within milliseconds of one another to minimize the margins for error. The actual conversion process was automated for this reason, sequenced by an array of computers and microprocessors. Though they accepted at face value that the machines worked, it still seemed like magic to them.

The disks above and below them exuded a silvery glow

and wraiths of white mist formed on the ceiling and floor. Tiny static discharges, like miniature lightning bolts, flared in the vapor. As if from a great distance came a whine, which quickly grew in pitch to a drone, then to a howl like a gale-force wind.

Brigid leaned against the wall. Her brain seemed to lurch sideways, and she closed her eyes, feeling tears cut runnels through the dried blood on her face. She wondered vaguely if the tears would make the jump with her.

Chapter 3

Though Kane didn't sleep, he dreamed.

He dreamed of the world's past, the nuclear war that had created the Deathlands, the remains of the U.S.A., unrecognizable to any who'd lived there before the nuke-caust. Then slowly, out of barbarism and anarchy, a new system came into being, bringing technology into its fortified cities and a predetermined, strict way of life for its citizens. What lay beyond the well-policed villes was now called the Outlands.

Kane's family was devoted to the duties of Magistrates, those charged with enforcing the rules in the Enclaves and in the still ruinous and wild Outlands.

The populations of the villes and to some extent the surrounding Outlands cooperated with this tyranny because of a justified fear and guilt nourished by the new doctrine. For the past eighty years it had been bred into the people that Judgment Day had arrived and humanity had been rightly punished. The doctrines expressed in ville teachings encouraged humanity to endure continual punishment before a utopian age could be ushered in. Because humanity had ruined the world, the punishment was deserved. The doctrines ultimately amounted to extortion—obey and suffer, or disobey and die.

The dogma was elegant in its simplicity, and for most of his life Kane had believed it, had dedicated his life to serving it. Then he stumbled over a few troubling questions, and when he attempted to find the answers all he discovered were many troubling questions—and the fact that humans were becoming little more than slaves.

What had become the most important question, the guiding mystery of his life, was to unravel the murky past and see where the future was headed, see it in time to avert some dread calamity.

Pigs, geese and cattle—first find out that they are owned.

Then find out the whyness of it.

That bit of ancient doggerel drove Kane, Brigid and Grant forward, kept them from accepting or surrendering to the forces arrayed against them. It had turned them into exiles on the planet of their birth.

Pigs, geese and cattle...

The nukecaust and the barons had reduced humanity to the status of barnyard animals.

First find out that they are owned...

Certain dark forces were utterly devoted to keeping the yoke of slavery around the collective necks of humanity, to keep them in the barnyard and troop willingly to the slaughterhouse.

Then find out the whyness of it.

Kane opened his eyes. All he saw were armaglass walls. These were brown, not amber, so he knew the jump was successful. He had made only a few gateway transits in the past three months, so he was always pleasantly surprised when he realized he was still alive and whole.

Intellectually he knew the mat-trans energies transformed organic and inorganic matter to digital information, transmitted it through a hyperdimensional quantum path and reassembled it in a receiver unit. Emotionally the experience felt like a fleeting brush with death, or worse than death. It was nonexistence, at least for a nano-second.

Grant and Brigid stirred on the floor plates. Bautu lay where he had been dropped. One of the most baffling features of mat-trans jumps was how a subject could start it standing up and end it by lying flat on his back.

The first jump they had made from Colorado to Montana had been marked by nausea, vertigo and headaches, all symptoms of jump sickness. Lakesh had explained that the ill effects were due to the modulation frequency of the carrier wave interfacing with individual metabolisms. It had since been adjusted and refined, but Kane wondered how the few hardy souls who had used the devices after skydark could have tolerated the adverse physical results.

Climbing to his feet, gritting his teeth against a brief wave of dizziness, Kane moved over to Brigid, who had both hands pressed against her head.

Voice tight with pain, she said, "Important health tip, gentlemen—don't jump if you're already suffering from a headache."

The heavy door of the chamber swung open and allowed DeFore and one of her medics to enter. DeFore was a buxom, stocky woman with deep bronze skin and ash blond hair braided at the back of her neck. Her aide's name was Auerbach, a burly freckled man with a red buzz cut. Following the sec protocols, he carried an SA-80 subgun. Both people wore white formfitting bodysuits, the standard duty uniform of the Cerberus redoubt.

DeFore's eyes swept around the chamber and settled on Brigid. "Where are Davis and Adrian?"

Helped by Kane, Brigid rose unsteadily to her feet. Her voice was level. "They didn't make it."

DeFore nodded toward the unconscious Mongol. "A prisoner or a guest?"

As he stood up, Grant snorted out a derisive laugh. "Is there any difference in this place?"

If DeFore understood his oblique reference to the way he, Kane and Brigid had been treated upon their first visit to Cerberus, she gave no sign.

"He's a prisoner," Brigid offered. "His name, as best as I can figure, is Bautu."

Briskly DeFore said, "Both of you need medical attention. Auerbach, call for a gurney. Grant, Kane—you know the drill."

Helmets under their arms, Grant and Kane walked out of the mat-trans chamber through a small recovery anteroom and into the control center of the Cerberus redoubt. The room was long, with high, vaulted ceilings. Consoles of dials, switches, buttons and lights flickering, red, green and yellow ran the length of the walls. Circuits hummed, needles twitched and monitor screens displayed changing columns of numbers. Cotta and Wegmann were on duty at the environ-op stations, and they gave Kane and Grant nervous nods as they passed by.

Kane glanced at the big Mercator relief map of the world that spanned nearly one entire wall. Spots of light flickered on almost every continent, and thin glowing lines networked across the countries, like a web spun by a radioactive spider. The map delineated all the geophysical alterations caused by the nukecaust and pinpointed the locations of functioning gateway units all over the world.

The two men stepped out into a wide, arched corridor made of softly gleaming vanadium alloy. Great curving ribs of metal and massive girders supported the high rock roof.

The Cerberus redoubt was built into the side of a Montana mountain peak, and could be reached from the outside only by a single treacherous road. The sec door was usually closed, so the gateway brought people and materials in and out. The trilevel, thirty-acre facility had come through the nukecaust in fairly good shape. It, and most of the other redoubts, had been built according to specifications for maximum impenetrability, short of a direct hit. Its radiation shielding was still intact. The redoubt held two dozen self-contained apartments, as well as a frightfully well equipped armory, a dormitory and a small dining hall. Cerberus was powered by nuclear generators, and probably would continue to be for at least another five hundred years.

The installation had served as the seat of Project Cerberus, a subdivision of Overproject Whisper, which in turn had been a primary component of the Totality Concept. Kane had often tried to picture what the place been like before the nukes flew—bustling with activity, purpose and people.

Now it was full of hollow corridors, empty rooms and sepulchral silences. The only evidence that it had ever been occupied before Lakesh and his staff of exiles had come to roost was the illustration near the main sec door.

Emblazoned on one wall was a large, garishly colored image of a froth-mouthed black hound. Three stylized heads grew out of a single, exaggeratedly muscled neck, their jaws spewing flame and blood between great fangs. Below the image, rendered in an absurdly ornate Gothic script, was the word Cerberus.

Even Kane, with his narrow education, knew the legend of Cerberus, the ferocious guardian of the gateway to Hades, the netherworld of the dead to the peoples of ancient Greece. It seemed an appropriate totem and code name for the project devoted to ripping open gates in the quantum field.

Grant and Kane turned into the last door on the left. It opened up onto a wide, white-tiled shower room. Each stall was enclosed by shoulder-high partitions. Rad-counter gauges were affixed to the walls beneath the shower heads.

They stepped into individual stalls, stripped off their body armor and piled it beneath the shower heads. The rad counters displayed only tepid yellow readings, not even a hundred roentgens, but they decided to scrub up all the same. Symptoms of rad sickness sometimes took days to appear.

If the area they had just jumped from had ever been hot, the rad level had fallen dramatically over the years. One of the mysteries spawned by the nukecaust was how hellzones could coexist cheek to jowl with "clean" regions. Reportedly much of Asia had been all but obliterated during the day-long nuclear conflict, and coastal areas were swallowed by tsunamis, giant tidal waves triggered by Russian "earth shaker" bombs.

Then again, much of what they had been taught about the nukecaust had turned out to be lies, so it was possible the devastation had been somewhat exaggerated so humanity wouldn't wonder if anything better lay over the horizon.

A mixture of warm liquid disinfectant and sterilizing fluid sprayed from the nozzle. Kane worked the decam stream into a lather and massaged it into his scalp and all over his body. When the needle of the rad counter leaned over into the far edge of the green zone, a jet of cold, clear water gushed down and rinsed him and his armor off.

After the decam process, Kane and Grant slipped into

white bodysuits handed to them by an attendant. They always felt a bit naked without the Sin Eaters strapped to their forearms, but their old habits had to be discarded here in Cerberus. Both of them had to continually remind themselves they were no longer Magistrates, enforcing the many and contradictory laws of Baron Cobalt. They were exiles now, as were all the personnel of Cerberus— except for one, and Kane wasn't sure if that particular one qualified as a person.

The dispensary adjoined decam, and when they entered they saw Bautu stretched out on an examination table, bound by canvas restraints. He was still unconscious, and DeFore was attaching gleaming electrodes to his shaved scalp. His head wound had been cleaned and treated by a liquid bandage. A film like a thin layer of skin had been sprayed over the bullet graze. The film contained nutrients and antibiotics, and the body absorbed it as the injury healed.

Brigid sat on the edge of a bed on the far side of the room. She had changed into a bodysuit that clung in all the right places to her tall, willowy figure. Her heavy mounds of reddish gold hair were tied back. The dried blood had already been sponged from her smoothly sculpted face, revealing a faint rosy complexion and a light dusting of freckles across her nose and cheeks. Her eyes weren't just green: they were a deep, clear, glittering emerald.

Auerbach examined the cut on her right temple. He murmured sympathetically to her and used an aerosol can to apply the liquid bandage. He made a comment that Kane didn't catch, and she laughed. He felt a quick, irrational flash of jealousy.

Baptiste owed her life to him—of course, he had put it in jeopardy in the first place, back in Cobaltville. He chided himself for his childishness and focused his attention on DeFore and Bautu. She plugged the electrode leads into a wheeled diagnostic scanner at the head of the bed and turned it on. Kane could make nothing of the flashing lights, the erratic jumping of a green line and discordant electronic noises.

Brigid rose from the bed and came over, touching the patch of thin film on the side of her head. Her bright eyes regarded the display monitor curiously. "Correct me if I'm wrong," she said, "but the electroencephalogram seems unusually, er, *unusual* for a Homo sapiens."

DeFore crooked an eyebrow at her. "So you're a doctor on top of being a historian? I'm impressed."

The sarcasm made Kane and Grant repress chuckles. Brigid sighed. "Reprimand accepted, *Doctor*. Now, tell me—"

"Yes, Baptiste, the readings *are* unusual. It appears the transmitter molecules released by the axonic end fibers of the brain's neurons aren't all crossing the synapse." DeFore's tone was brisk. "The ascending and descending neuron fibers aren't decussating normally. There seems to be a cross-current block, which may explain the patient's hypnopompic state of consciousness."

Frowning, DeFore leaned forward and squinted at the display indicators. "Evidence of some kind of brain damage."

"Being shot in the head will do that to a man," Grant commented.

"Except for a mild concussion, he's physically sound. The bullet didn't even crack the cranial casing. No, if it's brain damage, it's a strangely localized pattern."

"Explain," Kane said.

DeFore waved a dismissive hand. "Let me conduct a thorough examination and I'll try."

Kane opened his mouth to ask a question, but a reedy voice from behind interrupted him. "Allow the medics to attend to medical matters, friend Kane."

Kane turned as Lakesh entered. A wrinkled cadaver of a man, he was old, far older than he looked, and he looked very old indeed. His thin gray hair was cropped so short it was barely a patina of ash on his head. The network of deep seams and creases on his leathery face bespoke the anguish of keeping two centuries' worth of secrets. He wore a pair of spectacles with a hearing aid attached to the right earpiece. His eyes were a cloudy, watery blue.

Domi stood at his side, one arm slipped through his. She was a white wraith of a girl, with a provocative flare of hips. Her skin wasn't pale, but bone white, with no hint of pink, as if she were crafted from flawless porcelain. Her white hair was cut short and untidy and framed an angular, hollow-cheeked face. She wore a skintight belted jerkin of a silken red material that not only accentuated the ruby hue of her big eyes but showed off her long, gamine-slim legs to full advantage.

Like Baptiste, Grant and himself, Domi was another exile from Cobaltville. Unlike them, she was not ville bred but had been born in the Outlands, where postnuke-caust conditions had resulted in her type of albinism. Circumstances had thrown her in with the others, but she was not bound to them. She wasn't classified as a renegade or as a traitor to Baron Cobalt, nor did she have an active termination warrant hanging over her.

As an outlander, an outrunner, she was basically a non-person, and she was free to leave the redoubt at any time. So far, Domi had shown no inclination to do so. Despite the narrow strictures of life at Cerberus, it was still a much softer, safer existence than what she had known either in the Outlands or in the Pits of Cobaltville.

Besides, Lakesh had a peculiar fondness for her, due either to her rather endearing quality of innocence or her equally endearing habit of dressing provocatively.

Domi cast Grant a wide, toothy smile. Kane noted ruefully that Grant's return smile was a nervous twitch of the lips. Whereas Lakesh seemed unusually fond of the half-feral girl, Domi appeared to dote on Grant. It was understandable to the extent that she had joined in their escape—and had been instrumental to its success—because of him. Though Grant had no idea of Domi's age, it was fairly obvious he was old enough to be her father. He avoided being alone with her as much as possible. Kane wasn't sure if Grant distrusted Domi or himself. Probably a combination.

Suddenly ashamed of his own frivolity of thought, Kane snapped his attention back to what Lakesh was saying.

"I am truly sorry how cruelly you were used, Brigid. I can only hope your travails were worth it."

Brigid shook her head sadly. "Afraid not. The dialect the tribesmen spoke was incomprehensible. All I learned was that the rumors of a Mongolian warlord have foundation. Whether he has predark tech at his disposal is still an open question."

"Tell me what happened," Lakesh said gently, doddering over, and lowering himself into, a chair.

In a terse, colorless tone, Brigid told him everything that happened upon leaving the gateway installation and setting out across the Gobi. Her voice shook slightly when she reported how Adrian and Davis died.

"If it wasn't for Sverdlovosk, I would have died the same way, too."

Grant swung on her. "What do you mean?"

"He helped me to escape."

Kane scowled. "We lost two people, and you made a friend and brought another one home to visit. Of course, since nobody speaks his language, and according to the doctor, he's brain damaged, all he'll do is take up bed space—"

"Enough, Kane!" Lakesh said in a sharp, rapping voice.

Glaring toward him, Kane snapped, "It's not nearly enough, old man. You decide we're to act on rumors about a self-styled warlord a world away. Rumors that, when they had finally filtered into Cobaltville, were probably a year old and distorted beyond reality. Before my—" Kane paused, and when he continued speaking, his tone was venomous "—*exile*, I was told by Salvo himself the rumors were just that. In the Mag Division we always heard rumors. We learned not to put much faith in talk. Why do you?"

"Because I have access to intelligence your former fraternity did not have." Lakesh peered at him over the rims of his spectacles. "What upsets you about this the most, Kane? The loss of personnel?"

"Partly. It was a waste of resources. And you put Baptiste at risk."

Brigid spoke up angrily. "I volunteered, Kane. I wasn't ordered."

"That makes it worse," he grated. "Our numbers are small enough as it is. Now we're down to ten. Academics should not go out into the field until the field is secured."

Lakesh sighed heavily. "You are applying Magistrate Division protocols to a completely different set of situations, my friend."

An obscene comment leaped into Kane's mind. Before

it jumped down to his tongue, Grant caught his eye and shook his head. Kane turned the comment into a copy of Lakesh's sigh.

"At any rate," continued the old man, "it should be possible to wring some answers from our guest, brain damaged or not. We can hook him up to a language-interpretation program. His words won't be exact translations, due to his dialect, but the computer will recognize enough words to supply an English equivalent."

Grant waved to Bautu. "What if he's feeling uncommunicative when he wakes up?"

With Domi's help Lakesh heaved himself out of the chair. "That's why we have a supply of Pentothal and other psychotropics. Brigid, do you feel strong enough to accompany the rest of us to the control center?"

"Certainly. Why?"

"I owe you a look at what I fear we may be dealing with."

"Me, too?" chirped Domi.

Lakesh patted her arm with a gnarled hand. "Of course, darlingest one. We can't make a move without your valuable input—you know that."

Kane rolled his eyes.

Chapter 4

Lakesh sat before a four-foot ground-glass monitor screen. His liver-spotted hands played the keyboard as though he were a concert pianist.

Across the right side of the screen scrolled a constant stream of figures, symbols and numbers. The screen was black, yet the black swarmed with little points of brightness, like flickering dust motes. Near the bottom left corner was a curving sweep of blue green, mottled with wisps of white.

"What are we looking at?" Grant demanded.

"Our own benighted little home," Lakesh murmured, fingers still caressing the console keys. "Earth. Terra Obscura. This is a view from a satellite about 2,300 miles up."

Grant, Kane and Brigid all exchanged swift, startled glances. Domi looked disinterested. They were aware that in predark years, the upper reaches of the planet's atmosphere had been clogged with orbiting satellites, many of them designed for spying and surveillance purposes. According to legend, there were settlements of a kind in space, even on the moon itself. They were just as aware that ville doctrines claimed that all satellites were now simply free-floating scrap metal. For a time, in the decades following skydark, pieces of them fell flaming and disintegrating, once their orbits decayed.

Seeming to sense their wonderment, Lakesh said,

"There were literally thousands of satellites in orbit. All the major powers of the predark world put hundreds of them up there, over a period of fifty years. Did you think that every one of them fell down and went boom?"

"Hardly," Brigid replied dryly. "We just didn't know if there were any still operable and accessible."

"Very damn few," admitted Lakesh. "But those few are still transmitting. Fortunately Cerberus has the proper electronic ears and eyes to receive the transmissions. The satellite to which we've uplinked is one of the Vela reconnaissance class. Carries narrow-band multispectral scanners which detect the electromagnetic radiation reflected by every object on Earth, including subsurface geomagnetic waves. The scanner is tied into an extremely high resolution photographic relay system."

Kane stepped forward, standing behind Lakesh's chair, his eyes glued to the screen. He was filled with awe and a sense of despair. Earth seemed shadowy, dim, with a lost look to it as though the universe had forgotten about it long ago. He saw large areas of the globe lying under an impenetrable belt of dust and debris. In some places the belt looked like a dense blanket of boiling, red-tinged fog.

Shuddering inwardly, Kane stared at the thick, bloody haze clinging to the atmosphere. The clouds were the last vestige of skydark, the thirty-year-long nuclear winter.

The view on the screen tightened, penetrating the haze, and more details began to show. He saw whole continents spread out below him, forests appearing as ripples of green texture and seas that reached across vast expanses. He saw the high crags of the mountain peaks, and thousands of square miles of brooding desolation. Kane found the image inexpressibly sad.

It grew more so as he saw twisted ruins in the desolation, the scoured, rad-blasted bones of once great cities punctured by ugly craters. Around the cities were barren, empty vistas where nothing grew for hundreds of miles. He glimpsed a black and bare region that he knew instinctively was Washington, D.C., known for over a century as Washington Hole.

"It was a beautiful planet once," said Lakesh softly.

No one replied. The old man should know, since he had been born nearly fifty years before the nukecaust. Taking advantage of some new developments in making the body endure, he'd made it through all this time, though he'd spent a period in cryonic suspension.

He kept working the keys, and the image on the screen changed. A line of mountains appeared, and he said, "Ah, here we are."

As the aerial tour over Earth seemed to freeze, a green, irregular, elongated oval surrounded a section of the terrain.

"The former Mongolian People's Republic," Lakesh announced. "The computer-generated borders don't reflect the geophysical alterations since the apocalypse."

At the touch of another button, the country leaped upward. A tapestry of dark, oasis-spotted sand swelled on the screen.

"The southwestern Gobi Desert," continued Lakesh. "Also known as the Black Gobi. This photo was taken a year ago. What do you see?"

Kane, Grant and Brigid stared at the screen, straining to see anything other than tumbles of basalt, heavily eroded rock ranges and a sea of sand.

From a pocket in her bodysuit, Brigid took out the badge of her former office as an archivist, a pair of wire-framed, rectangular-lensed spectacles. Years of inputting predark data and documents, staring at columns of tiny type in Cobaltville's Historical Division had resulted in a minor vision problem. However, even with the glasses on, she couldn't pick out any unusual details in the image.

Impatiently Lakesh said, "Well? I'm waiting."

Domi ventured hesitantly, "Nothing?"

Lakesh laughed, turning in his chair and taking her hand so he could kiss it. "Excellent, darlingest girl. Nothing is all there is to see, and you saw it."

Kane repressed the urge to point out that since nothing occupied the girl's head, she would have a natural affinity for spotting the same. Impatiently he said, "Get to the goddamn point, old man."

Still laughing, Lakesh clattered over the keyboard again. The perspective on the screen changed, rushing downward, through a sky flecked with scraps of white clouds. The plummet halted over a place that was flat and bare, but held a structure in the center of it.

The image was blurred, but Kane saw a series of small, outlying constructions arranged in a circle around the dark bulk of a larger building. Rearing out of the sands was the suggestion of a wall.

"This was taken six months ago, at the extreme range of the photographic scanners." Lakesh tapped a key impatiently. "I can't enhance it further without losing resolution."

"There's been some excavation going on," Brigid observed. "Some old military or scientific installation?"

"Not by the proverbial long chalk," replied Lakesh. "I believe it is the ruins of Kharo-Khoto, once known to the Mongolian nomads as the Black City. It was a major commerce center six to eight thousand years ago."

Brigid moved closer, narrowing her eyes, examining

the image. ''The Tushe Gun feared that we were in his country to sap the flame from the Black City.''

Lakesh's eyebrow's rose. ''Indeed? The *flame* of the Black City? Did I hear you right?''

''You did,'' Brigid affirmed.

''So what?'' Grant asked. ''Some enterprising Mongolians want to clear away the sand and resettle the place. What's so critical about it?''

Lakesh was suddenly the scientist again. ''Look at this. It *is* critical.''

At the touch of a button, the image changed, shades of bright color blooming up from the central structure like the petals of an unimaginably huge flower. Hues of red, white, yellow, green, cyan, blue and even violet spread out across the ruins.

''This is a thermal line-scan filter of the area. Spectroscopic analysis indicates exceptionally high levels of radiation.''

''Is it a signature from a naturally occurring geothermal source, like a volcano or a hot springs?'' Brigid asked.

''No. This signature covers the entire electromagnetic spectrum. The white indicates infrared radiation, and visible light follows infrared. The phenomenon cannot be a natural one.''

''Lots of white,'' said Domi. ''Like snow or fog.''

''Or heat,'' muttered Kane, leaning forward. ''A hell of a lot of heat.''

''That's usually the byproduct of a high-density plasma discharge.'' Lakesh's tone was grim. ''The flame of the Black City, indeed.''

A sudden fear came over Kane. ''You said this region of the Gobi was used for military tests. Could the warlord have found old nukes buried beneath that city?''

"Unlikely. Kharo-Khoto has existed for thousands of years, and dates back to the Tanguat Empire. There was little archaeological work done on the site, even in the twentieth century. However, a Russian explorer named Kosloff reportedly unearthed a huge vault beneath the surface in 1923. Whatever he found there was never made public—at least not to the non-Soviet scientific community."

Lakesh swiveled his chair around, his eyes flitting from the faces of Brigid, Grant and Kane. Hesitantly he said, "There's something else."

"You mean this gets better?" asked Grant dourly.

"No. Worse. Much worse. I recognize that basic energy signature from my years of working on Overproject Whisper. The wavelength of the radiation is emitted by the essential working components of the gateway units, when the quantum path is opened."

"So there's another mat-trans system down there," Kane said. "Not commonplace, but not rare."

"I didn't say it was a mat-trans," Lakesh snapped, irritably waving at the big Mercator map on the wall. "If there was, it would be registered there. I said the basic spectroscopic energy form is similar. And those of us working for the Totality Concept used the same basic components in all of the technology. And where did the technology originate?"

Slowly, bitterly, Kane said, "The Archon Directorate."

No one really knew who the Archons were or where they came from. Until three months ago, neither Kane, Grant nor Brigid had even the vaguest inkling of their existence, let alone have any idea of the fact that the

Archons had influenced human affairs for thousands of years.

On the face of it, Kane would have seemed the least likely prospect to have stumbled over the evidence of their existence and works. After all, he and Grant had served for many years as Magistrates, enforcers of the ville laws and Baron Cobalt's edicts.

Both men followed a patrilineal tradition, assuming the duties and positions of their fathers before them. They didn't have given names, each taking the surname of the father, as though the first Magistrate to bear the name was the same man as the last.

As Magistrates, the courses their lives followed had been charted before their births. They were destined to live, fight and die, usually violently, as they fulfilled their oaths to impose order upon chaos.

Kane's life had taken another course, but he learned later he was following the secret path laid down by his father.

It hadn't taken much. A Mag raid on a slaghole in Mesa Verde canyon. An out-of-place computer system that was usually reserved for the ultra-elite administrators of Cobaltville. A strange device called a gateway, and a computer disk Kane palmed out of curiosity.

Seeking out Brigid Baptiste, a high-ranking archivist in the Historical Division, to decode it did bring some strange and cryptic information to light. And the threatening bits of data almost cost Brigid her life, and cast a shadow on Grant, too.

There was no alternative for Kane. He could join the baron's inner circle and let Brigid and Grant die, or save them and make all of them outcasts, exiles. Escaping Cobaltville, they had made their way to Cerberus, where survived the outcasts against this alien rule, and among them was Lakesh, Brigid's superior in the Historical Division. And Kane hadn't entirely made up his mind about Lakesh. After all, the man had been a part of so much that went on before that fateful conflagration. Or was it merely that he was a man used to decisive action, and the other a theorist?

Kane, Grant and Brigid were reclassified as outlanders, nonpersons, and they could never return to Cobaltville. As far as Kane was concerned, the war was over. The nukecaust had made the planet the property of someone—something—else, and humans like himself were exiles on the world of their birth.

Only Lakesh's theory that the nukecaust happened because of an alteration in the probability wave gave him even a dim light of hope. If the Archons turned the wave in a direction it was not supposed to flow, then perhaps the course could be redirected.

It was a small, almost ridiculous hope, but neither Kane, Grant nor Brigid had anything else on which to base a reason to continue living. Faced with the choice of bleak acceptance of the reality or a faint chance of salvaging humanity's future, they chose the faint chance.

It was the only human choice to make.

Chapter 5

In the dispensary, Auerbach had completed wiring Bautu to the computer module. A vocal outfeed cable encircled his squat neck, the direct digital sensor placed over his larynx. He mumbled and muttered, in a drugged state so close to sleep only a fractional difference in the medication kept his glazed eyes open.

DeFore attached the translation link to his ear and plugged it into the computer. Glancing toward Lakesh as he, Brigid, Kane, Grant and Domi entered, she said, "We've already obtained a sample of the dialect. Pattern analysis has yielded estimates on syntax, vocabulary and stochastics. We've got a highly simplified language substitute."

Lakesh thanked her and shuffled over to the computer. Into the oral interface speaker grid, he said, "I am your friend. You are my friend. Will you answer your friend's questions?"

Bautu's lips writhed and a rustling whisper came out. *"Tsa."*

From the computer, a harsh, electronic voice rasped, "Yes."

"Who is the Tushe Gun?"

The people in the dispensary didn't listen to the Mongol's voice, which was a thin, dry whisper, like old parchments being rubbed together. The computer's interpolator responded, "The Avenging Lama was is our chieftain. Brother. Black Hero. Priest. Not priest. One who knew holy words that is priest.''

Lakesh's eyes narrowed. ''How long ago?''

''Long ago.''

''Where is he from?''

''The black and dead city. Our country was rich and fertile. The Avenging Lama dwelt at the black and dead city. He could talk black words.''

''What are black words?'' Grant asked.

Lakesh turned slightly toward him. ''*Khara ugge...*'black words.' Magic formulas.''

Into the speaker he asked, ''Was the Tushe Gun king of all of Mongolia?''

Bautu's eyes slowly closed and opened. ''The Black Hero was ruler leader priest in the Black Gobi. He united all clans. China feared him and sent an army.''

''Was Kharo-Khoto destroyed?''

Bautu's head jerked back and forth. ''Yes. No. It died. It lived. It died. Lived. Black Hero died and lived. Brother found the flame and the ring. Lived again.''

Kane muttered, ''Gibberish.''

Brigid shushed him as Lakesh asked, ''What are the flame and the ring?''

''Treasures from Shamos. The flame. The ring. The air horse. The Avenging Lama lives again. The Black City lives again.''

''Tell your friend,'' said Lakesh. ''What is the flame?''

Bautu's head tilted to one side in a peculiarly strained fashion. Kane could see veins throbbing where the man's neck joined his shoulders. His mouth moved slowly.

''Buried deeply,'' rasped the electronic voice.

''Say again?'' Lakesh asked, adding in a soothing tone, ''Say it to your friend.''

''Buried deeply.''

"Is the flame buried deep beneath Kharo-Khoto, is that what you mean?"

"Buried deeply. Not supposed to remember. Brother buried them deeply. Cannot remember them."

Lakesh moved closer to the bed. He asked softly, "Why can't you?"

"Buried. Cannot remember."

"Remember them for me, your friend."

"Buried in the vault. Avenging Lama Brother I obey admire worship follow obey. Buried deeply. Avenging Lama spoke black words. Dragon's kiss. I obey admire worship—"

The diagnostic scanner at the head of the bed suddenly emitted a nerve-scratching squeal. The flashing icons and jumping, jagged lines showed Bautu's vital signs. Even Kane, with his limited medical knowledge, saw a sudden surge in brain activity and a highly elevated pulse and heart rate. Bautu was fusing out. He was shaking, his entire body trembling with some sort of tension, almost a convulsion.

DeFore reached quickly for a wheeled tray, snatching up a hypodermic. "He's fighting the medication! All metabolic functions are accelerating—"

Bautu jackknifed up at the waist. The belt restraints came loose with ripping, popping sounds. He reached up and clawed away the sensor electrodes attached to his skull, dragged off the vocal infeed from his throat. His mouth opened as if he were readying himself to voice a scream, but no sound came out. His eyes were wide, but they were empty black holes, mirroring no emotions, no thoughts.

He lunged from the bed, arms flailing wildly. A sweep of his left arm slammed DeFore aside, knocking the hypodermic from her fingers. A backhand caught Lakesh across the side of the head and sent him staggering the width of the dispensary. He would have fallen if Domi hadn't darted forward, a white wisp of motion, and caught him.

At the same instant Domi moved, Grant and Kane bounded across the room and grabbed Bautu's windmilling arms. As soon as they secured grips, they realized they had made a mistake. The two men shared a brief eye exchange, acknowledging their error. Grant hissed, "Shit."

Never had they encountered so powerful a man, not even the most juiced-up jolt-walker back in the Pits of Cobaltville. Though he was shorter than either one of them, Bautu's lunging rush carried them both with him. They strained to slow him down, muscles tightening and bulging. Their feet scrabbled for purchase on the slick floor. For a long moment the only sound in the dispensary was their harsh, labored breathing. Then Grant said, between clenched teeth, "Somebody get a blaster—"

Bautu brought both his arms together as if he were clapping his hands. The backs of Grant's and Kane's heads smacked together. Air left both sets of lungs in explosive *woof*s. The two men reeled away in opposite directions. Kane's feet tangled and he fell heavily, striking his head on the floor. Brigid had to dodge aside to avoid being bowled over by him.

Auerbach jumped on the Mongol from behind, sliding his arms around his neck, trying to apply a choke hold.

Grant recovered his balance first and bounded toward Bautu, leading with his left fist. He pounded it into Bautu's lower belly, but the warrior was beyond pain. He kept walking with Auerbach clinging to his back. He slapped at Grant, and his open hand connected with the side of Grant's face, sending him stumbling against the wall. Bautu reached up and around behind him, fingers hooked like talons. The blunt, ragged nails raked Auerbach's face.

The red-haired medic howled, shaking his head with a spattering of crimson. Still, he maintained the pressure of the choke hold. Bautu made a gagging sound, staggering a bit on wide-braced legs. Kane shook the swimming pain haze out of his head and scrambled to his feet. Brigid plucked at his arm, spoke to him, but he shook her off.

Quickly he closed with the staggering Mongol, bringing his fist down on the bridge of Bautu's nose. Blood sprayed in liquid tendrils from his nostrils, and as he opened his mouth to gasp for air, Kane jacked his left knee up into the man's groin. Bautu uttered a grunt, but he didn't double over. Instead, his heavy fist pistoned forward in a straight-arm punch.

Kane leaned away from it, but the fist struck him below his left ribs, sending pain stabbing up and down his torso. Measuring the Mongol off, he drew back his right arm.

"You son of a bitch," he snarled, and threw his fist with every ounce of his weight and strength behind it.

The blow caught Bautu on the side of his jaw with the sharp sound of a whip's crack. The shock of impact jarred up the bone of Kane's wrist and into his shoulder socket.

Bautu's head snapped around. Blood spilled from his lips. His eyes rolled up, the lids closed and he lurched backward. He pawed feebly at the air as he collapsed onto his back, pinning Auerbach to the floor. The medic cried out as his head struck the vanadium alloy.

Cursing, Grant rolled Bautu's limp body to one side, allowing Auerbach to scramble to his feet. He held a hand over the raw, oozing mess of his left eye. Brigid stepped forward and kneeled beside the Mongol, peeling back an eyelid and fingering the base of his throat. The man's face was a swatch of bruised flesh and smeared blood.

"Damn it, Kane," she said. "What have you done?"

Kane stopped trying to massage the searing pain from his knuckles. "What do you mean?"

"He's dead."

"Bullshit." Even as he said it, he knew the woman had spoken the truth. He had seen enough—and made enough—corpses in his life to quickly recognize one.

Bending over Bautu, DeFore poked, prodded and examined him. Dolefully she declared, "He's deader than fucking hell, all right."

Kane shrugged, saying to Brigid, "Let the punishment fit the crime. He died an easier and quicker death than either Adrian or Davis, or the one that he had planned for you. If you feel like holding a wake, that's your business."

Brigid glared at him and stood. "I'm glad an individual human life means so much to you, Kane. I suppose that's why you were such a highly decorated Magistrate."

Kane scowled, but before he could respond, Lakesh shuffled forward, supported by Domi. Rubbing the side of his head, he announced, "A man that strong doesn't die from a punch in the jaw."

"You're quite right," DeFore responded. "And he didn't. My guess is a cerebral hemorrhage, an aneurysm. Ties in with the pattern of brain damage indicated by the EEG."

"That wouldn't account for his strength," said Grant. "Would it?"

DeFore's lips tightened. "In typical cases, no. It was

almost as if his entire metabolism was suddenly kicked into very high gear, like a sustained adrenaline rush.''

Lakesh made a clucking sound with his tongue against his cheek. ''A postmortem is called for. See to it, please, after you treat Auerbach.''

Grant helped DeFore heave Bautu's body onto a gurney. Out in the corridor Lakesh said, ''Brigid, after you get some rest, I will need your help to prepare a briefing jacket. We will have to wring the historical database for every byte of information about Kharo-Khoto and the legends regarding it.''

Kane eyed him darkly. ''I hope you don't intend to send us back to Mongolia.''

Lakesh smiled cheerfully. ''Not at all, friend Kane. Or at least, not right away. No, I think the first destination for your next field trip will be Mother Russia.''

Chapter 6

Cobaltville was built on the bluffs overlooking the windings of the Kanab River. The white stone walls rose fifty feet high, and at each intersecting corner protruded a Vulcan-Phalanx gun tower. Powerful spotlights washed the immediate area outside the walls, leaving nothing hidden from the glare. The bluffs surrounding the walls were kept cleared of vegetation except grass, a precaution against a surprise attack. On the far side of the river, tangles of razor wire surrounded cultivated fields.

Inside the walls stretched the complex of spired Enclaves. Each of the four towers was joined to the others by pedestrian bridges. Few of the windows in the towers showed any light, so there was little to indicate that the interconnecting network of stone columns, enclosed walkways, shops and promenades was where nearly four thousand people made their homes.

In the Enclaves the people who worked for the ville administrators enjoyed lavish apartments, all the bounty of those favored by the Baron Cobalt.

Far below the Enclaves, on a sublevel beneath the bluffs, light peeped up from dark streets of the Tartarus Pits. This sector of Cobaltville was a seething melting pot, where outlanders and slaggers lived. They swarmed with cheap labor, and the movement between the Enclaves and Pits was tightly controlled—only a Magistrate on official business could enter the Pits, and only a Pit dweller with a legitimate work order could even approach the cellar of an Enclave tower. The population of the Pits was as strictly and even more ruthlessly controlled as the traffic. The barons had decreed that the villes could support no more than five thousand residents, and the number of Pit dwellers couldn't exceed one thousand.

Seen from above, the Enclave towers formed a latticework of intersected circles, all connected to the center of the circle, from which rose the Administrative Monolith. The massive round column of white rockcrete jutted three hundred feet into the sky. Light poured out of the slit-shaped windows on each level.

Every level of the tower was designed to fulfill a specific capacity, with C Level devoted to the Magistrate Division. On B Level was the Historical Division, a combination of library, museum and computer center. The level was stocked with almost five hundred thousand books, discovered and restored over the past ninety years, not to mention an incredibly varied array of predark artifacts.

The work of the administrators was conducted on the highest level, Alpha Level. Up there, in the top spire, far above even the Enclaves, the baron reigned alone, unapproachable, invisible.

Below, in his office on C Level, Salvo stared out of the single window at the gray skies and tried not to think about the baron. His mood was equally gray. It was the start of the rainy season, and persistent downpours had turned the fields outside of the walls into quagmires. The lower squats of the Pits were suffering from intermittent flooding, since there were no adequate drainage or sewage systems down there.

At least it was a clean, nourishing rain, not falling from chem-tainted, toxic clouds. He found the thought a very small, very cold comfort. For a moment he studied his reflection in the heavy pane of water-streaked glass. He had a flat face that was almost round and his eyes were a deep brown that rarely, if ever, showed what he was thinking. Though someone had once compared his eyes to puddles of muddy water, he always tried to make sure those puddles held no particular expression. His hair was cut very short, and in places the scalp showed through. He noticed a few gray strands that hadn't been there three months before.

There were also new lines etched across his forehead. The lines were bisected by a livid, ragged scar running from his hairline almost to the brow of his left eye. The scar was three months old, too. The laceration dealt him by Kane had been easier to mend than his teeth. Ashamed of his dentures, he now practiced speaking with a minimum of lip movement. He had Kane to thank for that new habit, as well.

Abrams, the Magistrate administrator, had been seriously injured by Kane, too. He was still convalescing and Salvo had assumed, as senior Mag officer, he would take his place not only in admin, but occupy his position in the Trust.

Three months had passed, and he had yet to hear from Baron Cobalt about a new position. In fact, he had yet to hear from Baron Cobalt about anything.

On the one hand, Salvo understood he had failed the baron. He had inducted Kane into the Trust, and Kane had turned on them, escaped the ville and assaulted the baron himself. Though no specific orders had come down from the top level, Salvo knew he was charged with the responsibility of apprehending two of his best Magistrates and Brigid Baptiste, the archivist. But in the past three months there had been no rumors of them, not even a case of mistaken identity in the Outlands. It was as if the three people had never existed.

A madness born of frustration and fear sometimes gripped him. Frequently an imagined pounding on his door woke him from a fitful sleep. Was the baron simply waiting for an opportune moment to serve a termination warrant on him, to convene a disciplinary tribunal or to quietly exile him to the Outlands? Was Baron Cobalt playing some sadistic game with him, allowing him to relax, to believe that all was well, and then stretch out his hand to snuff out his life?

Salvo sighed, tried to focus his mind on a plan of action, but past events crowded their way forward. He knew how Kane, Grant and Baptiste had disappeared through the mat-trans unit the Trust had been foolish enough to place in the Mesa Verde slaghole.

To where they had disappeared was still the outstanding question. All of the functioning gateways had been checked, their records showing no indication of use, authorized or otherwise.

Somehow the three renegades had appeared in the Dulce installation, which therefore left open only a single possibility—they were transiting through a gateway not listed as active. Wherever the mat-trans unit was located, its quantum energies had been altered, by means unknown, so they couldn't be traced back to the jump point. And that meant they had the help of someone—or several someones—intimately familiar with the workings of the devices.

Salvo wasn't familiar with the intricacies of the gateways. He doubted there were a dozen people in any of the villes who were. Baptiste was, since she had delved into the Totality Concept database, but it didn't seem logical she had learned more than the basics.

The Preservationists would serve as a variety of culprits for a variety of crimes, but Salvo wasn't really certain they existed. They were straw adversaries, convenient for accusations and convictions of treachery and sabotage. A vast number of people had been executed for being Preservationists, but no hard proof of their existence had ever been forthcoming. Apparently they wanted to throw off the current serious restrictions on individuals, and were supposedly searching for historical background to the nuke war. Not that the order ruling them didn't have its opponents, he thought.

Salvo's suspicions focused primarily on one man—old Lakesh, the head of the Historical Division, and Baptiste's direct supervisor. He was also a fellow Trust member, an untouchable, one of Baron Cobalt's pets.

Salvo knew nothing about Lakesh, could find out nothing about Lakesh, because he was under the baron's protection. All Salvo knew was that Lakesh frequently disappeared for days on end, and didn't have to account for his missing time. His quarters were not equipped with the regulation spy-eye, and he enjoyed unlimited access to the baron's delicately shaped ears.

All he knew about Lakesh was that the old man knew far more than he about the Archon Directorate and the hybridization program. From his years in the Trust, Salvo had gleaned a few nuggets of half-digested truths—predark theorists had argued about the insurmountable problems standing in the way of communicating with extraterrestrials. They had claimed that human beings would have nothing in common with alien life-forms, no matter how intelligent.

The Beforetime theoreticians had overlooked the pivotal fact that aliens would acknowledge the same problem and take measures to correct it.

The Archons' solution was a long-range hybridization program, combining the genetic material of humankind with their own race—whatever they were—to construct a biological bridge.

From the little Salvo understood, the program had been instituted hundreds of years ago, long before the nukecaust. He wasn't sure why. He knew the Archons themselves were a dying race, probably on the verge of extinction before the skydark. He suspected that since Archon involvement in human affairs dated back many thousands of years, the nukecaust itself could have been a major component of their program.

After the teeming masses of humanity had been culled, the herd thinned, then the hybrids would inherit the earth, carrying out the agenda of the Archon Directorate.

Salvo sighed, running a finger absently over his scar. The only thing he could be sure of when it involved the Archons was that he could be sure of nothing. They and their human allies were masters of subterfuge, of contradiction, of concealment and deceit. When it came right down to it, he wasn't even sure if they existed. The baron and all the other so-called hybrids could be no more than a new breed of mutie, yet another strain of twisted genetics spawned by the nukecaust.

He knew he wasn't an educated man, not like Baptiste or other archivists. He certainly wasn't in Lakesh's class. But he knew that in ancient times, the term *Archon* was applied to a parahuman world-governing force that imprisoned the divine spark in human souls. Certainly the Archons, if they existed, did not use that word to describe themselves. Salvo couldn't help but wonder if the predark scientists who had hung that appellation on them were employing a cryptic code to warn future generations.

No, he was not and probably could not be sure of

anything about the Archons. Only a single certainty burned in his mind and his heart—he had to find Kane. Had to bring him back to Cobaltville, had to throw him or his corpse at the feet of Baron Cobalt. It was the only way he could ever redeem himself. Grant and Baptiste would be welcome additions, but Kane was the prize. Besides, he knew, without knowing how he knew, that where Kane was found, so would be Baptiste and Grant. There was a painful, gnawing, soul-deep void inside of him. He couldn't—or wouldn't—understand why only Kane could fill it.

He heard a shuffling of feet at his office door. He didn't bother to turn. He recognized the shuffle. "Come in, Pollard."

A burly, stocky man, blunt of face and manner, stepped into the office. He wore the Mag day uniform of pearl gray bodysuit, long black coat made of Kevlar weave and the dark night-vision glasses. The right sleeve of the coat was a bit larger than the left to accommodate the holstered Sin Eater.

Salvo gazed at the man's reflection and was able to read his expression. "You've come up blank. Again."

Pollard nodded curtly. "Yes, sir. None of our informants in the Outlands have any useful intel. As far as I can figure, when they climbed into the gateway, they went to the fucking moon."

Salvo wheeled, face and voice savage. "Shut up, you triple-stupe bastard! How many times do you have to be told?"

Pollard swallowed hard and murmured, "I apologize. Sir."

For perhaps the hundredth time over the past three months, Salvo regretted not having Pollard chilled when he had failed to apprehend Kane and his companions. He had pursued them into Mesa Verde canyon and witnessed them disappear from the mat-trans unit. Under other circumstances, the little Pollard had seen would have been far too much. Anything connected to the Totality Concept was of the highest security priority. Only members of the Trust had access to the data, and even they weren't privy to the whole scenario.

However, Pollard despised Kane, and Salvo needed a confidant and, if necessary, a pawn. Though Kane and Grant might not have been loved by their fellow Magistrates, they were respected and admired. Their abrupt disappearance and conviction in absentia of sedition and murder had seriously damaged morale in the Magistrate Division.

Salvo's cover story to the division was flimsy, and he knew all the Mags knew it. Only their years of conditioning and discipline made them govern their tongues. Pollard knew more than they, and he still didn't buy Salvo's version of how Kane, Baptiste and Grant had been turned by the Preservationists. He allowed his hatred of Kane, his wounded ego, to keep him from asking the wrong questions. He was content to be an active player in what was being privately referred to as Salvo's vendetta.

Salvo was fully aware that his semifictions regarding a handful of operable gateways hadn't persuaded Pollard—a blunt weapon he might be, but he wasn't stupid. Single-minded to the point of stupidity, perhaps, but so far he hadn't completely crossed the line.

Turning back to the window, Salvo said, "They're out there somewhere. And someone knows exactly where."

Pollard lifted the wide yoke of his shoulders in a shrug. "Our intel section receives daily reports from all the villes. Nothing."

"And from overseas?"

Pollard frowned. "If they're in another country, we wouldn't know about it yet. Information takes a minimum of six months to reach us from foreign soil."

Salvo scowled in frustrated anger. Pollard's six-month assessment was best-case. Communications and contacts with other countries had all but ceased since the nukecaust. Over the past eighty years, spotty, fragmented reports had filtered in about the conditions in Japan, the former United Kingdom and Russia. However, they were so piecemeal, so sporadic, no clear picture had ever emerged. Nearly a century ago, fear of a foreign invasion had been one of the rallying cries of the Unification Program. Except for a handful of old rumors about Japs on the West Coast and Russkies in Alaska, nothing solid had ever been found to support this fear.

The architects of the Program of Unification had then drawn their paranoia from within, spinning ghastly "what if" scenarios about mutie rebellions and hordes of outlanders marching on the villes. As was the case with the fear of foreign invaders, there was no foundation for it.

Agents of the villes dispatched to other nations hadn't fared well, either. They had to go in sterile, carrying nothing that could peg their point of origin. Only a few had been sent out. As far as Salvo knew, none had ever returned.

Glancing over his shoulder at Pollard, he demanded, "What else?"

"The full alert is still in effect, triple red throughout all the villes. Border patrols have been beefed up and reinforced by all the Mag Divisions. Deathbirds fly on daily recon missions over all outland settlements. The net is spread wide."

"It just hasn't snared anyone." Salvo's voice was grim.

Pollard shifted his feet uncomfortably, cleared his throat. "Sir, I was wondering—"

Salvo turned, angling an eyebrow. "Yes?"

"I was wondering what the baron's take is on all of this. I presume you're keeping him informed."

Salvo's eyes widened, narrowed, then widened again. Chuckling, he stepped closer. His right hand swung up and struck Pollard across the face, rocking his head back on his shoulders, sending his dark glasses flying from his face. They clattered to the floor.

Pollard didn't make an outcry or say a word. He merely stood, eyes expressionless, a red flush spreading over his cheek, a spot of blood forming at the corner of his mouth.

Calmly, softly, Salvo asked, "Anything else you'd care to presume?"

Pollard did not reply.

"I asked you a question. I expect an answer."

"No, sir. Nothing more." His voice was barely above a whisper.

"Good. The lord baron's 'take' on all of this is none of your concern. His thoughts, his feelings, his whims are none of your concern. You do my bidding as I do his. If he is displeased, you will know it by *my* displeasure. Are we agreed on that?"

"We are. Sir."

Salvo spun away, back toward the window. "Get out of my sight."

He watched Pollard's reflection in the rain-streaked window as the man bent to retrieve his glasses and hurried into the corridor. As soon as he was gone, Salvo surveyed the panoramic view of Cobaltville. The rain showed no sign of abating. In fact, it was coming down even harder than before.

He had no choice but to bide his time. But the opportunity would come, he knew. As sure as death, they would meet face to face again.

He balled his fists and struck the double-glazed pane of glass. It shivered but didn't crack. Not even the water droplets sliding down the outer surface jumped from the impact.

"Kane, where the fuck are you?" he muttered to the night. *"Where the fuck are you?"*

Chapter 7

Kane stood at the edge of the precipice, looking down into a deep dark. The sky over the craggy cliffs was a heavy, leaden gray. The rain had finally stopped, and the mountain air smelled clean and fresh, without the slightest whiff of a chemical taint. The rich scent of wet, grassy meadows and groves of trees rolled up from the foothills below.

He blew a wreath of smoke into the gathering dusk, glad to be out in the fresh air, noting ironically he was polluting it with his cigar. No one in Cerberus smoked but he and Grant, even though Lakesh provided them with cigars.

Hardly anyone used tobacco in any form nowadays. There were mild drugs available that were much safer, less offensive to others and just as sedative. But both Kane and Grant had learned to appreciate good cigars during their many Pit patrols back in Cobaltville, and having the freedom to enjoy them when they wanted to was one of the few advantages of being an exile.

Standing on a rutted asphalt road, he faced a deep abyss that plummeted straight down a thousand feet or more. At one time steel guardrails had bordered the lip of the road, but only a few rusted metal stanchions remained. Although he couldn't see them, he knew the skeletons of several vehicles rested at the bottom of the chasm. They had lain there since the time of the nuke or the big chill, weathering all the seasons that came after, like monuments to Beforetime desperation.

Behind him the cracked tarmac broadened onto a huge plateau. The scraps of a chain-link fence clinked in the breeze, enclosing the entrance to the redoubt. Nestled against the rock face of the mountain peak was a high gate, vanadium alloy gleaming beneath peeling paint. The gate opened like an accordion, folding to one side, operated by a punched-in code and a hidden lever control. It was slightly open now, allowing a feeble light to spill out.

Lakesh had told him that when the Cerberus redoubt was built, the plateau had been protected by a force field powered by atomic generators. Sometime over the past century, the energy screen had been permanently deactivated, so new defenses had to be created. Although they couldn't be noticed from the road, an elaborate system of heat-sensing warning devices, night-vision vid cameras and motion-trigger alarms surrounded the mountain peak.

Cerberus had been built over two hundred years ago, and no expense had been spared. All design and construction specs were aimed at making it a viable, impenetrable community of at least a hundred people. There were far less than that now, and for most of the people who labored there, time was measured by the controlled dimming and brightening of lights to simulate sunrise and sunset.

Kane found he could tolerate only a few days of the artificial passage of time before he grew claustrophobic and had to get out into the open. Rarely, if ever, did any of the staff follow suit. They were all exiles from the villes, brought there by Lakesh because of their training and abilities, and they were all terrified of being discovered. Lakesh always assured anyone who evinced anxiety that Cerberus was listed as utterly inoperable, completely unsalvageable on all official records.

So far, the old man's assurances had never been contradicted. The Montana mountain range known as "the Darks" was technically within Cobaltville's territorial jurisdiction, but the wilderness area was virtually unpopulated. The nearest settlement was over a hundred miles away, and according to Lakesh it consisted of a small group of Sioux and Cheyenne. If they knew about the installation, they ascribed a sinister significance to it and never approached. In fact, nothing ever approached. In the past three months, there hadn't been so much as a Deathbird air patrol within ten miles of the mountain peak.

Sometimes Kane wished Salvo would find him. He regretted not chilling the bastard when he had the chance. He regretted a lot of things, and as Salvo symbolized all of the regrets, he had the vague sense that if he erased the man's life he could erase his own guilt.

Then there were other times when Kane yearned to be back in Cobaltville, under Salvo's command, fulfilling his Magistrate duties as one of the baron's chosen. A Mag's obligations to the new order had been drilled into him for nineteen years, and that had been his justification for life, his reason for life, and his identity. All of it was gone, and it was natural to miss it, but he realized he missed Salvo, as well.

Hate can be as strong a bond as love, he mused, tapping an inch of ash over the edge of the precipice.

There was a link between Salvo and himself, one that he had been unaware of until his exile. Baptiste had told him of the private conversation between her and Salvo shortly after her arrest.

Salvo had declared his hatred for Kane, though he couldn't mention a single incident that had sparked it. "A lot of reasons, some of which even I don't understand," he had said to her. "Maybe he's yin to my yang, or vice versa. A more tangible reason is that my father and his father were bitter enemies."

He had also said, "If you are a Magistrate, family tradition and family honor are all-important. Our entire discipline is based on it. I am also a man of pride, and I must have what all men of pride must have—vindication. Revenge for the wrongs compounded upon my family name, my family honor."

Kane had no idea what wrongs his father had visited upon Salvo's family honor. Only Salvo could tell him that, and he doubted they would ever again have an opportunity for a face-to-face talk.

A breath of icy wind gusted up from the chasm, and Kane pulled his jacket tighter around him. Winter came early to such high elevations and tended to linger a very long time. In a couple of months, perhaps less than that, the mountain road would be clogged with snow, tripling the difficulty for a curious somebody to make his way up from the flatlands.

He glanced up at the backdrop of gray sky. For a generation following the nukecaust, the sky had been black twenty-four hours a day. The worldwide atomic explosions had filled the atmosphere with inestimable tons of dust and debris, severely diminishing the amount of sunlight reaching the earth. The thirty-year-long nuclear winter, the skydark, had caused many of the survivors to freeze to death in the long night.

Gradually the clouds of pulverized rubble had dispersed and settled, though judging by the satellite pix, there were still places on the planet covered by the residue of the nukecaust.

Kane often wondered just how many truly human people populated the earth, but there was no way to hazard an accurate guess. Even the intelligence-gathering apparatus of the villes couldn't learn with any certainty about what was transpiring in the rest of the world. Radio waves wouldn't reach across the sea because lingering radiation and atmospheric disturbances disrupted shortwave bands.

If it could be determined that the Archon Directorate had not entrenched themselves in Europe, the Near and Far East, he knew his resolve to fight would be strengthened.

As it was, the resistance movement based in Cerberus seemed not only futile, but downright ridiculous. He and Grant cooperated with Lakesh because they needed to keep busy. Kane was introspective enough to know that the anger that had motivated him thus far could not be sustained. Every day it required more effort to fan the flames of rage. He couldn't help but wonder what would happen if he one day discovered he couldn't keep that spark blazing—or worse, didn't *want* to keep it blazing.

He heard a soft footfall behind him and he whirled, wrist tendons tensing, hand ready to receive the Sin Eater that wasn't there.

"When you look into the abyss," Brigid said, "the abyss also looks into you."

Kane relaxed and watched Brigid approach him in her characteristically loose-limbed, almost mannish stride. "Another quote from Lakesh?"

Even in the dim light, Brigid's eyes shone bright with humor and intelligence. "Not this time. Nietzsche said that."

"Who's he? One of the guys down in maintenance?"

"He was a nineteenth-century philosopher. He also said, 'He who fights too long against dragons, becomes himself a dragon.'"

Kane exhaled a plume of smoke. "Very appropriate, if you apply it to our circumstances."

"He had an amazing intellect."

"What happened to him?" Kane asked gruffly.

"He died in a madhouse."

Kane was startled into laughing. "That's very appropriate, too. Except in our case, the whole world is a madhouse."

Brigid didn't return the laugh. "We're ready for the briefing."

Kane flicked the stub of the cigar over his shoulder toward the chasm. Its glowing end descended like a tiny meteorite, until it disappeared in the depths and the darkness. "Let's go, then. A good briefing is better than a good cigar anytime."

Walking side by side across the plateau, Brigid said quietly, "I didn't have the chance to thank you."

"Thank me for what?"

"Rescuing me."

"When?"

She sighed in irritation. "In the Gobi, remember? I know it was all of twelve hours ago, but—"

"Leather the sarcasm, Baptiste," Kane interrupted. "You're welcome. But my main function, and Grant's, is to rescue the truly essential personnel of this place. That's why Lakesh recruited us."

Brigid stopped abruptly. Kane walked on for a few paces before halting and turning to face her. She stared at him silently. Kane asked, "What?"

"Why are you so bitter and angry all the time?" she demanded. "All of us are equally important."

"And therefore equally unimportant," Kane replied. "Only some are more unimportant than others. You don't have to be angry or bitter to speak the truth."

"The Mag in you is taking over again."

"Lakesh wants me and Grant here because we're Mags. We're the professional guns he never had, the killer instincts he could never bring into play. We're the enforcement arm of Cerberus."

"And you resent him for that?" Brigid asked.

Kane shook his head. "Not for that, no."

"For something else, then."

Kane saluted the air, the mountain peak. "This world, this madhouse, is the legacy he and his kind of people left us. He wants us to pick up the pieces of the humanity he helped to break."

"He regrets it, Kane. You know that."

"I regret it, too, Baptiste. But his regrets are too damn little and about two centuries too late."

Brigid didn't reply, didn't respond. Kane felt the intensity of her gaze on him. She moved forward quickly, shouldering past him, stalking toward the sec door. "I can't talk to you when you get like this."

Kane waited until she entered the small opening allowed by the portal before following her. One day, he thought, I am going to have to reason out why I keep risking my ass for a woman who can barely stomach me.

He made his way along the corridors and down an elevator to the cafeteria, where most of the briefings were held. Lakesh, Grant, DeFore and Brigid occupied a table at the far end, cups and a pot of coffee before them. Like the availability of cigars, Cerberus had another advantage over Cobaltville in its supply of genuine coffee, not the bitter synthetic gruel that had become a common substitute since skydark. The redoubt had access to tons of the real thing, freeze-dried caches of the stuff secreted before the nukecaust.

Ignoring Baptiste, Kane took a chair next to Grant and poured himself a cup. DeFore riffled through a sheaf of papers, shaking her head in disbelief. A cloth-covered metal tray rested on the table in front of her. The cloth was draped over a round, damp object. "Impossible," she muttered. "Impossible."

"You performed the autopsy yourself," Lakesh said.

"It's still impossible."

Kane asked, "What is?"

Lakesh's rheumy blue eyes regarded him with wry amusement. "Oh, that's right. You missed the doctor's preamble. Kindly bring friend Kane up to speed on your findings."

Tersely DeFore inquired, "You remember what I said about an indication of brain damage in Bautu?"

Kane nodded, sipping at his black coffee.

"It was a localized, isolated part of the brain." With a flourish DeFore snatched the cloth away from the tray. In the center was a white, deeply furrowed, oval-shaped thing. Though it was wet and somewhat cut up, Kane recognized it as a human brain.

DeFore prodded it with a slender steel rod. "The temporal lobe, to be exact. Some sort of disinhibition of the limbic system occurred."

"That's what you were saying before you started saying 'impossible,'" Grant declared. "What's the limbic system and what's so impossible?"

DeFore glanced down at her sheaf of paper. "In layman's terms the limbic system is a collection of smaller organs within the larger organ of the brain. They regulate emotional responses. Some scientists have speculated that religious visions and telepathic abilities stem from the limbic system."

"What's the impossible part?" Kane asked.

"An outside agency apparently caused the damage."

"Do you mean an injury?" Lakesh's tone was incisive.

DeFore shook her head. "No physical trauma could account for this. Something stimulated and broke down the inhibitors of the limbic system. For all intents and purposes, Bautu was programmed to die if he consciously recalled a buried memory."

"Ah," remarked Lakesh. "Hence the 'buried too deeply' monologue. Not the Black City, but a memory. Perhaps a memory of the Black City itself."

"How could he be programmed to die?" demanded Grant skeptically.

DeFore poked the brain with the probe, pushing aside the edges of a convolution. Blood and cerebrospinal fluid slowly seeped out. "See that hole?"

Brigid turned her face away. "Ugh."

DeFore grinned. "Don't throw up yet, Baptiste. You haven't seen my prize exhibit."

From a pocket in her bodysuit, she produced a small transparent packet. At first glance it held nothing more than a square of white gauze. By squinting, Kane saw a tiny triangular object positioned on the center of the square. It was a very dark gray, almost black.

"I removed this from a fissure in Bautu's temporal lobe," announced DeFore. "It's so small, barely two millimeters, that the initial X ray almost missed it."

"What the hell is it?" Kane asked.

"An implant," Lakesh declared flatly.

"How can you be sure it isn't an organic growth of some kind?" Brigid inquired.

DeFore nodded. "A pretumorous growth was my first diagnosis. So I subjected it to an ultraviolet-black-light examination. It gave off a fluorescent green color. It's definitely a manufactured foreign body, but one designed to fool the immune system."

"I don't get you," said Grant.

DeFore tapped the packet with the probe. "Normally any foreign body implant results in a marked degree of tissue reactions. I found no evidence of damage in the peripheral nerves and pressure receptors. No evidence of either acute or chronic inflammation in the surrounding tissues."

Lakesh leaned forward, eyes blinking owlishly behind the lenses of his glasses. "Did you analyze it?"

"I haven't had time to perform more than a preliminary. However, I found that a metal core is covered by an organic membrane. The membrane consists of blood protein and keratin. It is apparently composed of organic material produced by Bautu's own body. That's why there was no indication of rejection."

Brigid asked, "What could be its purpose?"

"A monitoring device," replied Lakesh.

"Or a suicide switch," said Kane.

Brigid's eyes narrowed. "What about Bautu's display of superhuman strength?"

DeFore's full lips quirked in a mirthless smile. "That's the easy part. Elevated levels of epinephrine were found in his peripheral nerves, the brain stem and the adrenal glands. It increased his cardiac output and elevated his strength and resistance to pain. Unfortunately the curve of cardiac efficiency flattens out quickly. Bautu went into severe shock, like a stroke, judging by the broken blood vessels I found. That caused an immediate circulatory arrest of some kind.''

"You mean a heart attack?" Kane asked.

"Exactly. Your punch to his jaw had nothing to do with his death.''

Kane resisted casting Brigid an I-told-you-so look.

Lakesh asked, "Is it possible that when my questions delved into certain levels of his memories—breached them, as it were—I activated the implant, which in turn triggered a metabolic explosion, stimulating a magnified, preprogrammed flight-or-fight reaction?''

DeFore consulted her notes, frowning. "I don't know.''

"But is it possible?''

Slowly, reluctantly, she said, "Yes, it's possible. But what was done to Bautu was deliberate. Who could have the ability to implant a human brain without noticeable signs of invasive surgery?''

"A psi-mutie," declared Kane. "Telekinesis.''

DeFore shook her head. "Even the most advanced psi-mutie on record never had the powers to do something like that.''

"There are psionic mutations on record who could perform startling feats of psychokinesis," Brigid said. "And allegedly teleport matter. Perhaps the Tushe Gun is one such mutant.''

"Don't get your hopes up," DeFore replied ruefully. "I also found random traces of radiation exposure in Bautu's soft tissues. I think the radiation is more likely to have caused a neuro-cognitive dysfunction than the implant.''

Lakesh rapped his gnarled knuckles on the tabletop. "I think it's more likely that both of your hypotheses have foundation. Nor does it necessarily have to follow that mutants are involved.''

No one replied to that, but it was obvious to Kane everyone was thinking along an identical track. Mutants with obvious physical characteristics were dying out, partly due to the long campaigns of genocide waged by the baronies, but primarily because most the human muties had reached evolutionary dead ends.

The general supposition had always been that the muties, human and animal alike, were the unforeseen byproducts of radiation and other mutagenics. Lakesh had indicated otherwise, claiming that many of the hordes of muties that once roamed the Deathlands were the result of pantropic sciences, the deliberate practice of genetic engineering to create life-forms able to survive and thrive in the postnukecaust environment. As Kane, Brigid and Grant had witnessed, bioengineering was the specialty of the Archon Directorate.

One breed of human mutant which had increased dramatically since skydark was the so-called psi-mutie—people born with augmented extrasensory and precognitive mind powers. As Lakesh had said, these abilities weren't restricted to muties, since a few norms possessed them, as well, but generally speaking, nonmutated humans with advanced psionic powers were in the minority.

Folding his arms over his broad chest, Grant said to Lakesh, ''You claimed that city in the Gobi was putting out a lot of radiation. That's got to be where he was contaminated.''

''I didn't say he was contaminated,'' DeFore responded. ''Just exposed. None of the tissues showing the rad readings were damaged. He hadn't received anything approaching a lethal dose.''

Grant sighed in exasperation. "Lakesh said the place was hot. Didn't you?"

"After a fashion," replied Lakesh. "But there are different wavelengths, different levels of radiation which can affect a human being in ways other than a quick or lingering death."

Turning in his chair, he reached out and touched Brigid's shoulder. "My dear, will you do the honors and relate to us what you found in our database regarding Kharo-Khoto?"

Brigid interlaced her fingers atop the table and cleared her throat. Kane found himself irrationally annoyed. Because of her eidetic memory, she didn't need to consult notes like DeFore—or like the rest of them, for that matter.

She began speaking.

Chapter 8

"The database had very little in the way of hard, verifiable facts about Kharo-Khoto. Legend and reality became so intertwined over the centuries that it is impossible to find a defined demarcation between the two."

Kane and Grant exchanged bemused glances. If Brigid noticed, she gave no sign.

"Kharo-Khoto is in one of the most desolate parts of the Gobi, although just near it is an oasis. Curiously, no mention of the city is made in contemporary Asian texts, though it was widely known as a commerce center of the Tanguat people. There is no firm idea of how old Kharo-Khoto might be, though some historians have speculated that the Gobi was once a very fertile area, supporting many cities and great industries. Some sort of global cataclysm turned the Gobi into a desert, and there are many reports from the twentieth century describing the ruins of large cities. Local nomads told stories of such lost cities emerging after fierce sandstorms. Kharo-Khoto was evidently considered the capital of a vanished civilization, although what this civilization might have been has never been determined. Even the derivation of the name of the city is a mystery.

"Some time over the last two thousand years, Kharo-Khoto's ruler was Khara Bator Janiyn, known in Chinese as Hara-Tzyan-Tzyun. He was a warrior and a mystic because he could speak 'black words,' magic formulas and spells. He also possessed a vast and magical treasure, though there was not much specific detail regarding it. There were mentions of 'sacred flames' and an 'air horse' and other gifts from Shamos, which translates into 'black star' or 'evil luminary.'

"Khara Bator's power grew so great that the Chinese emperor feared him and dispatched an army to subdue the so-called Black Hero. Kharo-Khoto was besieged for a long time and withstood all assaults. The inhabitants had an abundance of provisions and drew their water from a well fed by an underground river.

"Allegedly the emperor of China himself arrived at the scene of the siege and somehow cut off the flow of water to the city—how this was done is not fully explained. Either the underground river was diverted or poisoned.

"In any event, Khara Bator determined to die fighting with his people rather than perish of thirst. He prepared for a final battle, but his favorite daughter persuaded him to flee the city while she opened the gates to allow the Chinese army to march unopposed into Kharo-Khoto.

"The warrior king and the remnant of his army left under the cover of darkness while the Chinese army assembled to enter the city at dawn. All the while during the flight, Khara Bator spoke his black words, and the fertile country around them was transformed into a barren waste.

"While her father transformed their land into a desert, the daughter threw Kharo-Khoto's treasures into a dried-up well. As dawn arrived, the Chinese found that what at sunset had been forests and meadows was a desert at sunrise. Raging, they stormed into the city to take vengeance and to loot, but they found it deserted, except for Khara Bator's daughter. They slew her and, rather than risk dying of thirst and hunger, they fled the dead city and country, leaving Kharo-Khoto's fabled treasure behind.

"For centuries afterward treasure seekers tried to find the treasure. On certain nights, the legends say, the treasure could be seen at the bottom of the well, but the Black Flame of Shamos rises up to protect it, killing all who are too close. I should note, however, there are no Chinese historical records to support any of this.

"There are very vague and spotty references to Kharo-Khoto over the following centuries. Supposedly Genghis Khan spent some time there, which is evidence that the city was occupied in the eleventh century at least.

"In 1907 the Russian archaeologist Kosloff was the first European to study the ruins of the ancient city. He mounted several expeditions and in 1923 found a massive vault beneath it. Though he claimed a significant find, a vast and astonishing array of artifacts, he didn't inventory them. He wasn't allowed to disturb or take anything from the vault, and it was sealed again after he and his party left it. I found a couple of cryptic references about mysterious maladies that struck down members of Kosloff's expeditions. The symptoms seem remarkably similar to radiation poisoning.

"The last historical mention of Kharo-Khoto in the database dates to the latter part of the twentieth century. By 1949 that region of the Black Gobi became China's primary weapons-testing site, due to the remoteness of its location. Its mysterious tradition also kept local nomads away.

"That tradition became even more mysterious when, in 1979, several prominent Chinese scientists disappeared there while they were doing some tests near Kharo-Khoto's ruins. They had utterly vanished, and despite the mobilization of a huge number of troops and search aircraft, no clue to their fate was ever found. Oddly that area was also the center of a UFO mystery at the time. Many sightings of strange lights skimming across the sky were reported in the general vicinity. Just so you'll know, the tribesmen in the region called them 'air horses.' The Chinese authorities called them 'hallucinations.'''

Kane stirred restlessly in his chair, scuffing his feet on the floor. Brigid cast him a quick, irritated glance and continued speaking.

''Before you ask, yes, the so-called Tushe Gun, 'the Avenging Lama' is also a figure of Mongolian history and tradition, though not quite as ancient as the tale of Kharo-Khoto. In the eleventh century Genghis Khan, Emperor of All Men, seems to have been the first man to have been elevated to the title of the Tushe Gun. After melding together the feuding Mongol tribes into an army, he swept over China and Iran. His sons moved farther west, into Russia and Eastern Europe.

''After the Khan's death, his immediate family established the so-called Golden Clan to maintain the ruling dynasty. In the fourteenth century they made Kharo-Khoto the capital of the Mongol Empire. As in the Khara Bator legend, the Chinese marched on Kharo-Khoto and razed it to the ground. Succeeding centuries saw it covered completely by sand.

''In the mid-eighteenth century a warrior chieftain by the name of Amursana made an attempt to reclaim Kharo-Khoto from the Chinese. Claiming to be both a descendant and a reincarnation of Khara Bator, he united the scattered Mongol tribes for a guerrilla war of liberation against their oppressors. For more than a year, he and his nomads fought a hopeless fight against superior forces.

"Amursana died in 1755, and legends sprang up that the liberator Khan would one day reappear as a warrior figure inspired by the gods, and something of a cult developed wherein people did nothing but wait Amursana's coming incarnation on the Gobi and a rebirth of the Golden Clan.

"In 1911, one Mongol chieftain determined to revive the glories of the Golden Clan and he, too, chose the ancient capital of Kharo-Khoto as his base. Born sometime in the 1870s, a man named Dambin Jansang was said to possess hypnotic powers and a gigantic force of will. His early years were spent studying occult sciences with Chinese and Tibetan mystics. As he traveled around Mongolia at the turn of the century, the conviction spread he was the reincarnation of both Khara Bator and Amursana. He was worshipped as a divine warrior, hosts of savage fighters gathered around him.

"He led a revolution against the Chinese and was invested with the title of the Tushe Gun. He became both the spiritual and military ruler of the Mongolian people. He was said to have possessed the ring of Genghis Khan, an ornament supposedly found in the underground vault of Kharo-Khoto. In that vault Jansang claimed to have made contact with the Sons of Intelligences of Beyond, who predicted his rise to power. Allegedly the ring of Genghis Khan allowed him to escape from grave dangers.

"The Tushe Gun's horde captured and sacked the Chinese garrison at the western Mongolian city of Kobdo. The story stated that the Tushe Gun's clothes were in shreds from rifle bullets, but that he himself was unharmed. The inhabitants were massacred, and he slaughtered ten people according to an occult ritual. With his victims' blood, he painted tokens of victory on the banners of his troops.

"After this victory, his reputation as the Mongol messiah was uncontested, and the Tushe Gun was appointed governor of the west. He soon became one of the richest and most powerful chieftains in the country. He was cruel to his enemies and was feared by his worshipers. Flaying people alive who had displeased him was one of his pastimes.

"In 1924 a combined force of Russian and Chinese troops set out for the Black Gobi to assassinate the Tushe Gun. This was not accomplished through force of arms, but through deceit and treachery. Dambin Jansang, the Avenging Lama, was shot by a man he trusted. He was decapitated and his heart ripped out. His head was paraded all around Mongolia to prove to the people that the revolution and their messiah were dead.

"In the years that followed, many people claimed to have seen the Tushe Gun, whole and mounted on his pony, riding across the wastes. Many Mongolians sincerely believed that one day the Tushe Gun would be reincarnated and ride out of the Black Gobi to rebuild Kharo-Khoto and resurrect the Golden Clan.

"And judging from what I saw and experienced, that seems to have finally happened."

Lakesh cleared his throat and lifted his spectacles so he could massage his eyes. "A fascinating account and just slopping over with all sorts of dire implications."

"How so?" Kane asked.

Lakesh held up a hand. As he spoke, he counted off his points on his fingers. "One—the Black Flame of Shamos. Some sort of device discharging plasma and radiation? Two—the treasure vault, containing a magic ring and an air horse. A psionic accelerator in the form of a ring and a flying vehicle? Three—the so-called black words. An alien language? Four—a fertile region transformed into a desert virtually overnight. Exposure to lethal levels of radiation?''

''Are you asking us,'' growled Grant, ''or telling us?''

''I'm telling you it appears that an ancient base of the Archons, forgotten and lost for thousands of years, may be involved.''

''And now remembered and found,'' Kane interjected. ''You're making quite a stretch, fitting all this magic mumbo jumbo in with the Directorate.''

''Think you so, friend Kane? The Archons have interfered with and influenced human affairs for many thousands of years. It makes historical sense that a city would have been built around and above one of their underground bases, and it would tend to explain why certain areas of the Black Gobi have been taboo to generations of Mongols.''

''Could the Archons have brought Genghis Khan to power?'' inquired Brigid. ''Maybe giving him a 'magic ring' and other weapons so he could terrorize the world and depopulate whole countries was part of their agenda to cull the herd.''

Lakesh smiled sadly. ''Why not? Traditionally, the Archons have always allied themselves with conquerors and despots. Reasons *can* be found for the success of peoples like Genghis Khan's Mongols. The new vigor of an expanding population that's perhaps threatened with displacement, their battle tactics—swift maneuvers relying on small, fleet horses with great endurance—and a culture that trained its mounted warriors from a young age to be consummate riders, archers and swordsmen. And perhaps it makes sense that more settled and secure groups had become complacent and found it difficult to repel them. Still, given the vast size of the empires conquered begs the question of how we are to explain without magic—or its technological equivalent—that Genghis Khan, an untutored barbarian, was able to subjugate peoples and empires far more advanced than he was.''

Kane pursed his lips and nodded reluctantly. The technology employed by the Archons was vastly different than anything available to predarkers. To date, the only offensive/defensive Archon weapon they had encountered was an infrasound emitter.

It had been the only artifact he, Grant and Brigid had returned with from the Dulce installation. By examining it, the Cerberus techs had rendered it inoperable, but they had learned it was a marvel of miniaturization, designed to convert electric current to ultrahigh sound frequencies by a maser. There was no denying something like it in the hands of a ruthless warrior like Genghis Khan would have been interpreted by his victims as a weapon of the blackest magic.

"The Tushe Gun wore a big dragon ring," Brigid said. "The scar on Bautu's head resembled the dragon's face."

DeFore frowned. "I didn't see a scar."

"The bullet wound obliterated it." She tapped the right side of her head. "The scar roughly corresponded with the location of the temporal lobe, where you found the implant."

DeFore's eyes widened. "Are you proposing Genghis Khan's magic ring was responsible for the implant?"

"I'm making an observation," Brigid retorted coldly. "Both he and the Tushe Gun said something about a 'dragon's kiss.' So I'm presenting all the facts in order to reach a provisional hypothesis. It used to be called the scientific method."

Impatiently Grant said, "Why would the Archons try to repeat ancient Mongolian history?"

"We could always ask Balam," put in DeFore with a wan smile.

Kane cast her a sour glance. Over the past three months, he had yet to make a second visit to Balam's holding facility. Recollections of the creature's fathomless black eyes and the mental message it had imparted still gave him occasional nightmares.

We are old, it had told them. *When your race was wild and bloody and young, we were already ancient. Your tribe has passed, and we are invincible. All of the achievements of man are dust—they are forgotten.*

We stand, we know, we are. We stalked above man ere we raised him from the ape. Long was the earth ours, and now we have reclaimed it. We shall still reign when man is reduced to the ape again. We stand, we know, we are.

Kane repressed a shudder. "Waste of time, DeFore."

Lakesh nodded his head. "We wouldn't get anything out of him but his patented 'we stand, we know, we are' telepathic message."

"Assuming the Mongols have laid claim to an old Archon installation," Grant said, "do you want us to take it away from them or destroy it?"

"Preferably take it away from them. At worst, the Tushe Gun is using it as a staging site for wars of conquest. At best, it could contain a means to successfully combat the Directorate."

"Even if the Tushe Gun is planning to revive the Golden Clan," Kane said, "so what? Asia is a bit out of our jurisdiction."

"You don't have a jurisdiction anymore," stated Brigid matter-of-factly. "For all we know, the Archons could be behind all of it."

Lakesh shook his head. "No, I doubt the Directorate

is directly involved in Mongolia. It seems, however, that the Russians—one of them, at least—are. That is where the first clue to this mystery may be found."

"How do you propose we get to Russia?" Kane asked. He instantly regretted the question when he saw Lakesh's thin lips twist into a supercilious smile.

"How, indeed, friend Kane."

Chapter 9

Like most other intercontinental locations, Russia was still a big unknown—except to the Russians, and they weren't providing information. What little scraps of intel had leaked out since the megacull close to two hundred years before had to be assembled like a jigsaw puzzle with most of the pieces missing.

It was a certainty that Moscow had been hit very hard, as had most of the other industrial cities. The entire country had suffered the nuclear winter like the rest of the nuke-ravaged planet, but because of its extreme northern latitudes, it was believed that for over thirty years, temperatures rarely rose above five degrees Fahrenheit. Speculation had it that more Russians died during the big chill than during the actual holocaust. Other than that, the conditions in Russia could only be inferred from very old reports.

Supposedly a form of the old Stalinist industrialization regime had been revived, at least in the century following the nukecaust, but even that Intel was too fragmented to be reliable. It was word-of-mouth, too little detail separated by too many years, though a militia unit called the Internal Security Network had been identified. As Kane and Grant were aware, rumors of a Russian base in Alaska had circulated for years, but were never found to have any solid basis beyond lingering paranoia.

In the control center the main monitor screen showed

only a sweeping, vast snowscape, an infinity of wind-swept whiteness. Old craters, the rad levels still too high to allow snow to settle on them, pockmarked the ground. Though they resembled a pattern of dots, Kane realized that some of the larger craters might have been a quarter of a mile in diameter.

The image dissolved, replaced by another view of the white wasteland. The terrain was scored by roadways and railroad tracks. In the distance a tiny cluster of dark, stalk-shaped objects reared from the ground. A suggestion of spired minarets could be seen atop a few of them.

"These are the most recent—and best—satellite photos we have obtained of the Moscow vicinity," Lakesh said. "They were taken some thirty years ago, and obviously some rebuilding has been going on."

"How could you get pix of Mongolia and not of Russia?" asked Kane suspiciously.

"That country's atmosphere is still too densely ionized for a satellite recon," Lakesh answered. "At this point the ionization blanket is probably a seasonal phenomenon, but we are unable to time the satellite's flyovers to coincide with the clear periods. We were lucky to get these views."

"But we don't have an idea of the current level of their society," said Brigid. She was making a statement, not asking a question. "We don't know what they have or what they don't have."

"We know *one* thing they have, at least. A mat-trans gateway."

Lakesh pointed to the tiny light glowing on the sprawling Mercator map on the wall. "That's the place. An outer suburb of Moscow called Peredelinko, about twenty miles from the city center."

Grant eyed the light, then Lakesh distrustfully. "You're sure?"

Lakesh smiled. "Do you recall me telling you that after the first mat-trans successes, we built the units in modular form so they could be shipped to and assembled in other locations?"

"Yes," answered Kane, "but I assumed you meant the redoubts."

"That's where the majority of them went, yes. But a few went to other places. Peredelinko, for one."

"Why?" asked Brigid.

"*Glasnost, perestroika,* a thawing in East-West relations. An overt sharing of material goods, a covert sharing of technology."

"If America and Russia got on so well," said Grant, "there shouldn't have been a war."

"No, there shouldn't have been. You know my thoughts on that."

Brigid, Kane and Grant did know his thoughts, but they didn't pretend to understand them. According to what Lakesh had learned from Operation Chronos, not only was the holocaust preventable, it was not *supposed* to have happened. Operation Chronos had disrupted the chronon structure and triggered a probability wave dysfunction. Lakesh didn't believe that the past was a fixed object, immutable and unchanging.

"At any rate," Lakesh continued, "the gateway unit is inside a dacha."

Kane squinted. "A what?"

"A kind of country house," explained Brigid.

"Exactly," Lakesh said. "It was a dacha given to the American diplomatic staff. That was the cover story, at least. In reality, it was to prove to the Russians that the Totality Concept technology worked."

Grant glanced again at the map. "So they knew about it."

"Of course. Many Russian electrophysicists and quantum theorists were involved in aspects of Overproject Whisper. Peredelinko itself had been a kind of artists' and writers' commune, at least for those adhering to the party line. Later it became something of an enclave for scientists."

"How do you know if the gateway still works?" inquired Kane.

"We still receive a positive read on the phase-transition inducers. However, the target autosequence initiators show a negative."

"And that's bad," stated Grant blandly.

Lakesh shrugged. "Not necessarily. It could just mean a sensor isn't transmitting a green signal as it should."

"What if the thing's inoperable?" Grant demanded. "We could jump there, and if the receptor coils aren't powered up—"

Lakesh gestured sharply. "If we can't verify the jump at this end, we'll choose the abort option and transmit you to an alternate unit."

"'Alternate unit'?" echoed Kane incredulously. "Like where? Cobaltville?"

"Perhaps. Dulce, maybe. At least you'd know your way around."

Kane's eyebrows knitted together. "Not funny, old man."

Lakesh smiled impishly. "Don't worry, friend Kane. The worst-case scenario is that we'll hold your patterns in the digital security interlock until we can establish a transit line back here."

Grant made a low, growling noise deep in his throat

and glared at the door leading to the jump chamber. "I *hate* those fucking things."

Lakesh consulted his wrist chron. "It's better than walking. Now, I have to be back in Cobaltville early tomorrow, so I won't be here to see you off. Collect what ordnance you require from the armory, but I insist you do not wear your Magistrate armor."

"Why not?" Kane asked.

"According to Brigid, this man Sverdlovosk had knowledge of the baronies and of gateways, so it stands to reason other Russian officials you may encounter will, as well. There is no reason to advertise your point of origin and former fraternity, even if you are no longer affiliated with it."

"Assuming we're able to make the jump, what do you expect us to do over there?" inquired Grant.

Lakesh regarded him calmly, unblinkingly. "I expect you to spy, friend Grant. I expect you to return with enough hard data regarding Russia's connection with the Tushe Gun so we can formulate a plan of action."

Kane, still frowning, said with a deliberate slowness, "We don't speak Russian."

"I do," declared Brigid, imitating his cadence of speech.

Lips compressing in a tight white line, Kane said, "You're doing it again, old man."

"Doing what, friend Kane?" Lakesh sounded genuinely puzzled.

"Sending an academic out into a hellzone. What are you trying to do—wash away your guilt in her blood?"

Lakesh's shoulders stiffened. "What about *your* guilt, friend Kane? Do you believe it can be washed away by the blood of Salvo or even the baron? Do you think our fight should lay only with them?"

Kane took a swift, dangerous step toward him. The old man didn't move, nor did his placid expression alter. Kane thrust his head forward, his glaring eyes only a few inches from the lenses of Lakesh's spectacles.

"How is it," he said in a low, quiet monotone, "that such a goddamn genius, such an expert on history, such a tactician, always manages to say the wrong fucking thing?"

"And it's a measure of your growing maturity that you don't try to kill me each time I do. The superego triumphing over the id."

Lakesh broke the eye contact, turning and shuffling toward the door. "It's quite cold in Russia, even this early in the fall, so I will inform the jump-prep crew to provide you with the proper dress. There will be a map, though based on landmarks two centuries old, prepared and ready for you, as well as the standard survival equipment. You will embark at 0800 tomorrow morning."

With that, Lakesh exited the room. To his departing back, Grant muttered sarcastically, "And good luck to you all."

Brigid faced Kane, her eyes bright with a cold, emerald anger. "Why do you keep baiting him? Why do you behave toward him like he's an enemy?"

Softly Kane answered the question with one of his own. "Why are you so sure he isn't?"

Brigid gritted her teeth in exasperation. "He's not Baron Cobalt."

"No, he's not. In many ways he's Baron Cobalt's mentor."

"I think I know what you're suggesting."

Kane shook his head in response. "No, you don't, Baptiste."

He didn't try to explain his reasons, since they were

only half-formed and too personal. Everything he had believed in had been revealed to be a lie, part of a centuries-spanning deception, so he had no reason to believe that Lakesh was always forthcoming with the truth.

"What you are suggesting," Brigid snapped, "is that you are disorganized mentally and emotionally. The only time you act like you're together is when you have a blaster in your fist."

She turned sharply on her heel and stalked out of the control center. Grant murmured, "Wasn't good, Kane. She could be right."

"She very well could be. So could I."

They walked into and down the corridor to the armory. It was a huge room stacked nearly to the ceiling with wooden crates and boxes. The walls were lined with a half-dozen, tall, glass-fronted cases. M-16 A-1 assault rifles were neatly stacked in one, and an open crate beside it was filled with hundreds of rounds of 5.56 mm ammunition. There were SA-80 subguns, Copperheads, and 9 mm Heckler & Koch VP-70 semiautomatic pistols complete with holsters and belts. Stacked neatly in a corner were bazookas, tripod-mounted M-249 machine guns and several crates of grenades. Every piece of hardware, from the smallest-caliber handblaster to the biggest-bore M-79 grenade launcher, was in pristine condition.

They went through the crates and the cases, picking and choosing from their lethal contents. Both of them took four grens apiece—an implode, two incendiaries and a high-ex. They attached them to the combat harnesses they would wear beneath their coats. They clipped three 20-round magazines for their Sin Eaters to the harnesses, as well.

Grant didn't speak as he carefully inspected the ordnance—he had that grim, hooded look in his dark eyes Kane knew well.

"Something on your mind?" he asked mildly.

Grant didn't answer for several uncomfortable moments.

"I asked—"

"I heard you," Grant retorted tersely.

He's getting mulish about something, Kane thought. And there was nothing on earth more intractable than a mulish Grant.

"You're wondering the same thing I'm wondering," he said.

Grant gave him a sharp, angry look. "And what the hell would that be?"

"It would be that we're running off to fight an old fart's private war. And it's not enough to know *who* we're fighting anymore—it's *why* we're fighting. Otherwise, we might as well be back in Cobaltville, burning down slaggers in the Pits."

For a second Grant scowled at him, his eyes distant. Unhappiness seemed to settle on his broad shoulders like a heavy cloak. After a few moments of silence, he moved visibly to shake it off. Returning his attention to his combat harness, he said, "I know why. Death is always simple."

"But not the ways of dealing with it," Kane replied. "Or even facing it."

Grant draped the harness over his arm with an angry slap of leather and a clank of metal buckles. "You don't have to go on this op, you know. You don't have to go on any op. This isn't a Mag duty call. You haven't sworn an oath. You can bow out, stand down, find yourself a remote little spot and live in a tent with a stickie slut for all I care. I don't give a shit anymore."

"Yes, you do. You need me at your back—old, tried and true—not an unreliable historian."

Grant stared directly into his eyes. His voice was a husky whisper. "At this point, Kane, I'm starting to wonder just how reliable you really are."

He turned away, saying, "I'm going to get some rest. If you're going with us, 0800 comes awfully early."

Grant strode out of the armory and down the quiet corridors. The vanadium alloy sheathing on the walls and floors absorbed sound, so a sepulchral silence always seemed to shroud the interior of the redoubt.

He walked past the electronically locked door to Balam's cell, and he grimaced. Like Kane, he had never visited the entity's confinement facility a second time. His initial reaction to the creature had been a primal, mindless urge to kill it. Lakesh had claimed at the time that his xenophobic response was quite natural and human, but Grant didn't have the inclination to go near the thing ever again.

His quarters at Cerberus weren't quite as spacious as his flat back in the Enclaves of Cobaltville, but they were a bit better appointed. The bed was much larger and very comfortable. He draped the combat harness over the back of a chair and went into the bathroom.

He stripped and stepped into the shower stall. As he stood beneath the bracing jets of cold water, he knew he had been out of line with Kane. He had no right to pass judgment on him. Kane held himself solely responsible for their exile, and his self-anger sometimes surfaced as overprotectiveness toward Baptiste or as a tendency to provoke Lakesh.

Undeniably Kane was responsible, but Grant didn't blame him. He had served with and fought back-to-back with the man for many years, and he owed him his life several times over.

True, the peeling away of Grant's Mag identity and his Mag purpose had been hard to endure, especially during those first weeks in Cerberus. Now, when he thought of his years as a Magistrate, it brought only a brief, sad ache. He had never been one to plan for his future, and he had become well-conditioned to disappointments in his life, so he was stoic in the face of physical and emotional pain.

Grant had followed Brigid Baptiste's lead, who was the most adaptable of the three of them, and he buried himself in the new work Cerberus offered. It was an exciting experience to rediscover his capacity for independent thinking, to contemplate and explore new concepts.

Unlike Kane, he made a concerted effort to get to know the other Cerberus personnel—Bry, Farrell, DeFore, Banks and the others. Most of them were brilliant and wayward members of different divisions in other villes, who had fallen afoul of barony laws in one fashion or another. Through Lakesh's machinations, they ended up in Cerberus instead of executed.

But old Mag habits died very hard. On occasion he still thought of his fellow exiles as slaggers, as criminals, and of Lakesh as a dangerous subversive. He managed to push all of it to the back of his mind, storing it with his memories of Cobaltville and all the other things that were past and he wasn't particularly anxious to think about.

Grant twisted the chrome handle on the shower-stall wall, cutting off the flow of water. He toweled himself off, pulled on his white briefs and stepped out of the bathroom. He stopped in midstride, stomach muscles jumping in adrenaline-inspired spasms. He stared at another subject he wasn't particularly anxious to think about.

Domi reclined on the bed, on her belly, one hand cupping her chin. She was naked except for bright red stockings that encased her long legs from toe tips to upper thighs. She grinned at him, a speculative, insolent play of her lips and a flashing of flawless teeth. He couldn't help but notice that her eyelids and lips were painted the same cool shade of aquamarine.

Those marvelous, strange red eyes held him and they glinted like rubies on either side of her delicate, thin-bridged nose. Her voice was soft and throaty. "Waiting for you. Again."

Grant cleared his throat. "You're wasting my time and yours. Again."

Her pale blue lips made a moue of disappointment, and she closed her big eyes. "You don't want me. You reject me. Boo-hoo."

Her lips twitched, her eyes opened. "You lie. Big-time you want me."

Domi slowly rolled over onto her back, her head hanging over the foot of the bed. Grant struggled to think clearly. He found his eyes shifting from her face to the small, hard-tipped breasts that resembled porcelain doorknobs, past them to her soft, slightly rounded belly and then to the naked juncture of her curving thighs. Her eyes never left his.

It took him longer than he wanted to force his gaze away from her nudity. He knew from past experience how difficult it was. Although Lakesh, and presumably other men in the redoubt, found Domi's flirtatious manner and revealing mode of dress entertaining, he was troubled by it and he wasn't sure why. There had been other women in his life, some through the line of duty involving prospective, baron-approved mates, and others through passions discovered in the course of a mission.

Domi could have been one of the latter, but she was a child. Because of her sexual servitude to the Pit boss of Cobaltville, the late and unmourned Guana Teague, Grant viewed her as a victim. Both of them had taken a hand in Guana's bloody demise, though Domi gleefully accepted the lion's share of the responsibility—she had cut his throat.

As far as Grant was concerned, sharing in the chilling of a human being, even one as deserving as old Guana, wasn't a sufficient foundation upon which to build a relationship. Besides, he was genuinely fond of the girl, and he doubted she would be satisfied with an uncomplicated, strictly physical relationship for very long. Her emotions were too strong, too simple. She would be incapable of separating the act of sex from true love.

Wearily Grant said, "We've been over this before, Domi. I'm too old and you're too young and the twain will never meet."

Domi laughed, a warm, fluid sound. She raised her left leg, smoothing the scarlet stocking. "Think of interesting color combination. Your black on my white. My white on your black. Think how nice."

"I'm trying not to," he murmured to himself. Louder and more decisively he said, "Get your goddamn clothes on and go."

A sudden emotion flashed through her eyes like a streak of crimson lightning. She quickly twisted back over on her stomach. "Colors! That be it. You think snotty doctor bitch DeFore more in your color scheme."

Grant nodded thoughtfully. "Now that you mention it—"

Domi sat up sharply, kneeling in the middle of the bed.

Her pert, taut breasts pointed at him. Nostrils flaring, she exclaimed, "Knew it! Take that bitch outside, kick her fat ass off cliff!"

Grant brought a hand to his forehead. "Shit. I've had enough of this behavior for one day."

A quick lunge brought him to the bedside. He yanked up the edges of the top sheet and flung them over Domi's head. He grasped the excess cloth in both hands as she struggled and squealed surprised curses. She was trapped inside the sheet like a small animal inside of a bag, and Grant easily swung her off the bed and carried her over to the door. He opened it with one hand, then gently placed her on the floor.

"Go to bed," he said sternly before slamming the door and loudly locking it.

As he turned away, he heard her voice. "You big-time bastard. But you get ready. I be back." Then she laughed, a sound full of warm, liquid humor.

Grant groaned. Now he really did have something to blame on Kane.

Chapter 10

At 0755, in the anteroom connected to the jump chamber, the three of them inventoried their ordnance and other equipment. Kane and Grant wore their gren-laden combat harnesses over black high-necked sweaters. Both of them were shod in heavy-treaded, fleece-lined boots. They stuffed gloves and woolen scarfs into the pockets of their ankle-length, black Kevlar-weave coats. The Mag-issue coats offered a degree of protection against penetration weapons and they were insulated against all weathers, including acid-rain showers. Trans-comm circuitry was sewn inside the lapels, terminating in tiny pin mikes connected to a thin wire pulley. If they were searched, the transceivers would pass a cursory inspection. Long combat knives, the razor-keen blades forged of dark blue steel, hung from sheaths at their hips.

They made sure the Sin Eaters were secure in the rather bulky holsters strapped to their forearms. The big-bored automatic handblasters, less than fourteen inches in length at full extension, had magazines carrying twenty 9 mm rounds. When not in use, the stock folded over the top of the blaster, reducing its holstered length to ten inches.

When the weapons were needed, they need only tense their wrist tendons and sensitive actuators would activate flexible cables within the holsters and snap the pistols smoothly into their waiting hands, the butts unfolding in the same motion. Since the Sin Eaters had no trigger guards or safeties, the blasters fired immediately upon touching their crooked index fingers.

Brigid wore a long, fur-collared leather coat with voluminous pockets. Inside one pocket was a flat case containing emergency medical supplies, including hypodermics of pain suppressants, stimulants and antibiotics. Snugged in another pocket was her side arm of choice, a stub-barreled Mauser with an extended magazine holding fourteen rounds of .32-caliber ammunition.

Grant had disapproved of her choice, pointing out that the blaster had an accurate range of only twenty-five meters and its semiautomatic rate of fire was unreliable. Brigid had countered that the Mauser weighed considerably less than the H&K VP-70 she had been using, and its recoil was negligible, though she did admit it possessed less stopping power.

Bry came in from the control center. A small man with rounded shoulders and curly, copper-colored hair, he handed Brigid a folded map, a trans-comm unit, a rad counter and a square metal-and-leather case containing survival rations, such as concentrated foodstuffs and bottles of purified water. As Brigid hung the case over a shoulder by its straps, Bry said in a strained voice, "You know we're unable to receive a read on the autosequence initiators on the Peredelinko unit."

Brigid nodded, sliding the map into an inner pocket of her coat.

"Since we can't synchronize the matter-stream modulations, you three may suffer a bout of extreme jump sickness."

Kane tested his Nighthawk microlight, thumbing it on and off. "Why?"

Bry made a smoothing motion with the palm of a hand.

"If the modulations are synchronized, you *slide* along the quantum path to your destination." He knotted his hand into a fist and punched the air. "When they aren't synchronized, you more or less *slam* into your destination."

"We've had jump sickness before," said Brigid. "It's tolerable."

Bry shuffled his feet uncomfortably. "This time it may be bad."

"How bad?" Grant asked, scowling.

"No way of telling, sir. Could be nothing more severe than you've already experienced—headaches and a temporary touch of nausea."

"Or...?" prodded Kane.

Bry's eyes flicked nervously back and forth, from one face to another. "Or an incapacitating weakness that may last several hours, hallucinations and overall a debilitated physical condition."

Brigid patted the pocket containing the medical kit. "That's why we have this."

Wetting his lips, Bry said hesitantly, "One more thing—"

Kane snorted. "One more? This just gets better and better."

"You understand how the mat-trans unit in this facility is the only one with no transit feed connection to the others? Its jump lines are untraceable."

"Yeah?" Grant rumbled dangerously.

Bry gestured feebly to the control room. "That's a two-edged sword with the Peredelinko unit. We aren't sure if we can achieve a retrieval lock. So, if conditions warrant, remain close to the chamber and hit the LD button."

The LD button—Last Destination—was a fallback device designed to bring jumpers back to their point of origin if they materialized either in hostile environments or at the incorrect transit point.

"And if they don't warrant?" challenged Kane.

"Conduct your mission. When you return to the Peredelinko chamber, simply encode this unit's coordinates in the normal manner."

"Simple, actually," said Brigid.

Kane gave her a sour smile. "It's always been so, hasn't it?"

She didn't even look at him. Picking up a fur hat from the table, she turned toward the door leading to the mattrans chamber. "Gentlemen, the motherland awaits."

Kane started after her, then noticed Grant hanging back, glancing watchfully toward the control center.

"Waiting for someone?"

Grant smiled ruefully. "No. And yes."

"Are you coming with us, no and yes?"

"Why do you ask?"

"No reason. Just thought I'd try to be reliable."

They went through the anteroom and entered the gateway chamber. Right above the keypad encoding panel, in faded maroon letters, was an imprinted notice—Entry Absolutely Forbidden To All But B12 Cleared Personnel. Every time Kane saw it, he always wondered who the B12 cleared personnel had been and what had become of them—whether they had jumped from the redoubt in desperation and left the B11 and below personnel to die slowly or go mad from isolation.

As Kane closed the heavy armaglass door behind them, the lock mechanism triggered the automatic jump initiator. All three of them took deep, calming breaths. He glanced toward Brigid, but she refused to make eye contact, still giving him the silent treatment. He knew he had offended her the night before, but he doggedly told himself he didn't care. Baptiste was too clinical, too fixated on logic and reason to ever truly understand him. He sometimes wondered why he had sacrificed everything for a woman who treated him most of the time as though he were a mentally deficient jolt-brain. Maybe one day he would find out—but he doubted it.

Then the familiar vibrating hum arose, climbing to a high-pitched whine. The hexagonal metal disks above and below exuded a shimmering glow that slowly intensified. The fine mist gathered and climbed from the floor and wafted down from the ceiling. Tiny crackling static discharges flared in the vapor. The mist thickened, curling around to engulf them.

Kane peeled back the cuff of his coat, looking at his wrist chron. "I just thought of something—"

He never finished. He felt as if a ten-ton meat cleaver crashed down on the crown of his head, splitting scalp and skull, wedging deeply between the hemispheres of his brain. Implode grens detonated behind each eye.

His consciousness skidded and reeled over impossibly curved and deep abysses. It was a confusion of speed, distortion, a plunging, spinning whirlpool that was all inside the confines of his head but immense enough to encompass the entire galaxy-flecked universe. Round and round, faster, lurching, rolling, caught helplessly in a torrent of energy that somehow was not energy, a raging flame that didn't burn but chilled with a cold deeper than a gale whipping from the lifeless vacuum of space.

There were colors he had never seen before, never known existed, sounds that he couldn't hear but caused him soul-deep agony. He felt as though his mind were the size of a quivering atom, driven through a mad, roaring, icy void.

Then he saw himself and he saw Baptiste and Grant,

and though they didn't look like themselves, he recognized them, knew them.

Kane glimpsed himself crouching in a primordial jungle, clad in animal skins and frightened. His father was Grant, his uncle was Baptiste and his brother was Salvo.

He saw himself, Baptiste and Grant, their faces painted blue, fighting the armored legions of Rome, reeling back, gashed and defeated.

He saw a walled city exploding with flame, and he stood back-to-back with Grant, exchanging sword strokes with a massed horde of red-handed butchers who owed allegiance to Attila.

He saw Baptiste, a beautiful captive dragged at the stirrup of a Norman lord's horse, and he tried to cut her free, only to be cut down himself by the bone-shattering fall of a spiked mace.

He saw himself struggling against the hands that forced his head down cruelly on a bloodstained headsman's block in Kilmainham Gaol, and the smirking man who had betrayed him to the British was Salvo.

He saw himself dressed in fringed buckskins, standing on a narrow parapet and sighting down a long Kentucky rifle. He was praying for one clear shot at Generalissimo Antonio López de Santa Anna. The elaborately uniformed caudillo had aquiline, aristocratic features, but his cold dark eyes were the eyes of Salvo. Though Kane couldn't see them, he knew Brigid and Grant were somewhere within the crumbling adobe walls of the old mission on the Bexar River.

He saw himself astride a pony, galloping wild and fierce, feathers in his long, streaming hair as he rode down on the blue-clad *wasicun* soldiers at Greasy Grass. The white soldier chief blubbered in terror, and though

Kane's people called him Pahaska, he knew he was really Salvo.

The chaotic montage of images seemed to slow, and a sleet storm of emotions swept over him. Kane knew the agonies of defeat and the pain of wounds and the bitterness of love and trust betrayed. Through it all, he recognized Grant and Baptiste and all the bodies that had carried their souls throughout the changing ages, throughout the long track of savagery, valor, loyalty and deceit. And always, in the bloody scenes of the strife, their spirits were together, living and battling and dying, being reborn and somehow always finding one another again. And now they had found each other again, perhaps for the final time—

With a convulsive effort Kane opened his eyes, and the motion felt as if it blew the top of his head off. He felt as if he were painfully clawing his way up out of some deep chasm. He strained every particle of his battered consciousness to understand, to see.

The last tendrils of mist were clearing away, and he could feel the tingling static discharges from the raised metallic disks beneath his body. He lay on his back and he couldn't move. It was as if something had sucked the strength out of him. His mind rolled with confused questions. Through the blurred swirl of his vision, he tried to see the color of the armaglass.

Before he could fully focus, bile arose in a burning column in his throat, and he just managed to turn onto his right side before it spewed explosively from his mouth. Fortunately he had eaten very little before the jump, so after the first ejection of liquids and stomach acids, he only dry-heaved for a few moments.

Drinking in gasps of cool, stale air, wiping his running nose with the sleeve of his coat, Kane painfully hitched himself up on an elbow, squinting through the dim light. He saw Brigid curled in a fetal position on the far side of the six-sided chamber. Her mouth sagged partly open, her eyes were closed and she whimpered softly to herself like a small, frightened animal. Tears glistened on her cheeks, and her shoulders quivered.

On the other side of him, Grant coughed, groaned and tried to blink his eyes open. A thread of blood worked its way out of his right nostril. In a voice tight with pain, he grated, "Fucking fireblast."

Kane pushed himself up in a half-prone position, putting his back against the earth-toned armaglass wall, silently enduring an attack of vertigo. He massaged his throbbing temples with trembling hands. It felt as if the walls of his cranium had been scoured with fistfuls of sand. His stomach lurched and boiled and twisted in cramps.

"So this is what slamming instead of sliding feels like." Kane's words were a hoarse, barely audible rasp.

Grant squirmed his way up to a sitting position, resting his forehead against his knees. His breathing was labored. "My head feels like a slaghole full of stickie piss."

The simile made Kane's stomach slip sideways again. "Did you dream?"

"I did something…probably in my pants." His muffled voice was flat, toneless. "Oh, God—please don't let me puke. If I start, I probably won't stop."

Kane looked over toward Brigid. She was still curled up on the floor, but the small sobs had ceased. He called her name, but she didn't respond. He forced himself to his hands and knees, surprised and irritated by how weak he was. As he crawled over to her, he realized the chamber was slightly smaller than the one in Cerberus, around three-quarters the size. He knelt beside her and gently shook her by the shoulder. "Baptiste?"

She didn't respond, so he lightly slapped her cheek, noting with dismay how parchment pale she looked. Brigid's eyelids flickered, then opened. Blinking, she stared up at Kane in complete disorientation, her emerald eyes clouded by confusion and tears.

Then her hand shot up and closed around his wrist with a fierce strength, her nails biting into his flesh. She lunged into a sitting position, clutching him in a desperate embrace. In a thin, aspirated voice, she whispered, "I saw you die, Kane. *I saw you die!* You were trying to save me—"

Kane was too stunned to speak. He had already discounted his vision during the transit as a dream, a nightmare, just another symptom of jump sickness. He didn't want to speculate that it might have been anything else. He refused to speculate that it might be anything else.

"Just a dream, Baptiste," he said softly. "A hallucination, like Bry warned us about."

Some of the tension went out of her body, and she pushed herself away from Kane, her eyes scanning his face quickly, intently, as though she were convincing herself that he truly was who he was supposed to be. Inside him, Kane felt a jolt as he saw the longing in her eyes, knew it to be a reflection of the longing in his own soul. Then the moment was gone. She turned away quickly, wiping at the tears on her cheeks. "I'm all right now," she said in a monotone. "I hallucinated."

She tried to stand up, staggered and swayed and would have fallen had Kane not reached up and steadied her. "Take it slow," he said. "We're all in rocky shape."

With a wan smile she leaned against the wall, rubbing

her forehead. "My head is splitting. Anyone need a pain reliever?"

Grant replied, "I'm feeling a little better. Let's give ourselves a few minutes to recover on our own before we juice ourselves up."

The three of them remained where they were for a while, and at length the pain in Kane's head abated though his stomach was still tied in cramped knots. Carefully, as if he were ninety years old, he climbed to his feet and stumbled on rubbery legs to the heavy door of the chamber. He noticed immediately that the handle was bent in the middle. Obviously some terrific force had been exerted upon it. He looked over his shoulder at Grant. "How are you feeling?"

The big man uttered a sigh and placed his hands flat on the metal disks, heaving himself erect. "Like 220-odd pounds of steamed shit."

He reeled dizzily for a second, running a hand over his face. He dabbed at the blood on his upper lip and frowned at the spots on his fingers. "Anybody else bleeding?"

"Only you," replied Kane. He looked questioningly at Brigid. "As far as I know."

"Remember that shot of infrasound you took in Dulce?" Brigid asked. "It ruptured and weakened the subcutaneous capillaries in your nose. Whenever you experience a sudden pressure change, there will be some minor hemorrhaging."

Grant leaned a shoulder against the wall. "Figures." He inhaled deeply, exhaled slowly and asked, "Are we ready to face the motherland?"

"As we'll ever be," answered Brigid flatly, moving away from the door, her hand reaching inside her coat pocket for the Mauser.

Kane and Grant exchanged curt nods, tensed their wrist tendons and the Sin Eaters slapped into their waiting palms with faint whirs of tiny electric motors.

Grasping the door handle, Kane lifted and turned it. Instead of the solid chock of the lock solenoids disengaging, the sound was an odd, strangely tinny click. Slowly, a few inches at a time, he toed the door open.

There was no adjacent recovery anteroom beyond. The jump chamber opened directly into a small control room, barely twenty feet across. Kane saw a single, simplified master control console running the length of one wall and he recognized a few of the basic command panels from Cerberus. Many of the indicator lights were dark, and the walls showed black soot streaks from a long-ago fire. One section of the metal-and-plastic console was warped out of shape, sagging slightly toward the floor.

He stepped into the room, surveying it with quick, alert glances. The light source was a dim triple neon strip on the ceiling. Only intermittent pieces of it glowed. Most of it was melted, dangling down like congealed noodles. In the corners he looked for functioning vid spy-eyes. He saw one, mounted on the north wall, but a close examination showed him it was inoperable. Quietly he announced, "Looks clean."

Grant moved out, blaster at the ready. Brigid followed him, sweeping the short barrel of the Mauser back and forth.

"Small," she said. "Not like the redoubt specs Lakesh showed me."

"This isn't a redoubt," Grant reminded her. "Its a dutch or whatever."

"Dacha." Brigid eyed the master console. "Fire damage to some of the sensor outfeed circuits. No wonder we couldn't get a read on the autosequence initiators. A minor miracle there was an open transit link at all.''

"Let's wait for the hosannas until we find out for sure where we are," Kane said. "For all we know, we were routed to one of the alternate units Lakesh mentioned."

He walked swiftly to the double set of sec doors. They were painted a very pale shade of green, though patches of it were scorched and pitted. The green control lever in the frame was in the down, or closed, position. He put his ear to the door, knowing that most sounds couldn't penetrate the thick, sound-absorbing vanadium alloy.

Kane assumed a combat stance in front of the doors while Grant moved to position at the control lever. Kane nodded, and Grant threw up the lever, jamming it hard into its brackets. With a squeaking hiss of pneumatics, the pair of doors slowly swung outward. Kane tensed, finger crooked around the hair trigger of his blaster. He didn't really know what to expect, but he was surprised by the sight revealed by the opening doors.

Chapter 11

He looked into a short earthen tunnel. Its floor was tightly packed dirt. The walls and low ceiling were supported by an arrangement of square wooden timbers. The feeble light from the control room penetrated only a few feet into the tunnel, so Kane fished his microlight from his pocket and turned it on. Grant peered around the door frame, taking his night-vision glasses from his coat and slipping them on his face. The specially treated lenses of the Mag-issue glasses allowed him to see clearly in deep shadow for approximately ten feet, as long as there was some kind of light source.

The narrow amber beam of the tiny flashlight illuminated a plastic box-switch on the wall near the right door. He clicked the switch, and a few naked bulbs on the ceiling glowed to grudging life. A barred gate blocked the end of the passageway.

Kane strode into the cramped tunnel, tasting the very cool, sour air. With the bore of the Sin Eater leading the way, he walked to the barrier in the far wall. The bars were made of high-grade vanadium steel as thick as his index finger. The crossbars were three inches apart. The top, the sides and bottom of the gate were set flush in a concrete frame. The barrier was secured by a keypad quad-electronic lock, and not even one of his grens would breach it. The lock didn't look like part of the original door, as if it had been installed later as an additional security measure.

Coming up behind him, Grant asked, "Can it be opened?"

Kane shook one of the bars in frustration. "Not by force."

He turned at Baptiste's approach. "I hope a Syne is among the odds and ends you thought to bring along."

She dipped her hand into a pocket of her coat and produced a small metal device shaped like an elongated circle. The Mnemosyne was an electronic lock decrypter. Brigid placed the Syne against the keypad, thumbed a stud on its surface and initialized the decryption mechanism. It emitted a faint, very high-pitched whine. The tight-band, high-power microwave frequency overrode the lock's microprocessors, and with a snap of metal the locking bolts clacked aside.

Gingerly Kane pushed with the barrel of his blaster, and the barred door swung silently open. "Handy little gizmo."

Brigid pocketed the device. "Me or the Syne?"

"Both, so far."

As the gate swung open, an overhead neon strip fluttered and came on. The three of them walked through the door and into a small, concrete-walled chamber, like a ten-foot-square cube. The floor was still dirt, but slightly moist. A rusted metal cabinet was affixed to the wall by screws. It gaped open, showing only empty, warped shelves. Just on the other side of the locker was a heavy wooden door. It bore an ordinary knob made of aluminum.

Kane gripped it and twisted it cautiously. There was no resistance or stiffness in the lock, and the hinges squealed slightly as he pushed the door open. By the light of his Nighthawk, he saw the foot of a black, wrought-iron spiral staircase, corkscrewing up into darkness. The steps and handrails were flecked and flaking with rust. The air was considerably colder now, and not quite as stale.

Grant craned his neck, peering upward. "That's a long climb." His breath plumed out before him.

"And probably a bastard cold one, too." Kane placed his miniature flashlight between his teeth and tugged on a pair of black leather gloves. Brigid did the same and donned her fur cap. Kane attached the microlight to his left index finger by its tiny Velcro strap, wearing it like a ring.

Uneasily Grant said, "I'd hate to make that climb and find out we're not in Russia, after all."

Kane scaled the first few treads of the stairs, testing them. "It feels cold enough to be Russia." The steps creaked a bit, and little rust showers sprinkled down from the undersides, but they seemed solid enough.

They began climbing, Kane taking the point as always. It was an ingrained habit from his years in the Mag Division. When he acted as pointman, he felt electrically alive, sharply attuned to every nuance of his surroundings. After a few turns of the staircase, no light from below penetrated; in fact, it was just a tiny pinpoint of pale yellow far below. He paused long enough to put on his dark-vision glasses. Though the Nighthawk microlight emitted a powerful beam, the illumination it cast didn't pierce the shadows more than ten feet above him.

The longer they climbed, the higher they went, the colder it became. The staircase squeaked and groaned alarmingly during their upward progress. Kane estimated they had climbed for some ten minutes before he reached the final curve of the spidery iron spiral.

He stepped out onto a wide metal platform about a dozen feet square. A section of floor plate, joined to another by a weld, gave slightly beneath his 180 pounds. He called down behind him, "The end of the trail."

Brigid's voice wafted up. "What's up there?"

Kane shone his light around. The needle beam touched a blank metal wall, haloing a wedge-shaped handle and a pair of deadlock bolts. Both of them were pushed to one side. "A door. Unlocked."

With a nerve-racking tremor of the platform underfoot, Grant and Brigid joined him on the landing. She looked around, saying softly, "This shaft is deep. We must have climbed two hundred feet."

"Hell of a construction project," Grant commented, "burying the gateway that far beneath the duchess."

"Dacha," Brigid corrected automatically.

"Get ready," Kane said, stepping to the door and grasping the handle. He turned it. It resisted, metal grinding stiffly against metal. Taking and holding a deep breath, he put all of his upper-body strength into the turn, pushing at the same time with a shoulder.

The door popped open, and a shockingly frigid rush of air swept over him. Off balance, he stumbled forward through the doorway, and his first glimpse of what lay beyond it tore a startled *"Shit!"* from his lips.

He froze, flinging out a hand to anchor himself to iron gridwork. He waited for the tight fist of fear to relax its grip on his reflexes. His rigid training subsumed the surprise and fright swarming through his mind.

Eyes stinging from the icy lash of the wind, he surveyed his position and he disliked it immensely. He was at least seventy-five feet above the overgrown ground. It was patched whitely with small drifts of fresh snow. Standing inside of an enclosed box made of bolted-together sections of rusty grillwork, he felt trapped, as though he were in a cage. It was barely large enough to accommodate him. Looking between the intersecting metal slats, he saw a few rocks, a lot of weeds and very little else. A night bright with stars and a cloud-covered moon shone overhead.

By its uncertain light, he saw a fenced perimeter encircling the area for a hundred yards all around. The fence line ran along the crest of a small ridge, and though he couldn't be sure, it looked as if lengths of razor and barbed wire were stretched between the ten-foot-tall posts.

Glancing over his shoulder, he saw the door he had forced open had been disguised to look like an oversize chimney flue. In fact, the entire shaft was made of red, mortared brick, just like a chimney.

He muttered, "This makes no damn sense at all."

Grant poked his head out of the doorway. "What doesn't?" He looked up, around and from side to side. "What is this?"

"That's what I want to know," Kane replied. "Let Baptiste out here. Maybe she'll have a notion."

Grant withdrew back into the shaft and allowed Brigid to step out into the grille-enclosed box. She didn't appear overly surprised.

"Lakesh said there was a house here," she said, touching the bricks. "A mansion, judging by the size of the chimney. I'll bet we're standing where the attic used to be."

Pointing past the cage, she said, "See, if you look really closely, you can just make out the outline of a structure on the ground."

"What happened to it?"

"Destroyed, burned down. Who knows? Obviously

somebody must have known the chimney led to the mat-trans unit and took pains to secure it. Demolishing the house would have been the first step."

Pacing around the box, Kane said, "There isn't a way out."

"There has to be." She gestured to the chimney beneath the little enclosure. "Look."

By peering between the slats, Kane saw a series of U-shaped iron rungs set into the exterior of the chimney, leading down to the ground. They were dark and discolored by time and exposure. "And I thought your eyes were bad, Baptiste."

He dropped to his knees, exploring the grille with his fingers. Grant poked his head out. "What's going on?"

Kane didn't respond for a moment. Inserting his hand between the flat iron strips, he touched an object that clinked and clanked. "Found a lock. Feels like...yeah, a combination lock, latched on the underside."

Putting his face close to the slats, he said, "Not enough room to work our hands down there, even if we wanted to try to figure out the combination. We'll have to shoot it off."

He tried jamming the barrel of the Sin Eater between the narrow spaces, but the diameter of the bore was too big. He made a wordless utterance of disgust. Brigid tapped his shoulder. "Let me."

Obligingly Kane stood and moved to the far side of the cage. She knelt down, Mauser in her hand. The slender barrel slid in easily between the slats. Turning her face away, she squeezed the trigger twice. The reports were flat, lackluster cracks, like fingers snapping. The whine of the bullets ricocheting from steel slicing through the chill night air was much louder. She bent down, peered through the grille and announced, "Done. And with less noise than that cannon of yours."

She rejoined Grant back on the chimney platform while Kane struggled to raise the floor grille. Hooking his fingers around a pair of crosspieces, he heaved, wrestled and finally managed to lift the section up on hidden hinges. He slammed it upright with a painfully loud clang.

"If I knew you were going to make that much noise," Brigid said irritably, "I would have suggested you use your grenades."

Kane swung his body through the opening, his feet groping for and finding the first rung. He pushed his blaster back into the forearm holster and went down, hand over hand. The icy wind slashed at him, whipping his coattails about. He estimated the temperature was probably in the high teens, but the wind-chill factor dropped it to the single digits.

The ladder rungs were sunk deeply into the brickwork, and unlike the spiral staircase, seemed rock solid under his weight. He guessed the ladder was of more recent workmanship.

He alighted at the base of the chimney in waist-high weeds. Something crunched underfoot and, kicking at the turf, he uncovered a chunk of charred wood, fire hardened to the consistency of stone. The digging toe of his boot revealed a streak of stained white in the dirt. By the time the other two joined him, he had pulled a big square of white plastic out of the half-frozen ground. Several words were imprinted on it, and though Kane couldn't decipher them, he recognized exclamation points and the meaning of the red skull symbol.

Brigid glanced at it curiously. "That settles the question of whether we're in Russia or not."

"What's it say?"

Brigid's brow furrowed in momentary concentration. "I can speak Russian easier than I can read it. Let's see… Forboding—no, Forbidden Zone! Trespassers Will Be Put To Death Without Trial! By Order Of Internal Security. Signed Major-Commissar Zimyanin."

Grant looked around uneasily, tugging up the collar of his coat. "You figure this major-commissar burned down the house to camouflage the gateway?"

"Possibly," answered Brigid. She pointed to a tiny series of numbers beneath the skull insignia. "A long time ago. That's the date of the notice—ninety-some years ago."

Kane dropped the square placard and consulted his wrist chron. "Nine twenty-seven. Why is it so dark?"

"Different latitude and longitude," Brigid replied. "We're about ten hours later than in Cerberus."

Kane nodded. "That's what I was wondering. I was getting ready to ask about the time difference right as we jumped."

Grant stamped on the ground. "Dawn is a long time away. What do we do until then?"

Brigid drew the map from her pocket. Unfolding it, she traced a wavery line with a gloved forefinger. "We're here. Peredelinko itself was a medium-sized ville before the nukecaust and if it survived, it's only a mile or so away. It's on the route we'll have to take to Moscow, so maybe we can find some transportation there that will at least get us to the inner suburbs."

Kane looked toward the fence. Some of the support posts had fallen down, leaving gaps wide enough to walk through. Beyond the fence, on the other side of the ridge, a tree line massed blackly against the sky.

"That looks like a damn wilderness to me," Grant

commented. "Maybe we should wait until daybreak. Even if there's a path in there, we'll have a hell of a time finding it."

"I'd rather find out now," said Kane.

"Me, too," agreed Brigid. "We can always come back and make camp."

Grant sighed, acknowledging he was outvoted. "Let's do it, then."

Brigid quickly checked her rad counter. The reading hovered at midrange green. "Safe enough."

A gibbous moon, between half and full, moved in and out of heavy clouds as they walked across the weed-choked ground and up the slight slope to the fence line. Most of the strands of barbed wire were completely encrusted with rust and broke easily when they applied pressure. The three of them stepped through a wide-open space between a pair of fallen posts. The fur-trimmed hem of Brigid's coat snagged on a spur of razor wire, but Grant quickly and easily disentangled her. Outside of the perimeter they found another plastic sign promising death to interlopers.

They moved quickly and quietly toward the trees, Kane a few yards ahead, pausing now and then to test the air for sounds or scents. He heard nothing but the rustle of wind-whipped foliage and smelled only damp vegetable matter. A very brief snow flurry whitened and wetted their hair and clothing.

Right at the edge of the tree line, in a shallow coulee, they found a path. It was a cramped draw, meandering in and then out of the border of the woods. Though it was narrow, Kane saw the faint tread marks made by a wheeled vehicle. There were also the impressions of shod horse hooves.

''These tracks weren't made recently,'' he murmured to the others. ''Days, maybe even weeks ago.''

''It's a sign of some kind of habitation, at least,'' Brigid observed.

They began walking again, the trees offering something in the way of a windbreak. Grant continued to check their backtrack, a part of Magistrate training that was now ingrained, unconscious habit. The towering chimney was out of sight, concealed by the dip in the terrain and the woods. Within half a mile they reached a cracked and furrowed ribbon on an old blacktop road. The asphalt had a peculiar ripple pattern to it, and weeds sprouted from splits in the surface. Kane and Grant had seen the rippling effect before, out in the hellzones. It was a characteristic result of earthquakes triggered by nuclear-bomb shock waves.

On the other side of the road was a grove of larches. They moved into the damp gloom between the tree trunks, avoiding places where the undergrowth was tangled and thick with thorns. They splashed through a tiny, shallow creek that was edged with a thin layer of ice. Suddenly Kane came to a halt, hand signaling behind him for silence, though Grant and Brigid had been too preoccupied with their cold feet to be talking.

''Listen,'' he whispered. ''Hear it?'' His face knotted in concentration. ''Like hammering.''

Grant listened blankly for a moment, then said, ''I don't hear anything.''

They huddled in silence but heard nothing except the sigh of the wind. Kane moved forward again, the other two allowing him the point once more. After marching another few minutes, they noticed that the larches no longer grew so closely together. They passed sawn and chopped-away stumps.

Kane stopped again and went to one knee, gazing intently ahead. Brigid and Grant followed suit on either side of him. In a clearing several wooden houses were scattered, some with thatched roofs. All were small and ramshackle. None of them showed lights. Windows and doors were boarded up or open and dark. In the center of the clump of houses, rearing from a bare patch of dirt, was a stone-walled well.

Kane, Grant and Brigid crouched at the edge of the clearing, watching and listening. They heard a very faint scraping sound, far off somewhere, then nothing but the wind. There were only shadows moving among the ruined structures, caused by moonlight filtering through breaks in the scudding clouds.

Kane eased out into the clearing, walking heel-and-toe in the characteristic way of a Mag penetrating a potential killzone. Grant and Brigid followed him in single file, giving him a twelve-yard lead.

Kane approached the nearest house at an oblique angle and looked in through the open door. A gust of wind set it to banging, and he realized that was the hammering sound he'd heard. He shone his microlight into the place, seeing nothing but empty, dusty dark, stripped of all signs that it had ever been inhabited. Circling the house, he noticed the barren remains of a fair-sized vegetable garden in the rear. The furrows were overgrown with weeds.

Two more houses were similarly deserted, and both of them had cultivated ground in the back. Some distance away he saw a big, rambling barn, most of it intact. He strode toward it, gesturing for Brigid and Grant to pick up the pace.

The doors were missing, and Kane speculated that looters had removed them and the hinges and carted them off. At the cavernous opening, he paused, waiting for his

companions. The amber light from his flashlight illuminated dimly only part of the blackness within the barn.
Brigid came to his side, adding the glow from her own
microlight to his.

"What are we doing here?" Grant whispered.

"This place looks like it had been a thriving ville.
Where did the people and the animals go? And why?"

"For all you know, this place has been deserted since
skydark," hissed Grant.

Brigid shook her head. "No way. This place has been
deserted for a long time, but not that long."

"Maybe when Major-Commissar Zimyanin secured
the dacha, he moved all the people out of here, afraid
they'd be mat-trans jumping to hell and gone."

"Doubtful," said Kane quietly. "That was nearly a
century ago. This place was abandoned only in the last
couple of years, five at the outside."

"So what?" Grant's whisper was harsh, exasperated.
"Not everything you stumble over is a mystery you have
to solve, you know."

Forcing a patient note into his voice, Kane intoned,
"First of all, judging by the tracks we found, somebody
hangs around here. And they own a wag or a horse, or a
horse-drawn wag. Second, this barn is the most likely
place in the area to keep them. And lastly, if nothing else,
we can spend the night here out of that bastard cold wind
and even light a fire without it being spotted."

Grant considered his companion's words for a silent
moment. His simple "Oh" was contrite.

Kane stepped over the earthen threshold. He immediately smelled mustiness and the cloying stench of something dead, something a long time dead. The interior of
the barn seemed saturated by the charnel-house reek.

Queasiness reawakened in his stomach, and his mouth filled with sour saliva.

He stopped in midstride, fanning his microlight around. The needle of light touched gray shapes dangling from the rafters by lengths of hemp. The shapes were wired-together animal skeletons, and he had trouble identifying them. It took him a second to realize that horse skulls had been attached to dog vertebrae, and the jawbones of cows were affixed to the fleshless, horned heads of goats. He heard a sudden, shocked intake of breath from Brigid and a mumbled ''Fucking fireblast!'' from Grant.

A big, low table, crudely fashioned, occupied the center of the barn. It was one of the doors, supported on four corners by the bleached thigh bones of either cattle or horses. Kane moved deeper into the darkness, the beam from his flashlight striking dull reflections from metal. A large brass bowl served as the centerpiece for the makeshift table. It was round and very deep, discolored by verdigris.

At the edge of the makeshift table, Kane leaned forward, directing his penlight into the bowl. Old dark stains thickly coated its curving inner walls. Piled neatly inside of it were small, delicate bones. Resting atop them an equally small and delicate skull grinned up at the shadows overhead.

Kane felt his heart pound wildly as he stared, transfixed at the skeletonized remains of a human infant, who could have been no more than six months old. He wasn't aware of Brigid coming to his side, clamping a hand over the cry of horror bursting from her lips. The sound she uttered was as though from a stab wound.

A scraping noise echoed from somewhere deep in the gloom, too deep for his small light to pierce. The sound came again, accompanied by the scuff and scutter of feet. The foul miasma he had scented upon entering the barn seemed to fill his nostrils.

Two eyes the color of old ice gleamed out of the shadows on the far side of the table. Something sucked the stale, stinking air. And chuckled.

Chapter 12

Even with their lights, none of them could quickly categorize, identify or otherwise recognize the shape shuffling out of the murk. There was no use to call it any other name than a thing.

It stood, swaying slightly on the opposite side of the long, low table, regarding them quietly. It chuckled again, a hollow, neutral sound.

The Sin Eater filled Kane's hand, and its comforting weight helped to make his eyes and reasoning centers work in tandem again. His unblinking stare took in the tall, cold-eyed form. The face was heavily rouged, thickly caked with an orange powder. Bright red pendulous lips were quirked in a toothless rictus that might have been a smile. The black outlines of its eyelids revealed a successful experiment with a burned match. The sweeping eyelashes were so long, so fluttery, they were obviously artificial. The eyes were a pale, nearly colorless gray. The whites showed all around the iris and lent a hypnotic intensity to the hard, thoughtful stare.

Framing the pear-shaped baby face was a fall of long tresses, of different colors and textures, as if several heads of human hair were woven together to make a grotesque wig. The creature's garb was a mismatched collection of rags and tatters, some of them moldering and rotten with age. Jutting out between the folds of cloth was a long, thick pink cylinder. After staring at it for a shocked second, Kane realized the enormous erection was fashioned from wax.

The thing waved a hand sporting very long, very curved black fingernails and said, *"Dobniy vyecher, tovarishs."* The voice was lilting, soft, though it carried a masculine timbre.

The words had no meaning to Grant or Kane, but Brigid responded quickly, *"Spaseebah."*

"What did he—it—say?" Kane side-mouthed to her.

"'Good evening, friends.'" Her answering whisper was brusque. "I said thanks."

At the sound of their voices, the mascaraed eyes widened. *"Angliis?"*

"Nyet," Brigid said.

"Amyerikis?"

"Da."

The thing tittered in wild excitement, flinging one taloned hand in front of its rouged lips. Both Kane and Grant found the hyperfeminine gesture thoroughly repulsive.

"What the fuck is it?" Grant growled. "Man or woman?"

Brigid voiced a halting conglomeration of consonants. The creature giggled again, lifted the frayed hem of its robe and twirled in a clumsy, coquettish pirouette.

"I think I'm going to throw up again," said Kane grimly, finger tensed on the Sin Eater's trigger.

The thing spoke for a long time in its lilting soprano. At one point it caressed the wax phallus in an openly lascivious manner. Brigid frowned during the monologue, nibbling her lower lip. When the torrent of words ceased, she said softly, "Try to keep your stomachs in one place. It's a man. Sort of. Used to be."

"What?" Grant demanded.

"His name is Koshelav. He's a Skotpsi."

"I thought he was a Russian," said Kane.

With a weary smile Brigid replied, "He is. The Skotpsis were a religious sect which flourished in Russia four hundred years ago. The cult traces its origins back to the pagan goddess Cybele, whose priests wore women's clothes and castrated themselves as sacrificial offerings at her altars. After the cleansing the cult enjoyed a brief revival. He claims he is the only priest left."

Despite the cold, Kane felt sweat form at his hairline. The infant and probably the animals had been sacrificed during Koshelav's insane rites. And he had a clue as to why the village was deserted.

Grant came to the same conclusion. "He probably chilled the villagers and their animals. Let's blast the crazy son of a bitch and move on."

"Wait," said Brigid. Waving her hand to the dangling skeletons, then to the bowl containing the bones of the child, she asked Koshelav a long question containing an accusatory note.

Koshelav's eyes blinked, and he shook his head so vigorously that his makeshift wig nearly slipped from his bald pate. He vehemently said, *"Nyet, nyet!"* over and over.

When Koshelav stopped speaking, Brigid shook her head in frustration. "I don't know whether to believe him or not. He claims Peredelinko was a Skotpsi ville for many, many years. They lived in peace here. Then a new regime took power in Moscow and classified everyone here as undesirables, as perverts, as spies. They suffered through a long reign of terror. The villagers who were not murdered fled the place. As the high priest, he stayed behind, lest he violate his oath to Cybele. The bones are those of his own animals, and the child's skeleton is his son's. All were killed by the police. He dug them up.''

Eyeing the wired-together skeletons dangling overhead, Grant asked, ''Why'd he mix and match 'em, then?''

''For one,'' replied Brigid impatiently, ''he's obviously insane. For another he switched the remains according to gender, female skulls on male bodies or vice versa, in accordance to Cybele's necromantic rites.''

''So he's not a murderer,'' Kane remarked. ''Just a fused-out ghoul. That makes me feel a whole lot better.''

Koshelav spoke again, this time in a tone hushed with reverence. Grant started to speak, but Brigid shushed him into silence. When Koshelav's words trailed off, he inclined his head, putting his hands together, the tips of the long, ragged nails touching.

''He says he had been praying to Cybele to send him new acolytes,'' she translated. ''And his prayers have at last been answered.''

''I don't think so,'' muttered Kane.

Grant whispered, ''If the dumb bastard castrated himself, how could he have a son?''

Brigid lifted an eyebrow. ''Good point. I'll ask him.''

She spoke to Koshelav. The man acted as though he hadn't heard. Head still bowed, he turned and shuffled into the gloom. Brigid called out after him. Koshelav continued shuffling, out of the range of the two microlights. Kane stepped swiftly after him, around the edge of the table. ''Hold it, chief.''

With shocking suddenness, the shadows around, behind and above them erupted with a flurry of movement. The pungent odor of rot grew perceptibly stronger, like a wave. Something brushed the crown of Kane's head. He ducked instinctively, his hand rising to shine his light overhead. A loop of thin, flexible wire encircled his wrist. The wire tightened, and a jerk from above snatched his arm up, shooting a streak of pain into his shoulder socket. At the same time, he heard Grant and Brigid cry out behind him. He turned on his toes, wrenching at the wire.

In the dim, wavering light he saw Grant, his arms flying up to horizontal positions, pointing in two directions. His wrists were snared by loops of wire, and they were pulled simultaneously by two ragged figures on either side of the barn.

Brigid clutched at her throat with both hands, her teeth bared as she gagged for air. Her hat fell off, and Kane glimpsed a glinting strand of wire stretching up from the base of her neck into the shadow-shrouded rafters.

He pressed the trigger of the Sin Eater, and bursts of orange flame smeared the darkness. The rapid-fire roar was nearly deafening. Pieces of bullet-chopped wood showered down, and a dangling skeleton danced and flew to flinders under the barrage.

The tension on the wire around Brigid's throat relaxed. She dropped to her knees, followed half a heartbeat later by a ragged, robed body plummeting down from above. A flailing leg struck her a glancing blow on the shoulder, knocking her onto her side. The body hit the floor with bone-crunching finality.

Another wire loop whispered out of the darkness and wrapped itself around Kane's right forearm. His gun hand was wrenched painfully across his torso, the Sin Eater pressing against his ribs. For a fraction of a second he considered the ludicrous picture he presented, standing on his toes, one arm straight up, the other wrapped around his torso, as though he were frozen while performing some bizarre semaphore dance.

Koshelav shouted from somewhere deeper in the barn,

and a half dozen more wigged and rouged figures flounced out of the murk from all sides, rags and tatters flapping. They carried long wooden poles, once the handles of hoes and rakes, with loops of knotted baling wire attached to the ends.

Kane struggled, kicking at the nearest figure. His boot connected solidly with a knee; if they were all Skotpsis, there was little point in aiming for the groin. The man went down, raising a terrific squalling, plucking at his leg. His wig fell off and lay on the floor like the carcass of a small, shaggy animal.

A very hard object struck Kane in the back with breath-robbing force. Only the tough cushioning of the Kevlar-weave coat and the sweater beneath kept his spine from being damaged. If not for the biting grip of the wire on his left wrist, he would have been knocked to all fours. He swayed, toes digging into the dirt, like a marionette operated by a deranged puppeteer.

In a helpless rage Grant watched as a Skotpsi dealt Kane the fierce blow with the butt of the wooden handle. The wire snugged around his right wrist had fouled in the mechanism of his forearm holster and prevented the Sin Eater from sliding into his hand. The tiny electric motor that operated the spring cable whined impotently.

He saw Brigid, half-prone on the ground, snap desperately at the stinking air and try to pull open the noose around her throat.

Grant struggled, yanking both arms upward. He received sharp, painful tugs as a response. He heard a titter of malicious, triumphant laughter and he snarled. Muscles bulging beneath his coat, he strained to drag his left arm toward him. The pulling pressure increased, and if not for the glove, the flesh around his wrist would have been lacerated. He maintained the tension for a few seconds, then relaxed his arm.

The Skotpsi holding the pole on his left stumbled back, pulling Grant with him. With all the speed and strength his training had bred into him, he leaped toward the ragged man. The surging strength of that unexpected lunge pulled the man on his right off his feet. He howled as the pole slid through his hands, inflicting painful friction burns on both palms.

Grant snatched the end of the wooden handle gripped in the hands of the Skotpsi on his left. He thrust it forward, like a spear, with all his strength and weight. The blunt end of the stave caught the man directly on the bridge of his nose, right between his black-lined eyes. Delicate bone splinters drove through his sinus cavities, then into his brain.

The Skotpsi uttered a peculiar cawing noise as blood spurted in a torrent from his nostrils. He twitched in a spasm and toppled backward, slamming against the barn wall, his wig falling forward over his face.

Spinning on his heels, Grant yanked the pole from the dead man's clenching and unclenching hands. As he spun, he swung the wooden handle in a short, humming arc. The arc ended against the Skotpsi hanging on to his right wrist. The blunt end smashed into a rouge-reddened cheek, cracking the bone with a sound like a wet twig breaking.

The robed man cartwheeled and thudded down on the packed dirt of the barn floor with an impact that drove all signs of life from his eyes.

Encumbered by the pole still attached to his left wrist, Grant tried to free the Sin Eater from the coil of wire around his forearm. An avalanche of squealing forms struck him from all directions. Clutching hands gripped his arms, his neck. Long nails clawed for his eyes, raking away his dark-vision glasses.

Brigid managed to insert her fingers into the strangling noose around her throat and work some slack into it. Even as she did so, a shrieking knot of Skotpsis flung themselves out of the gloom, bearing down on her. She shouted in Russian, telling them that she and her friends meant no harm. She might as well have saved her breath.

As the first figure reached for her, she performed a backward somersault, intending to come out of the roll on her feet. Her reflexes and muscle tone were in excellent condition, but she wasn't a trained hand-to-hand combatant, despite a few tricks she had learned from Kane and Grant. Her long, heavy coat skewed her timing, misplaced her center of balance, and when she rolled erect, she lost her footing. She stumbled backward, and only the barn wall prevented her from falling.

For a split, frozen second she surveyed the scene in the barn. Grant was struggling with three Skotpsis, who were trying to force him down on the ground. Kane was snared in a tough wire web, and three more of the ragtag cultists charged her. A clinical segment of her mind noted that not even twenty seconds had elapsed since the wire garrote had tightened around her neck, yet in that short span of time, the Skotpsi's surprise tactics had effectively neutralized their individual defensive measures. She recalled the old axiom that a battle like this was either won or lost within the first minute.

She didn't waste time trying to draw her Mauser. One of the three Skotpsis lowered his long-tressed head and rammed it into her lower belly, carrying her up and backward, with the intention of pinning her against the wall. She cupped her hands and slapped them swiftly and sharply against the sides of his head, over his hair-screened ears.

The Skotpsi screamed at the agonizing concussion against his eardrums. He let her go and fell to his hands and knees. Brigid tried to twist away from his two companions. One of them kicked out, and her legs went out from under her. She sprawled half across the table, the vibrations of her falling body sending the bone-filled bowl skittering toward the edge.

The two cultists were in such a hurry to lay hands on her that they jostled into each other. One was shouldered aside, and the other reached out and gripped her left ankle. He dragged her toward him. Brigid raised her right leg and rammed the heel of her boot into the painted face. The Skotpsi fell, blood gushing from split lips. His jaw hung askew. Brigid kicked his limp hand from her ankle.

The third tattered scarecrow voiced a sobbing shriek of outrage and hurled himself over the fallen bodies of his comrades, hands wide, fingernails curved to rake the flesh from her face. It was Koshelav himself.

Brigid planted both feet on his sternum, and using the momentum of his wild rush, her lithe legs levered up and flipped him over her. He grunted as he rolled across the splintery surface of the table. The bowl banged to the floor, scattering the small bones.

Koshelav rolled off the table and dragged himself to his feet. His wax phallus was broken in half. When he noticed the breakage, an angry titter bubbled past his lips. He settled his wig firmly on his head and opened his mouth to speak.

Kane, still hanging like a puppet, suddenly sagged against the grip of the wire around his left wrist. He drew his legs up, clear of the floor, bending them at the knee.

Koshelav whirled at the sudden movement, just as Kane pistoned out his legs.

The thick treads of his boots smashed full into Koshelav's face. With a mushy snap of bone and cartilage, Koshelav's body rocketed backward, his rags flapping as though he stood in a stiff breeze. Even as he flailed away into the dimness, the unexpected drag on the wire around Kane's wrist overbalanced the man on the other end of it crouching in the rafters.

He fell headlong, hitting the hard-packed dirt with his face. Kane sat down hard on the ground with a grunt of forcefully expelled air. Gasping, the man tried to push himself up. Almost casually Kane kicked him in the side of the head, rolling him over into the gloom. He made no movement afterward.

Simultaneously Grant used the butt of the snare pole around his right arm as a bludgeon, whacking one of his assailants across the torso, sending him staggering toward the open door of the barn. With a sinuous twist of his body, he tore free of the two cultists. They yelled in dismay, clawing wildly for him.

Grant broke the length of wood over a bewigged head, and as the man sagged to the floor, he thrust the sharp, splintered remainder into the third Skotpsi's belly, jerking it free with a snarl. The man went to his knees, screaming, hands clapped over the crimson gushing from punctured flesh and stomach muscles.

Brigid drew her Mauser and fired off a 3-round burst into the gloom, not knowing if the bullets hit anyone, but hoping the noise of the shots would unnerve the Skotpsis enough so they would consider cutting their losses and scattering.

The tendon-stretching pull on Kane's right wrist immediately slackened, and he jerked his almost numb arm backward, dragging a clattering pole from the shadows. He bellowed, came to his feet in an angry rush, squeezing the trigger of his blaster. The triple reports filled the barn with a roaring violence.

One of the cultists jumped at the shots. He lifted the hem of his robe and began a slap-footed run toward the barn entrance. Grant took a few steps in pursuit, thought better of it and stopped to disentangle the wire noose from his wrist and the cable spring mechanism of the holster. The Sin Eater slid into his palm, and it required a great effort to resist the savage temptation to empty the entire magazine in a 360-degree firing pattern.

Kane clawed the wire loops from his wrists, glaring around, making an automatic body count. Out of the ten ragged figures sprawled all over the barn, four would never rise again, Koshelav among them.

Grant planted the bore of his blaster against the head of the man who kneeled and whimpered and tried to staunch the flow of blood from his ripped belly. "You fucking slagger. Here's your termination warrant."

Grant was all Mag again, infuriated by the very notion that such low-life scum would dare to lay violent hands on him.

"No!" Brigid's voice was very sharp, though a trifle hoarse from her near strangulation. "We're the intruders here!"

"He assaulted a *Magistrate!*" Grant's tone vibrated with a bloodthirsty rage. He was totally caught up in a Mag's righteous fury. "They called down the thunder and now they'll earn and learn what it *means!*"

"You're not a Magistrate anymore!" Brigid shouted. "If you were still a Magistrate, you'd have to chill me, chill Domi, chill everybody in Cerberus. *You're not a Magistrate!*"

Grant's lips twitched in reaction to her words. By degrees the maddened flame in his dark eyes guttered out. With a wordless snarl of disgust, he wheeled away from the sobbing, wounded Skotpsi.

Kane had watched and listened to the exchange with a cold, ironic smile on his face. He knew exactly how Grant felt, because his own ingrained Mag pride was offended, and only blood and lives could redress the insult.

He took a very deep, very calming breath. "Is everybody all right?"

Both Brigid and Grant answered with brief affirmatives.

"Good. And in case anybody was wondering, I've changed my mind about spending the night."

He directed the beam of his Nighthawk microlight around. As he half expected, the amber glow revealed cunningly concealed hiding places all over the barn. He marched toward the black inner recesses of the structure. Brigid called after him, "Kane, there may be more of them back there."

Kane hefted his Sin Eater. "I sure as hell hope so, Baptiste."

Chapter 13

There wasn't much to see except piles of garbage, empty food cans and heaps of straw. In an enclosed stall, he found a horse, a big sorrel obviously used as a dray animal. It wore a rope halter around its head, and it was in a vicious temper, on edge from the smells and sounds of blasterfire, as well as the scent of fresh blood. When Kane approached, it laid back its ears, rolled its eyes and back-kicked the wall. The sound of a metal-shod hoof striking wood was startlingly loud.

"Kane?" Brigid shouted anxiously.

"It's all right. I found a horse."

"What kind?"

"A mean one."

In a partitioned alcove that served as a tack room, he saw a leather harness hanging from hooks on the wall, and where there was a harness, there had to be a wag. A rear door opened onto the outside. The cold air hit his face with a slap that was very cleansing after the close, stinking atmosphere of the barn. He found a two-wheeled box cart, its rails propped up against the wall. The wheels were old rubber tires with worn treads.

He went back inside to fetch Grant and Brigid. They had herded the surviving Skotpsis together to huddle shoulder to shoulder, blubbering and weeping. Whether they sobbed because of the pain of their injuries, grief for their dead comrades or simply out of bitter disappointment that a planned sacrifice had gone awry, Kane wasn't inclined to ask.

He reported what he had found. "I need somebody to help me hitch the horse to the wag. Volunteers?"

There was no response. Kane studied the expressions on their faces and declared, "Grant, you'll do. Baptiste can cover the dickless wonders."

Grant, who had retrieved his dark-vision glasses, cast him an angry look. "I don't know anything about horses or wags or hitches. Brigid is our resident expert on everything. Let her help you."

"If we leave you alone with these jolt-brains," Kane replied flatly, "you might be tempted to chill them all, if even only one of them looks at you crossways."

"So?"

"So, the whole countryside could be crawling with them. For all we know, cutting off their tools and dressing up like gaudy sluts is the fashion rage among Russian men nowadays. I don't want us to be targets of a blood hunt. We need to focus on what's ahead of us, not behind."

Grant let out his breath in an expletive-seasoned sigh. "Let's do it."

At the stall Grant warily eyed the horse and slowly swung the gate open. The horse backed up, champing its teeth. "Keep it covered. If it tries to bite or kick me—"

"I'm not going to chill a horse on your account. Show it who's boss. Pretend it's Domi."

"Kiss my ass." Grant reached for the halter nervously, and the snorting animal tossed its head, snapping at his hand. "Goddamn nasty son of a bitch!"

"You would be, too, if you had to live with these slime-slags."

Kane waited until Grant had secured a grip on the

horse's halter before hauling the harness down from the wall. There wasn't enough room in the stall for the animal to rear up, but it whinnied angrily and tried to stamp on Grant's feet. He directed a steady stream of curses and threats at it.

"You won't get him to cooperate that way," Kane stated. "Talk nice and slow to him. Treat him like a baby."

"You mean like I treat you?" Grant muttered darkly. But he followed Kane's instructions, and after a minute of speaking in a low, crooning tone, the horse was calm enough to be led from the stall.

Once outside, they harnessed the animal to the two-wheeled cart. Kane had anticipated a time-consuming and frustrating process of trial and error trying to figure out the intricacies of the harness. Fortunately, with only a couple of mismoves, they managed to hitch the horse to the wag in less than ten minutes.

Kane stepped back into the barn. "Stay out here with the horse. He seems to like you."

The Skotpsis were still huddled together, but their weeping was now only a collection of irritating sniffles. "Tell them to stay where they are until we're gone," Kane said to Brigid. "Otherwise they're liable to get seriously dead."

Brigid conveyed the message in terse Russian. The only responses she elicited were sullen, up-from-under glares. "Want me to repeat it?" she inquired.

"Fuck 'em. They've been warned. Let's go."

When they got outside, Grant was already in the driver's seat of the cart, experimentally tugging and testing the reins. Brigid climbed into the back. Kane lingered at the open door of the barn. She heard a faint click and saw him make an underhanded tossing motion. He turned and approached the wag. "Keep a tight hold of those reins."

"Why?"

An instant later a hell-hued flare erupted inside the barn. The chill air shivered with a thundering concussion. The horse neighed shrilly, half rearing, and the wag lurched forward. Grant sawed on the reins, shouting, "Whoa! Goddamn it, *whoa!*"

"That's why," said Kane calmly, sitting down beside Brigid.

Hungry flames roared through the barn, illuminating its dark, dank interior with the brilliance of an exploding star. All of them felt the jolt of searing heat. Long threads of light gleamed between the planks of the exterior wall. Screams of fright wafted over the loud crackle as various combustibles caught and were consumed.

To Brigid's accusatory stare, Kane said, "They'll have plenty of time to get out. With any luck the fire will spread to the rest of the ville, smoke out this rat's nest once and for all. It's worth the sacrifice of an incend."

To Grant he waved an imperious hand and announced grandly, "Let us be off."

Grant, staring over his shoulder at the rising tongues of flame, murmured, "Cold-blooded but stylish."

Kane leaned back, folding his arms over his chest, smiling modestly. "Something you're born with, you know. You either have it or you don't."

Brigid looked away from him, shaking her head in exasperated weariness. Lowly, she said, *"Dasvidaniya."*

A FOOTPATH LED to a wide, two-laned ribbon of blacktop. A river ran alongside it on the left, swirling around half-submerged boulders. On the right side of the potholed road, the forest was heavy and dark, massive pine trees growing so close together that the boughs were intertwined.

The conflagration of the barn smeared the night sky with a wavering glow that could be seen for miles, the light peeping through the branches of the tall pines.

"It'll burn itself out soon," Kane said reassuringly.

"If it doesn't fire the whole ville, then the woods," retorted Brigid. "It may draw attention we don't need."

"You worry too much, Baptiste."

"One of us better, don't you think?" she snapped.

The cart rocked and jounced over the cracks and faults in the roadbed. After a mile or two Grant learned how to control the horse with tugs on the reins and clicking noises with his tongue.

Within a half an hour the winding blacktop angled away from the river, climbed up a hill, then dropped down. Fog swirled and eddied in front of them as the wag rolled down the promontory, descending into a shallow valley. Ahead mist hung heavily above masses of shrubbery and brush that grew in tangled madness on both sides of the road. The horse splashed through puddles of stagnant water, covered with a scum of sickly looking green.

The only sound, other than the rhythm of hoofbeats and the creak of the cart's axle, was the infrequent, sad trilling of a night bird. The sounds increased the atmosphere of desolation, made the silence of the small valley even more sinister and mysterious.

By the glow of her microlight, Brigid checked her rad counter. "Getting a low-end yellow reading. The closer we come to Moscow, the higher the rad count."

Though there was no obvious sign of bomb damage, all of them knew that the Americans had employed a significant number of neutron weapons during the nukecaust. Damage from explosive warheads was minimal, though the spread of lethal radiation had been vast.

Kane checked his wrist chron. Even though it was still set on Montana time, he quickly performed the calculations. "Getting on to five o' clock. Sun ought to rise soon."

Grant, in the driver's box, glanced to his left and his right. Even his dark-vision glasses couldn't penetrate the mist. Ghostlike shadows of dead trees thrust their gaunt skeletons above the undergrowth. The chill wind had died completely, but he still felt cold. The air was dank and clammy. The horse reacted to the oppressive atmosphere by laying its ears back and shying from every shadow.

As the path inched and climbed its way out of the valley, the horse seemed to grow more apprehensive. It shortened its stride, taking slow, cautious steps, ignoring Grant's jerks on the reins.

Kane turned around to face Grant. "What're you doing?"

"I'm doing nothing," complained Grant. "It's this contrary pile of soap bones."

Despite Grant's prompting, the horse stubbornly kept decreasing its speed and length of stride. Finally it came to a complete halt, ears cocked forward, standing stiff legged and alert. Grant slapped the reins against the animal's rump, but except for a nervous quiver, it still refused to move. Kane looked past the horse, into the thinning mist, feeling the back of his neck tingling.

He slid out of the cart, the Sin Eater filling his hand. "Something's ahead," he whispered.

Brigid climbed down onto the road, Mauser in her fist. She moved around to the left side of the wag, standing slightly behind the wheel.

From around a bend in the path, a halo of dim light

appeared from the fog. As it grew closer, they heard the tramp of feet. A figure appeared, walking casually, a rifle slung over a shoulder. He held a lantern high in his right hand, and its light glinted from a silver disk pinned to the earflap of his fur cap.

He didn't see the horse and wag until he was nearly ten feet away. When he did, he skidded to a clumsy halt and hastily unslung the rifle from his shoulder. Even in the feeble light, Kane and Grant recognized the blaster as an old Soviet AKM, an improved version of the even older AK-47.

The man was young and slender, barely out of his teens, with the silky beginnings of a mustache on his acne-spotted face. He was bundled up in a dun-colored greatcoat. He shouted a question in a very nervous voice. Kane framed him in the sights of his Sin Eater, but Brigid stepped around the wag, responding to his question with a calm voice. The Mauser dangled by her leg, concealed by the folds of her coat.

"Stay where you are," called the man. He had trouble holding the rifle and the lantern at the same time, but he was clearly loath to relinquish either.

"Don't shoot," Brigid said. "We mean no harm."

"Who are you?"

"Visitors. Is this the way you treat strangers you meet on the road, point guns at them?"

The man lowered his rifle and lifted the lantern so the pale beam washed Brigid's face. He didn't appear too reassured by the sight of a strange woman. Or perhaps it was the two men in black, wearing sunglasses on this dark night, that unnerved him.

"Who are you?" he demanded again.

"I told you, visitors. Who are you?"

"Private Petaya of the Internal Security Network, Ramenki bureau. What are you doing on this road?"

Brigid tried one of her smiles on him. Ramenki was one of the inner suburbs of greater Moscow, so they were on the right route. "We are traveling to Moscow."

"From where?"

She gestured behind her. "From back there."

The answer caught Petaya by surprise. He made an odd sound, half nervous chuckle, half snort of derision. "There's nothing back there but Peredelinko. And it is a forbidden zone."

"Forbidden to whom, Private?"

"To all...except for members of the network."

"Precisely."

Petaya stared at her in unblinking surprise. "You are agents?"

"Yes, a special investigative unit."

"Investigating Peredelinko?"

"Yes. It is deserted."

Petaya sighed and the barrel of the rifle lowered. "That's good, that's very good. Captain Ivornich has been asking Central for months to dispatch investigators. I was afraid you were one of them."

"Them?"

"Skotpsis. They've been known to waylay travelers, sometimes sneak this way into Moscow for victims. I patrol this road once a week, looking for signs of them. I am very glad to hear they are finally gone."

"They are, Private. Now we must be on our way."

Eagerly Petaya offered, "I'll go with you so you can report to the captain."

"Not necessary."

"My shift is nearly done. By the time we reach my station, it will be time for me to go home." He threw her a friendly, ingenuous smile. "There will be hot coffee for us, too."

He turned and started up the road at a sprightly pace. When he was out of hearing range, Brigid told Grant and Kane of the conversation. Grant couldn't help but chuckle. "Investigators, huh? He's not that far off the mark."

The horse responded to the reins again, and they set off after the young man, following his lantern like a beacon bobbing in the mist.

Quietly Kane asked, "What happens if we're questioned by the kid's superior? If their setup is anything like the Mag Divisions, he'll want to see our orders."

"It's too risky not to stop by," Brigid whispered. "Hopefully they'll be bogged down by just enough ville-type bureaucracy to give us the chance to brazen our way through."

The condition of the road improved the longer they rolled along it, though they saw wide, barren swathes forevermore poisoned by radiation, turned into perpetual dust fields. They topped a rise just as dawn broke up the dark sky with pink-and-orange brushstrokes and Ramenki lay before them. The community seemed little more than several rows of old two- and three-story houses divided by a river that flowed beneath a rickety covered bridge.

Most of the houses and buildings seemed structurally sound, but in dire need of cosmetic attention. Pitted walls, peeling paint and ugly black patches shone through the cornices. The streets were deserted, and there were no lights. All the windows were shuttered. Garbage littered the gutters and alley mouths, its odors strange but still foul. Small, darting creatures foraged in the rubbish.

After a bend in the road, they saw a pale blue light glowing over the arched entrance to a low, stone-walled building. A sign suspended from cast-iron moorings was imprinted with a single word in Cyrillic—Militsiya. Brigid translated it for Kane and Grant. ''Police.''

Petaya made for the steps leading up to an iron-bound wooden door, waving at them to disembark. Grant reined in the horse at the curb. ''I'll stay here,'' he said lowly.

''Good,'' Kane whispered. ''I'll leave my trans-comm channel open so you can listen in on whatever there is to hear.''

''Don't talk to anyone,'' Brigid instructed him. ''Pretend you're a mute, if you have to.''

As Brigid and Kane walked toward the entrance, she spoke low, barely moving her lips. ''Let me do all the talking, no matter what happens.''

''Of course.''

''I mean it, Kane. You'll have to follow my lead if things turn nasty. Act taciturn.'' She smiled, adding, ''That shouldn't be too much of a stretch.''

The interior of the police station was as barren as the exterior. It consisted of a cramped, stuffy common room that held a pair of battered metal desks and several chairs. Bulky, old-fashioned black telephone units were on the desktops. Sheets of coarse pulp paper were everywhere, tacked to the walls, scattered on the desks, wadded up on the scuffed, unvarnished floor.

An old cast-iron stove glowed red in a corner. Atop it was a coffeepot, and the heady aroma set up a longing in Kane's taste buds. Beside the stove was a door, standing slightly ajar. Beyond it barred cell doors could be seen. The snores of sleeping men floated out.

Captain Ivornich stood up from behind a small desk when they entered. Not even the dull maroon uniform blouse, high boots, jodhpurs and wide black gun belt that girded her slim waist could conceal the svelte figure swelling beneath.

Kane's breath caught momentarily in his throat. Despite her lack of cosmetics, she was very lovely. The woman's black hair, pulled back severely from a remarkably high forehead, fell down her back as straight as a frozen flow of India ink. Her oval face was of marble whiteness, and her deep violet eyes were slightly tip-tilted, hinting at Asian ancestry.

She was a bit shorter than Baptiste, but very slender and muscularly athletic in build. She was perhaps as much as five years older, but her complexion was smooth and unlined. Her eyes, rich with suspicion, flicked back and forth between Kane and Brigid, finally settling on him. Kane immediately sensed an electric tension spring up between the two women.

Petaya spoke quickly and respectfully to Captain Ivornich. She listened to him impassively, then declared, "I have heard nothing of a special investigative unit dispatched from Central. Let me see your credentials." Her voice was husky, her tone accustomed to giving commands and having them obeyed.

Coldly Brigid said, "We are part of a covert-operations team. We were not issued credentials, as a standard security measure. You should know that."

Ivornich's black eyebrows shifted. Gazing at Kane, she asked, "What is your name and rank?"

"Irrelevant," interjected Brigid, a note of arrogance in her voice. "We need not establish our identities to you. It is enough for you to know that both of us hold ranks higher than your own."

"Indeed. Then why did you stop here?"

"A simple courtesy, to apprise you that Peredelinko

should no longer be of concern to you. All the Skotpsis are gone.''

"To where?"

"Does it matter, Captain? They are out of your jurisdiction. That should make you happy."

Ivornich nodded. "It does, if true. With only myself, Petaya and one other officer, our resources were strained trying to keep tabs on them. Thus, I am very happy to hear your report. So will your superior, no doubt. To whose authority do you report?"

Brigid's mind raced, though her slightly scornful, slightly superior expression remained intact. Ivornich's question was very reasonable under the circumstances, and trying to evade it would arouse her suspicions further. "Sverdlovosk."

The black-haired woman's face registered a surprise very close to outright astonishment. Her eyes widened, and her smooth brow furrowed. "Piotr? I mean, the colonel?"

Brigid only nodded. A bit of the tension ebbed, but it didn't vanish completely.

Irritated, Ivornich demanded, "Why didn't he tell me? I've been after him for months to send agents from Central down here to clean out Peredelinko. Why would he not let me know in advance so we could coordinate our movements?"

Brigid shrugged, as if the matter was of little importance. "As you know, his duties require his absence from Central for long periods. He approved the investigation before his latest trip."

Ivornich frowned. "You know about that?"

"About what?"

"The project."

"Of course."

Ivornich's frown became a tight smile. "Of course." She touched the telephone unit on her desk. "And, of course, Colonel Sverdlovosk has yet to return from his latest trip, therefore I cannot contact him to verify your story."

Brigid stiffened. "You call me a liar?"

"Not at all. But if you are who you say you are, then you understand the security protocols and proper channels. Moscow Central agents traveling the countryside without identification is not particularly unusual, I grant you. Not riding in an official network vehicle can be easily explained. But you and your silent comrade pique my curiosity. You speak with an accent I cannot place, and that piques it even more. You claim your rank exceeds mine, yet you are considerably younger than myself, and I know I rose very quickly in the hierarchy of the network, despite my posting here."

Ivornich's voice was very calm, very matter-of-fact. Though Kane didn't understand a word she said, his pointman's seventh sense—a subtle prescience of impending danger—caused his hand to instinctively ready itself to receive the Sin Eater.

The phone jingled discordantly. Ivornich deftly spun the receiver to her ear, spoke a word, then listened intently. She dropped the receiver back into its cradle with a clatter.

Showing her white teeth in a half grin, she said, "However, my curiosity must remain unsatisfied for the time being. But only for a short while. The colonel is returning to Moscow this morning. You may meet him personally and make your report, at the railhead in Ilyamanof Station. You do know the area?"

"Of course," Brigid said, the image of the numbers on the crates in Mongolia startlingly clear in her mind.

"Tell me."

"Twelve."

"Exactly." Ivornich's smile widened, though her eyes remained cold.

Brigid turned confidently toward the door. "Then we shall be there."

Kane also turned, but Ivornich spoke sharply and though he didn't know what she said, something in her tone conveyed that she had addressed him. He cast her an over-the-shoulder glance, eyes masked by his dark glasses.

"Unlike your colleague," Ivornich said, her throaty voice humming with menace, with a grim humor, "you have the look of a professional, of one of us. I should know you, especially if you outrank me. Why don't I?"

Kane only glared at her. Brigid spoke up sharply, "Your security classification is not high enough, Captain, to know this man or even to speak to him."

Ivornich hooked her thumbs into her belt. "We shall see. Until then, keep this in mind—the worst kind of death is reserved for agents provocateurs. They rarely die easily or quickly."

Brigid and Kane walked out of the office. Grant, still seated on the wag, sagged with visible relief when they came down the steps. Kane whispered, "My, she *is* a bitch, isn't she?"

"Da," Brigid agreed gloomily.

"She didn't even offer us coffee."

"No, but she did seem awfully interested in you."

"A purely professional interest, I'm sure," Kane replied blandly.

"What was all that gibberish about?" Grant asked.

As she and Kane climbed into the cart, Brigid said, "Let's get rolling and I'll tell you."

"Get rolling to where?"

"The railhead."

"I don't know where that is," retorted Grant.

Brigid forced a wan smile. "We had better behave like we do. I'm sure the good captain will put a tail on us to make sure we get there."

Grant snapped the reins, and the horse began walking. "So far," he murmured to the animal, "our first few hours in Mother Russia are turning out to be a whole lot of no fun."

Chapter 14

Lakesh stepped out of the elevator, through the archway and into the Historical Division. He passed archivists going off shift, and they greeted him with respectful, deferential nods. The only person who didn't nod was a black-coated Mag who had stepped into the elevator with him at the promenade. In fact, he went to a great deal of effort to pretend he hadn't noticed Lakesh.

The Mag remained behind in the elevator, and Lakesh knew he was whispering into his lapel trans-comm, reporting to Salvo that he was here, reappearing unannounced after a two-day absence.

Lakesh repressed a smile. The Mag, and others like him, were victims of forces too powerful and too insidious for them to combat or understand. The man wasn't an enemy. The forces that had made him a Magistrate were the enemies.

He walked through the long, broad corridors of the division, past scores of sealed doorways that led into hundreds of chambers and antechambers. All of them were filled with the relics of vanished cities and long-dead people. The quiet air smelled of dust and time—time past, time present, time future and time twisted out of shape.

Most of the storerooms were crammed to the ceiling with racks upon racks and shelves upon shelves of a vast number of books, magazines and technical manuals, articles of clothing, crates of paintings, pieces of statuary and sculpture—anything that had survived the nukecaust more or less intact. Lakesh pretended that he took pride in the fact that the Cobaltville Archives contained a greater volume of predark artifacts than any other ville in the network.

He entered the main work area, the chemically treated rainbow insignia on his bodysuit allowing him to pass through the invisible photoelectric field without activating alarms. A long row of computer stations, half-enclosed by partitions, all faced a long blank wall. Hidden behind the stone-and-steel-reinforced wall was a bank of sophisticated mainframe computers, the heart and brains of the division's database.

Around him the archivists hurried to their machines. There were fifty direct-digital-control computer stations in the huge room, with sixty operators always on duty. The ten extra archivists were kept as a reserve force in the event that someone became too incapacitated—or in Brigid Baptiste's case—too arrested to handle his or her keyboard.

The warning buzzer sounded, and the monitor screens lit up. The room filled with the faint clatter of fingers on keys. Long rows of silent men and women became automatons who served as the revisionists and editors of human history.

Lakesh scanned the faces of the archivists and wondered how many of them wished they would drop down dead. It was impossible to tell from their facial expressions—somber and preoccupied, with perhaps a touch of cold intellectual resolve.

Their whole lives, from conception to death, were ordered for them, both at work and at home. Ville dogma, ville upbringing, convinced them how lucky they were to live on the bounty of the baron and not have to scratch out a starvation existence in the Outlands. As long as they obeyed the maddening and contradictory volume of rules, they had security, as well as medical and even retirement benefits.

It was the life Brigid had led, Kane and Grant had led, the only life they had known. Now they were forced to run and then run again, with prices on their heads that any so-called citizen could collect just by giving information about them. All because they had sinned by trying to learn a truth and develop a concept of larger destiny.

Lakesh stood and watched the workers for a few minutes. As senior archivist, it was his duty to pretend interest. The spy-eye vid camera on the ceiling transmitted his image down to the Magistrates' intel section.

When he felt he had put on a sufficient show, he shuffled into his private office. It was fairly spacious, but it didn't have a window, not that he gave a damn. He knew the Admin Monolith towered three hundred feet into the bracing Colorado air. Made of steel, aluminum, vanadium alloy, glass and rockcrete, it stood like a grim, foreboding deity over the residential Enclaves and the Pits.

Past generations had labored in buildings such as this, in office suites, in corporate headquarters, their life energy sucked away until nothing was left but flesh and bones. The war to leach away the human spirit had begun a very long time before January 20, 2001.

Lakesh had never worked in a tower or a skyscraper, never had a corner office with a view. He had spent nearly thirty years of his life in an underground installation beneath Archuleta Mesa, just outside of Dulce, New Mexico. During that time he had labored day and night, never feeling if it were actually day or night, on Project Cerberus, a major subdivision of the Totality Concept.

Sitting down behind his desk, he turned on his personal computer. Like all the machines in the division, it was equipped with a direct digital infeed to the mainframe database. Unlike all the other machines, it had no built-in governing hardware or security lock-out programs to restrict his access and thus alert a monitoring official.

He tapped in his clearance code and opened an untitled file. The symbols and numerical sequences appearing on the screen would mean nothing to an observer who didn't hold an advanced degree in quantum physics. Lakesh had received such a degree in his late teens from MIT, back in 1970. His education had been furthered in Dulce, handling technology that should not have functioned, yet did so beyond even a theoretician's wildest fantasies.

In his years at Dulce, first as a tech head then as overseer of Cerberus, he had learned—or rather, began the process of *un*learning—that quantum scientific principles were not a form of "new" physics at all, but a rediscovery of ancient knowledge. As a physicist he always sought symmetry, but rarely in nature were symmetries perfect—they were often slightly broken, almost imperceptibly flawed. It was a manifestation of a broken symmetry that now obsessed him.

During those last few years, he read the growing body of scientific theory that megalithic structures such as the dolmans of Newgrange in Ireland and Stonehenge in England were expressions of an old, long-forgotten system of physics. The theory, based on hyperdimensional mathematics, provided a fundamental connection between the four forces of nature. In the relativistic universe of Einstein, energy flows downhill—hot to cold—from higher to lower energy. A spinning celestial body, such as a planet, would have a connection to uphill and downhill energy flows, from an invisible higher dimension, to a lower one, in which humans lived and perceived their reality. Evidence indicated there were many vortex points, centers of intense energy, located in the same proximity on each of the planets of the solar system, and these points correlated to vortex centers on Earth.

Lakesh was sure some ancient peoples were aware of this, and manipulated these energies to open portals into other realms of existence. He suspected the knowledge was suppressed over the centuries, an act of repression he believed was the responsibility of the Archon Directorate or the secret societies in their employ. It was an axiom of conspiracies that someone or something else always pulled the strings of willing or ignorant puppets. He had expended many years tracing those filaments back through convoluted and manufactured histories to the puppet masters themselves.

Perhaps, he thought, studying the mathematical formulas on the screen, by employing hyperdimensional physics, the Archons go back and forth from our world to their own.

And if his hypothesis bore fruit, those naturally occurring gateways could be closed off, or used as peepholes to spy on the Archons as they had spied on humanity for aeons. Or even used as doorways into the past, where the seeds of humanity's enslavement had first been planted.

Though Lakesh rarely strayed beyond the borders of science, even theoretical, he had made a study of ancient history, scanning very old texts for clues to Archon involvement in human evolution. He didn't have to look very deeply before he realized that the so-called alien/ UFO phenomenon dated back before the twentieth century, when it gripped public consciousness. In fact, the historical records of nonhuman influence on Earth ran uninterrupted from the very dawn of mankind to the present day.

Always it was the same—human beings as possessions, with a never ending conflict bred between them, promoting spiritual decay and perpetuating conditions of unremitting physical hardship. And always secret societies were created by human pawns to conceal and to protect the true nature of humanity and its custodians—or masters.

Loathing once more rose up within him. No matter how deep the roots of their influence extended, the Archons didn't belong on Earth; they hadn't evolved here. They were from outside, and they needed something from humanity, perhaps as desperately as a leech needed blood. He still didn't know what. Even after all his years of research and study, his work was pitifully incomplete and inadequate.

With the loathing came guilt. He had helped the Archon Directorate to cull, to contain and control the masses of humanity and now he wanted freedom from his guilt and freedom for mankind. Humans, despite all their failings, had at least learned the concept of acknowledging that others of their kind had the right to freedom. True, they forgot easily and had to be reminded often— sometimes violently—but the history of respect for each other was there.

The Archons, wherever they came from, had no such history. Perhaps they knew nothing whatsoever of respecting the rights of other life-forms, inferior in their eyes, which they viewed basically as property.

However, he had come across cryptic references to other nonhuman entities that appeared to be, at least superficially, more benign than the Archons, and these entities were always connected in some fashion to the ancient megalithic structures in Europe.

He recalled the millennia-old legends of the Tuatha De Danann, wafting into Ireland on a city of light, with many treasures and superior weapons. They had built four great cities that were the centers of science and learning. The sites of these cities were allegedly entrances to the Bru', magic places not inhabited by humans. The Bru' na Boinne, Newgrange by the River Boyne, was the most important of these places—

The trans-comm unit on his desk emitted a rising and falling warble. He felt a jolt of fear and he fought it down. Physically he was nearly a hundred years old, chronologically a shade under two hundred and fifty, and he refused to be frightened by anyone or anything.

The trans-comm warbled again, then fell silent. It was a sound he hadn't heard in three months. It was a summons to Alpha Level, to a meeting of the Trust, the latest incarnation of secret societies acting as insulation between the Archon Directorate and what was left of humanity.

Lakesh saved his calculations and engaged his comp's encryption lock, though it was an unnecessary precaution. Not even Salvo would dare to audit his computer work. Nor could he understand it if he did.

Stiffly Lakesh arose from his desk and shuffled through the work area. His image as the venerable senior archivist, the devoted servitor to the baron, was important. Therefore, he always walked as if he were only a few steps from expiring completely. He actually could maintain a sprightly gait if he cared to—several of his joints were prosthetics, he was on his second set of lungs and his old, leaky heart had been repaired by surgery and was equipped with a pacemaker. Bionic replacements for worn-out joints and new organs were one of the benefits of sleeping in cryonic stasis for a century. To be of use to the Unification Program, he had needed to be as fit as cybernetic alterations could make him.

Once out of the workroom, he entered a short corridor leading to a storage area. The passage dead-ended at a locked door that supposedly led to a room filled with old printed matter. Lakesh inserted a key into the lock and clicked it open.

Inside the door was an elevator shaft just large enough to accommodate two men. He stepped onto the pancake-shaped elevator disk and pulled the door shut behind him. Automatic lock solenoids snapped into place, and the disk on which he stood shot upward. Every level of the Admin Monolith possessed a private, hidden elevator, known only to members of the Trust.

The disk hissed to a pneumatic stop, and Lakesh opened the door, striding down the ramp and into the baron's suite, the puppet master's alcove. All the strings of power in the ville extended down from this level.

The foyer was magnificent, as was every room in the suite. Glittering light cast from many crystal chandeliers flooded every corner of the entrance hall. At the far end of the foyer, flanking huge, ivory-and-gold-inlaid double doors, were two members of the elite Baronial Guard. Their impeccably tailored uniforms consisted of polished black boots, short white jackets and red trousers.

The guards opened the doors, and the one on his left said courteously, "The lord baron awaits you in his private lounge, sir."

The doors shut behind him, and as he expected, he saw nothing but a deep, almost primal dark. The baron's level was the only one in the monolith without windows. Lakesh walked forward, heading toward the dim golden glow of a single light shining over an open door. When he saw the light, he realized the baron had not called a meeting of the Trust.

Baron Cobalt sat alone in a room so completely sound-proofed that the ears grew weary of trying to catch a whisper of outside noise. No one ever came to the baron's private audience chamber unbidden. In fact, only Lakesh's special status as one of the original architects of both the Totality Concept and the Unification Program allowed him to be alone with the hybrid ruler of Cobalt-ville, the eyes and hands of the Archon Directorate.

Baron Cobalt wasn't unprotected, however. He sat inside the curve of a small, horseshoe-shaped desk. Rows of buttons and toggle switches lay within easy reach of his delicate fingers. If Baron Cobalt pressed one button, his guard promptly appeared. If he pushed another button, his personal staff came.

Very few people outside of certain members of the Trust knew what the baron looked like. It was part of a tapestry of mystique, of deception and of deliberate mis-information.

Baron Cobalt's excessively slender body was draped in a one-piece dark golden robe that accentuated the pale gold color of his skin. It was stretched tightly over a narrow, hairless skull so elongated that it resembled an upside-down teardrop. Very small ears were set low on the sides of his head. His face seemed to consist primarily of delicate brow arches, prominent cheekbones and a very long, very sharp chin. The large eyes were slanted, and the big irises were a beautiful yellowish brown in color.

He wasn't tall and in fact looked very fragile. If his muscles had little strength in them, then the power of his will and his station more than compensated for his physical shortcomings. What he willed to be always came to pass.

"My good friend. My trusted friend." The baron's lipless mouth barely seemed to move, but the musical fluting of his voice filled the entire room.

Lakesh inclined his head. "My lord baron. How may I be of service to you?"

Baron Cobalt shifted uneasily in his chair. "You may help me to understand the nature of a problem. It has vexed me far longer than it should have, yet I cannot come to a resolution or wipe it from my mind."

"What is the problem?"

The baron's long, artistic fingers suddenly clenched, hooking like an eagle's talons. His mouth writhed, contorted as if he were trying to repress a scream or a sob. He husked out a single word, "Kane."

He repeated it, stretching out the syllable as if it were taffy. "Kayyyynuh."

The baron's beautiful eyes blinked, brimming with sudden tears. Lakesh kept a tight rein on his shock, not allowing it to register on his face or demeanor. He looked at the tears with great interest. It never occurred to him that members of the Hybrid Dynasty could weep.

In a savage whisper that sounded nothing like his controlled, musical contralto, Baron Cobalt hissed, "He laughed at me!"

The baron's slender frame trembled. "He humiliated me, he assaulted me—*he laughed at me!*"

One of his hands touched his short neck, rubbing it gingerly. "I can still feel the brute's paw around my throat, holding me helpless. I tried to reason with him. I told him that the ideal solution to a better world lay in the creation of a better human, and that I represented the better human. I explained that once the superior life-form was in power, then the final depopulation of the old type of human could be realistically, profitably and painlessly carried out.''

The baron dragged in a ragged, harsh breath. Tears spilled from his eyes, splashing over his jutting cheekbones. ''He didn't care. Do you know what he said to me, the filthy apeling? I shall never forget it. He said, 'You're not a god-king, you're not divine. You're not even a good employer. You're a laboratory monstrosity with an attitude—a vampire living off the genetic material of human beings. You have to take baths in chemicals and gore. You're *disgusting* is what you are.'''

Lakesh knew Kane had violently confronted Baron Cobalt in Dulce, but he had never heard the details. He was a bit shaken by the intensity of emotion, and he now understood why the baron had isolated himself for the past few months. He had been as humiliated as a demigod could possibly be by a lower life-form who not only refused to worship him, but even sneered at his claim of divinity.

The baron spoke quickly, the words tumbling over one another in their haste to leave his lips. ''I said to him, 'Much of that superior genetic human material derives from your father,' and that made us related, after a fashion. He didn't care even about *that,* Lakesh! Why? Tell me *why!*''

Lakesh spread his hands in a puzzled gesture. ''Who can say, Lord Baron? He is human.''

Baron Cobalt cleared the tears from his face with angry swipes of his hands. ''But I am human, too, and I don't understand what he wants, why he said what he said, why he *did* what he did. I meant him no harm.''

Choosing his words carefully, Lakesh said, ''You said

it yourself, my lord. He is the old type of human, and you are the new. He simply could not understand.''

"How could he not understand that we, the oligarchy of barons, represent the most singular achievement of biological pioneering in the history of this planet?'' The baron's tone was plaintive, distressed.

"Very few old-type humans can grasp the staggering implications of the project, my lord. They cannot stretch their ordinary minds to encompass its detail.''

The baron eyed him haughtily. "Yet you understand.''

"I am a scientist. I have lived most of my life in a scientific environment. Long ago I realized the inherent limitations of man, and therefore accepted this most ennobling of human goals...the creation of the superior human.''

It was an answer Baron Cobalt expected and accepted. "Yes, the drive to improve the strain of humanity began long before I was born, long before the holocaust. Hitler's Aryan breeding farms, for example. Of course, selective mating to produce the human of the future's better world required too much time. A new thinking that led to the same end at a much swifter pace was plainly demanded. Hybridization was an absolute necessity after the nukecaust. I can see that. You can see that. Why cannot others see it?''

"Perhaps,'' Lakesh said slowly, knowing he was treading on very dangerous ground, "they cannot see what you and I see because they are obsessed with freedom.''

Baron Cobalt's small nostrils flared. "An ideological term. They should be concerned with other things than primitive concepts of physical liberty. Besides, none of them would know how to use freedom if they had it, would they?''

"Indeed." Lakesh smiled, realizing the baron had missed the point entirely, and that revealed the weakness, the Achilles' heel that every hybrid, perhaps even every Archon carried somewhere within them.

Baron Cobalt, bred for brilliance, had emotional limitations placed upon his enormous intellect. He was a captive of his Archon hive-mind heritage, the captive of a remorseless mind-set that didn't carry with it the simple comprehension of the importance to humans of individual liberty.

Smug in his hybrid arrogance, the baron didn't understand the primal beast buried inside the truly human psyche, the beast that always gave humans a fair chance of winning in the deadly game of survival of the fittest. Indoctrination and conditioning could be spread only so far, and the Archons and their bastard half-breed spawn could not acknowledge it. Pride, hubris, would not allow it.

The sweeping supraorbital ridges on the baron's brows lowered. For an instant his eyes glittered, cobralike. "Kane must believe he is free, do you not think so?"

Lakesh shook his head. "He is running, hiding, my lord. That is not freedom."

"Perhaps not to you or I. But to an apeling like him, escaping my justice must be the most liberating experience of his wasted life. He must answer for the destruction he wreaked in Dulce. The project's timetable was unforgivably altered, you know."

"Surely," Lakesh said smoothly, "the responsibility of finding Kane and his confederates lies with the Magistrate Division."

"True." Baron Cobalt steepled his long fingers beneath the point of his chin. "And Salvo has yet to produce results. I want those results."

Warmly, reasonably, Lakesh replied, "I sympathize,

FREE BOOKS!

FREE GIFT!

AND YOU CAN GET
FREE BOOKS <u>PLUS</u>
A FREE GIFT!

NO COST! NO OBLIGATION TO BUY!
NO PURCHASE NECESSARY!

PLAY "LUCKY 7"
AND GET FIVE FREE GIFTS...

HOW TO PLAY:

1. With a coin, carefully scratch off the silver area at the right. Then check the claim chart to see what we have for you—FREE BOOKS and a gift—ALL YOURS! ALL FREE!

2. Send back this card and you'll get hot-off-the-press Gold Eagle books, never before published. These books have a total cover price of $18.50. But THEY ARE TOTALLY FREE, even the shipping will be at our expense!

3. There's no catch. You're under no obligation to buy anything. We charge nothing—ZERO—for your first shipment. And you don't have to make any minimum number of purchases—not even one!

4. The fact is thousands of readers enjoy receiving books by mail from the Gold Eagle Reader Service™. They like the convenience of home delivery... they like getting the best new novels before they're available in stores... and they love our discount prices!

5. We hope that after receiving your free books you'll want to remain a subscriber. But the choice is yours—to continue or cancel, anytime at all! So why not take us up on our invitation, with no risk of any kind. You'll be glad you did!

SURPRISE MYSTERY GIFT!
IT CAN BE YOURS <u>FREE</u> WHEN
YOU PLAY "LUCKY 7".

PLAY "LUCKY 7"

Just scratch off the silver box with a coin.
Then check below to see the gifts you get.

YES! I have scratched off the silver area above. Please send me all the gifts for which I qualify. I understand I am under no obligation to purchase any books, as explained on the back and on the opposite page.

164 CIM CCNF
(U-M-B-09/97)

NAME

ADDRESS   APT.

CITY   STATE   ZIP

7	7	7	**WORTH FOUR FREE BOOKS AND A FREE SURPRISE GIFT**
🍒	🍒	🍒	**WORTH FOUR FREE BOOKS**
⬤	⬤	⬤	**WORTH THREE FREE BOOKS**
🔔	🔔	🍒	**WORTH TWO FREE BOOKS**

Offer limited to one per household and not valid to present subscribers.
All orders subject to approval.

PRINTED IN U.S.A.   © 1991 GOLD EAGLE

THE GOLD EAGLE READER SERVICE: HERE'S HOW IT WORKS

Accepting free books places you under no obligation to buy anything. You may keep the books and gift and return the shipping statement marked "cancel". If you do not cancel, about a month later we will send you four additional novels, and bill you just $15.80—that's a saving of 15% off the cover price of all four books! And there's no extra charge for shipping! You may cancel at any time, but if you choose to continue, every other month we'll send you four more books, which you may either purchase at the discount price…or return to us and cancel your subscription.

*Terms and prices subject to change without notice. Sales tax applicable in N.Y.

BUSINESS REPLY MAIL

FIRST-CLASS MAIL   PERMIT NO. 717   BUFFALO, NY

POSTAGE WILL BE PAID BY ADDRESSEE

GOLD EAGLE READER SERVICE
3010 WALDEN AVE
PO BOX 1867
BUFFALO NY 14240-9952

NO POSTAGE
NECESSARY
IF MAILED
IN THE
UNITED STATES

my lord. I, too, was betrayed, by one of my own archivists. However, dwelling upon it would prevent me from devoting my full attention to my work—''

''*Kane* is my work!'' Baron Cobalt's voice rose to a high-pitched screech, nothing modulated or musical about it. He knotted his hands into fists, and his lean form stiffened, as if he had received a severe electric shock. ''And from this moment on, he will be *your* work, as well! He will be the work of all of the divisions, of all of the villes!''

Lakesh tried to keep his face from mirroring his astonishment. To witness Baron Cobalt losing his serenely detached control and screaming like an enraged, frustrated human child was shockingly unexpected.

''I will not allow it, do you hear?'' The screech dropped to a sibilant hiss. ''For the past three generations, humans have been taught a gospel of weakness and they must not learn how to understand and hate and fight again. Kane could teach them how. The human race must not be allowed to rebel and turn against the doctrines.''

Anger lived in Baron Cobalt's voice, as well as outrage. But genuine fear hummed there, too, the fear that the pendulum would one day swing back in mankind's direction, that humanity would eventually recover its sense of identity and correct the overbalance.

''Lord Baron,'' Lakesh declared, ''Kane is not a revolutionary, nor a visionary. He is simply a criminal. An outlander. He does not deserve your personal attention.''

Baron Cobalt's voice dropped to a low, gloating croon. ''I know what he deserves. And I know that he will receive it. If I do nothing else, I will make certain of that.''

The baron's golden eyes bored into Lakesh's. ''And you,'' he continued, ''will help me.''

Chapter 15

Grant and Kane had visited some old predark villes where attempts at rebuilding had begun, but none of those places had received the full devastating fury of nuclear weapons like Moscow. Entire city blocks were completely barren and empty of movement.

The day dawned bleak and gray, but the wind didn't rise appreciably and the temperature, though low, was bearable. The cart rolled along the paved, litter-choked streets, between bombed-out ruins and tumbled-down apartment buildings. Some areas were nothing but acre upon acre of scorched and shattered concrete, with rusting rods of reinforcing iron protruding from the ground like withered stalks of some mutated crop. On the horizon a clump of high towers topped by spires and minarets was outlined against the sky.

Brigid used the map to fix their position in relation to the rail yard. Despite her eidetic memory, it wasn't easy, since so many of the landmarks noted on the map were missing. She directed Grant to cross over a two-lane highway. It was early yet, so there wasn't a dangerous amount of traffic, but all of them were surprised by the number of gas-powered vehicles on the road. In America, in the villes, such transportation was reserved for the elite. When they looked closer, they saw that many of the wags that rumbled up and down the blacktop bore the silver-circle insignia designating them as official Internal Security Network vehicles.

On the other side of the highway, a big sign spanned the width of a broad avenue. Brigid read the words aloud, "Nikulino Street Marketplace. Good. We're only a few blocks away from Ilyamanof Station."

Kane eyed a truck idling at the mouth of an alleyway. "We should just ditch the horse and buggy and grab some real transport."

"We're supposed to be security agents," Brigid reminded him. "Not thieves."

"In that case," said Grant, "we'll requisition what we need, in the name of the state."

The signs of habitation, if not civilization, became thicker. One entire lot was covered by tents. Music came out of a big tent, played on an accordion. Some of the tents were elaborately embroidered. One was colored so luridly, it obviously contained everything an undiscriminating shopper could want—liquor, food, gambling, women and the dubious privacy of canvas-walled boudoirs.

The smells were strong and pungent, even biting. It seemed as if every other door had a sign above it advertising that vodka in some form could be purchased or bartered. Brigid couldn't help but wonder if only alcohol made life tolerable in nuke-blasted Moscow.

There were wags, mostly oxen drawn, and a few buggies, but most of the people they saw walked in a trudging, downcast gait. The reason was the parade of sec network men and women, wearing drab overcoats and toting old Kalashnikov autorifles. The sec agents gave them and their wag hard, piercing stares as they rolled by, but said nothing.

Still, their attention made Kane nervous. He didn't

think much of Brigid's provisional plan to pretend they were network operatives themselves. "They'll be tailing us right to the rail station," he told her. "We need to get ourselves lost."

"If that's where Sverdlovosk will be," she replied, "that's where we need to be. He helped me get out of Mongolia alive."

"And he might help all of us get dead here in Russia."

"He's the only lead we have," she retorted doggedly.

Grant said, "We're foreigners, hated Americans. We're here to spy, remember? That's not exactly a well-respected pastime in any country."

Brigid frowned. "My feeling—my *instinct*—is that whatever Sverdlovosk and maybe even Ivornich are up to in the Gobi, it has very little to do with the good of the state."

Kane opened his mouth to voice an objection, then shut it again. He often relied on his instincts to decide on a certain course of action. In fact, obeying his instincts had resulted in all of their exiles from Cobaltville. He exchanged a quick look with Grant. By the wry half smile on the big man's face, Kane figured he was remembering the same thing.

He sighed in resignation. "All right, Baptiste. You speak the lingo, you met the bastard. Your call. For now."

Vendors opened up food stalls, and the primary items seemed to be vegetables, particularly potatoes. A few merchants sold small household items, and the prices posted on everything made no sense to any of them, even Brigid. Overall, the Nikulino Street Marketplace reminded Kane and Grant of the Tartarus Pits. Both of them became slightly wistful with nostalgia.

The wag came abreast of a lot enclosed by a split-rail

corral. Inside the crude fence milled livestock—sheep, goats, pigs, a few cows and a couple of horses. The air was redolent with the rich aroma of manure. A beefy man wearing a leather apron and a wool cap pulled down low over his head whistled and gestured to them.

"Stop," Brigid directed Grant. "Here's where we can ditch this rig and get a little spending capital."

Grant reined the cart to a halt at the curb, and Brigid hopped out, speaking to the burly man. He uttered a few grunts and walked around the horse, studying its withers, the hooves, peeling back its upper lip to inspect the animal's teeth. Grant noticed the man had no ears beneath his stocking cap, only hacked-off nubbins with bits of fleshy lobe attached.

He and Brigid began talking, the man punctuating his side of the bargaining with energetic gestures. Kane saw one of the overcoated sec men standing across the lane, watching and listening to the exchange with great interest. Sidling up to Brigid, he murmured, "We've got no time for this. Whatever he offers, take it."

Brigid shot him a steely glare, but ducked her head and held out a hand. The beefy man immediately produced a roll of paper currency from an apron pocket and counted out ten notes. They were printed on a fibrous wood pulp and absurdly colored, featuring a badly out of register engraving of a stern, fatherly man with a white beard.

Grant climbed off the cart, gave the horse a farewell pat and the three of them walked away. Brigid riffled through the bills. "He would have paid more, you know."

"You're as bad as a Pit jolt merchant," Kane snapped. "No matter what he paid, it was still a clear profit."

Pocketing the money, she replied, "If I'd accepted his first offer, he would've become suspicious."

Kane rolled his eyes. "But three officers of the Internal Security Network haggling over the price of horseflesh is perfectly acceptable? We were being watched, you know. If it's reported to Ivornich that we stopped to sell livestock—"

"We'll deal with that when—or if—we have to," Grant interrupted. "Let's find the railway station."

The avenues opened up, became broader. People were beginning to file into the market district, and they seemed to be of every shape, size and color, sporting every kind of garb. Grant, Kane and Brigid mingled with them, deliberately seeking crowds.

"A pretty diverse bunch," Grant commented.

"Russians were only one of over a hundred nationalities in the old Soviet Union," Brigid said.

The building styles were as diverse as the population. Old buildings dating back to well before skydark, newer ones that were throwbacks to earlier styles, duraplast domes and great, squatting stone masses with no discernible architectural design.

They tramped the thronging streets, past shops, past brothels, gambling halls and saloons. There were many eating places, all spilling exotic odors into the street. Although they were hungry, they decided against sampling any of the food.

"We don't want to risk contracting Uncle Vanya's revenge," remarked Brigid cryptically.

They crossed the Boulevard Yagovard and passed into the squalid side lanes that fringed the marketplace. People slunk in and out of alleys, prowling for jack, a bottle, a pinch of narcotics. No one molested them. Kane glanced over his shoulder and commented, "If we had shadows, I think we lost them in this place."

Their route led them beneath an elevated railroad trestle. A cumbersome-looking steam locomotive chugged overhead, filling the air with a prolonged grumble. On the other side of the trestle, they saw a confusing network of railroad tracks crisscrossing around huge dark warehouse sidings. They picked their way over the rails and the greasy gravel toward the main terminus.

As they approached, the sun slowly broke through the gunmetal gray cloud cover and touched what little color remained on the peeling yellow paint of the railroad station. Peering through the sooty windows of the waiting room, they saw varnished benches, a scuffed linoleum floor and twin chalkboards for arrivals and departures. An old woman, white hair bound in a scarf, drowsed behind the ticket-window grille. They looked up, then down the tracks, seeing nothing but oily wooden cross ties, rusty rails, cinders and a lot of soot. They saw no trains or people.

There was only a man dressed in a uniform of heavy black twill pushing a broom on the opposite side of the platform. Grant, Kane and Brigid entered and crossed the waiting room. The man kept sweeping, even after Brigid spoke to him.

He grunted something in reply and hooked a thumb over his shoulder, brooming his way along the platform.

"What was that about?" Grant asked quietly.

"I asked him where to find track twelve," she answered.

"And?"

She gestured. "Thataway. In the old factory complex."

"That's real helpful," grated Kane.

With Brigid in the lead, they left the platform and walked between two sets of tracks, toward a rail yard adjacent to the station proper. They wended their way through a maze of shunts, past empty flatcars and rusted machinery, toward a collection of dirty warehouses.

They heard the train before they saw it approaching. The three of them hunkered down behind an embankment and watched. It was the same old steam engine they had seen crossing the trestle at the outskirts of the market-place. It was several tracks away, reducing its speed as it slowly rumbled toward a large, dark building that stood isolated beside a double railway spur. Around and behind it were other big buildings, probably part of the old industrial park.

Its rusty brakes squealed as it came to a rattling stop alongside the building. Two men climbed down from the cab, and even at a distance of a hundred yards, they could see they were wearing the overcoats and disk-decorated fur caps that identified them as sec network officers.

Brigid's body suddenly stiffened. "See that?"

"What?"

"The number on the building, right above the door."

Kane and Grant looked, but saw only smears of grime and dirt that might have been anything. Brigid said, "It's the number twelve."

"Where'd you get this reputation for poor eyesight?" Kane asked.

"I'm astigmatic and farsighted. I can see things far away perfectly."

The sec officers didn't walk a post but simply took up guard positions on opposite sides of the door. Kane studied the facade of the building. A row of windows ran some six feet up all around the dingy walls. He looked again at the guards. One of them lit a cigarette, and the other stifled a yawn.

After a quick, whispered conference, they decided to risk approaching the warehouse. They walked in a crouch at the bottom of the embankment until they reached a point where a small, tin-walled storage shack blocked them from the view of the sec officers.

Patiently they worked their way toward the warehouse, keeping to cover as much as possible, stopping frequently to watch and listen. Almost thirty minutes passed before they stood in the shadow of the building's west wall. Grant, the tallest of them, tried lifting open all the windows. The last one was unlatched, and he slid up the wooden sash. He investigated the frame with his fingertips, searching for alarm wires. Then he slowly chinned himself upward, took a quick look and lowered himself to the ground.

"There can't be anything important in there," he whispered. "Only two guards, windows not locked—"

Brigid nodded uncertainly. "You may be right. There's only one way to find out, though."

Making a stirrup with his hands, Kane heaved Grant up to the opening. The fit was tight and he struggled, wriggled and kicked his legs to work his shoulders, then his hips through the frame. Under any other circumstances, the sight would have made Kane laugh.

Brigid followed next, lifted up by Kane and helped inside by Grant. Gripping the edge of the windowsill, Kane pulled himself up, his boots finding traction on the rough-textured wall. The narrow metal frame caught at the small bulges made by the gren- and magazine-laden combat harness beneath his coat. For a second he was caught fast and he squirmed and cursed.

From somewhere in the dark interior, he heard Grant's amused whisper, "Not so damn funny now, is it?"

Kane struggled free, grunting, "I didn't think you were funny—"

"Yes, you did. You thought it was funny and you thought I didn't know."

Lowering himself to the gritty floor, Kane looked around. The light peeping in through the grime-streaked windows was sufficient for their dark-vision glasses, though Brigid took out her Nighthawk microlight. The interior of the warehouse was high and cavernous. A length of railroad track ran into it from the outside, beneath a closed pair of wide, cross-braced doors. Big wooden crates were piled to the ceiling, some of them unmarked, but others stenciled with the Cyrillic numeral 12. All of them silently and carefully surveyed their surroundings.

On a long trestle table rested a high stack of six-inch thick, paper-wrapped slabs, four feet wide, ten feet long and perfectly rectangular in shape. Kane, Brigid and Grant soft-footed their way over the dusty concrete floor to the table, walking around it, examining the slabs. Kane tore a corner piece of the paper away. Beneath it gleamed a glassy substance, somewhat translucent and a pale ocher in color.

"Armaglass," Brigid whispered, a frown line deepening on her forehead. "A lot of it."

"I didn't know Russians manufactured this stuff," Grant commented softly.

"I didn't know anybody *could* manufacture it anymore," interjected Kane. "The stuff still in use in the villes was left over from before skydark. It's not good for much, is it?"

"Shielding," said Brigid. "One of its properties is that

it goes opaque when exposed to certain levels and wavelengths of radiation. That's one of the reasons it's used in the mat-trans gateways, to block energy overspills.''

Grant pursed his lips. ''Then it would be useful in Kharo-Khoto, since Lakesh said the place was very hot.''

''We don't know if Sverdlovosk has anything to do with armaglass,'' Kane argued.

''He's supposed to show up at warehouse twelve in the rail station,'' replied Brigid. ''So this has something to do with him, all right, even if the armaglass is not bound for Mongolia.''

''What do you want us to do?'' Kane demanded. ''Hang out here and hope Sverdlovosk arrives, and if he does, you'll pop out and say, 'Hey, remember me?'''

''What do you suggest?'' Brigid's tone was flat.

''Do a recce. Grant and me will split up, check out the zone. You can stay here, just in case your pal does show up.''

Brigid thought it over for a moment, then nodded. ''Agreed.''

''Find a dark corner to wait in. Monitor us on your trans-comm.''

Before they left, Grant and Kane ate a protein bar apiece from Brigid's survival pack, washing it down with long drafts of purified water. Climbing through the window a second time was no easier or dignified than the first. They went to the rear of the warehouse, made certain their trans-comm frequencies were open and in sync, then walked off in opposite directions.

Kane kept his Sin Eater leathered as he trod a path through high weeds and scattered machine parts. Most of the rusted hunks of metal were so corroded as to be unidentifiable. He walked behind the row of warehouses, sensing that most of them were long-ago abandoned. He saw and heard very little except for the infrequent cheeps of birds roosting in the eaves of the big buildings.

As he crossed an overgrown strip of gravel alley between a pair of warehouses, he heard the roar of an engine from the direction of the rail yard. He saw an open-topped jeep, painted a dull ocher, tearing up a muddy road ribbon beside one of the tracks. Immediately he sensed triple-red danger. He was exposed and he knew the two uniformed sec network men in the vehicle had spotted him.

The jeep skidded to a halt at the mouth of the alley, and the men climbed out, looking toward him suspiciously. They carried Kalashnikov rifles in shoulder slings. Kane was about twenty yards away from them, hidden from the waist down by weeds. He continued to casually cross the alley, as if he had every right to be doing so. Running would only catch the eyes of the officers immediately.

He reached the other side of the alley and veered to the left, toward the compound of an old factory. Judging by the mounds of slag, the great litter of steel scrap, it had been a smelting plant at one time. Into his lapel transceiver, he whispered, "Triple red. I think I've been made. Stand by, observe radio silence until you hear from me."

A big building stood behind the slag heaps. It had no door and was probably an easy place to become lost in. A harsh voice shouted behind him, the words quick and incomprehensible. Kane continued to walk at a steady pace. He didn't turn his head, but the Sin Eater slid smoothly into his palm.

The shout came again, buzzing with an angry, puzzled note. He kept walking. He heard the faint metal-on-metal click of a firing bolt being pulled back. He dived to his left, rolled behind a pile of iron posts and came up running an erratic zigzag pattern. The first shots whined over his head just as he had fallen. A second volley banged loudly on the iron posts, ricochets whining off in all directions.

Kane ran faster, hearing feet pounding behind him. The building loomed massively before him. A stuttering burst of autofire kicked up clods of dirt all around him. He stopped running, pivoting on his right heel, leading with his blaster. The Sin Eater roared, one round from the 3-round burst smashing into an officer's shoulder and twirling him around in a bright spray of crimson. His companion cried out and threw himself to the ground.

Kane turned and dashed behind a mound of slag, then raced for the open building. He heard the shouted Russian of the sec agents behind him, calling to the guards at the front of the warehouse. Once reinforcements arrived, they would fan out and cover the area, but that would take time.

As he sprinted into the building, a rattling hail of bullets drummed on the outer wall. He loped through the murky emptiness until he reached the far side, eyes darting back and forth, seeking an exit. He leaned against the corrugated metal wall and listened. He heard nothing on the other side of it.

Sidling along the wall, he found a loose section of tin and yanked it carefully away from the wood cross brace. He managed to ease his body through the small opening and found himself in a wilderness of grotesque iron shapes. He moved through them swiftly, doubling back toward the warehouse where Brigid was waiting.

Armed uniformed men marched all over the perimeter. He had no idea where they had come from. When he reached a position where he had a fairly unobstructed view of the rail yard, he saw a large covered truck parked near one of the warehouses. A silver circle was painted on the cab door. He considered hailing Grant to warn him, but discarded the notion. He might be in hiding, and even the whisper of sound made by the transceiver circuit engaging could give him away. Thinking of his partner, Kane shivered.

Kane gazed for a moment at the truck, wondering if he and his companions had indeed tripped an alarm somewhere inside the warehouse and called up the hounds. If so, Baptiste was in grave danger, trapped inside of the place.

Cursing the daylight, he began moving again, sometimes in a crouch, often crawling on his belly through the high weeds. The men searching for him were nearby, but they were not yet too close.

Finally he reached the rear of the warehouse, crept beside the west wall until he reached the window. It was still open, and he heaved himself up and through it, feet-first this time. He dropped lightly to the floor, on the balls of his feet.

Kane started to speak into the transceiver when he heard the step behind him. There was a short crackle of noise, and paralyzing pain lanced into the back of his neck, flooding and overwhelming the nerve endings throughout his entire body. He tried to whirl, to bring up his blaster. Instead, he shambled clumsily, dimly aware he was falling to one side.

"Ah. I see one of you took the bait."

The voice spoke in precise English. He caught a fragmented glimpse of Captain Ivornich's slender, compact figure. She smiled at him over the black, sparking object in her right hand.

Then there was nothing at all, nothing but a colorless void.

Chapter 16

With a shocking suddenness, Kane awoke. One moment he was floating in a comfortable sepia sea of unconsciousness. In the next moment it was as if a great hand snatched him up by the scruff of the neck and flung him into a cold and miserable reality. He felt something hard against his back and a stiffness in his neck.

For an instant that felt as long as an eternity, he fought against a surge of panic. When it passed, he cracked his eyelids and saw his lap. Then he opened his eyes and forced them to focus on his surroundings. He was in a small, square metal room with flat gray walls. The room was evenly, almost intimately lit from some invisible source. He saw no doors or windows, and there seemed to be no ceiling. In front of him stood a small desk. Piled atop it was his coat, sweater, combat harness and holstered Sin Eater.

He looked down at himself. He had been stripped except for his pants. Naked to the waist, he was seated in a high-backed wooden chair, his wrists tightly bound to the arms by leather cuffs. Long wafers of metal ran along the wood beneath his arms. His bare back pressed against a wider metal plate. It didn't feel uncomfortably cold, so he figured he had been sitting in the chair long enough for his body heat to warm the metal. Carefully he leaned to the right, looking down. The square chair legs were bolted solidly to the floor.

He gathered his muscles, straining them against the cuffs, testing their strength. A wave of icy agony coursed through him, streaking up his arms, over and across his back. He writhed, not able to bite back a cry of surprised pain. Slowly the wave receded, easing away.

A woman laughed. "How do you like our attitude adjuster, outsider?" The language was English, and somehow it didn't surprise Kane.

"Effective," he said, surprised to hear how steady his voice sounded. "It'll work the kinks out of your back for sure."

Boot heels clacked on the floor behind him. He looked up at Captain Ivornich as she walked around the chair and stood in front of the desk, leaning one hip casually against a corner. In her right hand she held a small box molded from metal. Two buttons, one green, one red, studded its surface. Clipped to the belt around her waist was a black plastic instrument. Two metal prongs protruded from one end. Kane recognized it as a stun gun, which delivered an incapacitating electric shock.

"I suppose I should thank you for not shooting me," he said politely.

The woman's eyebrows arched in mock wonderment. "Really? I wouldn't if I were you."

Her thumb depressed the red button on the box in her hand. Icy jolts of voltage rushed through Kane's back, up his arms. He cried out, muscles twisting in a brief spasm. The agony went away, and Kane sat there, sweating and gasping.

"Do you still wish to thank me?" Ivornich asked.

Kane refused to respond.

"Good. Save your breath. You have a lot of screaming yet to do."

She leaned forward slightly. "You will tell me two

things—how much classified information you know about the project and *how* you know.''

"Know about what?"

"Colonel Sverdlovosk and District Twelve for starters.''

"I don't know the colonel at all."

Ivornich sighed. "Give me some credit. I trapped you like a rabbit in a snare. I fed you a story about the colonel arriving this morning, when in actuality the call I received was to apprise me that he would be late in returning. It seems he had a bit of transportation trouble in Mongolia. His vehicle went missing.''

"That's a shame," Kane said inanely.

"You were under surveillance almost to the moment of your apprehension. By the way, your companion received a very poor price for the horse.''

"She figured as much."

The woman ignored his comment. Turning slightly, she lifted the holstered Sin Eater. "Unusual design. It appears to be a customized, reframed Spectre autoblaster, dating back to the late 1980s. Is it a standard side arm for those in your profession?''

"Profession?"

"American spy. Or insurgent." She dropped the blaster back onto the desktop with a clunk. "I grant you we know very little of the conditions in America since the nuclear war.''

"Then we're even."

"By no means. I suspect you and your companions did not come here simply to look around. How did you get here, anyway?''

Kane shook his head. "You wouldn't believe me."

"Probably not," she agreed. "I do believe you were

sent here from one of the so-called baronies to get information. Which one?"

"Which one what? Which barony?"

"Yes."

"I'm what you might call an independent contractor."

"What does that mean?"

Kane pretended not to have heard her. He made a casual show of looking around the room. "Can you give me an idea of where I might be, or is that classified, too?"

"You are in the Territorial Police substation on Previnsk Street, under the jurisdiction of District Two."

"What is District Two?"

Ivornich held up four fingers. "Our national government consists of four major superstructures or districts. Each of these have clearly delineated responsibilities. Labor. Security. Mutuality. Politics. A general policy-making body is made up of executives from all the districts. Don't you have something similar in your baronies?"

"Similar," Kane admitted. "We call them divisions."

"A typically American militaristic mind-set."

Kane threw her a derisive half grin. "Look who's talking—*Captain*."

A line of confusion appeared on her smooth brow. "Look who's—ah, I see. You meant that as a joke, didn't you? Glad to see it. A sense of humor is an absolute necessity in situations like these."

"It's gotten me into trouble before."

"I don't doubt it," she replied wryly.

Her thumb tapped the red button. The jolt of electricity surging through the arms and back of the chair was very brief, but he winced just the same.

"The current can be increased to become quite, quite painful," she declared. "Even lethal."

"I figured that out myself."

"In your country this would no doubt be considered a vile, inhuman torture, would it not?"

Kane pretended to consider the query thoughtfully, recalling some of the bloody techniques practiced by the Magistrates to wring information out of a prisoner. "Actually, no. In my country, this little attitude adjuster of yours would be laughed at because it's so ineffectual and merciful."

"Really?" Ivornich seemed surprised, even a bit disappointed. "According to the American history I was taught, criminals were treated very leniently, coddled even."

"Not anymore. Not for a very long, long time. Of course, almost everyone in my country is now treated like a criminal, and not very leniently, either."

"Including yourself?"

"Especially myself."

"What was your crime?"

Slowly, reluctantly, Kane replied, "I asked all the right questions."

"Did you receive answers?"

"Oh, yes." The bitterness in his voice was undiluted and undisguised.

"I, too, seek answers, outsider," Ivornich said.

"Then ask the right fucking questions, Captain," snapped Kane.

Ivornich's lips compressed in irritation. "I did not gain the appointment of territorial commander because I am a woman and therefore soft. The council invested eight years of training and education in me to manufacture a tool. The tool is of the hardest forged steel. You cannot match your steel against mine.''

Kane sighed and said reasonably, ''I don't want to, Captain. Maybe we can agree to an information exchange. Tell me where my friends are—''

Anger flared in Ivornich's violet eyes. Her thumb hovered over the red button. ''You are in no position to ask for anything.''

Kane responded to the anger with his own. ''Just because I'm an American does not make me an enemy. The war is long over. There's no reason to continue hostilities that burned themselves out nearly two hundred years ago.''

Ivornich made a disdainful spitting noise. ''Idiot. I don't give a damn about old political differences, or building new bridges of understanding between our respective nations.''

''Then what *do* you give a damn about?''

''A rise to power,'' she stated coldly. ''A rise which does not need to be diverted by factors such as yourself and your friends. You are a mystery, and I hate mysteries. They tend to give me headaches, and I feel a very severe one coming on.''

''I don't care much for mysteries myself. But I'm here to solve one.''

''Which is?''

Kane considered evading this query as he had the others, but he needed to drop a few crumbs of information in order to gauge her reaction, to find out if she was truly involved with Sverdlovosk and his project.

Carefully he said, ''The Black City. The sacred flame. The Tushe Gun.''

Captain Ivornich's cold marble face didn't alter. She continued to eye him suspiciously. ''Nonsense words.''

Voice dropping to a half whisper, he added, "The Archon Directorate."

He saw by the sudden change of expression on her smooth face he had said the wrong thing. Brusquely she said, "You've wasted enough of my time. If you will not provide me with straight answers, I will not provide you with any more of it."

Though her tone was heavy with menace, Kane detected an undernote of warning in her eyes and voice.

"Do those two words mean something to you?" he asked.

"No."

"What about one of them, then? Like Arch—"

Ivornich's thumb depressed the red button. Like a bolt of lightning, pain ripped through Kane's nervous system. His nerves seemed to catch fire, electric with agony. He writhed and convulsed and cursed.

When the contortions and the pain ceased, he sat shivering, bathed in sweat. Ivornich leaned forward until their faces were only inches apart. Softly she said, "I don't enjoy this. I am certain you do not, either, so speak no more nonsense to me. Do you understand?"

Kane drew in a shuddery lungful of air and nodded.

Ivornich cleared her throat, straightened up and asked, "Do you have a name?"

Exhaling a deep, unsteady breath, he said, "Kane."

"Kane? Just that one name?"

"Just Kane. My family name."

"No first name?"

He forced an ironic smile to his lips. "If I do have one, I don't know it. And you, Captain? Do you have a first name?"

The woman nodded. "Lenya. However, I do not use it much anymore."

"You prefer Captain?"

"I do. I've risen fast and far in the Internal Security Network. So many of my superiors, my peers, perished in the last two revolutions, the council had no choice but to promote me. I'm still rising, still going far. Survival and success. That's how to get ahead."

"I appreciate the advice. Maybe it'll help me survive the revolutions brewing in my country."

"Ah." Her eyes widened. "Tell me about them."

Kane tried to gesture. "They haven't happened yet."

"Is that why you are in my country, to learn from the experts?" Lenya Ivornich's tone was amused. "You could not have come to a better place. History has always conspired to tear Russia apart through internal strife, throughout all the great ages of change."

"Or," Kane ventured, "Russia conspired against history."

"You speak of the war. The holocaust that should not have happened."

"Yes. The nukecaust, the skydark."

"You believe my country started it?"

Kane opened his mouth to reply, then shook his head. "I don't know. That's what I was taught. I believed it most of my life. Now I'm no longer sure. I'm undergoing something of a revolution myself. A revolution of the mind."

Ivornich frowned at him. "Explain."

Hesitantly he replied, "I don't know if I can. How long does it take for the mind to finally realize it has been conditioned, tricked, deceived and betrayed? How long does it take to comprehend independence, freedom, responsibility?"

Ivornich gazed at him steadily, then the corner of her mouth quirked in a smile. "You intrigue me, Kane. Perhaps you are a spy, perhaps not. Why should the Americans now make such an effort to enter Russia, take such a risk?"

"I don't represent a government, Lenya."

She didn't react to his use of her first name, but she didn't object to it, either. "Then what is your mission?"

Kane shook his head again. "That's not the right question."

Captain Lenya Ivornich's violet eyes went cold. She stared hard at him, lifting the metal box in her hand so he could see it. "If you are a spy, you will die. If you are not, there might be a difference in your sentence."

Kane shrugged, meeting her stare unblinkingly. "I am what I am, Captain."

Her thumb brushed the red button. Kane tensed, keeping his eyes on her face. Then she dropped the control box to the desktop and stood up, spine stiffening, shoulders squared. Reaching out, she stroked his cheek, a quick, perfunctory caress. In a whisper so faint he barely heard it, she said, "Cooperate with me, Kane."

Then, with her left hand, she made a sharp, beckoning wave. Kane heard a click and he saw a portion of the gray wall open as if by itself. Two uniformed sec men stepped through. He realized the door was apparently operated from the outside, which meant that somewhere behind the walls was either a one-way window or an observation chamber so everything that had been said or done was witnessed or recorded.

Ivornich pointed to Kane. "Take him out back and shoot him." She spoke in English for his benefit, then repeated the command in Russian.

One guard swiftly loosened the leather cuffs around Kane's wrists while the other covered him with a stubby black Makarov handblaster. He was hauled to his feet, arms wrenched behind his back and steel handcuffs snapped around his wrists. The captain turned her back, not looking at him as he was hustled out of the room.

In a dim stone corridor outside the gray interrogation room, the guards pushed Kane before them to the right along the dank passageway. In complete silence they walked down a steep flight of steps, the clammy cold radiating from the stone and seeming to penetrate to Kane's bones. The stairs ended in another dark corridor. It turned to the left, then pitched downward. Kane felt that he was descending to the bowels of Mother Russia herself, and he wondered how the route he was marching could possibly fit the definition of "out back."

He was pulled to a stop at a rust-streaked iron door. The door creaked open, pulled inward from the other side, and the guards shoved him into a small, musty, murky room. It was all square blocks of grim gray stone. He prepared himself to receive a kick or a kidney punch, but neither came. The door clanged shut behind him, and he turned to face it.

Dim light filtered down from a barred window high overhead, casting most of the cell into deep shadow. A tall, slender man stepped out from a wedge of darkness beside the door. He wore a maroon tunic, khaki jodhpurs and high black boots. His curly blond hair was turning ivory at the temples. His brown eyes were surrounded by crinkles, and deep lines creased the weather-beaten skin on either side of his sharp nose.

He looked at Kane intently. When he spoke, his voice was strong but pitched low. "I am Colonel Piotr Sverdlovsk. No one can see or hear us in this room. Now tell me who you really are and why you are here."

Chapter 17

A little of the predawn snowfall had settled on the field adjacent to the old factory complex. Between the railroad tracks and the gloomy facades of the warehouses, patches of snow turned to brown slush as the temperature rose.

Grant, prone in the muck fifty yards away from the number-twelve warehouse, awaited Brigid's next signal. He was as motionless as a fallen obsidian statue, not even breathing deeply. Though he lay in a shallow channel beside a length of track, he did nothing to betray his position to the pair of Internal Security Network men patrolling the perimeter around the complex.

Upon hearing the first crackle of blasterfire, he had gone to ground and waited. And waited. He had received Kane's trans-comm message and he assumed Brigid had as well. From his position he watched as several sec officers carted Kane's limp body out of the warehouse and dumped him in the back of the canvas-covered truck. They were obviously obeying the orders of a black-haired woman bundled up in a woolen coat.

Grant waited for other officers to lug Brigid out, but instead, a wounded man was helped into the truck. The woman climbed into the cab behind the wheel and drove away, leaving four men and a jeep behind.

He was puzzled and irritated. He hadn't given in to the urge to call Brigid, hoping she was still hidden somewhere inside the cavernous warehouse. He had been on the verge of rising and investigating when his trans-comm circuit opened and he heard a very faint nonverbal signal—Brigid tapped out a code on the transceiver of her own comm unit, evidently fearing to speak.

She repeated the tapped-out message and closed the frequency. She had told Grant not to reenter the warehouse. She was hidden in the rafters. When she was in no danger of being overheard, she would contact him again. Wait. Just wait.

So Grant had waited, for over an hour, watching the sec men come in and out of the open double doors of the warehouse. They stood in front of it now, talking and smoking hand-rolled cigarettes. A small locomotive, puffing and hissing, clattered along the track behind Grant's position. The officers cocked their heads toward it as the whistle gave a mournful wail.

Grant tried very hard to look like a bump in the ground as the locomotive, moving in reverse, rumbled past him. It backed up toward a single boxcar waiting on a siding about a hundred yards away. The men in the engine cab paid no attention to anything but what lay behind them. Carefully he turned his head as the engine crawled toward the boxcar. A squat-bodied man jumped out of the cab and approached the coupling of the car, not looking in any other direction. At that moment Grant's trans-comm circuit opened with a faint crackle. Brigid's voice, whispery and tight, asked, "Grant, do you copy?"

With the thumb and forefinger of his right hand, he drew out the pin mike from his coat's lapel and replied softly, "I copy. You safe?"

"For the moment. The officers are gone. I think they've given up."

Grant gazed toward the warehouse. Two of the sec

men pulled the double doors shut, locking it with a chain and padlock. "They have."

"They got Kane," Brigid said grimly. "Captain Ivornich was with them."

"I saw. They dumped him in a wag and drove off."

"To where?"

"I don't know."

She was silent for so long, Grant almost called her name. Then she asked, "Was he alive?"

"I believe so. He was unconscious, though."

A small sigh of relief was transmitted through his coat's transceiver. "Are you able to reach the warehouse?"

Eyeing the sec officers as they milled around the door, he replied doubtfully, "Maybe. Might take me a little while. I'll have to go the long way around."

"All right. I'll go to the window where we entered. When you're well on your way, signal me and I'll meet you around back."

Grant closed the circuit, releasing the pin mike, allowing the tiny spring and pulley sewn inside his coat to retract it into the lapel. Carefully he belly-crawled along the channel parallel to the warehouse, continuing to sneak looks both at the sec officers and the man attaching the boxcar to the locomotive. None of them so much as glanced in his direction.

When he reached a point where he was facing the building's east wall and out of sight of the guards in the front, he heaved himself to his feet and skulked toward the far corner. He crossed the fifty yards with a long, ground-eating stride and he almost made it.

A uniformed man stepped from around the rear wall. He didn't see Grant immediately, but when he did, he came to a clumsy halt, his feet skidding in the slippery slush. He tried to unlimber his Kalashnikov rifle, but the strap fouled in the collar of his coat and he lost his balance. Flailing his arms, he went down like an empty gunnysack. He scrambled to his hands and knees, still struggling with his blaster's shoulder strap.

Grant rushed forward, leaped into the air and landed on the astonished officer's back, left hand cupping the man's chin while his right forearm came across the windpipe and hauled back. The rifle slipped off the officer's arm and hit the ground without going off.

Putting all of his upper-body strength into a backward wrench, Grant heard a crunch of gristle and cartilage. The man uttered a small aspirated gurgle, stiffened, spasmed and died. Panting, Grant dropped him face first into the muck and looked around to make sure no one had witnessed the brief struggle. Gathering a fistful of coat in one hand, he dragged the corpse along the wall and around the corner. The man had evidently decided to make a final perimeter patrol, and his comrades would miss him very soon.

He rolled the body into a stand of weeds, kicked enough muck over it to hide the human outline and, carrying the Kalashnikov under an arm, he crept quickly to the west corner of the warehouse. The way was clear. Into the pin mike, he whispered, "Now."

Almost immediately he saw Brigid's booted feet come through the open window, followed an instant later by the rest of her. She had lost her fur hat somewhere in the warehouse, and her heavy mounds of hair tumbled freely about her shoulders. Staying close to the wall, she ran very lightly, almost soundlessly toward him, looking back only once.

When she was around the corner, she acknowledged

the rifle in Grant's hands with a nod. "Did you chill the man who had that?"

"What do you think?" Grant glared at her aggressively. "Kane could be just as dead by now, so you'd better find it in your heart not to pass judgment."

She didn't reply, but she declared grimly, "We have to find him."

"How? The mission is compromised, and what little cover story we had is blown to hell. The only way to find him is to give ourselves up and hope we'll be taken to the same place he is."

Brigid nodded. "They've probably taken him to the nearest militia station."

"Probably. First things first, though. We've got to find a way out of this dump."

The shrill whistle of the locomotive pierced the cold air. Grant and Brigid's eyes met. Quickly they moved along the rear wall to the corner. The iron wheels of the engine turned slowly on the track, finding traction as it pulled the freight car behind it. A puff of white vapor floated from the smokestack.

"We'll have to run for it," Grant said. "Run and not look back. We've got to reach that boxcar before it's in view of the guards around front."

"I'm a good runner," replied Brigid confidently. "You know that."

"That I do. But you tend to get distracted easily. If you hear me shooting, don't look around, don't stop, don't even slow down. Understood?"

"Understood."

Grant drew in several deep breaths. "Go."

They lunged from the cover of the warehouse wall, racing across the open ground toward the train. The clank and increased wheezing of the machine helped to muffle the pounding of their feet on the muddy turf. Brigid was faster and she obviously held back so as not to outdistance Grant. He was a little annoyed but appreciative of her consideration.

Legs pumping, they jumped across the shallow channel and sprinted alongside the tracks. The stock of the Kalashnikov bumped painfully against Grant's upper thigh. The chuff-chuffing of the locomotive grew louder as it picked up speed. The freight car rumbled and rattled past them. They crossed the tracks, leaping nimbly over the cross ties to get on the far side of it, in order to be blocked from the officers' view. The sliding door was open. Grant and Brigid sprang for it, snatching handholds and wriggling their bodies inside.

They sat and caught their breath. The car had been used to haul cattle in the recent past. The wood-plank walls exuded the stench of animals, and there were piles of fairly fresh manure on the floor.

"Now what?" Brigid asked, gulping the air.

Grant peered between the slats of the freight car's wall. The warehouse complex and the collection of sec officers slowly receded. "Let's get to the locomotive and question the engineer. We'll force him to take us as close as he can to the security network station."

Brigid lifted a questioning eyebrow. "That'll mean climbing around on the outside of the train."

He smiled wryly. "You're a fine runner. Time to find out just how agile you are, too."

She stood up. "Let's get to it."

As the train chugged at a moderate twenty miles per hour through the rail yard, Grant and Brigid eased themselves out onto the exterior of the swaying car. The spaces between the horizontal sections of the side wall provided them with secure foot- and handholds.

On the roof of the freight car, they walked spraddle-legged and stumbling, ducking their heads beneath the spark-shot layer of vapor wafting back from the smoke-stack. Reaching the lip of the car, they lay flat and looked down over the coal tender into the open cab of the locomotive.

There were only two men, both in dirty overalls, one the engineer and the other the fireman, who shoveled coal into the gaping maw of the firebox. Brigid and Grant waited until the man scooped up a shovelful and turned away before they moved. Grant went first, swinging himself over and down, landing with a crunch atop the pile of coal, starting a miniature avalanche. The locomotive made too much noise for the sound of his landing to be heard.

Brigid slid down next and clambered over the black lumps of fuel, into the exposed rear section of the cab. At that moment the coal shoveler turned away from the firebox. Mauser in hand, Brigid yelled at him in Russian, telling him to freeze.

The engineer didn't hear the command, but the fireman, a stockily built young man with blunt features, threw the shovel toward her. He missed, but she didn't. She squeezed the trigger of her handblaster as soon as the shovel flew from his hands. The .32-caliber bullet took him in the meat of his right shoulder, spinning him against the engineer. He fell down on the sooty floor plates, writhing and squawking.

The engineer, a heavyset man, was about fifty with a silvery beard. He kept his hand on the throttle even as he twisted himself around, his dirty face stamped with shock and fright.

Brigid ordered the fireman to his feet and out of the cab. He sat down unhappily atop the coal in the tender, hand clapped over his shoulder. Blood seeped slowly between his grimy fingers. Grant inspected the wound, saw it wasn't serious and covered the man with the Kalashnikov.

Standing beside the engineer, Brigid placed the bore of the Mauser only a few inches from his right ear. Speaking loudly, she demanded, "Where is the nearest Internal Security Network station?"

The man gaped at her as if she were insane.

"Answer me," she commanded, prodding his ear with the blaster.

"Previnsk Street," the engineer blurted.

"How close can you get us to it?"

"The rail runs over the street, but it is a direct route. There are no stops."

"We'll make one," she replied. "Do what you have to do to get us there, but play us false and you will die."

The engineer regarded her bleakly for a second, nodded in resignation and turned a valve wheel. The locomotive continued to chug along, but it couldn't travel very fast through the rail yard. The track wasn't designed for rapid traffic, and there were three points to be switched over. The linemen in the yard moved lazily to change them, and Grant cursed impatiently beneath his breath. The train finally worked its way past the main terminus and joined an artery wending its way through the city proper.

Pointing to the sullen fireman, Grant asked, "Do we need this slagger?"

Brigid cast the young man a quick look and gestured with her blaster. "You. Jump out. We're not going fast enough for you to be hurt."

Reluctantly, hand still over the bleeding hole in his shoulder, the fireman rose and climbed down the steps of the cab. He hesitated, then leaped off into the weeds. He shouted something as he did so.

"What did he say?" Grant asked.

Brigid smiled without humor. "He promised to rape and kill me when next he saw me."

Grant looked over the side, past the freight car. The fireman was still rolling across the ground. He considered trying to pick him off with the Kalashnikov when he stood up, but the young man stayed down until the train was out of rifle range. Or, Grant considered hopefully, the bastard had broken his neck in the jump.

The train continued to gain speed. Buildings and hovels and ruins flitted past.

"How far now?" Brigid asked the engineer.

He shrugged. "Two kilometers, more or less. We must pass a checkpoint."

"Will you be obliged to stop?"

The engineer nibbled at his lower lip and didn't respond. Brigid dug the barrel of the Mauser into his ear. "Answer me."

"No." The man sighed out the word. "It is a checkpoint for passenger trains, not freight."

The locomotive chugged its way deeper into a metropolitan area. They seemed to be traveling infuriatingly slowly, but the engineer claimed their speed was right at the legal limit. To exceed it would draw attention. Brigid didn't argue with him.

Leaning to the right to look out the open cab window, the engineer cried, "They've closed the checkpoint!"

Brigid translated, and Grant climbed down from the coal pile to take a look ahead. A barrier of wood painted in red-and-yellow stripes bisected the tracks. At least a dozen armed sec officers stood on either side of the rails.

"They're onto us," he grated. "How?"

"The fireman probably," Brigid replied. As the engineer reached for the brake lever, she swatted his hand with her blaster.

"We must slow down," he told her pleadingly, nursing his knuckles. "It is the law."

"Ram it," she ordered. "Increase our speed."

The burly man's swart face locked in a mask of bewildered anxiety. "But it is not permitted—"

"Ram it!"

The engineer twisted the throttle wheel, feeding more heat to the boilers. The locomotive shuddered and hissed as it struggled to pick up speed. He yanked on the whistle cord. Long shrills of warning sounded. Grant crouched down in the tender, behind its iron walls, finger on the trigger of the rifle.

The locomotive's cowcatcher drove into the striped barrier with a crash, sending fragments of wood and splinters spraying in every direction. The officers beside the track shouted unintelligible commands as the train rumbled past them, but they heard no blasterfire.

Far from being relieved, Grant was at first confused, then worried. He yelled to Brigid, "They didn't shoot at us! That means they've got an ace on the line waiting for us."

She nodded in terse agreement. To the engineer, she demanded, "How soon to Previnsk Street?"

"Very soon. A minute."

Because of the racket of the clattering wheels and the hissing of steam, the warbling of the trans-comm unit in her pocket was so faint she dismissed the sound at first. When it was repeated, she cast a quick look toward Grant. He was staring at the transceiver tab on his lapel in surprise. He met her gaze. "I'm getting a signal."

"Me, too," she replied. "You take it."

Grant pulled out the pin mike, automatically engaging the circuit.

"Grant? Grant!" The voice was distant but unmistakably Kane's.

"Where are you?"

"About a quarter of a mile ahead of you. On the tracks."

Grant poked his head over the side. In the distance he made out a dark shape spanning the width of the rails.

"You've got to stop," Kane continued. "They've brought up heavy artillery to blow the train to scrap metal if you don't."

Grant didn't respond for a handful of seconds. Kane's voice demanded angrily, "Goddamn it, did you copy that?"

"Yeah, I did. What happens when we stop? Are we under arrest, scheduled for immediate execution or what?"

"Or what. I can't explain now, but you won't be harmed. We won't be prisoners."

A dozen possibilities, a dozen scenarios whirled through Grant's head in a fraction of an instant. But if Kane was in his right mind, unaffected by drugs or other influences, he would allow himself to be roasted to death before playing the Judas. Judging by his voice, he sounded clearheaded enough.

"You want me to believe the Russians want to be our friends?" he asked.

"No. Not friends. But not enemies, either. At least not now."

The blocky shape straddling the railroad tracks acquired a definite and identifiable outline as the locomotive rolled nearer. It was a light field cannon resting on big rubber tires. The ten-foot-long barrel was aimed directly at the front of the engine. Grant figured the artillery piece fired armor-piercing, high-velocity rounds and could certainly do want Kane said it could—blow the locomotive to scrap metal. He counted at least twenty sec officers standing on both sides of the tracks.

"Acknowledge!" Kane's tense, worried voice lashed out of the transceiver like the snap of a whip.

"Acknowledged," responded Grant. "We'll comply."

Turning to Brigid, he repeated the gist of the conversation. She hazarded a quick look out of the cab window. In a monotone she declared, "We have no choice."

She ordered the engineer to lay off the steam and start braking. He breathed out a heavy sigh of relief and quickly obeyed her.

By degrees the train clanked and clattered and screeched to a shaking halt. It continued to hiss clouds of steam even at rest. Grant left the rifle in the coal tender and he and Brigid stepped down on the left side of the locomotive, fingers laced at the backs of their necks. Grant glared at the dozen blaster bores pointing at him.

Somebody barked an order, and Kane stepped forward, wearing his black coat, looking damnably calm and fresh. Captain Lenya Ivornich walked beside him, one arm through his. Both of them smiled at Brigid and Grant, but they didn't smile back.

"Put your hands down," Kane said. "You look like you're doing calisthenics."

As Grant lowered his arms, he growled, "Now what? Torture or jail or both?"

A quartet of officers parted, moving aside, allowing the lean figure of Colonel Sverdlovosk to push his way forward. "Actually," he said coolly, "I thought we all might have an early supper. I'm sure you've worked up quite the appetite by now, running all over outer Moscow with your silly American knees bent.''

He bestowed upon Brigid a wide, welcoming smile, took her gloved hand in his and pressed his lips to it. "And you, Baptiste, are even lovelier than I imagined. I look forward to renewing our friendship."

Chapter 18

The low-ceilinged room was lit by flare-mouthed kerosene lanterns. Heavy purple drapes masked the windows, admitting no light in or out. The dining room was big, scattered with nearly two dozen cheesecloth-covered tables. A pleasant wood fire blazed in the hearth. A gramophone, obviously a reproduction of the machine that had been popular in an earlier century, played an old-time folk tune, full of melodic violin strings.

The place was an anachronism. Ivornich had claimed it was an accurate copy of the type of eateries favored by the social elite during the days of Czar Nicholas.

The restaurant was completely empty except for Ivornich, Kane, Brigid, Grant and Sverdlovosk. Upon entering the place by a back-alley door, Ivornich had commented cryptically, "You can relax in here. You're much safer here than you would be in official custody."

Only the three strangers had been served food, bowls of a rich, meaty stew Sverdlovosk had prepared and called beef Stroganoff. He didn't eat. He drank from a bottle of vodka and strutted back and forth around the room, frequently stopping at their table to encourage them to eat. He was a happy man. As he walked, he laughed and slapped his thigh and laughed again, looking toward them as they ate. They tried to ignore him and appear unconcerned, even though all three of them had been completely disarmed. Even Grant and Kane's Kevlar-weave coats were confiscated.

"It is *so* funny," Sverdlovosk said in English. "You don't realize yet how funny it really is."

Grant scowled as he stared, side-mouthing to Kane and Brigid, "It does my heart good to see a thoroughly tickled man."

Kane pushed his empty bowl away and poured a tumblerful of vodka from a decanter on the table. He tasted it, made a face, then downed the contents of the glass in one gulp. Turning to the table where Lenya Ivornich sat nursing a goblet of wine, he said mildly, "Let us in on the joke, why don't you?"

Ivornich shook her head, glanced at Sverdlovosk in irritation and sighed. The colonel kept chuckling and striding back and forth, swinging the bottle in one hand like a dinner bell. For the past forty-five minutes he had brushed off all of their questions and imbibed the liquor, immensely relishing its effects.

Crossing the room to Ivornich, he draped an arm about her slim shoulders and pointed to the three Americans, closing one eye as if he were sighting down the barrel of a gun. "See them, Lenya? Did you ever dream that the solution to our problem would drop into our laps, borne across the sea by the wind of the wolf?"

She tried to shrug off his arm. "No, Piotr, I did not."

To Kane, in a whisper, Brigid asked, "What did you tell them?"

"Damn little. I thought I was being a good tight-lipped, tight-assed Mag. They tortured me some—"

Brigid's eyes widened. "Tortured you?"

He shook his head scornfully. "Persuasion techniques that wouldn't force a Pit slagjacker to tell you the time of day. I mentioned the Archon Directorate, told Sverdlovosk a bit about where we're from, and he got all happy."

Sverdlovosk danced clumsily over to their table, pouring vodka from his bottle into their glasses. "Drink, my comrades, and I'll tell you a funny story."

He pulled up a chair and dropped into it. "You came here to find out what was going on in the Black Gobi, with warlords and armies."

"There doesn't seem to be any point in denying it," Brigid said.

"That's where the joke comes in," replied Sverdlovosk. "You can give me the final pieces I need to complete the puzzle and win the prize."

Then he was off into gales of laughter again. Grant had a fair bit of patience, but it was wearing thin. "If you don't mind," he said sharply, "we'd like to hear the punch line of this fucking hilarious joke so we can all laugh along with you."

"Why not?" Sverdlovosk swigged another mouthful of vodka, wiped his lips with a sleeve and announced, "Captain Ivornich and myself are executives of District Twelve."

Kane angled an eyebrow at him. "She told me there were only four districts in your government."

"District Twelve does not officially exist. Even mention of it to those who are not themselves members is a capital offense."

"What's the function of the twelfth district?" inquired Brigid.

"To find predark secrets, predark tech. To *keep* predark secrets, predark tech. Specifically to secure any and everything related to the Totality Concept researches, like the gateway units. I'm sure you have something similar to District Twelve in your baronies. Else you would not be here, enjoying my company.''

It wasn't a question, but a statement, so none of them felt obligated to respond to it.

"There is a phenomenon occurring in the Black Gobi," continued Sverdlovosk, "in the city of Kharo-Khoto. As I'm sure you've guessed, the phenomenon is not a natural one."

"You're right," Brigid said dryly. "We guessed it. Do you have any ideas—or speculations—on the nature of the phenomenon?"

"Oh, I do indeed. And I did not rely on my judgment alone, sound though it is." He smiled at Brigid, but this time his smile had very little warm humor in it. "But I digress. A bad habit of mine when I'm off duty."

Unsuccessfully swallowing a belch, he leaned forward and slammed the base of the liquor bottle atop the table, using the bang to punctuate his next words. "I'll begin at the beginning. I will ask you to listen without interrupting."

Despite the man's ebullient mood, all three outlanders noticed that Sverdlovosk's rawboned face bore lines of strain, great and immediate. Kane shot a sideways glance at Lenya Ivornich and saw the same thing swimming in her violet eyes.

Sverdlovosk leaned back in his chair. Wearily he said, "My country's present form of government is less than two years old, only the latest incarnation of several versions that were conceived, implemented and then discarded since skydark. What we have now is a corrupted synthesis of social democracy, Marxism and friendly fascism. This version will end soon, too, either by another revolution or by collapsing beneath the weight of its own bureaucracy. It is inevitable, and that inevitability was one reason District Twelve was created some two decades ago, simply to ensure that some sort of covert continuity bridges successive governments. It is quite maddening, this…unceasing turmoil.''

Sverdlovosk paused, frowning, and Ivornich spoke up helpfully. ''What he's trying to find the English words for is to describe how we have lived in fear of a return to the anarchy of skydark, and how desperate we are to prevent it, by any means necessary.''

Sverdlovosk nodded toward her politely. ''Thank you. I am always pleased to have words I did not mean put into my mouth.''

Ivornich flushed at the sarcasm, either from anger or embarrassment, and Sverdlovosk turned back to his captive audience. ''Actually what she said is fairly accurate as to our basic motivations. Fear. At any rate when I was assigned District Twelve duties several year ago, my main function was to pore over old intelligence files in search of hard data and references to the Totality Concept projects. Very few predark records still existed, but I gleaned sufficient information to understand that although the fundamental foundation for the concept's researches were primarily American, bits and pieces of it were shared with Russia. As I understand it, one of your predark Presidents publicly acknowledged his intent to share the SDI technology with my country.''

''SDI?'' repeated Grant quizzically.

''Strategic Defense Initiative,'' Brigid explained. ''Colloquially known as the Star Wars program. It was about the only aspect of the Totality Concept projects which the general public ever heard anything about. The SDI program was part of Mission Snowbird.''

Sverdlovosk smiled thinly. ''Precisely. And did I not ask you not to interrupt? In any event the report filed by

Major-Commissar Zimyanin regarding the gateway unit he discovered beneath the Peredelinko dacha was my starting point. Obviously it is still functional or you three would not be here. Poor Zimyanin. He secured the place as best he could in those wild old days, and his reward was to be shipped off to oversee a slave-labor camp in the Yukon. He knew too much to keep around, I imagine.''

Rising from his chair, Sverdlovosk paced over to the hearth, warming his hands near the dancing flames. Kane glanced again at Lenya Ivornich. She met his gaze unblinkingly. The eyes in her marble-smooth face were flint hard and flint cold.

Very quietly Sverdlovosk said, "So many wonders, so many scientific marvels created by men. And in the end none of it mattered.''

Sighing, he rubbed his hands together. "Through my investigations, I learned other things. I came across mysterious references to the origin of the Totality Concept technologies. It was something the Americans called the Archon Directive. I didn't understand what it meant. Who were the Archons? What was their Directive? What did it have to do with the Totality Concept? Very strange. The Archon Directive.''

He let the words hang in the air for a moment, like the solemn echo of the clang of a distant bell.

"Inasmuch as I had no idea of its meaning, I could not pursue it, given the fragmentary nature of the intel I was working with. Later I found that another gateway unit existed within China's former sphere of influence, out in the southwestern Gobi. In order to find the installation, I saw to it that an old predark military air base in Mongolia was reactivated. I went there and enlisted the aid of the nomadic tribesmen, specifically the clan ruled by Boro Orolok. I promised them food, medicines, weapons if they would search the Black Gobi for anything unusual. After a few months Boro's search paid off. He found the underground gateway installation.''

Sverdlovsk turned away from the fire. "As did you, Baptiste. You and your companions knew it was already there, just like you knew about the one in Peredelinko. However, I could not enter the installation. The sec door defied all my attempts to breach it. Just as well, I suppose. I am an old-fashioned fellow, and the very notion of having my essence transmitted to a distant point like a radio wave makes me incontinent.''

"Forgive yet another interruption," declared Brigid, "but I never got around to thanking you for allowing me to escape. I am grateful.''

Sverdlovsk grinned, exposing yellowed teeth. "Interruption forgiven. However, by the time I've finished my tale, you may feel that your gratitude is not only premature, but misplaced.''

Grant's body suddenly went taut, like a drawn bowstring. "That sounds like a threat, Colonel.''

Sverdlovsk looked at him in wide-eyed wonder. "Really? I did not mean it to sound so. Miscommunication, perhaps. My English is not perfect.''

He joined them at the table, picked up the bottle and upended it, swallowing the last few mouthfuls of vodka. He patted his stomach. "I am relaxed and perhaps a little drunk. My belly is full of hot vodka, and my head swirls with ideas. I shall continue—with your kind permission.''

Kane didn't bother to repress an exasperated sigh.

Sverdlovsk ignored him. "Where was I? Oh, yes. During the search for the gateway, Boro's youngest son came across the ruins of Kharo-Khoto. The son's name is—or was—Shykyr. He explored the place, since it loomed large in Mongolian legend. He discovered an underground vault beneath the ruins. When the discovery was reported back to me, I paid the tribe to begin excavations. I hoped the vault was yet another Totality Concept installation, or at the very least held relics of historical value. I had read of Kosloff's explorations, of course, so I provided the necessary digging equipment and left the Mongols to their work. I returned to Russia."

Sverdlovosk sat back down in the chair, his eyes flicking to each face. "Many months passed. Progress reports became sporadic, then they finally ceased altogether. I returned to Mongolia and found much had changed in my absence. Boro Orolok had abdicated his position. Shykyr was now the undisputed chieftain and had assumed the title of the Supreme Chief. Quite the promotion for a sixteen-year-old boy. He had forged an alliance between several western and northern tribes, and their united objective was to restore Kharo-Khoto to its former mythical glory and use it as the magical capital city of the new Golden Clan.

"I was still on friendly terms with Boro and I sought him out. He had changed from a happy, freedom-loving savage to an embittered drunkard. He told me that his son had bathed in the Black Flame of Shamos and undergone a terrifying transformation into a creature that was neither half man nor half god, yet the same and not the same. He was very confused on this point. He claimed Shykyr was the reincarnation of Khara Bator, Temujin, Amursana and Dambin Jansang. He hinted that it was not just a spiritual reincarnation, either. It went beyond the metaphysical. Furthermore, Boro accused his son of stealing the souls of his tribesmen, using the dragon ring of Genghis Khan."

Sverdlovosk's lips compressed, and he shook his head

ruefully. "Crazy Tartar talk, I figured. Superstition. He described a few of the artifacts that had been found in the subterranean chamber, but they were filtered through his own uneducated frame of reference and made no sense to me. I asked him to visit the vault again and take photographs with a camera I would provide, but he refused, saying he would never enter such a devil's workshop again. So I asked him to draw pictures."

Sliding a hand inside his tunic, Sverdlovosk withdrew a paper packet bound with twine. He tossed it onto the table. "Boro executed the drawings from memory. Traditionally a Mongol's powers of observation and recollection are phenomenal, since they have to rely solely on their memories to find water and game, without the benefits of maps or signposts. Look them over. Judge them by content, not by style or technique."

Brigid untied the twine and unfolded several sheets of the coarse-grain wood-pulp paper. Each one was covered with pencil sketches. The three of them looked at the first sketch, and Kane felt dread spring into his mind. It was a symbol, a thick-walled triangle bisected by three black vertical lines. The lines somewhat resembled stylized, round-hilted daggers.

"According to Boro," commented Sverdlovosk, "that symbol was everywhere inside the vault. Something tells me it strikes a chord in you, Comrade Kane."

Kane didn't acknowledge the comment either with words or his expression. He examined the second sketch. It looked like a pair of solid black cubes, a smaller one balanced atop the larger. A stick-figure representation of a man stood beside it, giving the impression that the two cubes were around twelve feet tall. All three of them recognized that drawing, too.

The other drawings depicted jumbles of geometric

shapes—ellipses, oblongs, cylinders, cubes and triangles. Some looked familiar; others were completely indecipherable.

While they inspected the pencil sketches, Sverdlovosk continued. "Obviously what lay beneath Kharo-Khoto was far more arcane, more ancient than anything connected to gateway units. I was familiar with the myths surrounding the vault, but when I offered my input, I was not permitted entry. When I learned that a number of the tribesmen were suffering from symptoms similar to radiation poisoning—much like members of Kosloff's expedition—I ingratiated myself with Boro's people, providing drugs, medicines, that sort of thing.

"By now Shykyr had upped the ante of his self-proclaimed divinity and adopted the title of the Tushe Gun, the Avenging Lama. He took notice of my contributions, and we worked out a bargain. I would see to it that he received the matériel he needed to restore the power of Kharo-Khoto, and Russia would benefit—an alliance of convenience, as in the old days."

Sverdlovosk looked toward the sheets of paper in the hands of his three guests. "Have any of you ever seen anything like that before?"

"Perhaps," answered Brigid cautiously.

Sverdlovosk's eyes narrowed. "Perhaps. And perhaps you can give me an idea of what they might be."

"Perhaps," Brigid said again. "You've never been in Kharo-Khoto?"

"In the city proper, in an area designated for visitors. But never to the vault. I presume that is where most of the matériel I supply ends up."

"If you have a military base nearby," ventured Kane, "why haven't you simply taken the place? According to Baptiste, the tribesmen were poorly armed."

Ivornich and Sverdlovosk exchanged swift glances and then dour smiles. Ivornich said quietly, "To involve the military would mean apprising our superiors of what is going on in Kharo-Khoto. They do not know."

"Yet," interposed Sverdlovosk, "it is a secret undertaking, the full details known only to Lenya and myself. As District Twelve executives, we are above reproach. Our orders are not questioned by our subordinates."

Kane grinned wolfishly, fixing his eyes on Ivornich. "What was it you said, 'Survival and success. That's how to get ahead'?"

"Exactly," she said stolidly, stonily. "Piotr and I have no intention of being dispossessed by the next revolution."

"Is that marked on your calendars, or what?" Grant asked darkly.

She shrugged. "It might as well be. Actually we're a bit overdue. It will probably come in the next year or so. A famine is projected for next winter."

Still grinning, Kane folded his arms over his chest. "So, Colonel, you and the captain hope to build a power base with whatever lies beneath Kharo-Khoto. Once you find out whatever it really is, of course."

"I already know one thing, American." Sverdlovosk's voice had lost all of its bantering tone. "I cannot sleep easily at night knowing that a legion of ignorant barbarians might have in their dirty hands the power to destroy a large portion of the world and poison the rest of it."

Neither Kane, Grant nor Brigid responded.

Sverdlovosk demanded, "What is the Archon Directive?"

"Kane said 'Directorate', Piotr," Ivornich corrected.

"Thank you, my dear. Well, Kane? What is it?"

"The Directorate or the Directive?"

"Both," Sverdolovsk said wryly.

Kane's grin widened, but it was a hard, humorless grin. "The Archon Directive was the predark commanding body of an ultrasecret agreement between a panterrestrial race and segments of several world governments. It was by following the Archon Directive that the Totality Concept was implemented. The major objective of the Directive was to orchestrate the nukecaust."

He reached out and tapped the sheet of paper decorated with the triangle-and-vertical lines sketch. "This was—*is*—their insignia."

"Kane!" Brigid's voice was full of alarmed warning.

As though he hadn't heard her, Kane calmly went on. "The Archon Directorate, separate and distinct from the Directive, now rules what's left of the earth. All from the shadows, of course."

He indicated the drawing of the two cubes. "We saw something very much like this in an underground complex in Dulce, New Mexico. We can't be certain, but it's probably an energy generator. The rest of the stuff—hell, it's anybody's guess. Flying saucers, radio gear, plumbing fixtures, who knows?"

"Kane—" Brigid began urgently.

"Kane what?" He enjoyed the expression of stunned incredulity that had settled on Sverdlovosk's face. "Who gives a shit who knows about it? Why shouldn't we let the colonel and the captain in on this? They should have an idea of what their ambitions have gotten them tangled up with."

"Panterrestrial race?" Sverdlovosk's voice was an unsteady rasp. *"Aliens?"*

"Aliens, yeah, but not necessarily from outer space. Maybe originally, but they've been here a very, very long time. They think they have the more legitimate claim on

Earth, since they supposedly raised us up from the ape. Oh, I almost forgot—their primary goal is to hybridize the human race, make the future generations half-breeds, so to speak. That's the destiny they've plotted for us.''

Sverdlovosk stood up so suddenly, so violently, his chair clattered over backward. Eyes wild, his lips worked, but no sound came out from between them. He stabbed a shaking finger toward the calm Kane.

"Well, Colonel," he said mildly, "I think I've given you the *real* punch line to your private joke.''

Sverdlovosk gripped the sides of his head and raised his face to the low ceiling. He bellowed, "Yes! Yes, yes, *yes!*''

He capered around in a small circle, performing a dervish dance of delight. "That is the answer. It has to be! Alien technology!''

Ivornich came to her feet in a rush, and both of them exchanged a heated babble of Russian. Sverdlovosk turned on Kane, spreading his arms in an eloquent gesture, as though inviting an embrace.

"Kane, my ugly American comrade! The final piece of the puzzle! How can I ever thank you?''

Kane stared at him, eyes wide in surprise. "You believe me?''

"Why shouldn't I? Russia certainly had its share of encounters with these Archons of yours in the past. Have you ever heard of Tunguska? No matter. So the Archons did it, did they?''

"Did what?'' asked Grant.

"Blew it up. The world.''

"Not exactly,'' said Brigid, shooting Kane an acid glare. "They put the wheels in motion, but we still don't know what they actually—''

"For nearly two hundred years, my people have been

taught that the charge we began the holocaust was simply propaganda. Most of us suspected otherwise, and it was a terrible psychological burden. And now to find out that it really *was* propaganda—well, I for one am beside myself with joy."

"There's more to the story than that," said Brigid in annoyance. "As usual, Kane simplified everything to the point of imbecility."

"There is always more to every story, my lovely young woman," declared Sverdlovosk. "Particularly the one in the Black Gobi."

Grant shook his head in frustration. "So now you know. How does that help you in your little endeavor out in Mongolia?"

Sverdlovosk leaned forward, palms flat on the surface of the table, thrusting his head forward. "You misspeak, Comrade Grant. Not 'your little endeavor'. At this juncture it is far more accurate to state, '*our* little endeavor.'"

He husked out a chuckle. "And that is the true punch line to my private joke. I give you permission to join the laughter."

Chapter 19

The Bykovo airport lay some twenty miles southeast of central Moscow. According to Sverdlovsk, it was the only one of four major airfields around Moscow that had survived the nuking marginally intact. The port itself had been rebuilt and repaired from concrete, duraplast and vanadium alloy.

Riding in the back of an open-topped jeep, Grant and Kane noted a number of medium-sized prop aircraft and a pair of gargantuan personnel-carrying transports.

From the driver's seat Sverdlovosk declared, "This is all we could salvage of our once majestic air force. As it is, keeping these few machines in operating order is an almost insurmountable task. They are, after all, over two hundred years old."

Kane and Grant thought of the Deathbirds, the retro-engineered Apache 64 attack choppers used by the Magistrate Divisions, and sympathized with the Russian mechanics. In the villes it was difficult to find people with the proper technical expertise to keep the Birds airworthy. It was even harder to find accomplished pilots. Grant had been one of the few truly gifted Bird jockeys.

Brigid, in the passenger seat, eyed the position of the sun. She guessed it was a few minutes shy of ten o'clock, and the morning sky was cloudless and sunny, the thermometer ten degrees higher than it had been twenty-four hours before.

The previous evening they had been driven—under guard—to a secluded safe house outside the city. They had been given separate rooms, and though they were comfortably appointed, the doors were locked and sentries posted. They didn't have the opportunity to talk among themselves, even over the trans-comms, since Sverdlovosk saw to it Brigid's unit was confiscated and Grant's and Kane's coats taken.

At least all of them had enjoyed a fairly restful night and they took advantage of the en suite bathrooms to clean themselves. Sverdlovosk had suggested they do so, saying cryptically that it might be their last chance for quite some time.

Then they had been served an early-morning breakfast by the silent sentries, who stood by while they ate, making sure they didn't appropriate any of the cutlery.

After they had finished, Sverdlovosk arrived, returned Grant's and Kane's coats and announced it was time to begin their journey. He had jovially but steadfastly refused to answer any of the questions put to him, saying only they would learn everything in time.

He braked the jeep to a halt before a huge metal-walled hangar. Four khaki-clad, AKM-wielding troopers bracketed the open double doors. Sverdlovosk led the way inside the hangar. Inside was a gray transport plane, looking for all the world like a humpback whale outfitted with a pair of wings.

Affectionately patting the riveted metal skin of the craft, Sverdlovosk said, ''This is a Tu-114 turboprop cargo and troop carrier. It was converted back in the 1980s to an early-warning recon ship. They used to be known as Mossbacks.''

''Why?'' asked Brigid.

''I haven't the faintest idea.''

Judging by the prideful smile on the Russian's face, he expected them to be impressed—and they were, though they tried hard not to show it. Because of the 250-mile-per-hour winds that once swept regularly over the rad-ravaged face of America, aerial travel had been very slow to make a comeback. Unpredictable geothermals in the hellzones and chem storms quadrupled the hazards of flying. Even the Deathbirds, their manufacture dating back to the last decade of the twentieth century, had only been pressed back into service thirty or so years ago.

For all intents and purposes, winged craft were obsolete in the Deathlands of America, and though all three of them had seen predark pix of the machines, they were overwhelmed by the power suggested by the sheer bulk and wingspan of the Tu-114.

Small forklifts raised crates into the open cargo hatch in the plane's belly. The crates were all marked with the number twelve. Several of them were long and flat, fitting the contours of the slabs of armaglass they had seen in the warehouse.

Kane looked up at the cockpit and through the port he saw Lenya Ivornich in the copilot's seat. She wore a headset and seemed engrossed in checking out the instrument panel systems. She suddenly looked up, caught his eye and smiled at him warmly.

Sverdlovosk went to the foot of the set of metal steps rolled up against the plane. "We're right on our departure schedule, so if you will board and find seats for yourselves, we'll get under way."

None of them moved.

"We know where you want to take us," said Kane. "We don't know why."

"The why is simple, Comrade. You have no choice. Should I remind you that in your short time in Russia

you've impersonated official personnel, trespassed on restricted property, seriously wounded a security network
officer and killed another? The last charge alone warrants
immediate execution.''

Kane almost sneered, but he managed to bring it out
as a go-to-hell grin. "Don't lean on us, Colonel. This
venture is either a cooperative effort or it isn't.''

"And if it isn't?" challenged Sverdlovosk.

"Then you're wasting your time and resources hauling
us to Mongolia. We won't identify a single artifact in
Kharo-Khoto.''

Sverdlovosk chuckled. "Yes, you're right. I shouldn't
pressure you. The awareness that I am in a position to
do so if need be is enough.''

"That's right. Return our property to us as a show of
good faith. Then we'll show ours.''

Sverdlovosk shrugged. "When we reach our destination. You have no need of weapons while we're airborne.
Surely you cannot argue with that.''

Kane made brief eye contact with his companions, then
bounded up the stairs leading to the Tu-114's passenger
compartment. The others followed him. It was strictly a
no-frills, utilitarian aircraft. The seats were hard and stiff
backed, not designed for anything approximating comfort. There were only six of them. Kane, Brigid and Grant
occupied the three seats nearest the cockpit door. The
other three, in the rear, were taken by a trio of alert-eyed
sec officers.

They buckled in, and the cargo doors slammed shut
from beneath with muffled thumps. Shouts from outside
announced the plane's readiness for immediate departure.
Sverdlovosk pulled the thick, rubber-sealed outer hatch
closed and entered the cockpit. A moment later came the
loud, vibrating drone of the four engines powering up.

The gray behemoth lurched from the hangar and onto the paved airstrip. Brigid, seated next to Kane on the aisle, gripped the armrests of her chair tightly. Her knuckles stood out like ivory knobs.

"Are you nervous, Baptiste?" he asked.

"What do you think?" she answered curtly. "I've never flown before."

"Nothing to it. A crate this size is a hell of a lot safer than a Deathbird."

"What happens if we crash?"

"Don't worry. Depending on our altitude and airspeed, if the smash doesn't kill you instantly, the burning fuel will. Either way, it's quick."

The Tu-114 taxied to the tarmac and accelerated down the runway with a deafening roar of the turboprop engines. Then, with a bump that jarred all of them in their seats, the landing-gear wheels left the ground and the whale-shaped craft nosed skyward. Sitting behind Brigid and Kane, Grant noted admiringly how the takeoff was remarkably smooth for such a cumbersome machine.

Kane looked out the window, watching the Bykovo airfield fall away below. The engines continued to purr powerfully as the big airplane climbed higher and higher.

"Say *dasvidaniya* to the motherland," he suggested to Brigid, whose eyes were squeezed shut.

She ignored him.

The Mossback continued to gain altitude, then it gracefully leveled off. The sky was a ceiling of unbroken azure. Mountains reared their snowy peaks on the far horizon.

The craft rattled and hummed as it soared steadily onward. The earth beneath was a vast, unending panorama of textured squares and rectangles of all colors and sizes.

Brigid finally opened her eyes and relaxed her grip on the armrests. "How high are we?"

Grant heard the question and leaned forward. "I'd say about ten thousand feet, give or take a hundred or three."

Her fingers clamped reflexively down again. Kane and Grant repressed the urge to laugh. Both men had put in plenty of flight time as Magistrates, though the Death-birds didn't have the speed, range or sustained altitude ceiling of the big cargo carrier.

The cockpit door opened, and Ivornich stepped into the passenger compartment. She had slipped the headset down to rest on the back of her neck. She held out several small paper-wrapped wafers.

"The cabin isn't pressurized," she said. "We'll be climbing to twenty thousand feet to get over the mountains and areas of ionization, so you may experience some discomfort. Chewing this gum will help to equalize the pressure in your ears."

Brigid took the sticks, eyed them dubiously and passed them around to her companions. "What's our flight time, Captain?"

"About four hours, if the weather holds. If it does not, considerably longer."

"It would have been faster to use the gateway in Peredelinko," Brigid replied. "I know the jump code for the unit in the Gobi."

"No doubt." Ivornich smiled. "But we could not have fit our cargo into it, and Piotr would have refused to set so much as his little toe inside it."

"You've made this run before?" Grant inquired.

Ivornich shook her head. "Never. But it's Piotr's tenth or eleventh trip. He's been going to Mongolia regularly for the past year."

"So he's expected there?" asked Brigid.

"To some extent. His official reason for returning so soon is to recover the wag you borrowed and left high and dry in the desert. It is military property after all, and despite the broad powers given to us by District Twelve, we still must account for equipment. Besides, he's making a delivery, as well, and that will allay any suspicions among his...customers."

"Customers?" echoed Kane.

Ivornich turned back toward the cockpit, lingering long enough to smile directly at Kane. "Get some rest. The flight is only the first leg of our journey. You and I will have plenty of time to talk later."

After she closed the door behind her, Brigid said, "I think you made quite the impression on her, Kane. What kind of torture did you say she used on you?"

Smiling a bit sheepishly, he replied, "I don't recall saying."

The plane sailed on, gradually gaining altitude, flying high above a cloud-wreathed mountain range. The plane bounced briefly from turbulence created by the mountains' geothermals, but the sec officers in the back were completely relaxed, talking and laughing among themselves. Kane figured they were Sverdlovosk's handpicked crew, men he could trust. He wondered if they even suspected their superior officer was involving them in an unsanctioned op.

After a while stuffiness and pain built in Grant's ears, a lingering aftereffect of the shot of infrasound he had been subjected to three months before. Unwrapping the stick of gum, he popped it in his mouth, chewing slowly. When saliva softened the substance, an unforgettable flavor of rotten apricots, with just a hint of battery acid, flowed over his tongue. He spit the half-masticated wad into his hand, glowering at it for a moment. Then he stuck it on the underside of his seat, deciding that ear pain was preferable to having the taste of the gum fill his mouth for the next few hours.

Though the cabin was heated, it was still cold at such a high altitude, so they kept their coats on and buttoned. Kane leaned toward Brigid and said quietly, "We need to go over a few things while we have the privacy."

As nervous as she was, Brigid Baptiste couldn't imagine being able to discuss anything intelligently. Then she considered that the man was trying to keep her mind off her flight-induced anxiety, and she silently thanked him for it.

"What do you think is going to happen when we arrive in Mongolia?" he asked.

"I don't know. But I do think the colonel has some kind of plan that involves us as pawns, not partners. What do you think?"

"I think the same thing. Don't you find it strange he accepted the story about the Archons so easily?"

Brigid, still holding tightly to the arms of her seat, looked at him questioningly. "You didn't expect him to believe you?"

"*I* didn't when I first heard it, and it came from the baron himself. I suspect he found more in those old intelligence files than he let on." He paused and added, "Besides, he has yet to ask you anything about Bautu."

"I noticed that," she replied dryly. "I've been waiting."

"Well, don't supply information."

"Who do you think I am?" she inquired sarcastically. "You?"

He stared at her for a long moment, his gray blue eyes going cold. "No, Baptiste. I think that's a safe bet."

With that, Kane slouched down in his cramped seat,

closing his eyes, resting his head against the window. Brigid squirmed and wriggled, unable to find a comfortable position. The plane lurched slightly. She bit back a startled gasp. Kane didn't stir, didn't so much as crack open an eye.

She thought about apologizing to him for the remark she had just made and the one the night before, regarding his tendency to oversimplify complex matters. She decided he had earned both. Still, she tried to imitate his relaxed posture and found that she could not.

The Tu-114 plunged on, a dark speck arrowing through the limitless blue sea of sky. Kane and Grant managed to nap, as did a couple of the soldiers. Brigid stayed wide-awake and tense. After a few hours the air became progressively rougher and the plane bounced and jounced on the turbulence. Scraps of clouds whipped over the wings. Suddenly the craft lost altitude, dropping like an elevator. Brigid clung to the chair arms, not enjoying the abrupt sinking sensation in the pit of her stomach.

The Tu-114 cut back its flying speed. Kane roused, looking out the window. The open land below was a vastness of parched grassland that rolled on to the horizon, a brown gold under the late-afternoon sun. The shadowy humps of distant crags and rock ridges rose out of the terrain. It was a harsh and bleak land, but not so harsh it couldn't support life. Herds of cattle and sheep grazed on the scrubby grass, and here and there were lines of trees along a blue river that curved around in serpentine coils.

The airplane circled a crude, unpaved landing strip, evidently one scraped out of a flat stretch of desert. During its second sweep, Kane saw three dun-colored blockhouses thrusting out of the soil like concrete pimples.

The hydraulic whine of the lowering landing gear filled

the cabin, then Mongolia rushed up to meet them. The Tu-114 shuddered and shook when it landed, the big tires bouncing over the rough ground. Slowly it came to a halt, and the engine noise faded. Soldiers rushed forward from the nearest blockhouse to jam wooden chocks behind the plane's wheels. Other troopers wheeled a stairway toward the passenger door.

Grant stood up first, beating Brigid only by a second. He announced, "A pretty smooth landing, all things considered. My compliments to the pilot."

Sverdlovosk emerged from the cockpit and twisted the latch on the hatch cover. "I hope you had a comfortable flight."

"Your hope is in vain," retorted Brigid.

Swinging open the door, Sverdlovosk allowed the three Americans to exit the plane first. They stood at the base of the stairs. The wind was very cold, but very clean, blowing off the Gobi.

When Ivornich had disembarked, Sverdlovosk ushered them all to one side, out of the way of the group of soldiers swarming onto the field to unload the cargo. The belly doors were already hanging open, and a man drove a forklift toward them, a wooden pallet resting on the prongs. The soldiers quickly began unloading the crates. One of them passed down a sealed leather satchel to Sverdlovosk.

Holding it in his right hand, Sverdlovosk directed them across the strip toward the largest of the blockhouses. It looked like a somewhat flattened cube, its dull and featureless surface sporting only one door and one window. As they drew closer to it, Kane noticed a gun turret on the roof.

Nodding toward a low range of hills in the west,

Sverdlovosk announced, "Here comes the local chamber of commerce."

A line of riders mounted on shaggy, squat-bodied horses came at a shuffling trot out of a pass in the foot of the hills. Kane did a quick head count. There were a dozen of the small, powerfully built mounted men. They wore fur hats and bandoliers of bullets and bright garb of wool and leather. Some of them carried long muzzle-loading rifles slung across their backs, and in their belts were stuck old-fashioned pistols. Grant, the armament expert, saw they were of First World War vintage, but the blasters were well oiled and tended. Scabbarded at their hips were short, curved swords. They were a bronze-skinned people, with sparse facial hair.

Ivornich rested a hand on the butt her holstered Makarov. "How do we deal with them?"

Sverdlovosk squared his shoulders. "Easy. Just act like you're disinterested in them. It's Boro Orolok and his retainers. They escorted me back here after my vehicle went missing. They're very polite, but they don't trust me."

"Then we'll have something in common," Kane commented offhandedly.

There was no shouting, no welcoming cries from the mounted men. They reined their animals to a halt in a crescent in front of Sverdlovosk and the others and simply sat there on their broad horses, which breathed heavily and blinked at them through long forelocks. The warriors eyed Ivornich, Kane, Grant and Brigid closely.

One man spurred his horse forward. He was heavyset, with a long, flowing mustache threaded with gray. His hair was braided in loops around his ears. His piercing eyes looked down at them, fixing briefly on Brigid. With a faint shock of recognition, she realized he was the same man who had ridden beside the Tushe Gun that night in the valley. An H&K VP-70 rode low in a gun belt around his waist. He smiled, showing strong, ivory-colored teeth and he rattled off a stream of incomprehensible gutturals.

Sverdlovosk replied in the same language, waving first to the plane, then to his companions.

"What are they saying?" Grant whispered to Brigid.

She shook her head in baffled irritation. "I wish I knew. If I did, Adrian and Davis might not have died."

Sverdlovosk looked toward her. "I told you a Mongol's power of memory is extraordinary. Boro remembers you, despite your rather disheveled condition the other night. He wants to know how you managed to escape."

Crossly Lenya Ivornich demanded, "Does that smelly Tartar speak any other language than this barbaric clucking?"

Sverdlovosk smiled crookedly. "Passable Russian."

"Good. Have him speak it, then."

Sverdlovosk obliged, saying, "Let us speak my tongue, so that my friends may join in our talk."

Boro Orolok grinned. "As you wish. And let us get out of this son of a whore wind."

"I can see he took to your language like a duck to water," Brigid observed wryly.

Gesturing toward the blockhouse, Sverdlovosk said, "In there it is warm, and we will have food and drink to allow our tongues to move more freely."

Boro grunted and swung down from the saddle. He waved to a pair of younger men to follow him. They were both slightly built and identical of facial feature, wearing the same type of thin, drooping mustache.

"His eldest sons," Sverdlovosk said in English. "Oborgon and Seng, the twins."

"How many sons does he have?" asked Brigid.

''Four.''

''Well, I know where Shykyr is. What happened to the other one?''

Eyes crinkling in amusement, Sverdlovosk said, ''You tell me, Baptiste. That's a question Boro intends to put to you, and you had best prepare a snappy answer. He named his third son Bautu.''

Chapter 20

The wardroom inside the blockhouse was a small warren of concrete, sunk twelve feet beneath the ground. Sverdlovosk, Ivornich, Brigid, Grant, Kane and Boro sat around the rectangular table, which occupied most of the floor space. Oborgon and Seng took up sloppy parade-rest postures in front of the open doorway. Unlike their father, they didn't remove their fur caps, though it was comfortably warm in the room.

A clay pot of greasy-smelling yak-butter tea simmered on a hot plate in the center of the table. A tray of biscuits sprinkled with gritty brown sugar was placed near Boro's left elbow. Only the Mongol helped himself to the food and drink. He sipped slowly at the tea from a chipped cup, not gulping it as everyone but Sverdlovosk expected. It wasn't proper Mongol manners to guzzle and devour a host's refreshments.

After a few minutes of polite conversation about the weather and grazing lands, Boro said in Russian, "We hauled your wag to the valley campsite, Piotr. It is out of fuel but undamaged."

"Good. I will retrieve it when I bring in this next shipment of matériel your son requested."

Boro brushed a crumb from his mustache. "My son—that is, the Tushe Gun—is still upset that the foreigner escaped. And he is even more upset that five of his followers were murdered in the sands. He is beside himself with worry about his older brother, Bautu. As all of us are.''

Brigid shifted uncomfortably in her chair. Sverdlovosk said sympathetically, "Yes, family is very important in this hard land. The clan is all.''

Boro grunted. His eyes suddenly fixed on Brigid's face. "Jade-eyed woman, who are you, where do you come from and where is Bautu?''

Brigid contemplated her reply for a long moment, rehearsing her words carefully in her mind. Gently she said, "I am a scholar. I and my comrades come from across the sea. From America.''

Boro nodded. "I have heard of it. A powerful country, once. A land that was the bitter enemy of both China and Russia. In the old days—before the skies went dark—we also hated the Russians and our own government in Ulan Bator who kissed the Russian bear's ass. We also hated the Chinese and their government in Peking. We hated a great many people. My forefathers were free nomads who owed allegiance to no one, belonged to no one and recognized no borders around our country.''

Boro Orolok was not boasting, merely making a statement of fact. "Now we are nomads again, but my people still hate those who wish to interfere with our way of life, to enslave us to rules and laws and property.''

"We don't want to interfere or to enslave," replied Brigid. "We wish to stop the enslavement of people. We don't want war to come again. There has been enough death.''

"You have answered two of my three questions," said Boro. "Now answer the third. Where is my son?''

Brigid felt perspiration collect on the palms of her hands. She continued to meet Boro's unblinking gaze, aware that Sverdlovsk and Ivornich, who had followed the conversation, were staring at her, too. Tension collected around the table like an electrical storm.

Suddenly Kane leaned toward her, and smiling politely toward Boro, asked softly, "What's going on?"

Without looking at him, she replied, "He wants to know where Bautu is."

"Then tell him exactly what he wants to know. No more, no less." A note of warning underscored Kane's quiet tone as he straightened up.

Stubbornly Boro asked, "Where is my son?"

Inhaling sharply through her nostrils, Brigid held her breath for a second, then stated clearly, "Your son is a guest in America, in my home."

Boro's slanted eyes widened, then narrowed to slits. "You speak foolishness, woman. How did he get from here to your home in America?"

"Yes, Baptiste," drawled Ivornich with a sly smile. "How did he?"

"It is not easy to explain." Brigid gestured, drawing an invisible arched line in the air between two points. "We used a device which can cover great distances in a very short time. He was injured, so we took him with us to heal his wounds."

"A device which can cover great distances," Boro repeated doubtfully. "Like the air horse in the vault of the Black City?"

Brigid exchanged swift glances with Sverdlovosk. He inclined his head a fraction of an inch in a nod. "Yes," he said. "Like the air horse in the vault. Have you seen it soaring along the winds?"

Boro shook his head. "No, it is at rest. The wind has not yet blown strength into it. My son—that is, the Tushe Gun—studies the mystic formulas to restore the wind to it. When will Bautu return to the clan?"

Despising the slight quiver the falsehood caused in her voice, Brigid answered, "When he is healed. When my friends and I return to our home, he will return to his home."

"You did not kill him?"

"No," she said earnestly, "we did not."

Sighing, Boro reached for the pot of tea on the hot plate and poured himself another cup. "Perhaps it is just as well he is not here. He has not been the same since he felt the dragon's kiss."

Brigid said, "I do not understand."

Boro extended his right index finger. "The Tushe Gun wears a dragon here. It is the same dragon worn by Genghis Khan. When it kissed Bautu—and others in the clan—he changed. He became cruel, he ignored his father." Bitterness colored his voice. "He no longer heeded or obeyed me. He did only the bidding of his little brother, as if a stripling in a mask would know what is best for the clan."

"So you don't believe your son Shykyr is an anointed one? You don't believe he is a messiah of your people?"

Boro scowlingly considered the query for a moment, the cup of tea held before his lips. He took a sip and shook his head. "I do not know. At first I believed his claims, or I wanted to believe them. He was always something of a dreamer. But as he spent more time in that thrice-damned vault, tending to the sacred black flame, he changed. I fear for him and I fear him. He will not allow even me, his father, to see his unmasked face."

"And your other sons?" asked Brigid, nodding toward Oborgon and Seng. "Were they kissed by the dragon?"

"No!" Boro exclaimed vehemently. "I refused to allow it. Shykyr and I quarreled over it. Seng and Oborgon were born a bit slow-witted, you see. They are addled enough already.''

Brigid lifted her eyes toward the twins. Their black eyes glittered at her impersonally. ''Can they understand the language we speak?''

Boro snorted, blowing bubbles in his tea. ''They can barely understand their own tongue, let alone a foreign language.''

''Ask them to remove their hats.''

Eyebrows rising, Boro asked, ''Why?''

''Indulge a foreign custom. Ask them to take off their hats in the presence of ladies.''

''What are you driving at, Baptiste?'' demanded Sverdlovosk. ''They are our guests.''

Ivornich's face was a mask of puzzlement, but she said, ''It's a small enough request.''

Boro shrugged. ''So it is.''

He twisted in his chair and barked an order at his sons. The twins did not move. With a bit more heat in his voice, he repeated the command. Slowly, moving almost in unison, their right hands rose and scraped their fur hats away. Two small marks, a pale bronze against the deep bronze of their windburned skins, were visible high on their foreheads. The marks were identical to the one she had seen on Bautu.

Boro cried out in anger. He pushed himself up and away from the table, shouting at them in his own dialect. As he stood up, his sons' right hands dropped to their belts and came up gripping duplicate handblasters, two mammoth Webley Mk VI revolvers.

Lenya Ivornich cursed and clawed for the Makarov holstered at her hip. Two thunderous bursts of noise, flame and smoke gouted from the hexagonal barrels of the pistols. There was no subtlety, no artistry or skill about the murder.

The heavy .445-caliber bullets caught her in the center of her chest and the center of her high, white forehead. Part of her scalp floated away in a crimson haze as she tipped over in the chair, propelled by the double impacts. She was very dead by the time she hit the floor.

Before she did, Kane and Grant were in simultaneous motion, reacting with the tensile-spring swiftness of men whose lives always depended on their reflexes. Gripping the edges of the table, they overturned it, and crackers, cups, trays and tea cascaded to the floor. Pushing the table through the planes of cordite smoke like a flat battering ram, they smashed the table against Oborgon and Seng, sending them staggering through the doorway into the short corridor.

Flinging the table aside, Grant and Kane bounded toward the twins. One had fallen down—they didn't know which one—and the other had fetched up against the wall. They still gripped their blasters and they squeezed off a booming shot apiece.

Grant spun around in a half circle as the heavy slug caught him on the left hip, skidding off the Kevlar weave of his coat before burying itself in the door frame. The impact hurt him, bruised him, but didn't cause serious damage.

The round fired from the twin on the floor whipped well over Kane's head, plunging into the wardroom and knocking a saucer-sized crater in the far wall. With his left foot he stab-kicked the man's gun hand, the edge of his boot catching the barrel of the Webley and ripping it backward out of his fingers. As the gun clattered loudly to the floor, Kane's right boot arced up, connecting solidly with the underside of the Mongol's chin. His head snapped up and back, and continued snapping back until it struck the concrete floor with a cruel *chock*.

The other twin looked over his shoulder unhappily and said something in a tone more of disapproval than disappointment. Before he turned his head, Grant hit him hard and with such concentrated purpose that the corridor echoed with the cracking of the jawbone. Then he followed up with blows to the stomach, one, two, three times in a flurry of left-right combinations.

Even as he doubled over, the Mongol tried to bring his pistol to bear, but Grant secured a grip on the long barrel, twisting it toward the ceiling. He jacked his right knee into the Mongol's face. Releasing his grip on the butt of the Webley, the man went over backward, face a mask of blood, falling beside his brother.

Kane drew back his foot another kick, the barely controlled Mag instincts in him blazing. But he stopped in midmotion, trembling with the effort.

Neither of the twins was unconscious, but they were too dazed, too foggy with pain to do more than twitch and moan. Boro pushed into the corridor between the panting Grant and Kane. Lips quivering, he cried out, "Seng!" and dropped to his knees beside the man Kane had kicked. Brigid squeezed in, her eyes shining with shock.

"What the fuck was all that about?" Kane snarled, still shaking with adrenaline.

"I asked Boro to tell his sons to take off their hats," she stammered.

Grant glared at her in disbelief. "What? Why?"

"I wanted to see if they had scars like Bautu, in the regions of their temporal lobes. And they do."

Boro grabbed a handful of Seng's coat, shrieking in their dialect.

Seng looked past his outraged father, staring at Baptiste. In Russian he replied, "You foreigners will not defile our destiny, you will not use us to gain your own ends. The Tushe Gun will not allow it."

Seng's eyes flicked toward Boro. "You are a pawn, Father, of the foreigners. You know the code of the clan—you stand with an outsider, you die with an outsider."

Boro shrieked again, spittle flying from his lips. He slapped his son open-handed. Suddenly Seng's eyelids drooped, as if the cuff put him to sleep. He sagged in his father's hands. Then his eyes snapped open wide. The pupils enlarged, engulfing the irises. There was no emotion in them. His body shuddered, a terrible tremor racking him from the top of his head to the toes of his boots.

At the same moment, Oborgon convulsed, his own eyes wide and staring at nothing. Boro scrabbled back from them, stuttering in fear. The twins rolled on the floor, limbs flailing wildly, tendons and veins standing out on their necks and foreheads. Their mouths fell open as if to voice howls, but no sounds came forth. Their hands twitched, fingers curling and uncurling in spasms.

"Ah, *shit*," rumbled Grant. "Here we go again."

Abruptly, as if power cords had been pulled, Seng's and Oborgon's seizures ceased. Their bodies froze in contorted positions, muscles locked. Then, very slowly, they relaxed, settling on the floor. Boro grabbed their wrists, fingered the bases of their throats. A dry, raspy sob worked its way from his mouth.

"They're dead," murmured Brigid. "Cardiac arrest induced by the implants."

"Suicide switches planted inside of his own brothers," Kane said grimly. "The Tushe Gun is quite the holy man."

Boro took Seng's hand, pressing it between his own, rocking back and forth on his knees, keening wordlessly in grief. Brigid, Kane and Grant shuffled back into the shambles of the wardroom. Stepping around overturned chairs and broken pottery, they clustered silently around Sverdlovosk.

He sat cross-legged on the floor, cradling Lenya Ivornich in his arms. Her violet eyes were already glazed over, and blood and brain matter dripped from the back of her bullet-blasted skull to the floor. Carefully, using the thumb and forefinger of one hand, Sverdlovosk drew the lids down over her beautiful blind eyes. He laid her down, arranging her arms and limbs in dignified positions. When he stood up, he was dry-eyed, remote of expression.

"We're sorry," said Kane softly, knowing full well how inadequate and foolish he sounded. "I liked her."

In a faint, papery whisper Sverdlovosk said, "And I loved her. Success and survival, that's the way to get ahead."

"What was she to you?" Grant asked. "Your lover, your wife?"

Sverdlovosk uttered a short, bitter laugh. "Would that she would have been. Her death might be a bit easier to bear. No, Lenya was my daughter."

Brigid whirled away, squeezing her eyes shut on the tears suddenly springing to her eyes. She had nothing to say. She could think of nothing to say when a man's child had been brutally murdered in front of her very eyes and there wasn't one thing she had been able to do to prevent it.

Not only had she been unable to prevent it, but she knew very well she may have caused it.

Chapter 21

Boro's broad dark face glistened with tears. "Why? Why did they betray me?"

Sverdlovosk did not answer. Clumsily he patted the Mongol's shoulder. The two men stood in the windswept compound, united in grief, watching as troopers placed the corpses of their children in canvas body bags. Kane, Grant and Brigid stood slightly behind them, shivering as the sun and the thermometer dropped.

"All my sons are lost to me," said Boro.

"As is my only child," Sverdlovosk replied.

"Do you blame me, Piotr?"

"No, my friend. Nor do I blame Seng and Oborgon." The troopers lifted the body of Seng into a bag. "So much has the Black City done for your clan."

When the body bags were zippered, Boro called to a pair of his men. They came forward, leading his sons' horses. They heaved the canvas-shrouded corpses of the twins over the saddles, mounted their own steeds and the entire band slowly rode away, toward the hills.

"They will wait for me at the camp," Boro said tiredly, the straightness leaving his spine. "I will join them when we have decided what to do."

Sverdlovosk turned away as soldiers carried the bag containing the body of Lenya toward a small outbuilding. Everyone followed him back inside the blockhouse, down the steps to the wardroom.

Troopers had conscientiously repaired and cleaned up the damage as best they could. One of them had considerately spread a throw rug over the bloodstain on the floor. Still, Sverdlovosk took a place at the table as far as possible from the spot where Lenya had died. Unlike Boro, he had yet to shed a tear. Kane saw the hard glint in the Russian's eyes and understood why. He wanted vengeance first. A period of mourning would come later.

A bottle of vodka sat on the table, but no one seemed interested in it. Surveying the faces of the people around him, he announced quietly, "Time for total truth among all of us."

"You included?" asked Grant.

Sverdlovosk acknowledged the query with a short nod. "Baptiste—what is the significance of the dragon's kiss?"

She told him, not deleting or soft-pedaling a single detail, including how Bautu had died and the findings of the autopsy. Boro, already numb with shock and grief, didn't react, except to reach for the vodka bottle.

"There is only one conclusion," said Brigid. "The ring worn by the Tushe Gun is actually some kind of surgical instrument which directly delivers the implant into a subject's—or victim's—brain."

Sverdlovosk quickly translated, and Boro took a shuddery swallow of the vodka. His voice rough with anger and pain, he demanded from the Russian, "Who would have made such a monstrous thing?"

The question was echoed in English.

Staring at Sverdlovosk, Kane said, "I think you know, Colonel. I think you've always known more about it than you've let on."

"You think correctly." The Russian ran a hand over his deeply lined forehead. "There was far more to the report on Kosloff's 1923 expedition to Kharo-Khoto than was ever released, and I read the unexpurgated documents in their entirety. He submitted the theory—with a substantial degree of verification—that a major civilization once existed in the Gobi, predating even Sumeria. The Gobi civilization was said to have been technologically advanced, and the desert upon which it sat was once lush with vegetation.

"Kosloff hypothesized that the civilization, of which Kharo-Khoto was the hub, perished due to atomic radiation. Geologists who visited the region later discovered traces of radiation. Evidently the source of the radiation is in the vault and once more active."

Sverdlovosk paused, wetting his lips with his tongue. "Kosloff's theory—which was rejected by his scientific contemporaries—was that the Gobi civilization was created by a nonhuman race. It was a theory I would have rejected, as well, except that I had access to predark KGB records detailing military encounters with so-called flying saucers and entities known as the Grays."

"The Archons," stated Brigid.

"Yes, the Archons. Russian troops occupying Berlin during the close of World War II came across evidence of their alliance with the Nazis. Most of that evidence was on paper, scientific developments geared toward secret weapons, and it was appropriated by the Allies. A deal was struck with elements of the Third Reich's intelligence community to absorb their technological and principal scientific establishment. Thus was born the Totality Concept researches, and the Cold War between my country and yours. However, the Stalinist government had in its possession something more substantial than documents."

Sverdlovosk scanned the expectant faces around the

table. "Yesterday, in passing, I mentioned Tunguska. Does the word have any meaning to any of you?"

There were headshakes and mumbled negatives.

"Except for the nukecaust, it was the greatest explosion of destructive forces ever recorded in Russia. Just after dawn, on June 8, 1908, a monstrous fireball was first spotted over the Gobi, scorching its way across the sky. People in southern Russia saw it next, describing it as a huge cylinder, glowing a bluish white. At 7:17 that morning it exploded over the Tunguska River region in Siberia. People as far away as forty miles from the epicenter of the blast were burned, bowled over, killed by the shock wave. Closer to the river the devastation was even worse. Acres of forestland, herds of deer were instantly vaporized."

"What was it?" Brigid asked. "A meteorite?"

"Meteors leave craters. There wasn't one. Investigators at the site reported finding unusual pieces of shiny metal scattered around. People and animals within 250 miles of the area contracted a strange disease, from which they eventually perished. Of course, the scientists of the day did not recognize the symptoms of rad poisoning."

Sverdlovosk smiled slightly. "As usual there was much political turmoil in Russia at that time, so a thorough examination of the site was not undertaken until the end of World War II, nearly forty years later. The material found in Berlin was the impetus for the new investigation.

"At Tunguska, scientists found a canister buried deep within the earth. It was a lifeboat-type contrivance and held three creatures in a form of cryogenic stasis. Only one was successfully revived. According to the report, it telepathically imparted that their craft had intended to land in the Gobi. Their mission was a search and rescue, but their propulsion systems malfunctioned. The crew raced against time to save their ship, but they lost. A little less than a mile above Tunguska, the craft exploded into oblivion.''

"What happened to the survivor?'' asked Kane.

Sverdlovosk shrugged. "The report was not clear about that, whether Balam died, escaped or was traded.''

"Balam?'' demanded Grant. "That was its name?''

"It was the closest approximation the linguists could come up with. Why?''

Kane didn't want to address that question at the moment, so he asked another one. "Traded to whom?''

"Possibly to the U.S. Shortly after the creature was found, the Americans made a discovery of similar creatures and a relatively intact vehicle in a place called Roswell, somewhere in New Mexico, I think. The implication was that the Americans exchanged some of the technology found in the wreckage of the craft for Balam.''

Lakesh had related the Roswell incident, but he hadn't placed particular emphasis upon it and all of them silently wondered why. It seemed like a seminal event in the course of intertwined Archon and human destiny.

"When the situation developed last year in the Black Gobi,'' Sverdlovosk continued, "I put together what I had read in all of the reports and reached the provisional conclusion that an ancient alien installation existed beneath Kharo-Khoto.''

"And you and Lenya set out to secure it for your own ends,'' Grant said, "using your positions in District Twelve as covers.''

Sverdlovosk half smiled. "It's not quite as mercenary as it sounds. Lenya's mother was from Azochozki, a Mongolian Burist by blood, so there is a certain familial connection. She perished about twenty years ago in an uprising in Georgia. Lenya's husband was killed two years ago, during an attempted insurrection. We sought only to establish a power base for ourselves, far from the continual strife. Of course, to establish such a base you need power that is outside the control of the central council."

"But it's within the control of a Genghis Khan wanna-be," Kane countered. "That hardly seems like an equitable exchange, either living at the sufferance of an unreliable political system or beneath the rule of a would-be conqueror."

Sverdlovosk nodded to Boro. "From what he's told me, his son's control over the power pent up in the vault may not be absolute."

Boro, who had sat stoically through Sverdlovosk's recounting, took another noisy swig from the bottle. Lowering it, he said in Russian, "Our people have known about the magic of Kharo-Khoto since...since the reign of Tabun Khan, the five kings. But we are not city dwellers. We are hunters, herdsmen, raiders.

"Sometimes children would wander into the ruins of the Black City. My son Shykyr was one of them, and no matter how severely I warned him to stay away, he kept returning. You know how headstrong youngsters can be. He was fascinated by the history in its walls. As he grew older, his childish fancy for the place seemed to pass.

"Then, three winters ago, Piotr asked our clan to seek out and report unusual features in the Black Gobi. He gave us instruments to help in our search."

"Metal detectors, Geiger and rad counters," explained Sverdlovosk, translating the Mongol's Russian words into English.

"Unbeknownst to me," Boro continued, "Shykyr used

the instruments in the vicinity of Kharo-Khoto. He found the entrance to the legendary vault and he claimed he had found our people's true destiny hidden there, as well. He persuaded many of our young men to join him in the explorations. Then bad things began to happen.''

''What kind of bad things?'' asked Brigid.

Sverdlovosk put the question to Boro whose face registered sadness.

''A strange wasting sickness struck our people, our herds. Many of them died. After I told Piotr of my son's discovery, he flooded us with tools and food and medicines. He asked us to clear the city and to open the vault.''

Boro shuddered and made an odd pagan sign toward the ceiling. ''Would now that my son had been the first to perish of the sickness.''

''So you didn't know about the radiation inside the vault?'' Brigid inquired.

''Know that the buried bosom of the Black City spread a poison across our land, our people, our herds? Need you ask?'' Boro clicked his tongue scornfully. ''The change in Shykyr was gradual. He agreed to Piotr's deal, but only on the provision that we excavate the city alone and in our own way. Shykyr spent more and more time, days even, by himself in the vault. Then one day he emerged, his face and soul masked, wearing the hetman's knot of leadership on his shoulder and proclaiming himself the Supreme Chief.''

Boro inhaled and exhaled a slow, soft breath. ''Bautu, my eldest, opposed his brother's arrogant presumption. Then he felt the dragon's kiss and became Shykyr's lieutenant. I argued with him, beseeched him to reconsider his loyalty. But Bautu was now a reflection of Shykyr, who claimed to be a living reflection of all the great

Mongol leaders throughout time. I never quite understood what he meant by that. He said I could not understand because I had no sense of our clan's destiny.'' The last word hissed out contemptuously from Boro's lips.

As Brigid translated, Kane knew the Mongol was mixing half truths with deliberate exaggerations. The man had been in on his son's plan, at least at first, and now he regretted his cooperation. It was easier to pose as a helpless victim of circumstances rather than as a willing conspirator who had been betrayed.

The Mongols had given their lives, their devotion to survive in this hard land. All they knew was what belonged to them and kept at the price of their own blood. And if they could protect their land using the magic weapons of a long-dead ancestor, then so much the better.

He thought about the old days in America, long before the barons dominated all facets of human behavior. Old dreams of freedom and old hungers for a manifest destiny were no longer permitted. Only in this bleak Asian wilderness were the primitive needs to shape the future still indulged.

Perhaps if civilized man, organization man hadn't allowed transitory political systems to kill their sense of adventure, their sense of justice, to kill their awareness that all around them was a living, wonderful world, then Earth wouldn't have been such a sitting duck for the Archon takeover.

Grant, ever the blunt pragmatist, brought the subject back home. "All right, now we know the back story. Time to plan how to write *fini* to it."

"We must enter Kharo-Khoto," said Sverdlovosk firmly. "From this base, it is a half day's overland travel and a bit."

"You're expected," Brigid said, "but Shykyr is obviously suspicious of you. He won't allow any of your party near the vault."

"And," put in Grant, "he may have been psi-linked through the implants to his brothers and is aware of everything that happened here."

Brigid thought that over for a moment, then shook her head. "Unlikely. The implants are designed for psychological conditioning. The deaths of his brothers may be accidental, an unforeseen byproduct of the process."

"Boro claimed Seng and Oborgon couldn't speak Russian, but they did," Grant argued. "They could have learned it through thought transference."

"Even so, it doesn't necessarily follow that Shykyr saw and heard everything that transpired through the implants in the twins."

"But you don't know," prodded Kane. "We know damn little about true Archon tech. All the stuff we've encountered so far has been manufactured here, by humans, following the Archons' specs."

"You're right," she admitted. "But we do know that the Archons are psychically anchored to one another by hyperspatial filaments of the mind. But it's a passive link, probably subliminal. It's an evolutionary, organic feature of their brains. The odds of Shykyr possessing an artificial equivalent are very, very low, simply because of the difference in our brain structures."

"It's still a gamble," Grant declared. "I don't like the percentages."

Kane forced a grin. "What's another one-percenter to us?"

Grant returned the grin, though a little sourly. It was a private piece of philosophy between the two men from their long careers as Magistrates. Their half-serious belief was that ninety-nine percent of things that went awry could be predicted and compensated for in advance. But there was always a one percent margin of error, and playing against that percentage could have lethal consequences.

Sverdlovosk massaged his eyes with the heels of his hands. "We will do whatever is necessary, but the actual details can wait for a while. Let us rest, have something to eat and get back together in three hours. Boro and I have some…things to attend to."

Grant opened his mouth to object, then shut it when he saw the grateful glance Boro cast the Russian. The men needed to deal with arrangements for their dead children's bodies. Boro probably had clan funeral rites to perform, and Sverdlovosk was probably pained by having his daughter simply lie in a body bag in a storage shed.

Standing up, Sverdlovosk said, "There is a cafeteria in the building across the way. The fare is simple but filling. We will reconvene here at—" he checked his wrist chron "—0900 hours."

Accompanied by Boro, he left the wardroom. After a few moments Kane and Grant exchanged shrugs, then trailed after them. Brigid left the blockhouse, but didn't follow the men across the compound. She walked slowly in the opposite direction, head bowed against the cold breeze.

The night sky wasn't black, since there were few clouds. The constellations wheeled frostily overhead, casting the compound with a silvery light. At the corner of a distant outbuilding, out of the steady wind, she stopped to weep.

She hadn't cried for a very long time. She had suppressed the grief over the murders of Adrian and Davis, and the tears she had shed in the Peredelinko mat-trans chamber didn't count—they were symptoms of jump sickness, or so she hoped.

But she wept tears of guilt over the deaths of Lenya Ivornich, Seng and Oborgon. Her clinical nature, the cool scientific detachment she prided herself on, had completely blocked an understanding of the consequences of her cleverness. This was one time she couldn't pat herself on the back for her ingenuity in ferreting out a concealed bit of data. Her training, her oh-so-special intelligence had prevented her from calculating the obvious human factor. Kane, despite her criticisms of his lack of tactics, would never have been so strategically stupid. He would have made sure that the twins were disarmed, bound and gagged if need be, before checking them over.

She, on the other hand, had given in to the whim to perform a trick of intellectual sleight-of-hand to impress the natives. And three people had died violently, unnecessarily.

Brigid had no idea how long she stayed there, but finally the tears slowed and cooled on her face. Shivering and sniffing, she pulled back the cuff of her coat to check the time, only to remember that Sverdlovosk had yet to return her chron.

Kane's voice floated from around the corner, from the shadows. "We've a little while yet."

He stepped around the wall and handed her a covered mug of steaming liquid. "It's some kind of barley soup. The taste isn't so much, but according to Emil the chef, it's nutritious." Adopting a broad accent, he said, "Goot for der tissues."

Brigid accepted the mug gratefully, removed the cover and sipped at it. Warmth slowly spread through her. After she had swallowed several mouthfuls, she asked quietly, "How long have you been there?"

"Just a few minutes. It's too cold for anything longer." Kane shifted his feet uncomfortably. "It wasn't your fault, Baptiste."

Almost without thinking, she replied, "I should have been smarter. More careful. I knew about the implants, didn't I, knew what had happened to Bautu?"

"You aren't responsible for what the Tushe Gun—or whatever his name is this week—did to them. You can't be held accountable for what the boys did to Lenya, either."

Brigid swallowed the last of the soup, then asked in a small, sad voice, "It's not a happy life, is it?"

"Not today. Maybe later."

She smiled bitterly. "'Later.' Will there be any more of 'later' to be had?"

"I've never thought about it."

"Aren't you afraid you'll run out of 'later's?"

"Of course I'm afraid. But I put that fear behind me, because there's nothing to be gained from it." His voice softened as he added, "And nothing to be gained from guilt, either. You hear me, Brigid?"

She looked up at him quickly, peering through the steam rising from the mug. "I think that's the first time you've called me by my first name."

Kane's eyebrows crooked in ironic surprise. "Is it?"

"You didn't realize?"

"I say a lot of things I don't realize or mean, as you've had occasion to point out." Nodding to the mug in her hands, he asked, "You done?"

Brigid handed it back to him. "Yes. Thanks, Kane."

"You're welcome, Baptiste."

Chapter 22

The sheer number of yurts was unsettling. There were at least a thousand of the yak-hide domes covering the valley floor, sprawling nearly a quarter of a mile or more in all directions. A gray umbrella of smoke hung above the valley, the result of hundreds of cook fires.

They were lying on their stomachs on the rim of the bowl-shaped valley, looking down at the tent city in the late-afternoon sun. Peering through the eyepieces of a compact set of binoculars, Grant looked beyond the settlement. The thin black line of walls reared from the sands two miles distant.

"There it is," he grunted.

"And there is where we will find the Tushe Gun," replied Sverdlovosk. "Let us be off. Scouts have already reported our approach, and if we delay further we will certainly arouse suspicion."

He elbow-crawled backward, down the face of the slope. Before following him, Grant passed the binoculars to Kane so he could take a quick look at their objective. At this distance the walls of Kharo-Khoto looked like no more than a dark ridge rising on the terrain. There was nothing sinister or awe inspiring about it. He extended the binoculars to Brigid. "Want a look-see?"

She shook her head. "I'll be getting a very close look before long."

At the bottom of the slope waited the convoy of a

covered truck and Boro's mounted men. They had left the air base before sunrise and traveled across the barren landscape all day, with only a single noon break to rest and water the horses.

Sverdlovosk lowered the tailgate of the truck. Stacked inside were over a dozen wooden crates of varying sizes. The three troopers who had flown with them from Russia guarded the cargo with watchful eyes, fingers on the triggers of their AKMs.

When the three Americans joined him at the rear of the wag, Sverdlovosk announced, "From here on out, you will have to trust me unquestioningly. One misstep will get us all killed."

Kane said flatly, "So you told us last night, but you've yet to earn that trust."

"It's too late now, Kane," Sverdlovosk retorted impatiently. "You either trust me or you don't."

"We don't," declared Grant.

"What can I do at this point?"

"Give us back our weapons and equipment," answered Brigid.

The Russian blinked in embarrassed surprise. "I apologize. Why didn't you ask me last night?"

Softly Brigid replied, "We figured you had other things on your mind."

Sverdlovosk smiled sadly. "Very true. I appreciate your compassion."

"That's one item you did earn," Kane remarked.

Sverdlovosk spoke to a soldier in the truck, who passed him the leather satchel. Using the open tailgate as a table, Sverdlovosk unsnapped the catches on the case and withdrew their possessions. They inspected them and found them to be in working order. Grant and Kane took off their coats so they could strap the Sin Eaters to their forearms and attach the combat harnesses.

Brigid swept the area with her rad counter. When she pointed it toward the valley, she said, "Midrange orange reading. The place is very warm."

"If it wasn't for the medicines I provided," Sverdlovosk said gruffly, "most of the Tushe Gun's followers would be dead by now. As it is, a great number of them are sick."

From the bottom of the satchel, he produced a pair of fur caps, duplicates of his own, decorated with silver disks. Thrusting them toward Kane and Grant, he said, "Wear these from now on. Don't speak, just glare around and everyone will assume you are my lieutenants."

Grant seated the cap on his head. "My color is not exactly the Russian-soldier standard, you know."

"All the better. You'll intimidate the superstitious Tartars, since black is one of their high or holy colors." Turning to Brigid, he asked, "Are you ready, my dear?"

She jacked a round into her Mauser, slipped it into a coat pocket and heaved herself up onto the tailgate. "No, but it's too late to back out now."

"No, it isn't," Kane said stiffly.

"We went over it last night," Brigid reminded him. "If Boro recognized me, then the Tushe Gun or some of his followers will, too."

Helped by a trooper, Brigid climbed into the back of the truck. The lid of a long crate was lifted open, and she stepped into it. The night before, Sverdlovosk had ordered the construction of a specially designed box. The sides were slatted, and the edge of the lid bore nail heads all around, but it was actually secured by concealed hinges and a latch on the inside.

After she lay down in the crate, the troopers carefully

packed small items around her body, not only to add weight but to keep her from rolling from side to side when the box was unloaded and carried. The lid was lowered, and Kane listened for the click of the inner latch. When it came, he turned away.

The night before, he had rattled off a litany of problems with the plan—her crate could be buried beneath the others out in the open, where she would freeze to death, or opened before it was conveyed into the city. Brigid had listened calmly to his objections, proclaimed them reasonable, then quoted him his own one-percenter bit of doggerel.

Sverdlovosk lifted the tailgate back into its upright position. "A very brave young woman. She shares my Lenya's strength of spirit."

Kane was too considerate to mention that Brigid could very well join Lenya's spirit if anything happened to upset the plan.

Sverdlovosk climbed into the cab, behind the wheel, instructing Grant to ride on the running board beside him and to look fierce and forbidding.

"You may feel a little at sea," Sverdlovosk told them, "since I will be speaking either in Russian or their own dialect. Whatever happens, you must follow my lead, do as I do."

"And what happens if you get your head chopped off?" Kane demanded.

"In that case, Comrade, I give you leave to follow your own impulses."

Flanked by Boro's riders, the truck rolled across the sandy terrain toward the mouth of the valley. A bitter wind gusted from it, streaming out the manes and tails of the horses. Before they had covered half the distance, a warrior astride a piebald pony galloped out to meet them.

He stood in his stirrups and waved and shouted. Riding in front of the truck, Boro shouted back angrily in response. The warrior reined his horse to a halt, and his dark, slitted eyes fixed on Grant as the vehicle rumbled past him. He was a small but powerfully built man.

Hanging on to the side mirror, Grant returned the stare, noting that the Mongol's swart face looked both brutal and hungry. Just beneath the matted fur trim of his leather skullcap, he saw a faint round scar high on his forehead. Grant turned his stare into a glare, and the warrior's eyes flicked aside.

Sverdlovosk said, "That is Gombo. He wanted to know where Seng and Oborgon were, saying that the Tushe Gun would be displeased by their absence."

"What did Boro say to him?"

"Basically, 'Fuck you, I'm still their father.' The rest was what we'd agreed upon, that they'd fallen ill back at the base. Since there is so much sickness in the camp, it's not an unusual excuse."

They passed a small flatbed truck parked near some thorny underbrush. Sverdlovosk pointed to it. "That's the wag I allowed Brigid to appropriate. It looks in working condition, and that is good. I hate filling out lost-ordnance paperwork."

As they rolled into the valley, they smelled odors of smoke, grease and roasting food. At the engine sounds of the truck, women in long, gathered skirts, their bodies underneath stout and squat, rushed for the safety of their yurts. A child who had been playing between two yurts rushed after his mother, squalling in dismay.

Smoke-stained faces peered out from behind tent flaps as they passed by, skirting cook fires and makeshift corrals holding horses and sheep. In a larger pen they saw a number of people who lay or huddled on the ground. Their bodies were distorted, scabbed, the eyes covered by milky films. Some people seemed to be one single festering sore, pocked with rupturing, vile-smelling boils.

Grant looked away in disgust, recognizing the symptoms of advanced rad poisoning. The camp of the Tushe Gun seemed more like a huge, open-air death ward than the home of his adoring followers.

It seemed to take a very long time to drive through the valley encampment, and Kane worried about Brigid in her crate, even though he knew there were sufficient spaces between the wooden slats to allow free breathing.

At the far end of the valley, a half-dozen riders galloped forth from the direction of the city walls. The men wore black tunics, and their faces were smeared with black grease. When they drew closer, they gaped at Grant, and one of them jabbered at Boro. The Mongol replied in kind, gesturing toward the truck.

Hands clenching on the wheel, Sverdlovosk chuckled nervously. "These men will escort us to the Tushe Gun's yurt in the city. They're warrior-priests, the Avenging Lama's bodyguards. They wear the holy colors of Khara Bator himself. They will not search us, Grant, because they think you're one of them."

Grant allowed the fixed scowl on his face to slip a little. "Maybe I will be, if this plan goes sour."

The two miles of terrain between the end of the valley and the city walls was bleak and black, as if it had been exposed to open flames. Powdery sand and ash floated up in the wake of the truck's passage, irritating Grant's throat so that he nearly succumbed to a coughing fit. He and Kane had seen rad-blasted landscapes like this before, hellzones where invisible poisons had leached all life away.

The city walls loomed nearer and they were more massive than Kane or Grant had expected. They were made of blocks of a dead black stone that reflected no trace of the setting sun. The walls loomed twenty feet high, and sections were so eroded they had fallen altogether. The great pillars of the gate reared from the ground, and beyond them were roofless arches and crumbling buildings containing nothing but empty legend. A few yurts were scattered around the outer perimeter of the walls.

Kharo-Khoto was enormous, and Kane tried to picture it in its past glory, blazing splendidly with light and color and roaring with life. He visualized the barbaric chieftains from the wild steppes, coming here to bend their knees in the presence of the Black Hero. And now there was only silence and gathering twilight to fill the streets and shattered buildings. A broad avenue ran inward from the gate, and the truck followed it, rolling over sunken paving blocks, the hooves of their mounted escort clopping on the stone.

The avenue widened inside the walls, opening into a vast courtyard filled with the wreck and ruin of Khara Bator's palace. Great blocks of basalt and granite had fallen from the building, and the main vault of the roof was open to the sky. But the inner arches still stood, and fragments of fretted galleries stretched to nowhere. Broken statues lay in the dust, their features mutilated by the merciless hand of time. The carved eye sockets were filled with grit.

The effort to clear away centuries of accumulated sand and detritus had to have been monumentally backbreaking. Despite himself, Kane felt a grudging admiration grow for the Tushe Gun and his devoted followers.

Sverdlovosk steered the truck around a white yurt in the middle of the courtyard. A sear-faced man armed with a brace of automatic pistols stood in front of it, seeming to pay no attention to the vehicle. Nodding toward the dome, the Russian said, "Inside that tent is the well, which leads down to the vault. It is always guarded."

In front of the palace ruins they saw seven large yurts, bigger than any they had passed in the valley, arranged in a circle. In the center of the cluster squatted the largest of the domes. It was black, decorated with petroglyphs in crimson.

On either side of it stood long wooden poles ten feet tall. Red-and-black banners were wrapped around the shafts, the loose ends fluttering in the breeze. Affixed to the very tops of the poles were human heads, the necks severed cleanly. Though the sagging, immobile faces were spotted with dried blood, Kane and Grant recognized Adrian and Davis. Kane hissed in anger at the sight, but he was glad Brigid was unable to see them.

The black-garbed riders halted their animals and dismounted. A man took the horses' reins and led them to a rope picket line off to one side. Sverdlovosk braked the wag and turned off the engine, pocketing the key. Grant stepped down from the running board as Boro and his men climbed from their saddles, turning their horses over to the men with blackened faces. Boro walked toward the center yurt while Kane, Sverdlovosk and Grant waited beside the truck. It was warmer within the city walls than in the valley, and the air smelled cleaner.

The tent flap opened, pulled from the inside. Boro spoke to someone in the interior, then turned and beckoned the three men to join him. Moving single file, they ducked their heads and entered the yurt. It was surprisingly well lit, the floor covered with carpets bearing elaborately woven geometric forms. One such design that Kane saw repeated was a red triangle bisected by three vertical lines.

The light shone from several small square panels hanging from the domed roof of the tent. They exuded a steady blue-yellow glow. Dimly lit by the panels, the Tushe Gun leaned forward on his seat of cushions at the shadowy back of the yurt. Grant and Kane tried hard not to stare.

The Tushe Gun was dressed colorfully in high boots of dyed red leather, blue leggings and a black silk tunic decorated with dragons worked in golden thread. Red gauntlets encased his hands and forearms. A fur-trimmed cloak of green fell from his shoulders to the backs of his ankles. The green complemented the smooth mask of carved jade covering his face. He made an imposing, dramatic figure, but there was something not quite right about him.

The Tushe Gun appeared taller than his fellow Mongols, with a broad chest and equally broad shoulders, but shorter legs, which was often the case with this body type. Yet even at a glance, his legs and arms seemed disproportionate compared to his torso. Overall, the impression was that there was something unnaturally out of balance in his build.

On the index finger of his right hand glinted a massive silver ring that covered an entire joint. It resembled a snarling, ferocious dragon's head, fanged jaws agape. A necklace of small gold beads hung from his neck to his waist. Around his hips was a tasseled cord of interwoven rainbow colors. Attached to the cord was a long, sheathed saber, the scabbard set with dozens of multihued gems.

Behind the curved eyelets, a glittering gaze studied them.

Sverdlovosk dropped to one knee, and after a brief hesitation Kane and Grant followed suit, ducking their heads and sticking out their tongues as the Russian had earlier instructed them to do. Only Boro didn't kneel in submission or respect. Kane assumed that as the Tushe Gun's father, he was exempt from the prerequisite groveling.

The masked form spoke in a peculiarly sibilant voice, the timbre hard and liquid at the same time. Boro shook his head and replied in an angry and contemptuous tone.

The hands of the man in the mask caressed the pommel of his saber. They were small hands, slender and almost delicate in shape. The green mask shifted away from Boro's angry face. Wordlessly he pointed toward the door flap of the yurt.

Boro sneered, hawked up loudly from deep in his throat and spit on the carpeted floor. Wheeling, he stamped his way out of the tent, violently flinging aside the door flap.

The Tushe Gun said in Russian, "You may rise."

Sverdlovosk climbed to his feet, Kane and Grant standing together on the right side of him.

The Tushe Gun's eyes flicked back and forth from the two Americans. "Who are they?"

"Gifts, Avenging Lama. They cannot understand our words, so I will speak candidly. They came from across the sea, like the other interlopers. I tricked them into accompanying me."

The green jade face nodded thoughtfully. "And what do you expect me to do with these gifts of yours?"

Sverdlovosk cast a warm grin toward Grant, and clapped Kane on the shoulder. "They have come to douse the sacred flame, so I would suggest you kill them."

"And what do you wish in return?"

"Only your trust. If you prefer, I will kill them for you."

The masked man said quietly, "No, I think not. Bautu was premature in killing the other outsiders. I think it would be wise to let the dragon kiss these two."

Kane and Grant, not understanding a word, smiled deferentially at the Tushe Gun. Much later, recasting this scene in his mind, Kane had no trouble guessing what had transpired.

Chapter 23

The Tushe Gun spoke one word, as sharp and as loud as a gunshot. Sverdlovosk immediately dropped to his knees as if he had been pulled by a string. Grant and Kane, after a mystified moment, did the same.

They resisted the impulse to look around, not even when they heard the rustle of the tent flap and the sounds of scuffling feet. They knew a number of men had entered the yurt—they could hear them breathing, smell their rank, unwashed-animal odor. Short, terse phrases burst from the Tushe Gun's half-concealed mouth. Kane's pointman sense triggered a distant alarm, and he began to raise his head.

Immediately they were bowled over by a swarm of bodies hitting them from behind. Hands grabbed at them, knees dug painfully into the smalls of their backs. Their arms were yanked upward and loops of rawhide slipped around their wrists.

Instinctively Kane stiffened his wrist tendons, hand ready to receive the weight of the Sin Eater. His hand felt nothing but air, and he realized in an angry, humiliating rush that Sverdlovosk had sabotaged either the electric cable motor or the tension actuator. He heard Grant snarl out a curse and knew his companion had just made the same discovery. The two men fought and wrestled, but the five black-garbed, black-faced men were very strong. The smallest statured of them was an equal match for either one of them in sheer muscular power.

Kane managed to launch a back-kick and he took savage pleasure in the shiver of impact running up his leg as his foot landed solidly. A moment later he received a kick on the jaw, and the floor spun crazily around and the light dimmed. Tasting blood, he was only slightly aware of a strip of leather being forced over his head and face.

Hard hands clutched his coat and dragged him up to his knees. Both he and Grant now had leather collars around their throats. They were cinched tight by rawhide leashes, which allowed just enough air to ward off unconsciousness. Loops of plaited leather bound their wrists.

When Kane's vision cleared, he saw one of the black-faced bodyguards sitting against the hide wall, trying to staunch the flow of blood from a flattened nose. The other five men stood behind them, short-bladed swords in their fists.

Sverdlovosk stood next to the Tushe Gun, gazing down sorrowfully. In English he said, "It had to be done, Comrades."

Kane spit out blood and a chipped-off fragment of molar. "Survival and success?"

"I'm glad you understand."

Grant strained against the hands gripping him, then made a strangling noise when a man gave the leash a sharp tug. When the choking pressure relaxed enough for him to speak, he said, "You son of a bitch. This is what you and Lenya had planned for us all along—sacrifice us to curry this masked asshole's favor."

Sverdlovosk sighed. "It is what *I* had planned, true enough. Lenya opposed my opportunism, so do not think ill of the dead. She was always more like her mother than myself. Lenya was interested in all of you, respected your courage. She was strangely attracted to you, Kane. With her passing, I see no reason not to revive the original strategy. It is very sound.''

"What about Baptiste?" Kane demanded.

"That's the simple beauty of it," replied the Russian. "Her part of the operation will continue without alteration. I only need one of you to identify the items in the vault, and inasmuch as she seems the most intelligent of the three of you—certainly the most attractive—she will serve my purposes adequately."

"What happens to her afterward?" Kane's voice was hoarse, hushed from the effort to keep from shouting in rage.

"To employ your vernacular, afterward will have to be played by nose."

"Ear," Grant corrected him. "And what happens to us? Do we end up as porch posts, like Adrian and Davis?"

Sverdlovosk smiled. "Surprisingly enough, no. At least not right away. The Avenging Lama has other plans for you." He puckered his lips. "The kiss of the dragon."

The Russian bowed to the masked man and backed away from him. The Tushe Gun gazed down steadily at Kane and Grant. They met his gaze defiantly. The eyes focused on Kane, staring unblinkingly through the openings in the layer of jade. His eyes widened until his jet black irises were completely surrounded by the whites. His lips moved beneath the mask, and a whispering, altered voice came forth.

The Tushe Gun spoke quickly, the syllables tripping over each other so rapidly the words were unintelligible.

For a moment Kane thought he heard, almost unimaginably distant, the rustle of leathery wings, the beat of a faraway drum or heart. The close, clammy air of the yurt seemed to vibrate. He remembered what Bautu had said about the Avenging Lama speaking black words.

He took a long, swift step toward Kane, raising and extending his right fist. The malevolent silver dragon swelled in Kane's vision, like a monster dredged up from an almost but not quite forgotten nightmare from his childhood. He leaned away, shrinking back. Callused hands gripped his hair cruelly, pressed his face between them. A knee jammed into his rib cage kept him stationary and upright. The strip of rawhide binding his wrists had some play in it, but his arms were held too tightly to work at the slack.

Out of the corner of his eye, he glimpsed Grant struggling, but the point of a sword blade pricked his throat, and he subsided with a growled curse.

From between the gleaming jaws of the dragon slid a thin, half-inch-long filament. It was finer than a strand of silk thread, barely thicker than a human hair. The end of the filament touched Kane's right temple, just below his hairline. He felt a sharp, exquisite sting, like a pinch.

The Tushe Gun drew his fist back, and the tiny metal thread withdrew into a recess above the curved reptilian tongue. His chanting continued, a mantra of monotony. The yellow-gem eyes of the dragon suddenly flashed with a pale golden glow. The glow became a shimmering halo, spreading from the eyes, dancing in a miniature borealis around the horned head.

The filament popped out of the open mouth again. A minute dark speck, almost too tiny for the unaided eye to detect, was attached to the end of it. DeFore's words streaked through Kane's mind like a wind-whipped fire.

I found that a metal core is covered by an organic membrane. The membrane consists of blood protein and keratin.

With a surge of horror he realized Baptiste's speculation that the dragon ring was a surgical instrument was probably more accurate than she ever dreamed. The filament had sampled his genetic structure, and whatever stunningly complex and miniaturized mechanism was inside the ring had manufactured an implant with his own blood and cells as a nonrejectable sheath. It wasn't sorcery, but it was no less terrifying—functioning biotechnology reduced and compressed to an unbelievably small scale.

Accompanying the surge of horror came an equally powerful surge of panic. He stopped straining against the hands holding him. He sagged, shifting his weight to a dead, limp mass. As the men tried to haul him upright, they momentarily repositioned and loosened their grips.

Kane's battle-trained muscles, tested and refined in a hundred situations, exploded in a perfect coordination of mind, reflexes and skill.

He acted without thought, somersaulting back against the legs of the bodyguards behind him, pulling loose the leash. He knocked one of them off his feet, causing another to trip over him and sprawl facedown, a short-bladed sword falling from his hand.

As Kane rolled, he wriggled and squirmed, working to drag his hands down over his hips. After a chafing gyration, he brought his wrists down to his ankles. He came out of the somersault in a deep squat, the length of plaited rawhide hooked at the heels of his boots.

A jabbering bodyguard kicked him hard in the chest. Kane went with the force of the blow, falling backward. As he fell, he strained against the leather bindings, jerked his arms and dragged his hands over the heels and soles of his boots. Thrashing over, he sprang for the fallen sword, deftly plucking it from the floor by the blade and opening a small cut on the palm of his glove. He came to his feet in a yelling rush. His yell was echoed by a shout of anger and dismay from the black-faced bodyguards. They piled forward in a mob.

He tossed the sword in the air, caught the grip in both hands and flicked out the blade, the tip dragging across a throat. The man stumbled back, a hand clapped to the side of his neck. A bright arterial jet spurted from between his fingers, splashing one of the glowing light panels with an artless crimson pattern.

"Kane!" Grant's lionlike roar filled the yurt. He struggled to get to his feet. Sverdlovosk towered behind him, a handblaster held high. He slashed the barrel viciously across the back of Grant's skull. Even over the cries of fright and anger, the sound of metal striking bone was loud and ugly.

Grant flopped face first to the floor, and Kane acted with the desperate swiftness of a man who has long lived by the speed of hand and eye. He swung the sword in a backward arc, the razor edge of the blade chopping into the horizontal wooden pole from which the door flap hung. Hands still bound, he tore the heavy square of hide down, and before the bodyguards could reach him with their swords, he swung the flap over their heads.

As the Mongols slashed at the folds of yak skin, Kane flung himself out of the yurt and into the courtyard, happy on the one hand to see it full of lengthening shadows, cursing himself on the other hand for leaving Grant. But they had worked together long enough to subscribe to the discretion-is-the-better-of-valor school of survival.

Kane ran, using the sword blade to slice through the

strips of rawhide binding his wrists. He didn't waste time trying to claw his Sin Eater free of its holster. He rushed toward where Sverdlovosk had parked the truck, acting on the impulse to free Brigid.

When he reached it, he saw he was too late. A line of clansmen unloaded the cargo, stacking the crates on a low-slung, wooden-runnered sledge harnessed to a pair of ponies. The Russian troopers stood by, overseeing the labor.

Sverdlovosk's voice penetrated the din in the courtyard, bellowing commands in Russian. Kane swerved away from the truck, racing toward a tumble of stone, his body curved in a half crouch. The shadowy form of a man loomed up in front of him, and he saw the glint of steel.

Kane tried to sidestep and felt the dull impact of the sword point as the man stabbed at him, targeting his heart. The tough fabric of his coat resisted the steel tip, and though he was pushed off balance, Kane returned the thrust with his own weapon.

The eighteen-inch blade struck his attacker at an upward angle, sliding between his ribs, grating on bone. The man coughed and convulsed in a death spasm, folding over the sword and wrenching it from Kane's hand. He didn't bother trying to withdraw the sword. He spun on his heel, running toward the area where the horses were picketed.

Vaulting over a cracked block of basalt, he heard shrill, keening cries from behind him. The stone walls of Kharo-Khoto threw them back in wailing echoes. He glanced back over his shoulder. Through the milling crowd of Mongols and Russian soldiers dashing after him, he glimpsed a blank jade face.

He unbuttoned his coat, fingers groping over the grens

clipped to his combat harness. Sverdlovosk could have defused them, but Kane had no choice but to hope they would serve the purpose.

He gripped a metal-shelled egg, detaching it from the harness, thumb flipping the priming pin away. He did it all by feel, not knowing if he had an incend, an implode or a fragger in his hand. Under the circumstances he really didn't give a damn.

He lobbed it back in a looping overhead throw and he heard it clink twice against rock.

A blaze of light suddenly illuminated the area in front of him with a white, incandescent glare. A tremendous cracking roar, half explosion, half windstorm, slammed against his eardrums. The shock wave of the concussion was slight, but he felt invisible hands tugging at his coattails, trying to yank him backward.

A spout of oxygen, dust, rock particles and powdery sand swirled around his face, irresistibly sucked back toward the wedge of instant vacuum created by the detonation of the implode gren.

He lunged over a toppled statue, and for an eerie split second, his body hung motionless in midair, suspended perpendicular to the fallen sculpture. Then the whirlpool effect created by the implosive device collapsed in on itself, and his momentum interrupted, he fell heavily across the statue. At the same time he felt and heard tiny fragments of stone pattering down all around him.

Knuckling the grit from his eyes, he rolled to the ground and staggered to his feet. He didn't look behind him to gauge the destruction wrought by the gren. He knew what he would see—those closest to the detonation point would be mangled lumps of flesh, their eardrums shattered by the brutal decompression, their eyeballs pulled from their sockets, internal organs burst, blood from ruptured vessels springing out from every orifice, their lungs flattened wafers of tissue. Those at the far edge of the implosion's epicenter might be unconscious due to the sudden and absolute lack of oxygen.

In a sprint Kane reached the tethered horses. They were frightened and began to neigh and stamp their hooves. He rushed toward the closest one, untying the length of rawhide attached to the animal's halter and snatching a fistful of mane.

The horse whinnied in fright and rather than try to calm it down, he leaped onto its bare back and kicked its flanks, letting it bolt. Kane had always loved horses in general, but from a distance. Because of his ville-bred life, the closest he had ever come to the beasts was during duty patrols, either in the Pits or in the Outlands. And those had been dray animals, fairly docile, slow moving and phlegmatic.

The beast he clung to now was a war pony, fierce, high-spirited and skittish from the unfamiliar smell and feel of the rider. It went clattering and bucking across the courtyard with shrill cries. Kane gripped the halter with one hand, beating with his free fist at the horse's head.

Snorting in anger, it headed for a crumbled section of wall, running flat out. Kane bounced and jounced on its back, at first trying to turn, then giving it free rein. He had blurry glimpses of men streaming by and he barely heard their shouts over the drumming hoofbeats. He fought to maintain his balance, gritting his teeth against the spine-compressing jolts.

The horse galloped toward the split in the wall, sand spurting from its hooves. Kane hung on, dimly aware of the ruins reeling past. The animal reached the broken heap of rubble spanning the width of the gap in the wall.

Kane felt its muscles sliding and gliding beneath its

glossy coat. It leaped high in the air, higher, it seemed to him, than was necessary to clear the pile of stones, forelegs tucked beneath its chest, powerful hind legs catapulting it over the barrier.

Then his mount alighted gracefully outside the wall, but with a jolt that launched Kane straight up. It was impossible to maintain his grip on the halter or the mane, so he sailed headlong through the air, toward a cluster of yurts. He tucked his chin as he hit the ground, not trying to resist the kinetic force of the fall or to land on his feet. He rolled, reflexively slapping the ground to absorb the momentum and minimize the chance of having the wind knocked out of him. Shoulder and lower back throbbing, he rolled twice and came dizzily to his feet.

The horse galloped off, kicking its hind legs joyfully, tossing its head, neighing loudly, as if throwing Kane off its back was one of the high points of its life.

Outraged yells on the other side of the wall started him running again. He reached beneath his coat and drew his fourteen-inch combat knife. So far he was ahead of his pursuers, and for the moment none of them was in sight, but he knew he couldn't keep it that way.

A door flap was thrown back on the nearest yurt, and Boro looked out. Opening the flap wide, he motioned Kane toward him. Without breaking stride, he sprinted for the dome, diving through the opening, snatching the man's tunic and dragging him to the floor.

He pressed the point of the knife to the man's throat. Boro shook his head, saying, *"Nyet, nyet,"* letting Kane know he had no intention of giving him away. Hesitantly Kane released him, allowing him to rise and lace the door flap shut.

The sound of pounding feet came from outside the tent, and Boro pointed to the wall farthest away from the door, where horsehair blankets, rolls of fleece, cushions and other household articles were piled. Kane crawled quickly to the heap, lying down in a fetal position as Boro draped him in blankets and covered him with cushions. He lay motionless as Boro leaned indolently against the pile.

Peering through a small slitlike fold in the musty blanket over his head, he saw the door flap quiver, shaken from the outside. Before Boro could move, a knife blade insinuated itself through the hide and severed the leather lacings. A skullcapped warrior ripped the hanging aside, shouting a fierce question. He looked inquisitively around the dark interior of the tent. Boro shouted back, in a fury over the damage to his yurt. He half rose, gesticulating angrily, and the Mongol mumbled an apology and withdrew his head.

Kane smiled slightly. Estranged though he might be from his son, Boro Orolok was still the father of the Tushe Gun and deserving of a great measure of respect. Had he chosen another yurt to dive into, even an uninhabited one, a different occupant's denial wouldn't have been taken at face value and the dwelling could have been slashed to ribbons and set on fire.

Still, Kane realized that Boro hadn't offered him sanctuary out of unselfish charity. He kept the knife in his hand as Boro got up to fix the flap and return to remove his guest's camouflage.

Boro spoke to him urgently in Russian as Kane sat up. With hand signs and head shakes, he tried to indicate that he didn't understand. Boro continued chattering while Kane rolled up his right coat sleeve, unstrapping the holster from his forearm. With his microlight, he examined it and saw, with a relieved sigh, that Sverdlovosk's sabotage was minimal. All he had done was to disconnect the spring cable from the electric motor. He had lacked either the time or the technical expertise to do more extensive damage. Under the circumstances it had been sufficient.

With the point of his combat knife and his fingers, he manipulated the cable connection back into the motor's socket. He strapped the holster back on and experimented.

Boro stopped talking, eyes widening at the sight of the big blaster slapping into Kane's hand as if by magic. When he pushed the Sin Eater back into the holster, Boro began talking again.

Kane put a finger to his lips to shush him, then pulled the pin mike from his lapel. He switched the trans-comm to Brigid's frequency and got the result he feared—a crackling hash of static.

He released the miniature microphone and glanced gloomily at his wrist chron. The fact that it still kept perfect time did little to make him optimistic. It was 6:20 p.m., and at that very minute, Grant's brain could be heavier by one implant and Brigid could have been captured or trapped in a subterranean vault.

He used the knife to cut the leather collar away from his throat and looked sourly at Boro. The Mongol grinned at him broadly. An old Mag bromide popped unbidden into his mind. Aloud, he muttered, "The man who smiles has yet to hear the terrible news."

But Boro continued to grin.

Then his trans-comm circuit clicked open.

Chapter 24

Around her was the sound of hurrying feet, the clopping of hooves and the complaining tones of men not happy about performing strenuous labor so late in the day.

Above the voices Brigid heard the thud of heavy objects hitting wood and the grunts of exertions. Then her own crate moved, with a loud, long scrape, down the bed of the truck. It lurched, tipping down at the bottom, and through the vertical cracks between the slats she glimpsed flitting shadows of movement.

She lay without a quiver, breathing shallowly through her nose, not even stirring when the crate was heaved up and dropped on a hard surface. The booming impact echo filled the container, and the back of her head bounced off the floor of the crate. She didn't cry out, but her muscles went taut. Cool air sifted through the tiny spaces between the boards, and she inhaled it gratefully, quietly.

She felt the jerk of sudden motion, heard the tramping of horse hooves and the sliding sound of wood dragging over rocky, sandy ground. She saw nothing above her but a tiny sliver of sky purpling with twilight.

After a minute the forward motion ceased, and a man spoke. She recognized the arrogant tones of one of Sverdlovosk's troopers, a man named Kropotkin. She strained her ears. He was speaking to someone disrespectfully in Russian.

"This one first," he said, kicking the crate for emphasis.

A gravelly voice responded in flawed Russian. "Why is this one so important?"

"Why? It contains perishables. It is the Avenging Lama's wish that this one be delivered first."

One corner of the crate lifted a few inches. She heard a grunt, followed by a weary sigh. "Help me. It is heavy."

"Get one of your clan brothers to help you, Tengri. I must oversee the unloading of the rest."

Footsteps marched away. Tengri shouted a name, and other footfalls approached. Voices muttered and murmured over her. Her crate rose, moved unsteadily forward and her limited view of the sky disappeared, replaced a moment later by an odd bluish white glow.

Metal clinked and jingled. The rattle of heavy chains dragging over and around the crate filled her ears. For a handful of seconds she heard nothing else.

Then her crate was lifted, tilting slightly, accompanied by the creak of a hoist-type mechanism. Brigid found herself holding her breath as the crate rose higher, then dropped straight down in a slow, controlled descent.

The blue light dimmed, and the crate swung slightly from side to side, the top and bottom bumping and scratching against a rough surface. As the crate was lowered deeper, gloom thickened around it. Peering through the slats of the lid, she saw an occasional hint of golden light, like sparks flashing under a dark sea. A tingling thrill surged through her.

Filtering faintly from above, Brigid heard shouts and yells, an outcry of tumult. The steady, controlled drop halted with a squeak of the winch and pulley. Then it began again, a terrifying vertical plunge. The hoist mechanism clattered loudly, and her stomach tried to glide up her throat.

The descent ended abruptly with a jolting impact that sent vibrations of pain through her entire body, causing her forehead to slam smartly against the underside of the lid and the back of her skull to rebound from the floor. The air was nearly driven from her lungs.

She bit her lips, squeezing her eyes shut and waiting for the pain to recede. She lay quietly, listening for any sounds near her. There was nothing from nearby, but through the stillness faraway voices rose in harsh, wild screams of anger.

Dragging in a shuddery breath, Brigid opened her eyes and saw a golden shroud of light peeping through the cracks. She fumbled for the inner catch, finding it and snapping it aside. Before pushing the lid open, she pulled her trans-comm unit from a pocket and opened the comm circuit to Kane's frequency. All she heard was a muted cacophony of squawks and crackling squeals. When she tuned to Grant's frequency, she got the same result. She fought off the dread rising in her, assuming some energy force was interfering with the carrier wave. She put it back in her pocket.

Carefully, an inch at a time, Brigid pushed against the lid. A sensation throbbed in her flesh, just beneath her skin, then deeper, an uncomfortable tingling that stopped on the edge of actual pain.

She drew up her legs and slowly rose, lifting the lid with her. At first only a mist filled with dancing flecks of golden light filled her field of vision. Then her eyes pierced the vapor, and she stopped moving. What she saw crushed her under the weight of a great, heart-stopping awe. Intellectually she had some notion of what to expect, but emotionally she was unprepared for what she saw.

A veil of light like diluted sunshine moved all around her, shimmering in the air. She felt subtle energies prickling her flesh, penetrating it, caressing her bones. Automatically she checked the rad counter on the lapel of her coat. The needle was motionless on the far end of the green scale, then flicked far over to the red and back to green again, like a deranged metronome. The light was a tingling, buoyant, intangible web, and she could feel radiation rippling over her in tiny waves. Though the wavelength couldn't be measured or accurately registered on her counter, she was positive it was jamming her trans-comm frequency.

Brigid looked through the golden shimmer, stared past it, focusing her eyes on whatever lay beyond it. She stood at the bottom of a huge cavity, cavernous and circular in configuration. She guessed it to be fifty feet high, but she had no idea of its circumference. Directly above her yawned a round, metal-lipped opening, a shaft leading up to the surface. A sling made of chains and fleece-lined leather was heaped around the crate. She didn't waste time wondering what had distracted Tengri and whoever else had been operating the hoist. She stepped out of the crate, treading carefully and slowly.

It took her a few moments to adjust her eyes to the diffuse light, learning how to focus through it. Plates of dully gleaming alloy sheathed the floor. Many of them were buckled here and there, bulging but not showing splits. The whole floor tilted slightly to the right, about five degrees out of true. As if from a vast distance, she heard a rhythmic, familiar drone.

Massive wedge-shaped ribs of metal supported the roof and sides of the cavity. The huge arching girders bore strange hieroglyphs, arranged in neat, compact vertical rows. She walked very slowly, consciously keeping a tight grip on her emotions, on her mind, not allowing herself to become lost in conjecture and terror.

The lines of the vast chamber were deceptively simple, but when she tried to follow the curves and angles, she found her head swimming and her eyes stinging. There was a quality to the architecture that eluded the human mind, as though it had been designed on geometric principles just slightly at a tangent from the brain's capacity to absorb.

Looking overhead, she saw the gigantic shapes of six curved metal tubes running along the roof. One bore a crack in the dark casing, and from this jagged opening the golden light spilled out—a blaze of incandescence that illuminated the interior of the craft. And it was a craft—that much was certain—an enormous ovoid spaceship, not an underground installation. Kharo-Khoto had been built over a giant flying disk that had crashed here God alone knew how many millennia ago. It was buried by the drifting sand of ages and shrouded in Mongol myth and conferred divinity.

A few yards behind the cracked cylinder were the first short metal risers of a stair that led up to a railed gallery. What lay on the gallery she couldn't tell, but between her and the foot of the steps stood an oblong pedestal, barely three feet tall. Four small pyramids crafted from pale golden alloy were placed at equidistant points around it. Resting on their points was a smooth, crystalline ovoid, around five feet long. It seemed filled with a cloudy, smokelike substance.

Brigid approached it cautiously, drawing her breath deep. The tingling sensation all over her body began to burn with a slow, cold heat. When she put out a tentative hand to touch the crystal surface, she was ashamed of the tremor in it. At her touch, the vapor within the ovoid immediately cleared and she recoiled, clamping her jaws shut on an automatic cry of fright. She was terrified and she didn't know why. She had expected it, after all.

An Archon lay inside the transparent cocoon—or what was left of one.

The supine figure lay on its back, the short, thin legs close together, the arms crossed over the narrow chest, the inhumanly long, inhumanly delicate fingers intertwined. It was very short, very slender and it had been dead for such a long time that it had mummified.

Dark gray skin was stretched drum tight over a protruding shelf of cheekbones and arching supraorbital ridges. The face consisted primarily of two big, hollow eye sockets, set beneath a high, hairless cranium. The large, upslanting eyes had decomposed to nothing but tiny wads of desiccated black gum. The small mouth, repulsively reptilian in its compressed neatness, was a straight, lipless slash above a pointed chin. The nose was a pair of fleshless slits. It was encased from neck to foot in a one-piece, tight-fitting garment of a dark metallic-weave material.

Brigid had never scrutinized Balam closely back at Cerberus—he'd never permitted it, erecting a quasi-hypnotic shield to mask his appearance from the ape-kin who held him captive.

Her visual inspection of the mummified corpse only confirmed what she had suspected. There was an eerie calm forever frozen on its cadaverous face, a quiet repose that went deeper than mere dignity. A kind of placid malice was stamped there, too, a sense of superior purpose and pitiless logic, but no real passion of any kind.

She took her hand away from the humped crystal form,

and the smoky vapor within it immediately swirled around the figure of the Archon again, obscuring it from view. She touched the cocoon again, and the vaporous substance immediately faded away, revealing the corpse. The crystal ovoid seemed to function as a self-contained stasis unit, an encapsulated survival system that had malfunctioned. Carefully constructed, it froze a subject in an impenetrable bubble of space and time, slowing to a stop all metabolic processes.

Theoretically the Archon could have waited forever to be released—except this unit had malfunctioned, protecting the creature sufficiently from the air and the elements so it didn't decompose, but not preventing mummification of the tissues. It could have lain there like that for twenty thousand years or twenty.

Brigid walked next to the stairway, testing her weight on the first few steps, then walked up to the gallery. A transverse ramp overlooked a big, hollow bay. Within it, nestled inside a cradle of massive clamps, was a saucer-shaped object, perhaps twenty feet in diameter. It had a silvery, metallic appearance, as bright as a newly minted coin. The alloyed skin was perfectly smooth and seamless with no surface protuberances of any kind.

Descriptive adjectives bubbled through her mind— scout ship, chariot of the gods, air horse.

Bright symbols were painted in red on the gleaming hull. These were not the indecipherable hieroglyphs, but Khalkha prayer inscriptions, sacred formulas intended to confer the might of the wind into the air horse.

Her lips twitched in a humorless smile. One of the clansmen, perhaps the Tushe Gun himself, had failed to find the entrance hatch to the small vessel and hoped that by daubing mystic words on it the secrets of its windborne power would be revealed.

She left the gallery and returned to the lower deck. She walked deeper into the ship, footsteps ringing hollowly from the metal floor plates, the echoes captured and lost in the silence. Yellow shadows chased themselves across the high, convex ceiling. Shapes loomed up and out of the golden-hued mist.

One shape she recognized. It was twelve feet tall and looked like a pair of solid black cubes, the smaller balanced atop the larger. The top cube rotated slowly, producing the steady, almost subsonic drone of sound. A faint whiff of ozone pervaded the air around it. It was a duplicate of the power generator in the subterranean Dulce installation, and it obviously still functioned, even if the stasis unit did not. The machine must have been self-perpetuating to have lasted this long, feeding its energy cells from some power source she could only guess at.

Rising around her was a complexity of electronic relays and connections like no machines she had ever seen. The extent of the circuitry faded into the darkness where the golden mist didn't reach. The panels bore an intricate arrangement of keys and readout screens marked with the hieroglyphiclike symbols. In the center of one console glared a red, backlit triangle, bisected by three vertical, round-topped lines.

A metal-framed rectangle of deep, glossy black hugged the curve of the wall above the main console. It looked like polished obsidian, ten feet in length and three in height. Four chairs, apparently molded out of one piece, rose from the floor before it. They were small and too narrow to comfortably seat even her own neat rear end.

Opposite the console stood a vertical arrangement of armaglass slabs, forming a hollow cylinder. The slabs were bound together, held upright by ropes and rusty chains. She paced around them and found a wooden door, reinforced with crudely hammered-out lead sheets, forced between a pair of armaglass sections. The door was heavy, but it had no knob or latch. Working her fingers between the wood and the armaglass, she was able to tug it open a few inches and see what lay on the other side. Two thick metal pillars rose from the deck plates, each one six feet tall, and mounted on top of each was a sphere that looked as if it had been sculpted from quartz. Between the pillars the floor lifted slightly, like a dais. Atop it was an interlocking pattern of hexagonal metal disks, exactly like the emitter-array platforms of the mat-trans gateways.

Mystified, Brigid inspected the area around the armaglass enclosure, and she found wooden crates marked with the number twelve, a collection of picks and shovels, a makeshift table holding the remains of a meal of mutton and bread, medical instruments and tech manuals written in Russian. She recognized most of the instruments as simple blood-testing equipment, a microscope and a small-scale fermentation tank. A small bottle contained a handful of yellow tablets. The label on the bottle was printed in Russian Cyrillic, and though she couldn't be sure, she thought the tablets were pain medication. She also saw power cables snaking off randomly and to no obvious purpose, precision tools, rad counters and a stack of batteries.

Returning to the control console, she saw the subtle marks of recent use upon the panels. Someone had manipulated the banks of buttons and keys not shaped for human use. She studied them silently, ignoring the steady, icy prickles spreading deeper through her body.

After a few minutes of thought and examination, Brigid began delicately pecking at the console keys. The sequence she chose was largely guesswork, following the intricate linkages and the marks of fingers upon the buttons. On impulse, she passed her hand over the panel glowing with the triangle symbol. A shimmering image rippled across the dark rectangle, swam, shifted, then broke apart into countless separate yet similar black components, then swirled again to acquire a new shape.

It took only a moment for her suspicions to form about what she was staring at, and when she did, she felt no sense of elation over the discovery.

She couldn't be certain, of course, lacking specific training, but she felt she was looking at the building blocks of the genetic code of mankind displayed on the screen. Thousands of strands of DNA, double helix upon double helix, corkscrewed from one end of the screen to the other.

Now she knew the black secret of the Black City, the proud history of the ancient Mongols with their tales of sorceries and magic rings and treasure vaults, and her throat closed up. She was sick, covered with cold sweat and closer to despair than she had ever been in her life.

She might have reacted differently if she were dealing with a dead race's leavings, sifting through archaeological evidence of vanished customs, science and beliefs. She could have adopted a clinical, detached view, perhaps spinning out a reasoned treatise on the subject of a crippled starship crashing in Mongolia ages ago, and how it was the source of a great many Oriental myths and religions. But the Archons were still here, alive in their science, their technology, mastering a knowledge that had conquered the stars while protohumans still gaped in wonder at lightning and fire.

Out of this buried spacecraft very well may have emerged the first altered version of Homo sapiens on

Earth. She wondered if she was also looking at the answer to a riddle that had bewildered predark anthropologists—humanity's enigmatic origins.

All she had accomplished was to uncover irrefutable evidence that the Archons had indeed attempted to manipulate mankind's genes in the dim past in order to control his destiny, his dreams, his spiritual evolution. There was no way of knowing what had worked and what hadn't, or what had led to unexpected results.

A laugh broke the hush, a sound as out of place and as musical as a flute, but Brigid didn't find it pleasant. She spun around on her heel, hand dipping inside her coat for the Mauser.

The Tushe Gun stood there, holding a three-foot-long saber, the blade resting lightly on his crooked left elbow. He looked the same as he had the first night she had seen him, with his outlandish costume and blank, masked face. Yet she sensed a subtle difference about him even as her blaster came out and trained on him.

The laugh came again, from beneath the layer of jade. "Ah, behold the fox-bitch, who knows a great many small things, yet the one big thing still eludes her." He spoke in Russian.

A man's voice spoke from the golden haze behind him. "The great many small things she has learned make for one very great thing."

Brigid set her teeth on a groan. Sverdlovosk sauntered out of the fog. He wasn't smiling, but only because his lower lip was split and leaking a trickle of blood over his chin. A fresh bruise blued the right side of his face, from cheek to forehead. His eye was surrounded by puffy, discolored flesh. Behind him was the trooper Kropotkin, standing by but keeping his distance.

The sword in the Tushe Gun's hand lashed out in a

humming semicircle. Brigid tried to step back, even as the point of the blade caught the tip of her blaster, snatching it from her grip so fiercely the delicate tendons in her hand flared with a stabbing pain.

Even as the Mauser clattered to the floor plates, two men materialized out of the mist and slammed into her, pressing her tightly between them. Her arms were wrenched back at cruel angles, her shoulder blades feeling as if they ground against one another.

The musty smell of the Mongols tickled her nostrils, and she didn't struggle against them. Though they were slightly shorter than she, they were exceptionally strong, with muscles like bunched steel cables.

Brigid kicked herself off the floor, using the sturdy clansmen as braces. Her booted feet came up and connected solidly against the underside of the Tushe Gun's jaw, lifting him up on his toes and sending him staggering back against Sverdlovosk.

The Mongols instantly tightened their brutal grips, forcing her to her knees with outraged grunts and shocked curses. She caught a glimpse of the jade mask falling to the floor.

The Tushe Gun clawed it up, dropping his saber in the process. He held the mask with both hands for a moment, glaring over it in maddened fury.

Brigid didn't cry out in horror at the sight, though under other circumstances she might have screamed, both in repugnance and pity. The Tushe Gun's features weren't those of a sixteen-year-old stripling. They were unlike any man's.

His beardless face bulged in places, pulsing, as if tiny living creatures burrowed paths just beneath the swollen flesh. The left eye was much larger than the other, red rimmed, glassy and staring, leaking a viscous fluid not resembling tears.

The mouth was distorted, the corners curving down in a permanent frown, the flabby bottom lip wet with bubbles of saliva. The whistling sounds coming from it were repellent, obscene. The few teeth in evidence were crooked and irregular—some were square and white, others small, jagged and brown. The nose was more like a snout, the tip broad, splayed and upturned, one nostril very small and delicate, the other a gaping, hairy hole caked with dry mucus.

Even as she stared, unable to tear her eyes away, a lump of flesh suddenly jutted out above his right eye, stretching the skin. The Tushe Gun hissed, a liquid, slurping sound, as if in annoyed pain. He brought the jade mask up to cover his face.

She remembered the ancient tradition, the same in almost every religious culture, which held that anyone who looked upon the face of God would most certainly die—from the terrible beauty and glory, and awe.

There was no dread beauty or awe here. The Mongols on either side of her were horrified into speechless immobility by the face of their god-king. They didn't look as if they expected to be struck dead. They looked more as if they expected to be sick.

If it was true the starship had been used as a bioengineering birthing ward, then the Tushe Gun wasn't made in the image of man, Archon or the divine.

He had crawled from the womb of hell.

Chapter 25

Colonel Piotr Sverdlovosk didn't join the pell-mell stampede out of the yurt in pursuit of Kane. It was a waste of effort, and considering the grens the American would no doubt employ, quite possibly fatal. If the Tushe Gun wanted to join the largely futile chase, then so much the better. Maybe he would fall victim to Kane's weapons, and old Boro would step into the power vacuum. He was much easier to manipulate than his crazed son.

The Russian looked with distaste at the prone form of the big black man, lying facedown and trussed up like a sheep. He regretted pistol-whipping Grant, but having one of his bargaining chips loose on the hoof was enough.

Like almost everyone else who had achieved a position of authority in Russia, Piotr Sverdlovosk had come up the ranks the hard way, by tooth and claw, by knowing when to combine opportunity with profit. The only people he had ever cared about were dead, and though he mourned their loss, he had no intention of joining them anytime soon. At fifty-seven, he had outlived most of his peers and he planned to do more than simply survive in the amount of time left to him.

The situation in Kharo-Khoto offered too much opportunity and far too much profit to allow himself to be distracted either by grief, respect or even sexual attraction. As darling Lenya had been attracted to Kane, Sverdlovosk was drawn to the Baptiste woman. She was naive, true enough, almost innocent, but she possessed a remarkable intellect and an inner reserve of strength that aroused him.

He knew that by appealing to her intellect and taking advantage of her endearing naiveté he could manipulate her to support his plan to wrest away the Tushe Gun's dreams of empire and turn them into his own reality.

A harsh breath rasped out of the unconscious Grant. Sverdlovosk eyed him doubtfully, then he knelt down beside him, keeping his gun in hand. If loyalty was one of Baptiste's failings, then it wouldn't be to his advantage to allow both of her companions to die—particularly if he could save one of them from suffocating by simply turning him over.

Grabbing a handful of the man's coat, Sverdlovosk heaved him over onto his back so his breathing wouldn't be obstructed. The eyes were closed, and he leaned forward, placing a forefinger on his neck to time the pulse. It was steady and regular. A sudden sound outside the tent commanded his attention, a crumping of an explosion, intermingled with a whooshing clap of displaced air.

He wryly noted the noise as characteristic of an implode grenade, one of the death-dealing devices he had allowed the outsiders to keep in order to earn their trust. He could hear cries of anger and pain and what he thought was the Tushe Gun's voice raised in a flurry of furious commands. Sverdlovosk reached for the buttons of Grant's coat to relieve him of his combat harness.

Grant's eyes suddenly snapped open. He hissed "Survival and success" just as his upper body jackknifed from the floor, his head thrust forward.

Like a battering ram, the crown of Grant's skull

smashed into Sverdlovosk's forehead. Grabbing at air, Sverdlovosk toppled over on his back, his blaster flying from his hand. Before his body settled on the floor, Grant's legs darted forward, hooking around his throat in a scissors hold.

Teeth bared in a grimace of fury and exertion, Grant applied the pressure, devoting the strength in his powerful leg muscles into choking the life out of the man. Knots, lumps and ropes of sinew rippled along his massive legs.

A drawn-out, gagging gasp burst from Sverdlovosk as he clawed frantically at Grant's boots, then grasped his ankles and tried to wrench them apart. When that failed, he swatted out for his handblaster, but it was far out of his reach. His legs thrashed as if he were running in place.

Grant continued the relentless pressure. Sverdlovosk's eyes distended, his tongue slowly protruded, his face darkened. At the precise moment his clawing fingers went slack, Grant disengaged the scissors hold, lifting one foot and pistoning it full into the Russian's face. The man flopped over, limbs boneless and motionless.

His face bathed in perspiration, chest heaving, Grant glared around the yurt, saw the sword lying beside the black-robed, throat-slashed corpse and scooted over to it on the seat of his pants. By feel alone, he plucked the weapon from the carpet and used the blade to saw through the thongs binding his wrists. He kept an eye on Sverdlovosk while he did, his ear pitched to the sounds of distant tumult outside the tent.

He managed to slice through the rawhide with only a couple of nicks and he immediately lunged for the Russian's handblaster. It was a Tokarev 9 mm, with a full eight-shot clip in the magazine. He cycled a round into the chamber, then gingerly explored the tender place on the back of his head. He cursed when he saw blood shining on the fingers of his glove.

Sverdlovosk's blow hadn't rendered him senseless, but the gun barrel had lacerated his scalp and put him in a daze for a couple of minutes. Grant stood over the prostrate Russian, prodding him with a foot. A moan bubbled up past his cyanotic blue lips. His lower lip was cut and bleeding, and the stain of a bruise was slowly spreading over his face. But the treacherous bastard was still alive.

Grant aligned the man's curly-haired head with the bore of the Tokarev, finger tightening on the trigger. As he did, a shadow of motion slid over the open portal of the yurt. Grant whirled, leading with the blaster, flame, noise and a copper-jacketed bullet blooming from it. He had only the briefest of impressions of a jade face before the Tushe Gun hurled himself backward.

A loud shriek erupted outside the tent. With the short sword in hand, Grant bounded to the far wall, kicking the plush cushions aside. He slashed the hide covering in a two-stroke X pattern and ripped his way out of the yurt. He thought about tossing one of his grens behind him, just to test them, but he decided to exercise discretion and run.

He stayed in the shadows as he sprinted into the roofless palace, leaping across exposed areas. The sun was almost down, and the moon was nowhere in sight, so he fumbled in his pocket for his dark-vision glasses. Though he heard a lot of yelling, it was on the opposite side of the courtyard, outside the gates.

He encountered none of the Mongols, and he wasn't ashamed of his relief. Though small in stature, they were powerful and bred for war, not like the slagjackers and jolt-walkers he had dealt with back in Cobaltville.

Grant reached the base of a high inner wall where blunt blocks of stone had tumbled down. Behind him he heard voices, drawing closer. He quickly glanced at the wall's surface, then leaped atop a heap of basalt. He saw indentations in the weathered wall. Jamming the Tokarev in a coat pocket, he began to climb.

He dug his fingers into narrow niches and pulled himself nimbly upward, bracing himself with footholds. He climbed recklessly, clawing and kicking his way upward. It was laborious work, made doubly so because he was trying for speed. Sweat dripped into his eyes, and the cold wind chilled the moisture on his face.

When he reached the top, he chinned himself up to stretch out on the three-foot width and catch his breath. His throat felt raw, and his hands were sore. If not for the gloves, his fingers would have been torn and bleeding.

From his vantage point he cautiously surveyed the fortress ruins. A sand-swept flagstone hall lay below him, empty doorways gaping between fallen walls and broken ivory-inlaid columns. Dust and sand covered everything in shallow drifts. On the far side of the floor, surrounded by a wind-scoured colonnade, he saw wide stairs descending into shadows. There were footprints in the dust on the steps.

He raised his head to look toward the city gates. Though twilight was fading fast into full night, there was still enough light to show him the commotion in the courtyard a hundred yards away.

Men milled around a wide gap in the wall, some climbing through it, others strung out in apparent confusion. A handful trotted back in the direction of the Tushe Gun's yurt.

Grant laughed to himself. He had heard the detonation

of the implode gren himself, and he now figured that Kane had used it to escape the city. To where, he had no idea. The valley, populated with the Tushe Gun's followers and labor force, wasn't much of an option. According to Brigid, the gateway unit was about fifteen miles to the west, but he doubted Kane would make for that. No, he would go to ground somewhere, make a recce and work out one of his over-the-top rescue plans. And maybe get himself chilled in the process.

Raising himself up to a half crouch, Grant craned his neck to look toward the center of the courtyard, to the white yurt that concealed the well, according to Sverdlovsk. A horse-drawn sledge sat idle nearby, with only a couple of jittery-looking men around it. Even as he watched, more warriors appeared, signaling each other in agitation. He guessed they were carrying word of yet another outsider loose somewhere in their holy city.

He could barely see the truck from his position, so he had no idea if Brigid was still aboard it, encased in her crate, or down in the vault. After gauging the odds for a handful of seconds, he concluded it would be safer to contact her than risk raising Kane.

Drawing out the pin mike, Grant opened her voice-activated frequency. All he heard from the transceiver tab was a snarl of static, as if his signal was being jammed. He waited, frowning. Warriors were spreading out in the ruins of Khara Bator's palace, picking their way over the tumbles of broken basalt. A couple of them held burning torches aloft, closely scanning the ground for tracks. But none of them looked up.

The wavering firelight was uncertain, and though the ground was sandy, it had a surface layer of pebbles and gravel and so was unlikely to retain footprints very well. But these men were probably experienced trackers. They had to be in order to survive in this bleak land. Despite his situation, Grant couldn't help but feel a twinge of admiration for them. If the Deathlands had held a tribe of such people, then the Program of Unification would have been pushed back on all fronts, at the very least delayed for several years.

The warriors shuffled away, their backs to him. Grant released a pent-up breath, then whispered into the pin mike. "Kane?"

He waited for a response, but when one was almost immediately forthcoming, he nearly fell from his perch in surprise.

"Grant? Is that you?"

"No, it's Piotr, doing an uncanny imitation of Grant's voice. I'm a gifted impressionist on top of being a back-stabbing son of a bitch. Of *course* it's me."

Kane's relieved laugh filtered out of the transceiver. "Did you escape?"

"Sure."

"Good. Saves me the trouble of coming up with a rescue plan."

"Which probably would have backfired on your ass, anyway. Where are you?"

"Just outside the city walls, in a tent with old Boro. He helped to hide me. Where are you?"

"Still inside the city walls," Grant replied. "On top of a palace wall, in fact. How are we going to hook up?"

"You still have your light?"

Grant patted his side pockets. "Yeah."

"I'll move back into the city in about—let's see—five minutes. Find a position where I can reach you without drawing attention to yourself. When you're set, signal me with the light. If I'm in, I'll signal you back. Are you heeled?"

"I boosted Piotr's piece."

"I fixed my holster, so I'm primed."

"Fixed it how?" Grant demanded.

"It's simple, but you'll need some light. Wait till I reach you." Kane paused, then asked, "What about Baptiste?"

"I don't know. I tried but I couldn't raise her."

"Acknowledged. Five minutes, remember."

Grant let go of the pin mike and twisted his head around, looking behind him. The wall led to a crumbling enclosure, the remains of an ancient balcony or watch post. He turned around, and in a squat-walk, moved toward it. His dark clothing and complexion against the dark sky made him a scuttling silhouette, and it would require exceptionally keen eyes to see him.

Reaching the enclosure, he peered over what was left of the brick battlement. A high heap of bricks was piled directly below. Raising his eyes, he saw men streaming back into the city through the breach in the distant wall.

Grant removed the microlight from his pocket and tightened the band around the middle finger of his left hand. He waited, consulting his chron every few seconds. When the five minutes elapsed, he clicked the Nighthawk on and off, twice.

A pinpoint of answering light flashed from the courtyard, from a Mongol trailing after the other warriors. Even at that distance and despite the dim light, the body movements identified it as Kane. Grant watched the figure approach, then it walked out of sight behind a mound of chipped stone. Three minutes later his trans-comm clicked and Kane's quiet voice announced, "Set."

Moving over to the edge of the enclosure, Grant looked down. He saw Kane crouched between two square blocks of basalt. No one was around, so he whispered into the pin mike, "Go."

Kane took off the fur-trimmed cap, unwound the scarf from around his face, shrugged out of a quilted coat and then, with a short run, reached the pile of bricks. He bounded on top of it with a nimble agility, leaped, caught Grant's outstretched arm and swung himself up and over the battlement.

"Where'd you get all that crap you were wearing?" Grant asked.

Panting, Kane replied, "Old Boro. I made him understand what I wanted to do, and though he didn't think much of it, he helped me."

Grant grunted and rolled up his coat sleeve, exposing his Sin Eater and its powerless holster. "Show me what's wrong with this nuke-shitting thing."

Turning on his microlight, Kane bent over it. "Did you chill Piotr?"

"No, but not for lack of trying. You use a gren on these guys?"

"An implode. Chilled a few, maybe even the Tushe Gun himself."

"You didn't. He came back to his tent and saw I was loose."

Kane voiced a noise of irritation, working on the holster mechanism. "You think Sverdlovosk told him about Baptiste?"

Grant shrugged. "Depends on how pissed off the Tushe Gun is. If he holds him responsible for bringing us here, then probably not. If so, Petey-boy probably only spilled his own highly revised version of who we are and what we're doing here. Either way…" He didn't complete the sentence.

Kane finished it for him, grimly. "Either way, Baptiste

is hip deep in something that isn't bath oil. She can't count on Piotr to protect her and sooner than later, she's bound to be discovered." He straightened up. "Try it now."

Grant tensed his wrist, and the Sin Eater slid smoothly into his waiting hand. He immediately felt about ten times better.

"The way I see it," continued Kane, "is to put the arm on the Tushe Gun, use him as a hostage."

"Hostage for what?"

"For Baptiste, and for safe passage to the gateway."

Grant scowled. "I don't think that's how Lakesh visualized the conclusion of this mission."

"I don't give a shit what that demented old prick visualized." Kane's answer was a fierce, uncompromising whisper. "*We're* the ones in Mongolia with a horde of barbarians desperate for our heads to end up as gateposts."

Grant considered his partner's words for a moment, examining them from several different angles. His reluctance to agree with Kane stemmed from his Magistrate's training of never leaving a job undone. But as Kane had pointed out numerous times over the past three months, neither one of them had pledged oaths of obedience or sworn vows to faithfully fulfill the missions Lakesh assigned them. When everything was distilled down into its basic elements, the three outlanders had a duty only to themselves.

Grant pushed his blaster back into its holster. "Let's do it."

They clambered out of the watchtower and along the top of the wall, back toward the vicinity of the Tushe Gun's yurt. They had negotiated half the distance when they heard the trampling of feet below them, just around a turn in the wall. Both men went flat, lying motionless.

Around the corner marched thirteen men, following behind the Tushe Gun and Sverdlovosk and the trooper called Kropotkin. Long muzzle loaders were slung across the warriors' shoulders, short swords clanked at their sides and blaster butts protruded from belts. They were escorting the Tushe Gun and the Russian into the hall, toward the descending stairway encircled by the colonnade.

Staring hard at the Russian, Grant's lips drew away from his teeth in a wolfish grin. Sverdlovosk's steps were unsteady, and he dabbed continually at his mouth with a red-stained cloth. The light was too weak to be certain, but it appeared as if a great bruise discolored the right side of his face.

When the contingent reached the mouth of the stairway, eleven warriors assumed sentry positions around the colonnade while two followed the Tushe Gun, Sverdlovosk and the Russian soldier down the steps.

Kane tapped Grant's heel, and his partner turned his head toward him. They shared a brief hand-signal conference, then continued to creep along the top of the wall.

Farther along, the ancient barrier pitched downward at a forty-five-degree slant, terminating in a great heap of shadowed rubble. They had to climb down in almost complete darkness, which was both a boon and a handicap. Pieces of jutting stonework crumbled under their hands and feet and bounced off the rock pile with knocks and clacks.

The two men didn't pause in their descent. So much stone fell from the ruins, dislodged by wind and time, that the people who spent much time in the city had probably grown accustomed to the sound.

Wearily Kane and Grant lowered themselves to the uppermost point of the mound of rock and stood for a moment, flexing their legs and rubbing their arms. Then they stealthily picked their way down the pile of broken stone and masonry. Kane, the more surefooted of the two, reached the scattered base of it first.

He had just planted both feet firmly on the ground when a voice rose in a shrill alarm. A shadowy figure stood only a score of feet away, struggling to unsling a rifle. Kane and Grant reacted simultaneously. The Sin Eaters reflexively filled their hands, and 3-round bursts roared from both blasters. All six rounds found the target.

The warrior's cry of warning ended in a liquid gurgle as the 9 mm blockbusters tore chunks from his throat and sent a geyser of pulsing blood all over his torso. He collapsed heavily onto his rifle.

For a second there was no sound but the rolling echoes of the killshots. Then, from around the bend in the wall, came an outcry of startled voices, followed by the thudding of many pairs of running feet.

"Take 'em," Kane ordered.

Without having discussed it, both men knew they were sick to death of running like deer from hounds. Acting as prey didn't come naturally to them, either by training or inclination. Grant and Kane broke around the corner of the wall in a dead run, firing as they came, even before they had acquired targets.

Nine warriors rushed from the colonnade with full-throated screams, unleathering swords, pistols and shouldering rifles. One of the Mongols fell, struck by a shot from Kane's Sin Eater, then the firefight got under way in earnest.

The Mongols had an instinctive or inbred grasp of tactics. They spread out across the area, some trying to cut their quarry off from a retreat. Their blasters were old, but they knew how to use them.

Shots cracked and boomed. Kane was buzzed by bullets swarming around him like killer bees. He dived behind a carved pillar, half-buried on one side, triggering his Sin Eater. Three bullets took one Mongol down after hammering him between the eyes.

Grant went to his knees behind the fallen column, and his two autoblasters began to roar in a beautifully synchronized rhythm.

A man with muzzle loader was hit with a hollowpoint one-two punch, knocking him backward, the rifle blasting thunderously into the air.

A barrage of bullets spewed from four heavy pistols, thudding into the pillar and chopping out fragments but not penetrating it. Kane and Grant kept their heads down and kept firing. The thunder of the gunfire was deafening, echoed and magnified by the walls of the empty hall.

A keening Mongol raced directly for their position, swinging a curved sword over his head and working the trigger of a big black revolver. Kane shifted the barrel of his Sin Eater and let loose a triple burst. The warrior quivered, doubling over, bleeding from three wounds in his belly. He fell facedown barely four feet from the stone column.

A ball fired from a muzzle loader took Grant in the left shoulder and spun him off balance against the column. He fired the Tokarev in return, and two rounds pounded the man who had shot him off his feet, his limbs twisting and convulsing.

Grant dropped the Tokarev, feeling numbness spreading from his shoulder, into his arm nearly to his elbow. His coat's special weave had cushioned the impact, but absorbed only a little of the projectile's kinetic energy.

He saw Kane, still laying down a left-to-right pattern of fire, pitch a metal ball with his left hand. For Grant's benefit he shouted, "Gren!" then buried his face in his arms.

Grant dropped, too, arms over his head, bracing himself for the explosion.

One of the warriors saw the object bouncing across the ground, and he opened his mouth to scream a warning. A thunderclap blast slammed his words back into his throat.

For a microsecond the area was haloed in a red flash. Then flying tongues of flame billowed outward. The detonation of the incendiary grenade hurled fire-wreathed bodies into the air, the concussion shattering bones and rupturing internal organs.

A fine rain of sand, pulverized pebbles and droplets of blood drizzled down. Grant and Kane looked up, over their stone shelter. Two warriors thrashed around in blind agony, screaming as they tried to beat out the phosphorus flames on their clothes and hair.

Grant shot them quickly, one merciful bullet apiece. He and Kane climbed to their feet, surveying the killzone with swift, appraising stares. The guard unit was thoroughly neutralized, their bodies scattered like broken, bloody dolls. The air held a throat-closing reek of smoke and cordite. The sweetish odor of seared human flesh made both men want to hold their noses.

Looking behind them worriedly, Grant said, "There are a lot more in the city than these poor bastards. I think we can expect—"

There was no need to complete his thought. A wedge of men, at least half a dozen, piled around the far end of the wall in a milling rush. Two of Sverdlovosk's hand-picked troopers led the charge. Their AKMs were out, and when they caught sight of the outsiders, they shouted commands. The warriors behind them began to fan out warily but swiftly.

Grant plucked a gren from his harness, unpinned it and lobbed it around the curve in the wall. Eyes wide and fearful, the Russian soldiers dug in their heels and tried to stop, but the men behind them continued to push them onward.

The high-ex compounds detonated in a tremendous cracking blast, and a blinding burst of dust and sand erupted from the ground. The sound of the explosion instantly bled into a grinding rumble of a stony mass shifting. The groaning grating overlapped the ringing echoes of the detonation, then overwhelmed it.

The grinding noise expanded into a rumbling roar. As Kane and Grant watched, a long section of the wall toppled forward in a crushing cascade of bouncing blocks and spurting dust. All the men were engulfed, buried by the tons of down-rushing rock.

Kane and Grant stepped quickly away, shielding their faces from ricocheting chunks of stone. After the rolling echo of the crash faded, there came a stunned silence, stitched through with a clicking of pebbles and faint moans. Grit-laden dust hung in the air like a blanket over the fallen mass of rock.

In the hushed quiet Kane whispered, "Like you said...cold-blooded but stylish."

Grant shook his head dolefully. "I didn't expect that to happen."

Kane started walking toward the colonnaded staircase, aware of a gnawing anger at the capricious ways of history. Kharo-Khoto had watched the millennia crawl by, yet he knew that he and Grant could blow the city apart so completely it would not even exist as a legend.

At the top of the stairs they paused to pop fresh clips into their Sin Eaters. The steps were steep and wide, almost like separate levels, three feet across and four feet deep. They faded into a yawning black abyss.

Kane recalled what Baptiste had said about abysses staring back into you and fighting too long against dragons. An image of the ferocious dragon ring flitted through his mind, and he touched the spot on his head where it had kissed him. He chuckled, a harsh sound without much mirth.

"What's so funny?" Grant asked.

Kane looked up, past the shattered roof arches, to the pinpoint lights of the stars. "Right at the moment I can't think of a goddamn thing."

Chapter 26

At a command from their masked leader, the two Mongols beat her, but their heart wasn't in it. They seemed to be in a state of shock. Kropotkin held her in a full nelson, and she relaxed against him, letting his body absorb some of the impact of the blows.

Open hands cuffed her face a few times, and her teeth cut into her lower lip, filling her mouth with blood and salt. She was concerned over the head trauma inflicted only days before by Bautu, worried that sustained blows to the head could put her into a coma.

But the Mongols, Tengri and Wan by name, moved their pummeling attention on her body, punching her repeatedly in the stomach. Through the jiggling tears in her eyes, she saw Sverdlovosk turn away.

"Enough," said the Tushe Gun, speaking Russian.

The Mongols responded to the masked man's tone, but they obviously didn't understand his words. The warlord repeated his command in their dialect, and they obediently stepped away.

Brigid sagged, hanging limply in Kropotkin's arms. The soldier released her, and she fell to the cold floor plates, letting blood ooze from one corner of her mouth. The Tushe Gun said something else, and the Mongols bent over her, yanking off her coat, using knives to slice through the laces of her boots.

Brigid didn't resist. Constant waves of pain washed

over her. Her ribs hurt, her stomach hurt, her breasts hurt, her head throbbed with a blinding boom-boom beat. She didn't fight as Wan and Tengri stripped her, but she didn't cooperate with them, either. She refused to expend another fraction of her sparse energy reserves on a futile struggle.

Her pants were tugged off, her sweater cut away, as well as her underclothes. Tengri and Wan grabbed her arms, pulled her to her knees and dragged her across the floor to the armaglass enclosure. The Tushe Gun opened the door to allow them to manhandle her inside and drop her to the metal hexagonal disks. They stretched her arms out straight, held them there, while the Tushe Gun lashed leather cords around her wrists, then tied the nether ends to the bases of the metal pillars.

Brigid hung there, on her knees, between the quartz-topped columns like a nude scarecrow, her mane of hair falling forward over her face. Blood dripped slowly from her mouth, filling the cracks between the hexagons.

The Mongols shuffled away, and she carefully tested her bonds. They were very tight, as tight as they had been that night in the valley. She heard the scraping of feet on the floor disks beside her and she turned her head. The effort brought pain to her neck.

Sverdlovosk squatted down beside her and tenderly fingered her hair from her face. His bruised face was sorrowful, pitying. In English he whispered, "I am sorry, but I cannot help you this time."

Carefully she moved her bruised lips, her tongue feeling thick and heavy. "Why?"

"My position is in jeopardy. The Tushe Gun suspects my motives, and if I interfere with what he has in mind for you, I will die."

"What about Kane and Grant?"

Sverdlovosk shook his head. "They are dead. It is truly regrettable, but all of you knew the risks."

Brigid winced her eyes shut, then opened them again. Her emotions were frozen within her. "It's not as if you gave us many choices. What *does* the Tushe Gun have in mind for me?"

"I really do not know. But I do know I am powerless to stop him. Be strong, my darling. Face what comes with dignity."

"Fuck off."

He patted her bare back comfortingly and stood up. The Tushe Gun walked around her, standing over her, leaning his back against a sheet of armaglass. "Look at me, fox-bitch. Look at me."

Brigid did, slightly shifting her legs, drawing them closer together. The jade face stared down, blank, expressionless and nauseatingly pretty. Light glinted dully from the dragon ring on his hand.

"Do you know who I am, outsider woman?"

Calmly she said, "Your name, I am told, is Shykyr."

The green mask wagged from side to side. "You were told incorrectly. I am not Shykyr."

"Then who are you?"

"I am Khara Bator. I am Temujin. I am Chupatai. I am Kublai. I am Timur. I am Babur the Tiger. I am Amursana. I am Dambin Jansang. The blood of all the Altyn Uruk, the Golden Clan, flows within me. I know what they knew, feel what they felt. I am the living embodiment of the Yasa, the code of the conqueror."

The Tushe Gun paused to inhale a slobbery breath and said scornfully, "How could you understand, an outside interloper, a woman?"

As much as she wanted to, Brigid didn't laugh. "I

might surprise you with how much I understand. I understand far more than you know. Far more than you.''

His spine stiffened. "You are a liar."

"And you are a victim."

The Tushe Gun's shoulders jerked in reaction to her words. "What do you mean?" he demanded raggedly.

"I think I've got this place—and you—figured out." Brigid raised her voice. "Piotr, are you there?"

His response was a colorless "Yes."

"Listen to me. You'll find this interesting."

A flush of pain worked its way from her wrists into her forearms. Brigid tried to ignore it. "This is a space vessel, converted to a biotechnology facility for genetic engineering. It's been here for thousands of years, probably when the Gobi was a fertile region.

"The crew of this ship, whether it was their primary function or not, monitored the evolutionary process of the indigenous Mongolian tribes. For some reason the Archons chose a certain genotype within an extended family group for their eugenics experiments. Over the centuries they sampled and stored this group's genetic information.

"They altered DNA in tiny details, over many generations, isolated particularly desirable genes and spliced them with others. They preselected the makeup of the entire genetic blueprint. Then particular individuals could be chosen to carry this set of precisely planned characteristics."

"This is heresy," snapped the Tushe Gun.

"Science, Shykyr." Gazing steadily at the masked face, she declared, very sincerely, "Nothing in this so-called vault was created by your forefathers. It was used by them, perhaps even altered from its original purpose and design, but it all originated elsewhere. This is not a sacred place."

"You lie." The words issued menacingly from beneath the mask. "Khara Bator, the Black Hero, built his mighty city and treasure vault so that his clansmen would benefit from his wisdom when he was gone."

Brigid nodded. "Khara Bator built this city over the starship, probably as a continuation of many cities that had existed at this site over the centuries. By the time Khara Bator settled here, only one of the Archons survived. It was to his benefit, not yours, to maintain the mystery of the treasure vault among your clan. Perhaps some sort of homing instinct was bred into your genes, so succeeding generations of your people would always be drawn back here."

"You lie," said the Tushe Gun again. "This is where the spirits of my ancestors dwell, waiting to pass on their fire, their magic to those of their blood. I stepped onto this altar, and all of them reincarnated within the flesh vessel I provided."

Brigid bit back a groan. The pain grew more intense, but she would not let the masked man have the satisfaction of knowing how much she hurt.

"As best as I've been able to understand, you didn't step onto an altar, but a genetic mingler."

"A what?" asked Sverdlovosk, surprise vibrating in his voice.

"This so-called altar of Shykyr's is built along the same principles as a mat-trans unit. The mat-trans breaks down organic material, digitally phases it into a noncorporeal state, then reassembles it."

Brigid paused to delicately spit out blood. "The molecular matrix patterns—the genetic code—of Shykyr's antecedents is stored in some kind of computer memory. I stumbled across it, just like he did. This unit replicates the chemical composition of the genetic material in the database.

"So, when Shykyr inadvertently activated the unit, his body was modified to receive all the characteristics of the genetic patterns in the database. He was re-created on a biochemical level. Probably if anyone who did not share characteristics with his clan was exposed to the matrix, they would die—"

Brigid broke off suddenly when she saw the Tushe Gun lean forward. He whispered. "Tell us more, fox-bitch, of all the small things you know."

She took a breath. "You are manifesting the physical characteristics of all your ancestors' congenital qualities, good and bad. Perhaps you even experience some of their memories."

"Of course I do," the Tushe Gun said scornfully. "They are *my* memories from all of my incarnations."

"The tap-line of memories is what kept you coming back, isn't it? Looking for the unlocked knowledge your ancestors had of this place. But you absorbed only crumbs—thousands of years' worth of memories, hundreds of thousands of petty details, of pointless actions, with no clear frame of reference."

The Tushe Gun grunted, clenching his right hand into a fist. The dragon's head on his finger glinted. "Unwise were you to intrude upon that knowledge."

Brigid nodded toward his fist. "Let's discuss knowledge, then. You claimed the magic ring of Genghis Khan, the master of all men. You know what it does, but not how or why. When worn by Genghis Khan, it did indeed make him master of all men, by introducing a mind-control implant into the brain."

"It is a gift from the star Shamos."

"A gift? It was a trick, so Genghis Khan would do the

bidding of the Archons, to create a legion of sword fod-
der in bloody wars of conquest. He was a puppet. And
now, after long centuries, another puppet is born. *You*,
Shykyr.''

The Tushe Gun began a retort, but he bit it off, barely
able to repress a groan. Involuntarily his right hand lifted
toward his head.

''You're in an almost constant state of pain, aren't
you?''

The direct question took the Tushe Gun by surprise,
but he didn't reply.

''I'm not a medical doctor, Shykyr,'' Brigid stated,
''but I can make a prognosis. The strain placed upon your
metabolism has dramatically reduced your life span. Your
own genetic code is overwritten in favor of those codes
belonging to men who have been dead for centuries. Your
run for a destiny is only a dance toward oblivion. Piotr?''

''I'm still here.''

''There's nothing for you here, either. The radiation
leaking out of this place is of an unknown type, but long
exposure to it is fatal. Can't you feel it?''

''Yes,'' Sverdlovosk replied. ''A little fire that burns
in the blood.''

''Evidently Khara Bator knew this when he sealed off
the well. The so-called sacred flame turned the Gobi into
a wasteland. When the city was excavated by Shykyr and
his clan, the toxins spread again, killing them slowly.
You must appeal to him to seal it up again. Otherwise,
everything he cares for is doomed.''

Sverdlovosk did not respond for a long moment. When
he did, his voice was a barely audible whisper. ''I believe
you, Baptiste. I supplied Shykyr with what I thought was
needed to forge an empire, and it cost the life of my dear
Lenya. But I've run too far down the road of destiny to

turn back now. The return journey would not be worth the effort." He cleared his throat. "You will die and I will watch, and that is all there is to it."

Brigid shook her head in sad resignation. "You're fools. Both of you. Shykyr, you will be known in clan legends as the ruler who murdered his own people because his eyes saw only mad dreams and not the truth."

The Tushe Gun's arm shot out, his right fist tangling in her hair, wrenching her head back. He spoke so quickly, his words so charged with emotion, that Brigid barely understood him. His eyes burned, but there was a glitter of tears in them.

"Do you feel the greatness of time in my hand? All the long, long ages are gathered within it. A hand that will guide you into the dark."

He released her, stepping back, breathing deeply and harshly. "And you have already guessed the method and manner of that guidance."

He heeled about, stamping forcefully over the metal disks. Brigid heard the wooden door scrape shut, fitting unevenly between the sections of armaglass. She waited with a dull sense of dread for whatever was going to happen. Her soul felt shriveled, lost in a fog of hopelessness and defeat.

She thought of humanity—foolish, venal, deceived and battered humanity—and its glories and aspirations.

She thought of her mother, of Kane and Grant, and of Kane again. If he was dead, at least she wouldn't have to watch him die.

The quartz spheres atop the pillars suddenly glowed with a muted red halo. The hexagonal disks below her exuded a silvery shimmer, like heat waves rising from sunbaked ground.

Brigid felt no heat, only a creeping blanket of energy

that scratched to her nerves. As if from far away, she heard the drone of the generator increase slightly in volume. Her limbs began to tremble. Sparks that were more energy than light flashed through the facets of the prisms, crackling fingers darting from one sphere to the other and back again.

It seemed she heard voices, very faint, thready whispers that skittered along the edge of her consciousness. Grayed images penetrated her mind, and she felt her own mind merge with them. She strained at the cords binding her wrists, and made a convulsive effort to get to her feet.

Memories, layers of thoughts belonging to unknown people, plucked at her mind, and she glimpsed the pictures and emotions and textures of thousands of years past. She could make no sense of them, all flying fragments of remembrances and experiences.

Brigid felt globes of perspiration form on her body, rolling down her face, between her breasts, sliding over her stomach. A moan of pain and fright rose somewhere in her throat. She was only partly aware of it. It was as though she were tumbling headlong down a black tunnel, buildings, green fields and faces flashing by in kaleidoscopic images. She plunged through a thousand memories so fast she couldn't comprehend any one of them.

The pain from the beating suddenly exploded in a fountain of pure, undiluted agony. There were no preliminary warnings. Brigid cried out as her body twisted in rhythms of bone-deep pain. She was bathed in it, consumed by it, her soul shredded by it.

In the one tiny pocket of rationality and identity left to her, she realized the quantum energies unleashed by the mingler were transforming her, impressing new genetic patterns over the old. It was a process that would eventually kill her—slowly and in sanity-shattering pain.

Dimly she heard the Tushe Gun's voice ask coldly, "Do you like knowing the one big thing, fox-bitch? I hope so. There is more to learn. Much, much more."

And the level of agony doubled, then tripled.

She screamed, long, loud and hard, fighting at her bindings like a mad animal. Her body writhed, arched itself in bizarre, cramped postures. Even as she screamed, even as the long arms of agony rocked her in a fiery embrace, she vaguely heard another sound.

It was the sound of hell breaking loose and running on a rampage.

Chapter 27

As Grant and Kane entered the stairwell, they turned on their microlights, throwing the wide, curving steps ahead of them into amber-and-gray relief. Taking the lead, Kane hugged the wall, blaster barrel probing ahead. A dry, dusty perfume pervaded the passage. In the splotches of shadow, green jewels winked. On the walls glittered little squares of jade, part of an elaborate mosaic that had long ago been smeared out of recognition by the cruel hand of time.

Neither man spoke as they quietly wended their way on the down-curving stairway. Both were all too aware that they could face attacks from above and below them. They heard nothing but their own controlled breathing and the scuff of their boot soles on the gritty stone steps.

The stairwell made another gentle turn, then ended abruptly against a massive door. Rust flecked the iron cross braces of the bronze portal. It was nearly seven feet tall and very nearly that in width. Shining their microlights on it, they saw oil glistening thickly on the hinges, but no sign of a knob or handle.

"Thing must weigh out to a quarter of a ton," said Kane, playing his light over this dully gleaming surface. He stepped back. "See if you can open it."

Grant eyed the heavy slab of metal skeptically, but he placed his massive shoulders against it and thrust with all the strength in his muscular calves and thighs. He might as well have been trying to uproot a mountain. Like the rest of Kharo-Khoto, the door had been built on a heroic scale.

Turning, he ran his fingers over it, probing the sill. "There must be a hidden bolt or latch someplace."

"We can use a gren."

Grant cast Kane a doubting glance, looked at the door, then back again. "A gren?"

"Two grens, then," snapped Kane impatiently. "Or all we have left. Why not? It isn't made of vanadium."

Grant rapped at it with his knuckles. "Might as well be. This thing is solid. Besides, grens might start a cave-in. How deep do you figure we are?"

"At least a hundred feet. Whatever's behind that door must be—"

He closed his mouth and whirled, glaring up the stairwell. Grant waited silently, straining his ears to catch the sound that had alerted Kane. A moment later he heard it, an almost imperceptible crunch-click of feet treading the broad steps.

Kane extinguished his microlight, motioning for Grant to do the same. Ahead and above them a very faint illumination flickered against the shadows. Leaning toward Grant, Kane whispered, "Stay here."

He vaulted up the wide steps, taking long-legged strides on the balls of his feet. The sounds increased in volume, and the light grew in brightness. Halting, Kane carefully peered around a curve in the wall.

Five Mongols climbed down the stairs, moving as quickly and as stealthily as they could from level to level. They paused for a second at each one before moving forward again. They were all armed with handblasters, and the man in the lead held an old bulldog lantern with the shutter closed, allowing just a thin slice of light to peep out.

Only three step levels separated them from Kane, and he felt a flash of irritation for not realizing that they were being trailed. With his night-vision glasses, he could see the face of the man with the lantern. It was the Mongol called Gombo.

Raising the Sin Eater, Kane squeezed off a 3-round burst just as Gombo stepped down to the next level. The bullets struck the man directly behind him in the lower belly, swatting him double, driving the air out of him in an aspirated screech.

The warriors flattened against the stair wall and returned fire, Gombo dropping flat, his big blaster belching flame and thunder. Bullets tore white gouges in the stonework above Kane's head, sprinkling his hair with rock dust. He slid backward, grimacing at the ricochets whining all around.

When he was out of range behind a curve, he turned and loped back to Grant. "We're screwed," he told him grimly, "if we can't get that door open."

"I can't find the latch or spring catch. We're going to have to go with your plan."

"A gren?"

"Grens, plural."

Kane eyed the door again. "Let's use three, keep one back in case we can't open the door and we have to fight our way back topside."

"This is going to be a classic one-percenter."

Kane smiled thinly. "Good. I'm keeping track of them all, you know."

While Kane stood watch at the foot of the stairs, Grant swiftly doffed his coat and unbuckled the combat harness, removing the ammo clips and stuffing them into his pockets. He rearranged the grens on the harness, connecting their pull rings to the same hook. He hung the harness onto the iron cross brace of the door, the grens bunched together like a harvest of deadly fruit.

''The bastards are moving again,'' hissed Kane anxiously.

Shrugging into his coat, Grant moved up directly behind his partner, standing back to back with him. ''Set.''

Kane tensed his legs and breathed, ''Go.''

Kane lunged up the steps in one fluid movement, the Sin Eater in his fist blazing on full auto, playing the fireline back and forth. The Mongols were on the very next level and they began a screaming, stumble-footed retreat. The stuttering Sin Eater cut a swathe through the astonished men, stitching their chests, ripping holes in arms and legs.

Gombo and another man returned the fire with their big-bored double-action revolvers. Flame tongues lapped out of the barrels, and bullets knocked fist-sized chunks of stone out of the walls and the ceiling.

A hammer blow punched Kane in the stomach, smashing the air out of his nose and mouth, bending him double in shock and pain, numbing his mind and body for a split second.

In that moment Grant snapped off a single shot at the incend gren hanging between the high-ex and the fragger. It had a percussion-charge detonator, and a hard jolt was all that was required to set it off.

The 9 mm round penetrating its thin metal shell was a sufficiently hard jolt. The world dissolved in a blinding flash, a clap of thunder and a blooming burst of hellish light.

Chapter 28

Kropotkin heard the faint rattle on the other side of the big door, like faraway raindrops drumming on a distant tin roof. He cocked his head, listened and recognized the steady chatter of autofire, mingled with sharp, single-shot cracks.

He glanced quickly over his shoulder and just as quickly averted his gaze, restraining the impulse to cross himself. Shimmering, paper-thin wafers of light pierced the cracks between the upright slabs of armaglass. The nude figure with outstretched arms was a smudged silhouette on the other side of them. The colonel and the mad Mongol calling himself the Tushe Gun stood with two warriors beside the long control console, watching the flashing corona.

Kropotkin sensed his commander's unease, and it welled up within him, too. Unobtrusively as possible, he walked through the odd, gold-glowing haze to the massive portal by which they had entered the vault. He opened his mouth to report the sounds of blasterfire from without, but he said nothing.

He didn't even cry out in shock when the big metal door suddenly erupted from its frame, driven by a roaring torrent of superheated air and flame. The ponderous square of bronze and iron smashed squarely into Kropotkin, completely pulverizing all the fragile bones in his face, caving in his ribs, splitting his skull from hairline to his nape. He sailed backward with the door, his body momentarily spread-eagled against it.

When it tilted over and clanged down on the floor plates, Kropotkin was underneath it, its weight crushing every bone in his body, squashing all his organs to paste.

The cyclonic sounds of the explosions and the door banging down were physical assaults to the ear, the air shivering with a bass-register vibration.

Bricks and dirt pelted down from the ceiling of the stairwell, mixing with billowing rolls of noxious smoke. Layers of flame clung to the walls and steps. Sverdlovosk, Tengri, Wan and the Tushe Gun stumbled back, stupefied by the truly apocalyptic noise and the shock waves.

Through the horizontal mushroom of smoke plunged two drunkenly reeling figures. Twists of smoke curled from Grant's coat, and his face was skinned and abraded. Kane held a hand over his midsection, as if he were trying to bottle up pain, and blood streaked down his face from a laceration in his scalp.

They staggered to an unsteady stop just inside the vault, blinking, resisting the cough reflex. The brains of the two men were too numbed by the brutal concussion of the triple explosion to be impressed by what their eyes saw. Smoke blended with the strange, gold-flecked haze, like the eerie underwater scene of a sediment-filled lake.

They did register the presence of the four men standing near a complex of machinery. Sverdlovosk gazed at them with stunned, wondering eyes and he shouted something, but his voice didn't pierce the pained throbbing of their abused eardrums.

The jade-faced man seemed frozen to the metal floor, as were the two Mongols.

Grant's and Kane's eyes were drawn to the collection

of upstanding armaglass sections. Light pulsed from behind them, strobing in an almost hypnotic pattern. It looked like a homemade gateway, slapped together in a catch-as-catch-can manner.

For only a microsecond Kane's eyes registered a human outline behind the semitransparent walls. His mind replayed the brief, almost subliminal image of the kneeling figure inside the enclosure, and a horror flooded through him, washing away the groggy cobwebs.

Without a word he sprang forward, vaulting over the fallen, burning door, oblivious to the men at the console. Kane ran as fast as he ever had, legs pumping, feet spurning the metal floor plates. He caught a peripheral glimpse of one of the Mongols sprinting toward him, trying to intercept him, fisting a short-bladed sword.

The man's legs suddenly went out from under him as if he had slipped on an oil slick. As he went down, Kane noticed that his features were blurred by a wet, red smear. On the fringes of his hearing, he heard the hollow boom of Grant's Sin Eater.

Kane reached the door, noting absently that irregularly cut sheets of lead foil were nailed to it. Forcing his fingers into the crack where its edge joined with an armaglass section, he heaved back on it, the poorly planed bottom dragging along the floor.

He recoiled from the throbbing flare, raising his hand to shield his eyes, but he saw Baptiste, on her knees with arms outflung, as if she were humbling herself before a grotesque god. Her head dipped down toward the sparkling hexagonal disks beneath her.

He felt the feathery touch of energy as if he were breasting invisible waves of static electricity. Squinting, he saw that the bright skeins of plasma came not from the floor, but leaped and caromed from a pair of crystal orisms on either side of Baptiste. Little flames, gold and orange and greenish blue, danced over her limbs, creating a borealislike nimbus around her body. He raised the Sin Eater, not contemplating the consequences.

The blaster, still on full auto, spit a solid stream of rounds at the sphere on Baptiste's right. The bullets chipped out splinters, shards ricocheting away to splat into shapeless blobs on the armaglass. He maintained the pressure on the trigger. Empty shell casings flew from the ejector port, tinkling down at his feet.

The quartz prism burst in a nova of flying sparks and coiling ribbons of yellow plasma. The glow exuded by the floor disks dimmed instantly, and Kane shouldered his way past the door and onto the platform, dropping to his knees beside her, whipping out his knife to slash through the cord tethering her to the right-hand pillar. She slumped over, her body glistening with a sheen of perspiration. Blood shone on her face, black, blue and purple bruises marked her stomach, her ribs. Her eyes were closed, and her full breasts rose and fell in a spasmodic, uneven rate of respiration.

His brain clouded with a homicidal fury that he had never known before. He cut the cord binding her to the other metal post and caught her up in his arms. Her body was stiff, terrifyingly cold.

The other quartz sphere continued to crackle and spark, spitting arcs of energy in random, twisting patterns. One passed by Kane's cheek, fanning it with a hot, tingling shock. The spiral caressed an armaglass wall, leaving a smoldering scorch mark.

Kane tried to lift Baptiste in a fireman's carry, but her deadweight nearly bore him to the floor. Teeth bared, he hoisted her up under one arm, stumbling toward the chamber door. He almost made it.

A spear of energy sprang from the orb and impaled his back. He could do nothing but scream as agony overwhelmed him, filled his mind with nothing else, sweeping away all the strength in his arms and legs. When he felt himself falling, he pushed Baptiste out ahead of him.

Grant was there to catch her in his arms, preventing her limp body from slapping down on the hard metal deck. As he staggered back, trying to keep his footing, he saw Kane falling forward just inside the chamber, sparks showering colorfully from the back of his coat. Though his hearing was still impaired, it was penetrated by a sound he had never expected to hear from his partner—an unrestrained howl of agony.

Grant tried to maintain his balance under Brigid's slack weight and, overburdened, he felt rather than heard a *whup* of displaced air beside his head.

The second Mongol held a revolver in a two-fisted grip, shifting its barrel to align him in its sights. Grant fired from the hip, his arm crooked around Brigid's waist. One of the bullets punched his chest, crushing his sternum, the second lodged in his brain as he was folding and the third zipped between Sverdlovosk and the Tushe Gun, striking a spark from the bank of machinery.

The two men dived away in opposite directions. Rather than loose indiscriminate shots, Grant placed Brigid down gently on the floor. He slapped her sharply on both cheeks, with his left hand. Her head lolled around, and he struck her again—hard. Her eyes opened. No thoughts, no emotions were reflected in them. The expression on her face was dull, defeated, lifeless. He started to shake her, then a shadow of motion shifted over his shoulder.

A hard, thin object chopped lengthwise across Grant's lower back. The force of the blow sent shivers of pain into his kidneys, knocking him bodily forward, very nearly smashing all the wind out of him.

Fighting off the instinct to curl into a wheezing, gasping ball, he elbowed himself onto his side. His spine felt severed, but he knew it wasn't because he could still move and still hurt.

Gombo stood over him, both hands gripping a sword, and he lifted it for another downward stroke. The man's ravaged face was a clot of cooked tissue, peeled raw and covered by leaking blisters. His hair stood in charred, stinking clumps over his burned head. His clothes hung in smoking rags from his heat-seared body.

Only the coat had saved Grant from being cleaved in half, but his head was unprotected, and the next chopping stroke of the sword would mercilessly split his cranium. He brought up the Sin Eater—and a crushing weight slammed it down again, grinding his wrist bones into the floor.

Sverdlovosk stood on his gun hand, bringing all his weight to bear on his right foot. His left foot swooped up and smashed into the side of Grant's head like a club. He snarled something in Russian, a command.

Gombo scuttled close, sword held at a right angle to his body, positioning himself for a decapitation. He laughed, an animal, guttural sound like a throaty gargle.

Grant drew up his knees in a protective gesture. He shot both heels upward with a pistoning force into the Mongol's crotch. Lifted in the air, Gombo sailed backward. He hit the floor hard on the back of his head and neck, sword blade chiming against the deck plates. He made a convulsive effort to rise, then fell back and made no movement after.

Making a hissing noise, Sverdlovosk dropped, driving a knee into Grant's diaphragm, pushing the air out of his lungs. He wrapped his fingers around Grant's neck, thumbs pressing relentlessly against his windpipe. He was exceptionally strong, his strength pumped up to new levels by panic and terror.

Grant tried to free his right hand, still pressed beneath Sverdlovosk's foot, and he struggled to prise open the fingers digging into his throat. The Russian's sweat-sheened face twisted in a soundless snarl of exertion and a mad determination.

Piotr Sverdlovosk's expression suddenly changed, molding itself into a rictus of wonder and pain. A neat blue-rimmed hole appeared magically above his right eyebrow, and the back of his head broke apart. Through the pounding of blood in his ears, Grant heard that single, telling shot.

Sverdlovosk's fingers clamped down hard in a death spasm, then fell away. Grant hurled him aside with an open hand, turning over to see Kane clinging to the open door of the armaglass enclosure. His finger kept pressing the trigger of his Sin Eater, producing only the dry click-ings of a firing pin striking an empty chamber. Behind him bolts and arcs of energy flashed and coruscated wildly.

Gasping for breath, Grant scrambled to his feet and rushed to Kane. His blood-smeared face was blank with shock, with something beyond shock. He held himself with an unnatural stiffness, as if he were afraid to move, but he allowed Grant to support him and lead him, one baby step at a time, away from the door.

In a clear, distinct voice Kane announced, "I'm hurt."

"How bad?"

"I don't know." He spoke very quietly. "If I drop dead in the next second, I guess we'll find out. If tha happens, leave me and get yourself and Brigid out of here.''

Kane's words and his tone frightened Grant, but in a different way than mere fear. He tightened his grasp around Kane's waist. "We'll leave together."

"What about the Avenging Lama?" asked Kane hoarsely. "We can't leave him to seed."

"Forget about him."

"Forget, hell." Kane's voice thickened with emotion. "He tortured Brigid, did something unspeakable—"

Without warning, the man with the jade mask exploded from behind them. He raged between them in a whirlwind flurry of spinning kicks, elbow thrusts and hammer blows with the boss of his saber. He screamed and shrieked, and though neither outlander comprehended a single word, they understood him perfectly.

Grant reeled, caught himself and whirled. In an inhuman blur of speed, the Tushe Gun bent and pivoted gracefully. His foot caught Grant under the chin and sent him sprawling.

A laugh went up, mirth that was half an animal scream of sheer savagery. The jade face turned toward Kane, and he fancied its flat planes were sculpted into a mask of malignant glee.

The blade of the saber slashed out, like the razored tongue of a monstrous serpent. The tip bit into his coat sleeve. He lashed out with his combat knife and missed his target completely.

Off balance, Kane didn't try to recover. Instead, he let the momentum carry him forward to collide with the Tushe Gun. Their arms automatically clasped each other, their hands holding at bay the straining blades.

Kane looked into the mad black eyes and could smell the feral breath of the masked man. They locked for a long moment in a quivering embrace, bracing themselves on spraddled legs.

Kane knew he had made a grave tactical error. The Tushe Gun was much stronger and more than his match in a contest of strength. He was also too closely entwined with the man for Grant to make a lifesaving shot, even if he had stirred from the floor where the Tushe Gun's savaté kick had sent him.

On impulse Kane snaked a foot around his opponent's right knee, pulling forward with a hooked ankle. It cost him his balance, but the masked man's knee buckled at the joint.

Releasing his grip on Kane's wrist, the Tushe Gun tried to catch himself and spring back at the same time. Kane maintained his grasp on the man's forearm, using the elbow of his freed arm as a battering ram, whipping it forward, chocking it solidly into the hollow of his throat.

A gush of saliva spilled from the Tushe Gun's lower lip as he wrenched himself loose and threw himself backward, away from Kane's follow-through knife slash. Instead of gutting him, the blade opened a gash in his hip.

Struggling to draw in air, the Tushe Gun swung his saber in a flat, whistling, backhand semicircle. The clang of steel clashing against steel resounded loudly, and the knife was flicked from Kane's hand.

He didn't hesitate. He threw himself forward, shouldering the Tushe Gun backward, half lifting him from his feet. Kane's boots slipped and skidded in the pool of blood flowing out from Sverdlovosk's bullet-broken skull.

Kane fell, dragging the Tushe Gun with him. They grappled savagely, rolling on the deck. Kane battered at the green face with his left fist, pounding it repeatedly with hammering downward jabs from the shoulder. His mindless fury made him oblivious to the pain searing his knuckles and streaking up his wrist.

Crimson squirted from beneath the layer of jade, streaming in rivulets down either side of the Tushe Gun's chin. The mask acquired a hairline crack, then an entire spiderweb network spread across it.

The pommel of the saber crashed twice against the side of Kane's head, and for a moment his surroundings winked out of existence.

When they came back, he was on his hands and knees, fighting to gain his feet. The warrior-lama was erect and he kicked him in the face. Kane flopped onto the deck, tried to get up again. Another ruthless kick in the lower belly, then two, three, maybe four times.

Maybe more than that—he lost count. He made an effort to push himself up, but his arms folded beneath him. His strength was all gone, drained out of him by the kill-rage. He was sick and bleeding inside, and his body was one flaming torch of pain. It cost him much to breathe, to see, to even live. He knew if he closed his eyes, he would fall down a big, black, bottomless hole. Something caught at his throat, and he coughed reflexively, tasting blood.

He watched as the green mask turned and stared at Grant, who was climbing to his knees. The Tushe Gun leaped for him, a booted foot driving into the big man's belly. Grant folded around that foot, making no sound.

The Tushe Gun lifted his saber over his head with both hands and voiced a deep grunt of triumph. Holding the blade high, he returned to Kane. The polished sword dipped down, touched the base of Kane's neck where it joined with the shoulders, then whipped up high again. The Tushe Gun began to sing.

The song insinuated itself into Brigid Baptiste's empty mind. With a great effort she recognized it as a hymn in the Khalkha tongue, a musical declaration of personal liberty.

"High among the snow-clad peaks of the mountains stands a tent.

It is white as the sun white peaks, and from its entrance the Avenging Lama gazes along the horizon.

His stallion is white and swifter than the arrow and upon it he overtakes the wild deer—"

There wasn't much left of Brigid Baptiste—a few threads of memory, the odd little scrap of emotion. Broken pieces of another time, another place wafted through her frozen consciousness. They were vignettes, half-formed images that were all middles, with no beginnings or endings.

She saw herself lashed to the stirrup of a saddle, lying in the muddy track of a road. Men in chain-mail armor laughed and jeered above her, and long black tongues of whips licked out with hisses and cracks. Callused hands fondled her breasts, forced themselves between her legs.

Then she saw a man rushing from a hedgerow lining the road. He was thin and hollow-cheeked, perhaps nineteen or twenty years old. His gray blue eyes burned with rage. She knew him, she called out to him, shouting for him to go back, go back....

He knocked men aside to reach her, and a spiked mace rose above his head, poised there for a breathless second, then dropped straight down.

Her lips formed one word, a breathy rustle. "Kane..."

She wasn't truly aware of what her body did next, but

it levered itself to its feet, fingers closing over the leather-bound grip of a sword on the floor, stumbling forward in a clumsy half fall.

"The falcon on his strong wings hunts the wild swans, but the Avenging Lama is swifter than the strongest falcon."

She felt a resistance travel up her arm, then saw the jade face turn slightly toward her. The song ended, replaced by a wet, burbling laugh. Brigid staggered, pitched against him and fell atop Kane, her body draping his limply.

The Tushe Gun's laugh clogged in his throat. He stood, saber still hovering overhead, and looked down at the slash in his tunic from which his heart's blood was pumping. He cast his eyes down to the naked woman at his feet, saw the short sword in her hand and how the blade glittered redly in the light flaring from the armaglass chamber.

He sucked in a long, wet breath, braced his legs and swung the saber down at the soft exposed nape of the woman's neck. Then the cracked jade mask flew apart in spinning green shards.

Grant caught only a vague impression of the distorted face underneath, and then the face flew apart, too—the jawbone dissolving in a red-rimmed furrow as splinters of teeth erupted from the gaping mouth amid a liquid column of crimson.

The echoes of the Sin Eater's fusillade rolled and rang as Grant marched forward, stiff kneed, arm extended straight out, the blaster at the end of it continuing to spit fire and lead.

The Tushe Gun careened away from the 9 mm barrage,

body jerking and twitching under the multiple impacts. His boots slid and rasped on the floor as the bullets drove him into the open door of the chamber. Heels catching on the edge of the raised floor, he fell unceremoniously onto his back, legs kicking furiously.

A tendril of arcing energy brushed the saber in his hand. A sharp report shook the chamber, and the Tushe Gun writhed within a cocoon of blinding flame. A halo of smoke surrounded his body, but his crisped gauntlet still gripped his sword hilt. The blade was gone, melted and nearly vaporized by the plasma. Little blobs of semi-liquid steel clung to his blackened sleeve. The dragon ring was a splatter of molten droplets gleaming on the fingers of his right hand.

Grant shoved the door shut with a shoulder and leaned his weight against it, content for a long moment to see nothing, hear nothing and do nothing. Then he sleep-walked over to the motionless bodies of Kane and Brigid.

Kneeling down, he pulled her up and over, cradling her in his arms. Kane's eyes were open, glassy with pain and fatigue. Brigid's lips formed words over and over, repeating the same tiny, faint whisper. He ducked his head so he could understand.

She said, ''You were trying to save me, but I wasn't going to watch you die. I wasn't going to watch you die.''

''What's she saying?'' Kane croaked.

Grant didn't answer and he wasn't sure why. He smacked her face quickly. ''Pull yourself together,'' he whispered urgently into her ear. ''We're okay for now, but only for now. Pull yourself together.''

Her emerald eyes looked up at his face, and sudden joy shone in them. Then terror engulfed them, and she opened her mouth as if to scream.

Grant shook her. "You're all right, Brigid. You're all right. All of us are *all right*."

"Grant," she murmured hoarsely. "Where's Kane?"

"He's right here. All of us are here."

"So tired...hurt so much."

"We all do, but we've got to suck it up. We're not out of this yet."

Kane shifted slowly and carefully on the floor, making several attempts to prop himself up on his elbows. "When we get back," he said in a husky whisper, "I'm going to take your advice and do it."

"Do what?"

"Find myself a remote little spot and live in a tent with a stickie slut."

Grant rolled his eyes, then swiveled his head to survey the smoke-wreathed carnage, littered with corpses, empty shell casings and widening pools of blood. He glanced toward the bloodied face of Kane and looked down at Brigid. There was some color back in her face, and the defeated, drained look had gone. She smiled up at him wanly. Her smile was infectious, and almost miraculously he felt his exhaustion and pain ebbing away. He tightened his arms around her and said pridefully, "What a team."

Chapter 29

It took them longer than expected to pull themselves together. Brigid was in the worst shape, Kane following a close second. All three of them were shaky, weak and in pain.

While Grant helped her to get dressed, Brigid told him that Kane had received a direct shot of the plasma energy in the chamber, while she had been exposed mainly to its overspill.

Leaning on him while she stepped into her pants, she said grimly, bitterly, "The unit tinkers with everything that makes you *you*. It destroyed Shykyr long before it chilled him."

Kane, returning from an inspection of the area, said fiercely, "We should return the favor and destroy it."

Grant eyed him dourly as he held Brigid's coat so she could slip her arms through the sleeves. "This place—this ship—has been here for thousands of years. It survived the Chinese army, even the nukecaust. How do you figure to do it?"

Kane jerked a thumb over his shoulder toward the droning, two-tiered generator. "We didn't blow the one in Dulce because we didn't know what would happen. Let's find out now."

Brigid winced as she dropped her arms to her sides, and her and Kane's eyes met in mutual sympathy. "Knocking out the generator may not do anything."

"There's a lot of wild energy in here already," he replied, gesturing to the light pulsing within the arma-glass-enclosed chamber. "Maybe we can arrange a chain reaction."

Grant commented wistfully, "Wouldn't that be nice. But what can we use to start that reaction?"

Kane held his left hand out. A high-ex gren rested in his palm.

"Again with the grens. Or gren," rumbled Grant. "Even if that one itty-bitty gren can do damage, it doesn't have a timer on it. We'd get fried, too."

Kane grinned, dipped his right hand inside of his coat and brought out four paper-wrapped cylinders. Each one was about a foot long, and they were bound together by black tape. A coil of primer cord dangled from the center of the cylinder cluster. Both Grant and Brigid looked at him in surprise.

"Where'd you find that?" Grant demanded

"In a crate over there, along with some other exca-vating materials. When they unearthed and cleared the city, I figured they had to use demolition charges. Sverd-lovsk wouldn't supply them with anything too expen-sive or complicated, not when cheap, old-fashioned dy-namite would do the trick."

Grant laughed. "Leave it to you to sniff out anything that goes boom."

Kane angled an eyebrow at Brigid. "What about you, Baptiste? No objections to destroying a historical site or priceless artifacts?"

Her emerald eyes glinted with fury, with loathing. "Blow it to hell so no one can ever find it again, not even the Archons."

There was no need of further discussion. Grant and Brigid went to the stone-clogged stairway. She paused briefly beside Sverdlovosk's corpse and shook her head sadly.

Grant snorted. "Don't shed any tears for him."

"I won't. He met his destiny."

Though the first three step levels were cluttered with fallen blocks and rock debris, the passageway beyond was clear. Grant called the information out to Kane, who waited beside the base of the generator.

He placed the bound sticks of dynamite in the right angle where the lower tier disappeared into the deck plates and balanced the gren atop them. He hoped that when the dynamite detonated, it would set off the fulminate of mercury primer in the gren and quadruple the destructive power of the explosion. Still, the black cubes were made of an unknown metal, and he wished he had a canister of nitro-starch to spread around, as well.

Backing away, he played out the fuse, stretching it out straight. He set it afire with his lighter, a simple steel-flint device that he normally only used to light cigars. The end of the fuse sputtered, smoked and sparked. He turned and ran. He calculated that the yard-long cord had a burn time of approximately three minutes, a minute a foot. By his reckoning it had taken him and Grant at least that long to descend the stairs. Ascending them was a different matter altogether, considering their physical condition.

In the passageway they moved swiftly, though painfully, bounding from step level to step level, over and past the corpses of the Mongols, kicking loose stones from their path.

The three of them carried fully loaded blasters, since they had no idea of whom or how many they might meet on their way up.

Kane labored for breath, sweat cutting runnels in the

dried blood on his face. He ached in every bone and he coughed once, his mouth filling with blood-laced bile. The gnawing pain from the plasma-bolt discharge worked its way through his back and into his chest cavity. It steadily became unbearable. Every breath he took was an agony.

Still, he ran, shoulder to shoulder with Baptiste, for once allowing Grant to take the point. Their run-leap-run movements were like a mechanically repetitive ballet, danced out in the depths of a dead city.

Brigid stumbled, but Kane didn't give her the opportunity to fall. He clawed out at her hands, caught them and pulled her along with him. She looked at him once, and in the amber glow of his microlight, he saw in her eyes a pain so intense as to dwarf his own.

The darkness suddenly moved around them, the steps shifting beneath their feet. A tremendous explosion cannonaded up from the blackness behind them. A brutal column of concussive force rushed up the stairwell, slamming into them like an invisible tsunami, buffeting them up and off their feet. A black glob of smoke flung itself from the throat of the stairwell like a boulder launched from a catapult.

They flew up and out into cold, clean air, rolling painfully over the flagstoned ground. A series of consecutive hammering blasts thundered up. The colonnade around the stairwell shook and trembled. The walls showed cracks, and rifts split the ground. Rocks and mortar, shaken loose from the ancient walls overhead, sifted down. The ground heaved and shuddered. A fissure opened up around the mouth of the stairwell with a clash of rending rock and a distant shriek of rupturing metal.

Cornices and basalt blocks toppled down, one crashing into and knocking over the colonnade. They staggered to their feet and reeled, doing their best to maintain their balance and footing on the convulsing earth. All of them shared the same fear—that the chain reaction ignited by the explosives was atomic in nature. Sverdlovosk's story of the Tunguska disaster evoked visions of a miles-high mushroom cloud swallowing all of the Black Gobi.

The three of them dodged, ducked and ran, heading for the open courtyard. Blocks of stone dropped like bombs from the walls around them. A huge cube tumbled down from overhead, driving up jets of dust. Pillars that had been rooted in the same spot for millennia snapped off at the base like flower stems. Over the cataclysmic cacophony came screams of terror, pain and panic.

Skirting a low, quaking wall that shivered itself to rubble, Brigid, Kane and Grant found themselves dashing across the courtyard to the rear of the palace ruins. The walls collapsed, crashing inward, block after block, crash after crash.

With a roar like a hundred mingled waterfalls, the fortress of Khara Bator, the Black Hero, seemed to rise into the air, then collapse and scatter in exploding fragments. A reverberating, extended thunderclap rolled as the ruin imploded, walls folding in on themselves, roof arches breaking and cascading down in a contained avalanche.

They made for the city walls, slowing their mad pace only a trifle. Brigid cast a feverish glance over a shoulder, toward the vicinity of the well. The yurt that had covered it lay aflame on the ground, and plumes of black-and-yellow smoke, volume after volume, billowed up from the stone-ringed shaft.

They squeezed through a gap in the wall and went to their hands and knees just outside of it. The subterranean explosions tapered off, echoing faintly and finally ceasing altogether.

They hung their heads, panting, wheezing and hurting. At length, when Brigid was able to lift her head and focus her vision again, she saw Mongols fleeing the area around Kharo-Khoto, running toward the distant but comforting firelight of the valley encampment.

Grant tried to speak, but he had to make several attempts before he was able to ask, "What now?"

Brigid ran a trembling hand through her tangled hair. Hoarsely she said, "When we get back, we'll have to undergo a long decam period."

"If we get back," replied Grant, breathing less labored. "We won't win any popularity contests when the Mongols find out what we've done to their holy city."

Kane, face shockingly white beneath its coating of dirt and blood, made a vague gesture toward a collection of yurts. "Old Boro will ensure our safe passage to the gateway," he said between gasps.

"We chilled his son," panted Grant.

"He doesn't know that. Besides, his chieftainship is restored. That's better than a live but crazy son any day."

Grant turned his head and spit. "Even so, he may be the grudge-holding type. We're responsible for ruining the destiny of the Golden Clan."

Brigid shifted position, sitting down, resting her head against her knees. Softly she said, "As far as I'm concerned, destiny can take care of itself, just this once."

Take
4 explosive books
plus a
mystery bonus
FREE

**Don't miss out on the action in these titles featuring
THE EXECUTIONER®, STONY MAN™ and SUPERBOLAN®!**

The Red Dragon Trilogy

#64210	FIRE LASH	$3.75 U.S.	☐
		$4.25 CAN.	☐
#64211	STEEL CLAWS	$3.75 U.S.	☐
		$4.25 CAN.	☐
#64212	RIDE THE BEAST	$3.75 U.S.	☐
		$4.25 CAN.	☐

Stony Man™

#61910	FLASHBACK	$5.50 U.S.	☐
		$6.50 CAN.	☐
#61911	ASIAN STORM	$5.50 U.S.	☐
		$6.50 CAN.	☐
#61912	BLOOD STAR	$5.50 U.S.	☐
		$6.50 CAN.	☐

SuperBolan®

#61452	DAY OF THE VULTURE	$5.50 U.S.	☐
		$6.50 CAN.	☐
#61453	FLAMES OF WRATH	$5.50 U.S.	☐
		$6.50 CAN.	☐
#61454	HIGH AGGRESSION	$5.50 U.S.	☐
		$6.50 CAN.	☐

(limited quantities available on certain titles)

TOTAL AMOUNT	$
POSTAGE & HANDLING	$
($1.00 for one book, 50¢ for each additional)	
APPLICABLE TAXES*	$ _____
TOTAL PAYABLE	$ _____
(check or money order—please do not send cash)	

To order, complete this form and send it, along with a check or money order for the total above, payable to Gold Eagle Books, to: **In the U.S.:** 3010 Walden Avenue, P.O. Box 9077, Buffalo, NY 14269-9077; **In Canada:** P.O. Box 636, Fort Erie, Ontario, L2A 5X3.

Name:_____

Address:_____ City:_____

State/Prov.:_____ Zip/Postal Code: _____

*New York residents remit applicable sales taxes.
 Canadian residents remit applicable GST and provincial taxes.

GOLD
EAGLE®

GEBACK18

Don't miss out on the action in these titles!